The End

Raven River Academy

Ruby Vincent

Published by Ruby Vincent, 2020.

Chapter One

"This isn't how I thought I'd spend my Christmas."

Royal passed me a cup of tea. "You didn't have to come."

I gave him a look over the rim. "Of course I did. Where is he?"

"Fourth floor."

We left the cafeteria, weaving through the cold, sterile environment reeking of latex and disinfectant. Royal pushed the button for the elevator.

"Ember."

I peeked up at him. His face was chiseled, scruffy, and handsome, but it wasn't expressive. He was as hard to read as ever, all the same, there had to be a million thoughts going through his head. The night before, Nolan tried to kill him, his cousin was shot, and he discovered someone within the Horsemen was working against them. We had a lot to talk about.

"Royal?"

"About Hiro—"

"Don't."

We had a lot to talk about, but that wasn't on the list.

"Ember, he wouldn't have done this," Royal pushed on. I said he had more fearlessness than a person should. "You don't know his history. Believe me, it's impossible that he would have hurt Eli. There's an explanation and you have to hear it."

"I don't have to do anything," I snapped. "Except make sure he spends the rest of his life regretting what he did to my brother. And if you don't stop making excuses for him, you're next."

Royal crooked a brow. "What do you think you're going to do to me, princess?"

"Oh, I'll think of something special, baby." I rose up and kissed his jaw. "Just for you."

We stomped into the elevator, throwing glares and bared teeth at each other. How could I love someone so much and simultaneously want to run him over with a stolen car? That was an excellent question. Maybe it was like Mom said—love is only good with a little bit of hate mixed in.

The elevator dinged for the fourth floor. It wasn't hard to spot Julian's room. I safely pegged it as the one Pomona was pacing in front of. She caught sight of me.

"What are you two doing here?"

"We're here to see Julian," I replied.

"He doesn't want to see you. Go away!" Pomona made to go in the room and then spun on her heels. "What the fuck happened last night?! They're saying Nolan *shot* him. He's his best friend. He would never do that." She leveled a finger at Royal. "They're also saying the Angels crashed the party. This is your fault, isn't it? What did you do?!"

"What do you want, Momo?" I asked. "For us to leave or give you an explanation?"

"Both!"

That was hard since I wanted an explanation too. I was there. I witnessed it all from beginning to end, and last night still made no sense to me. Our plan was simple. Royal snuck Hiro and Cassius in through the gates, and they helped us trick Nolan long enough so he'd spill the names. Giving Royal up was never an option. I went to him after crossing off my list of suspects and Royal told me exactly what to say to Nolan, including giving up that he was a car thief. But Nolan...

I knew better than anyone that he was not a nice guy, but never in my lost-in-the-forest nightmares did I believe he was this. The guy we faced the night before was rotted with hate. He left his best friend bleeding on the floor and ran to who-knew-where to plot who-knew-what. The only thing I knew for sure was Nolan was not going to stop until the man who hurt his sister was brought to his knees. I knew he wouldn't stop.

Because I wouldn't if it was Eli. I would hunt them down and only death would have stopped me. Theirs or mine. If what Nolan is feeling is even a fraction of what I hold against the boys who attacked Eli...

Tea splashed on the polished tile, spilling from my trembling cup.

Hiro. I had feelings for him. Kissed him. Began to trust him. Allowed myself to imagine a future with him. And the entire time he harbored this secret. He attacked my brother. Blackmailed me. Forced me to steal to pay him. All the while he traded secret smiles with me across the lunch table. What do I do to a guy like that?

I didn't know. Everything I came up with wasn't nearly punishing enough.

"—didn't do a thing," Royal replied. "You can't blame this on us. Nolan had the gun. He tried to shoot me and his friend got in the way. Leo and Julian are saying the same thing. As much as the Raveners hate it, the Angels are innocent."

Royal wasn't exaggerating. The feeling the night before, as security and police swarmed the scene, piecing things together, was Royal and his crashers had to be responsible somehow, and Julian and Leo were confused. Nolan was a "good boy" from a "good family," he wouldn't do something like this.

Security trailed the gurney, asking Julian repeatedly if Nolan fired in self-defense before his mother lost her shit, yelling that her son needed to go to the hospital and to stop wasting time blaming Royal when they should be out looking for Nolan. There was no doubt their delay gave him the significant head start he needed to get away.

With everyone backing up that the Angels were not the aggressors, the police were forced to take Cassius and Hiro back to the OB instead of the police station. All they had them on was trespassing and, to my complete shock, it was Uncle Harrison who made clear he'd sue the department if they wasted a second of police time pursuing those charges when they should be looking for the guy currently on the loose with a gun.

The bruises on my neck coupled with Nolan's threats to have Eli's hands stomped if I didn't help him against Royal, stirred the familial protectiveness I often thought nonexistent. Though to be fair, it must have been that same protectiveness that moved him to assume guardianship of us. He wouldn't win uncle of the year anytime soon, but I could credit him with caring enough not to see us maimed and hunted down by a gun-toting maniac.

It was also a good thing he had the police escort Hiro out of the Estate and away from me.

Julian's door flew open. "Pomona, would you—" Gail's red eyes landed on us. "Royal. Ember. I'm so glad you could be here. How are you?" She seized us in a hug that almost made me spill the rest of my tea. "You've been through an awful ordeal. Julian and I appreciate you taking the time to check on him."

Gail turned on Pomona. "Julian needs more blankets. Would you ask the nurse? Thank you."

Pomona hesitated, looking torn between doing as she asked and questioning why Gail was hugging people she should despise. In the end, she chose the blankets.

"Oh, Royal." Gail got three kisses on him before Royal gently stepped out of her embrace. It was another strike against Rio Cruz that he couldn't accept affection. "Julian's told me everything. About Nolan, his sister, and the vendetta he has against you. I want you to stay with me until he's found and I won't hear any argument about it."

"Aunt Gail, I can't do that," he said automatically.

"I said no arguing."

I stood back, silently observing the battle of wills. I honestly couldn't guess who'd win this one. Royal made stubborn people look like pushovers, but Hart had this look in her eye like messing with her at the moment would have deadly consequences.

"We'll discuss this later," she said. "Come see your cousin."

Battle abated... for now.

Julian was sitting up in bed, messing with his phone. Surrounding him were flowers in every color and well-wishing greeting cards. He looked pretty good for a guy with a hole in him. He was wrapped tight in Egyptian cotton sheets and his bound shoulder and arm rested on memory foam pillows. If one were to get hurt, you'd want to recover in Raven River Estate Hospital.

The phone slowly came down as we entered the room. Julian's expression was inscrutable as he beheld his cousin.

"Hey, Ember," he said, though he wasn't looking at me. "How are you?"

"I'm fine. My throat's sore but the paramedics said I'd be okay."

He nodded, eyes peeled on Royal.

Gail moved over to her son. She tucked his sheets tighter just to give herself something to do. Every five seconds, she squeezed his hand or stroked his cheek.

Royal stepped up to the bed. "What you did, man, I won't forget it. I owe you."

"You don't—"

"Yeah, you do, and I will collect," Julian interrupted his mother. "And don't think this changes anything between us. I still don't like your ass."

"Julian!"

Royal shrugged. "That's a relief. I was afraid you'd want to walk down the hall holding hands."

"Royal!" Gail cried. "Both of you, stop this nonsense! Of course you like each other. You love each other. You're family and—" Gail burst into tears. "How can you behave this way!? Don't you understand what could have happened last night! You almost lost the other forever and what will this silly rivalry have mattered then?"

Red leaked into Julian's cheeks. What he felt exactly I couldn't say, but his touch was soft as he took her hand. "All right, Mom, don't cry anymore. It'll be okay."

"My baby." She fell on him, peppering him with kisses, and unlike Royal, he wasn't getting away. He was lit up like neon squirming in his straightjacket sheets. "Everything will be okay," she said. "Mrs. Harris will take over running the school for the rest of break and *all* of us will be home while you recover. Even your dad is flying back to be with you."

"Dad can stay where the fuck he is."

"Language," she reprimanded. Although, there was a lot less heat addressing his animosity to his father than to Royal. "Royal, sweetie, you'll stay here, and later on we'll go to your apartment and pick up whatever you need. I'll call Campbell right now to get your room ready."

She was on the phone in less than thirty seconds, telling her housekeeper to prepare for a guest.

I sidled up to him. "Amazing. Royal Cruz meets his match."

He chuckled. "Look at it like I'm choosing my battles. Besides"—he dropped his voice—"if I'm going to find out more about Nolan and where he's hiding, I'd do it better on his turf."

"—right here," Pomona sounded. "He's doing well. The doctors say he can go home soon." She walked in with more blankets and another visitor.

"I just don't understand how this could..." Sarah Ellison trailed off. "You," she flung, lips curling. "What are you doing here?"

Royal tensed up beside me.

"Sarah, don't." Gail ended her call quickly. "Leave it there."

"Gail, why would you let him in here after what's happened to Julian?" She stormed up to her sister. "Look at your son. This is the cost of getting involved with that boy!"

"That's enough," Gail barked.

"It is enough, Gail. It's time you stopped fighting me on this and accept that he is *not* family or worth your time. I've said it over and over again! You can't change what he is. He's just like his father. Nothing but a thug—"

I shot from Royal's side. He tried to grab me. I wrenched out of his grip, spun Sarah around and—

Smack!

"Ember!" Gail cried.

Sarah gaped at me, mouth open, jeweled hand covering her red cheek. "How dare you!" she shrieked.

"How dare *you*!" I shot back. "Nolan Ives shot Julian. One of your precious Raveners! And you know why? Because he was trying to kill your son!"

Sarah's eyes snapped to Royal, shining true surprise. Someone left out a few details when they told her what happened.

"That's right. He was aiming for Royal and Julian jumped in the way, saving his life. Maybe that makes you feel something in your withered, desiccated heart, but you're a cold bitch, so I doubt it! Just like Nolan, you're happy to attack Royal out of hatred for his father. It's all his fault, isn't it? You lost control of your life and Royal's arrival forced you to see you were another soulless, rich girl with daddy issues the size of a mansion and nothing to look forward to but a husband who ignores you and a shopping addiction to take the pain away."

I got in her face. "Rio is all you see when you look at Royal. The boy from the wrong side of the gates who coked you up and got you pregnant. That's why you push him away and desperately pretend he doesn't exist. Deep down, you're probably wishing Nolan finished the job!"

"Of course not!" Sarah shrieked.

"Then apologize!" I pointed to Royal, who stood there, face shadowed and eyes hooded. "And it better be a good one to make up for the last eighteen years."

Sarah's eyes darted from Royal to me. Her lips quivered, pressed tight together.

"Apologize now!"

"Ember." Gail put her arm around me and drew me away. "Calm down. There will be no more shouting or hitting." She looked to her sister. "However, she is right. Royal deserves an apology, Sarah. He was the victim."

I don't think she meant just the night before.

Sarah gazed at Royal and something flickered in her eyes. Then she turned away and shoved past us. She blew out of the door and the click-clack of her heels faded amid hospital noise.

Pomona gaped in her wake, a pile of blankets at her feet. "Son?" It seemed Sarah wasn't the only one missing information.

"Em," said Royal. Damned that I still couldn't tell what this man was thinking. Blank eyes reflected me as he held out his hand. "You should go."

"Yes, Ember, thank you for coming," said my headmistress, "but Julian needs his rest. I'll see you at school."

Royal grasped my hand, leading me to the door.

"Royal, walk her down and then come right back, please." Gail's voice was pleasant—as always. And it brokered no argument—as always.

Royal and I were quiet on the walk through the hall. I didn't see his mother anywhere as we rounded the corner for the elevators.

"Are you mad?" I asked softly.

"No." Royal grasped the back of my neck. He rubbed slow, soft circles under my ear, loosening the tension in my body. "You didn't have to do that, Em. I keep telling you I don't need you to save me."

"Yes, I did, and yes, you do. But it was only eighty-five percent about you. I really don't like that woman. She's got no right to look down her nose at you and run in there saying all that shit when last night you were almost killed. I should've slapped her twice."

Together we walked inside the elevator. Royal pulled me close as the doors shut. "Sarah's not going to change her mind about me. She doesn't want me in her life, and we're eighteen years too late for tearful reunions and one-big-happy-family bullshit. This is how it is. I'll stay out of her way and she'll stay out of mine."

I hugged him tight. "It won't always be like this. We're getting out of this place, Royal. I promise. You'll have a family that deserves you."

He ran his fingers through my hair—light, sweet, and soothing. But he didn't speak. I wasn't sure if he believed me.

"You can drive my car," he said as we left the hospital. "I'll get it from you later."

"Thanks. I wasn't trying to get kicked out but I should be with Eli." I sighed. "It is Christmas." *Quite a Christmas it's shaping up to be.*

Royal opened the driver's side door and shut it behind me. Leaning in through the window, his sweet, citrusy scent filled the car. "There's a present in the trunk for the little man. Maybe one for you too."

My lips quirked up. "Maybe? Well, I might have one for you. I'll give it to you when you come for the car."

He nodded. "Listen, about that stuff you said to Sarah and the thing about us running away together and being a family."

Stiffening, my hands white-knuckled the steering wheel. *No, Royal, please. I'm not ready for you to tell me my fantasies are just that.*

"Yes?" I rasped. "What about it?"

"The thing is... I love you."

My mouth fell open but nothing came out. Eyes huge, I stared at Royal as he kissed my gaping lips, backed out of the car, and loped off.

ELI SAT IN BED READING. His pile of unopened Christmas presents lay at his feet, waiting for my return to be torn apart.

He saw me and beamed. *"You're back. Finally. How's Julian?"*

"He'll be okay. Headmistress Mom is taking good care of him." I propped on the edge of his mattress. *"How are you? This isn't how I pictured our Christmas."*

"Curious. Did you think it'd be better or worse than this?"

I swatted his foot through the sheets. *"I wasn't prepared for a classmate to be shot. Another on the run. And Uncle Harrison to hug me of all things."*

Eli laughed.

"But as Christmases go..." Royal's confession whispered in my head. *"I've had worse."*

I put Royal's gift on his lap. *"Come on. Let's open these presents, get the cocoa brewing, and queue up a movie. For one day, we get to put everything else aside."*

"Merry Christmas, Em."

"Merry Christmas."

A great Christmas it turned out to be. Eli loved all of his gifts, including the ones from Royal, Cassius, and Clay. There was a gift in the pile from Hiro as well, but I took the manga and said I would explain later.

Clay hooked him up with new shoes. Cassius got him a multi-tool that was also confiscated under protest. And Royal got him the complete set of Artemis Fowl books.

"You have them all already," I said to his gushing.

"*Not with the new covers,*" he explained. "*I told Royal I wanted every version.*"

"Why?"

Sighing, he shook his head. "*You just don't get it.*"

Uncle Harrison and Aunt Violet didn't forget about us. We received joint gifts of an unsigned holiday card with a couple hundred in cash. The message was *buy whatever you'd like as a gift* and I was perfectly okay with that. I had my eye on a few things.

My presents I was afraid to open in front of him. There was a more than good chance they were naughty. To be safe, I texted the boys and, one after the other, they said I was safe to share with fourteen-year-old eyes.

Clay got me a silver charm bracelet with a dangling tiny fox. Cassius bought me a camera so I could one day build my own collection of old buildings. As for Royal, he gave me an entire notebook filled with drawings of me. Me eating breakfast with Camila, Brandon, and Gabriel. Me playing tennis with Eli. Me bent over my homework. It was all me drawn by the boy who swore he didn't draw for anyone.

My gifts for them seemed so boring in comparison. For Royal, I got a sketching kit, paint, and a canvas because I was certain he never gave painting a try. Clay hid crime novels amid his stack of textbooks, so I bought him a bunch along with a drawing I did myself of a possible future tattoo of our names entwined with a forest backdrop.

Cassius got the biography, tips, and tricks from the world's leading expert in con artistry, deception, and pickpocketing. I also gave him another tattoo sketch of us. I didn't forget Camila and gave her a

Florida survival kit of sunblock, guidebooks, a beach towel, umbrella, and a bunch of other silly things.

As Eli freaked over his presents, I piled my gifts in my lap, overwhelmed by the emotions coursing through me for the men who knew me so well. And if buried underneath was a twinge for the gift wrapped in fiery paper that I threw in the waste bin, I pushed it down.

Hiro's parents chose wrong. Hiro does not mean forgive.

THE REST OF WINTER break was uneventful.

The New Year's Eve party at the country club was canceled in light of the community not being in a festive mood, so there wasn't anywhere we needed to go. Eli and I hung around the mansion watching movies, reading, and prepping for our final semester. Uncle Harrison drove me to the police station to give my statement a few days after Christmas, and Aunt Violet dragged me to the mall to go clothes shopping. Other than that, we were left to our own devices.

I used my free time well, calling Hiro up to five times a day, leaving messages that said many colorful things, but the gist was he'd better face me and tell me who the other guy was that attacked Eli.

He didn't pick up a single call or send so much as a text. Cassius, Clay, and Royal had plenty to say in his place, but all admitted they hadn't seen him either. He dissipated into vapor Christmas Eve night.

"He has to show up for school," I signed. "He's not going to drop out in his senior year. When I see him, I will confront him."

Eli and I were in my room, stuck in the middle of packing to return to school the next day. The dorms reopened on Saturday and I would stake Hiro's room out all weekend until he showed up.

"Confront is code for..."

"Beat him into a shapeless mass of hair and ink."

Eli shook his head. "*Or maybe you should hear him out. I talked to Royal and Cas—*"

"Why are you guys talking behind my back?" I demanded.

"*This happened to me, Em. I don't have a right to know why?*"

I gritted my teeth. "*Don't make good points when I'm pissed.*"

He rolled his eyes. "*They're not saying he couldn't have done it anymore. After a week of silence, they can't deny that Hiro isn't looking too innocent. But they told me his history and how Mom and Dad took off with his college money.*"

"That is *not* an excuse."

"*No,*" he agreed. "*But they didn't both beat me, Em. One guy wailed on me and the other pulled him off. Thinking about it, Hiro must have been the guy who dragged the other away. It doesn't make it better, but it's possible he didn't know his partner was going to lose his shit.*"

"What is that supposed to mean to me, Eli? He didn't feel guilty enough to turn him in or stop blackmailing me. Whether he put his hands on you or not, he's got more than enough to pay for."

He nodded. "*You're right. Just don't fight anybody. It's up to me to decide how to handle it. I'll make them pay.*"

I kissed his cheek. "Actually, it's not, and you can stop listening to Cassius and start listening to me right now. Hiro and his buddy blackmailed me, threatened me, went after my brother, and then he looked in my face every day and lied. I will make him regret each one of those things separately and then all together, and I won't be kind about it. No mercy. No restraint. If you want a piece after I'm done, I won't stop you."

Eli wisely let it go.

The next day, Eli and I were loaded into the car for Raven River Academy. To say I had mixed feelings about returning was an understatement. I never wanted to be here. That I found and fell in love with my boys I wouldn't trade for anything. However, my life had only gotten more complicated since I passed through these gates, and as the daughter of notorious con artists, that was saying something.

My parents' message waited to be deciphered. Rio Cruz was a persistent shadow attached to my shoes. Nolan was out there somewhere along with the lurking traitor within the Horsemen. The traitor and his plans to bring down the gang I wouldn't care about if it wasn't almost certain he was the one giving out Royal's name as he did his business. He was starting a war and Royal was on the front line. How soon before I could get my boys out of this place?

Eli leaned on the door, reading from his new tablet. I tapped his knee.

"*Do you like the academy?*"

He scrunched up his face. "*What? Why?*"

"*I want to know. Do you like your classmates? Your teachers? The tennis courts and pancakes for breakfast?*"

Eli lifted his shoulders. "*Yeah, I guess.*"

"*Hart is nice,*" I admitted. "*Plus, she was quick on getting you an interpreter and note taker.*"

"*I like her. She's cool.*"

"*Do you want to graduate from the academy?*"

"*What's with the questions?*" he asked.

"*There's something I never told you.*"

Eli sat up straight. "*What is it?*"

I glanced at Aunt Violet and Uncle Harrison in the front seat. The two of them were deep in conversation about their past ski trip to Colorado.

"*I wanted you, Eli,*" I signed. "*To assume guardianship of you. For it to just be you and me with our own place. I'm eighteen and your sister, I had just as much right. I told the Child Services lady I was going to petition the judge, and she knocked reality in me. No judge was going to award guardianship to a single, teenage high school girl with no job, over a wealthy uncle and aunt living in the Estate.*"

"*I had to accept she was right, so I let Uncle Harrison do what he had to do. But I haven't given up. After I graduate, I don't see them letting me hang around the mansion for the next three years. They expect me to leave and I'm fine with that as long as you come with me. Do you want that? For me to be your guardian?*"

"*What about Mom and Dad? When we find them—*"

"*If we find them,*" I corrected. "*And if we convince them to come out of hiding, they'll be looking at jail time.*"

Eli dropped his head. He liked to forget about that tiny detail.

"*Yes,*" he replied. "*I want you to be my guardian. You are anyway.*"

"*Are you sure?*" I put the weight of the question in my narrowed eyes. "*Even if we got Mom and Dad back, you and I are on the first bus out of Raven River. We'd be leaving your friends and home for good.*"

"*Not for good. We'd come back to visit Rory.*"

"*Yes, of course,*" I gave in. "*We would come back for Rory.*"

"*I'll see my friends when we visit.*" His crinkle-eyed smile lit his face. "*Where are we going to live?*" Eli's eyes flicked to our aunt and uncle. "*And how will you convince them to give up guardianship?*"

"*Uncle Harrison confirmed Grandpa left us both trust funds. I'll make him an offer he has no reason to refuse. He'll allow me to withdraw the money—it doesn't even have to be all of it. Just enough to get a place for us and live on. He can go back to the child-free life he wants with Aunt Violet.*"

"*Think he'll go for it?*"

"*She will, for sure. Then she'll work on Uncle until he gives in.*" I smiled. "*Either way, I won't give up until he lets us go. There's a loft in New York waiting for us. You're going to love the plans I have for your room. I'm thinking wall-to-wall bookshelves.*"

Eli bounced in his seat. "*We can have a balcony and watch the sun set on the city. And I can enroll in a school for the Deaf.*"

"*Don't forget the insane movie collection.*"

"*And Saturday morning pancakes.*"

"Wandering the city and not recognizing a single person in the street."

"The park."

"The theater."

We fell on each other laughing. I was so happy; the seat belt was the sole thing preventing me from floating to the roof.

"You're going to have everything you want, little brother."

"Ember," Aunt Violet said. "Listen. We need to talk."

The smile melted off my face.

Uncle Harrison met my gaze in the rearview mirror. "I was unaware of the rule that eighteen-year-olds were allowed to leave campus when they pleased," he said. "I believe you will agree that while they're searching for Nolan, it's safer for you to remain at the academy. I will insist on it."

"I don't make leaving campus a habit," I protested. "Only when I have to."

"Like you had to attend the Thanksgiving party," said Violet. "With that boy who kept coming to the house."

"My boyfriend." It felt good to say that word.

"Was it your boyfriend who took you off campus a couple of weeks ago? The receptionist told me you were gone all day."

I goggled at the back of her head. "The receptionist? Why would she tell you that?"

She twisted in her seat. "We're responsible for you. We need to know where you are at all times. Why the academy allows you to sign yourself out is beyond me. You were gone for an entire day and no one knew where you were. How is that safe?"

Safe? Know where I am at all times? Who the hell is this lady? The Violet impersonator has got the looks down but apparently she doesn't know my real aunt doesn't care nearly this much.

"I went to Easthaven to do some Christmas shopping. It's not a big deal."

"Not a big— Harry, are you hearing this?"

"Easthaven," he sputtered. "You took it upon yourself to drive three hours outside of town and didn't think that warranted a phone call to let us know where you were?"

"You were with that boy, weren't you?" Violet added.

"My boyfriend," I corrected. "Yes, he drove me because the no-car situation was a bit of a barrier."

"This is unacceptable, Ember," said Harrison.

"Unacceptable," Violet agreed.

"What's unacceptable? I couldn't get what I wanted for Eli here, so I drove into the city. It was one time."

Eli tapped my hand. "*What's going on?*"

"*Aunt and Uncle have been replaced by aliens. Get ready to tuck and roll out of the car.*"

"As we've said, you can't just take off with your boyfriend and not tell us where you're going," Harrison responded. "It wasn't safe before and it's most certainly not safe now. Your aunt will receive a call if this happens again. So, it better not happen again."

"Okay. In two months when it's time to shop for Eli's birthday, can I expect one of you to drop everything and drive me to Easthaven?"

"Easthaven is too far a drive," Harrison said. "There's nothing there that you can't get right here."

"Exactly," Violet said. "In the future, you'll give us advanced notice and we'll do our best to have Monroe available to drive you."

"Are you saying I can't leave campus unless I'm driven by your chauffeur?"

"Yes," Harrison confirmed.

"*Definitely don't know who these people are,*" I told Eli. "*Just keep cool and smile. If we're patient, we'll find out what these imposters want from us.*"

He stifled a laugh. "*What do they want from us? Aunt Violet keeps moving, so I can't read her lips.*"

"*They want me confined to the academy. No more trips to East-haven.*"

"*What's the big deal? You're eighteen and since when do they care?*"

This is why I loved Eli. The kid knows what's up.

"Ember," Harrison pressed. "Do we understand each other?"

"Perfectly, Uncle, dear."

His eyes narrowed like he doubted the sincerity in that response. The man was no dummy. "Inform us in advance," he repeated. "If it's necessary, Monroe will take you where you need to go."

Of course, you and Aunt Violet will decide what is or isn't necessary. And getting Eli the perfect gift has already been downgraded on the list.

I didn't bother arguing. In their heads, they most likely believed they were protecting me. Plus, Uncle Harrison wasn't one to back down and Violet only lets me win arguments if I traded for equal or higher value.

Even so, I wouldn't be stuck here if it turned out I needed to go somewhere. There were many ways off this campus.

Soon we turned onto the dirt road leading to the academy. They dropped us off at the gates and let us take in our bags alone.

Saturday morning saw few cars in the lot and a smattering of students heading for the dorm building. We went inside and broke apart on the first floor. I brought my stuff to my room, tossed it on the bed, and left immediately for the boys' hall.

Royal opened up in nothing but his boxers. "He's not here," he said by way of greeting.

"Is he coming?"

He nodded.

"Let me in, Royal. He's done avoiding me."

Royal stepped to the side. I crossed the room and stretched out on his bed, expecting him to join me. He did.

I felt marginally better draping his arm over my waist. "How was the rest of break with your aunt and Julian?"

"We making small talk?"

"We can get heavy if you prefer."

He was quiet for a beat. "Fine. I stayed in my room for the most part. Left once to meet Rio and let him know what's going on."

I lifted my head. "What did he say?"

"He doesn't deny using and abandoning Viviana Ives. He said his intentions were romantic at the start, but then he found out she would inherit her entire trust fund when she married."

"That's pretty popular in the Estate," I muttered.

"Rio was just starting out taking over the Horsemen and he 'unwisely' believed an heiress was the easiest way to get the money he needed. Her father got in the way and you know the rest. He said when he left her, he believed she'd go back to her father and be fine. He didn't know she stayed in the OB until the news announced her murder."

"Did he feel any trace of guilt for what he did to her?"

"He felt something—but I wouldn't call it guilt that made him hunt down the man who killed her."

I froze. "He went after the pawnbroker? What did he do to him?"

"I don't ask those questions, Em."

He doesn't have to. Neither do I. The man ended up in the garbage with a pair of angel wings painted over his head.

"What's he going to do about Nolan?"

"The police aren't the only ones looking for him now," Royal said. "The guy bragged about a traitor plotting to take Rio and the Horsemen down. Rio is looking forward to getting the rest of the details out of him."

"I'd say I hope the police find him first, but Rio has a few of them in his pocket. I'd also say I hope Nolan does face Rio and force him to confront what he did to that innocent woman. He's well-named as a Horseman. Rio Cruz corrupts. All that he touches withers and dies like the first horsemen of the apocalypse, Pestilence." I flipped over. "Royal, don't you think it's time you told me the truth about the Horsemen and what they're planning?"

"Yes."

"Really?"

He cracked a smile. "You sound surprised. You're a part of this, Ember. After Christmas Eve, I can't pretend like you're not. But do you honestly want to get deeper in this than you already are?"

"If I'm going to get deeper with you, Clay, and Cassius"—I laced our fingers together—"I have to. Tell me."

"I will," he said. "Later. It's a long conversation and you're due another one today."

I sighed. "Small talk over."

"I didn't see it lasting long."

"Let me start. What did you tell Eli that has him believing Hiro deserves forgiveness?"

"The truth."

"What will you do when I don't give it?"

Royal drew back. "What do you want me to do?"

Holding his gaze, I said clearly, "I can't be a 'we' with him."

"Are you saying you want him out of the crew? He works for Rio, Em. It's not that simple."

"It is that simple. He'll make his money and Cassius will deliver it. That's all Rio needs. Eating with me, talking to me, and breathing my air is *not*."

"Can I ask you to hear him out before you make up your mind?"

"*You* haven't heard from him. No one has seen or talked to him, so why are you pushing that he must have a good explanation?"

"Because I know him," he said simply. "If someone told me you ran a guy over and then backed up and did it again, I'd say you must've had a reason."

"The guy I've thought about running over was you, and yes, you've given me plenty of reasons."

Royal laughed. A key turning the lock interrupted him.

I shot off the bed. "Royal, leave."

He didn't argue with me. Royal got up and reached for his clothes. He pulled on his pants as a duffle bag flew through the door. Hiro came through after it.

It wasn't fair that his beauty hit me on the heels of my rage. It wasn't right that light caught his hair, shining in those inky strands and found the curves and lines of his face. Angry Boy shouldn't make my heart skip a beat. Not when we met and not then.

Hiro noticed me and stopped dead. Surprise was quickly replaced by resignation. He knew this was coming.

Royal finished dressing and walked out. I was right behind. The door locked with a soft click.

I stepped toward Hiro and he moved back, maintaining distance.

"I called you," I began.

Hiro lifted his chin. That smooth face was impassive and those eyes vacant. "A few times. You went into serious, graphic detail. I don't know if it's possible to do half of those things."

"I'm a 'try and try again until I succeed' kind of person." I inched closer. My fists clenched and unclenched by my sides.

"Are you going to beat me up, Bancroft?"

"Yes."

"All right." He put out his hands. "Do what you have to do."

"Are you going to fight back?"

"No," he replied. "But can I ask you not to pull hair?"

My lips curled. *What the hell is with this nonchalant attitude? Does he think I'm messing around?*

I fisted his collar, dragging his lifeless brown orbs into the expanse of my vision. "It's no fun for me if you just take it," I hissed.

"Then I'll make it fun."

His hands came up and shoved me. I flew back, striking his desk chair, and charged him screaming. My fist smashed his cheekbone, snapping his neck around. He caught the second punch and twisted, yanking my arm up my back. Crying out, I kicked back and hit flesh. Hiro released me with a grunt and I spun on him, throwing another punch to the face that brought him down.

"Why?!" I screamed. Jumping on top of him, I forced him down as he tried to get up. "How could you do this!?"

I scraped a knuckle on his teeth punching him again. Blood that was his and mine ran down my fingers.

"I forgave you! Fell for you! And the whole time, you were the one who hurt my brother and blackmailed me!" Shaking him, I smashed his head on the floor over and over. "Every day, you lied to my face! Why?!"

"I— I'm sorry," he rasped.

"Don't say that! It means nothing coming from you!"

"Hurting him... wasn't a part of the plan."

"But hurting me was."

The first emotion bled into Hiro's eyes—pain like I'd never seen. "Yes," he whispered. "I wanted to hurt you... until I didn't."

Grabbing my hands, he pulled me off. "I'll explain everything," he promised through bleeding lips. "All of it. After, if you want to hit me, call the police, or turn me in, I won't fight you."

Rough, ragged breaths wracked my body. I didn't need the explanation. My soul ached to inflict more pain. To beat him until Hiro Saito was no longer the beautiful, vengeful angel that stole my heart and burned it to cinders. There was nothing he could say to ease the crushing agony of those nights in the mansion, sobbing into my pillow as I held the unopened gift I took out of the trash.

"You can't fix this." A tear dripped off my nose and splashed on his eyelid, soaking his lashes as his own. "You can't make it right. We should just skip to the end."

He nodded, eyes falling shut. "If that's what you want, Ember. Hart is in her office. We'll go now."

I didn't move. My hands shook in his grip, humming on rage and a screaming voice ordering me to get up and do it. Hand him over to Hart and wave as Ramadi carted him away.

He can give his explanation to her. Why should I sit here and entertain it? Pretend like there's something he could say that'd make delaying his justice worth it.

Slowly, I tugged free and climbed off of him, leaning against the bed. Hiro sat up too. Bruises were forming around his eye and cheek. Blood ran down his chin. We surveyed each other—physical and emotional messes—and I said, "Explain. I'm listening."

"Hurting him was never a part of the plan," he said immediately. "And I promise you, I didn't."

I scoffed. "So, you just followed him in ski masks to have a chat? With my Deaf brother who you can't communicate with? You didn't go out to that garden to talk, Hiro. This will get ugly again real fast if you keep lying to me."

"I did," he insisted. "I know sign language, Ember. Not a lot, but enough for a simple conversation and the alphabet."

"But you never—"

"*Told you,*" he signed. "*I wasn't talking to you before and I couldn't after.*"

I didn't have to ask what he meant by before and after.

"I started signing to Eli when we got him to the garden," he continued. "Everything happened so fast, I couldn't be sure if he noticed,

but if he did and I revealed I did too, the suspect list would've tightened up really quick."

"You went out there to *talk* to him. Code for threaten him like
you were doing to me."

"I wasn't going to make any direct threats," Hiro said. "I didn't
make any to you."

I fell silent, thinking of the vague ransom notes saying he'd ruin
my life and to pay or else. But it's true, no details were given on what
he planned to do.

Which is why I didn't take those notes seriously and Eli was hurt.

"I figured rolling up on him in masks was enough to freak him
out," Hiro continued.

"We've gone from beating my fourteen-year-old brother to scar-
ing and intimidating him? That's supposed to be better, Hiro?"

"No," he said clearly. "It's not. I'm not making excuses. I just want
you to know the truth. I deserve everything I have coming to me,
Ember."

"Nothing you say will change my mind." I said it because I had
to. For him and me.

He nodded. "I know it won't. Even so, you should know I was
only going to ask him about the message your parents left. Everyone
was focused on you but it was just as much of a possibility Eli could
tell us where they were hiding the money."

"But your *friend* had other plans?"

Hiro's face darkened. "He's not my friend." His menace chilled
me. "We wanted the same thing—our money back. So, we agreed to
do it together and smarter than the idiots shouting and threatening
you in the halls for everyone to hear. I made it clear I was in charge
but at the start he wasn't happy with how easy I was going on you. A
few notes in your locker wouldn't force you to pay, but that's where
Mallory came in. I had plans to fuck up your transcripts if you didn't

play along," he admitted. "If I couldn't go to college, neither could you."

I barked a mirthless laugh. "Beautiful symmetry, Saito. Well done."

"I didn't care about you then," he cried. "You were just a backwater rich chick standing between me and my future. And it never even got to that because the fucking bastard came along to corner Eli with his own plan. He jumped on him, pounding and beating his face in."

I hissed, heart squeezing at the vision of what he did to him. "Who is it? What's his name?"

Hiro looked away, jaw ticcing. "I was done after that. The notes. The money. All of it after Eli was hurt was him and only him."

"Who is it?"

"But I told him if he ever hurt you or Eli again, I'd beat the shit out of him myself."

I grasped his chin, jerking him to look at me. "Tell me his name!"

"I will," he said. "But before you run out of here and kill him—which you will. And before you turn us both in—which you should. I've given you the end. I also owe you the beginning."

"The sad tragic backstory that excuses your elaborate scheme to blackmail me, scare my brother, and destroy my future?" I spat.

"No, it's the sad tragic backstory that explains how I became the warped sack of shit that believed doing those things was okay."

Pressing my lips together, I released him, sinking onto the bed. The first real thing Hiro ever said to me spun on a constant loop through my mind.

"I'm the reason my parents are dead."

Despite everything he'd done, I found myself saying, "We don't have to do this part, Hiro. Seriously. I know what it means to talk about this and I won't force you to do it."

"You're not forcing me," he said. "I wanted to tell you before. I wanted to do a lot of things but I couldn't get closer to you."

We got closer all the same. In the little ways that matter. And now we're here.

Hiro moved to my side, propping himself on the mattress. We both gazed at different spots on the wall rather than each other.

His story came in a low, flat tone. "My parents moved here separately. They didn't know each other in Japan, and it was a joke between them that they had to leave the same home and fly across the world to meet each other."

"What brought them to Raven River?"

"Family. Mom's parents moved to Easthaven and then Raven River. My dad had a brother in town. There's a tight Japanese community here, they thought it'd feel like home."

I sensed a "but" coming. Of course there was a "but." This was not a happy story.

"But living in the OB is not paradise. Mom and Dad both had crap jobs and crap apartments. They spoke little English. When they met, got married and pregnant, they saw the same future for me and decided to do something about it.

"You know by now that the Horsemen is four gangs in one."

The seemingly non sequitur tripped me up, but I trusted it would eventually connect. "Yes."

"One of them is the gang that used to run my old neighborhood. The one my uncle ran as second and enforcer."

"Your dad's brother?"

He nodded. "Dad always knew his brother was up to shady shit. He had more money than a bartender should. But Dad didn't ask questions till he had to. The Eastside Crew's racket was simple. The OB is a dangerous place and there are other gangs who are far from friendly. They provided protection and loans. All about taking care of the community."

"Sounds familiar," I murmured.

"It's how Rio got them to unite. He sold the leaders the same dream and promised them the entire OB to live it," he explained. "Dad wanted in too, so Uncle Kenzo gave him an easy job of going store to store collecting payments. For that Dad made five times his salary."

Hiro dropped his head, staring up to the ceiling. "For years life was good. We had a nice place. Mom opened a daycare. They put me in tutoring, English classes, and soccer practice. I didn't know what Dad did of course. What seven-year-old knows anything about what their parents do? All I knew was every now and then, Dad would take me to visit different shops around the neighborhood. He'd either say to run around the store or play outside while he was working."

Drawing my knees to my chin, I hugged my legs. My fury leaked out of me bit by bit, unable to hold under his soft, haunting voice.

"There was one older woman," he said, "who owned a restaurant with her son. He always got angry when dad and I came in, but she'd shush him and send him away. She would smile at us, and sometimes, she'd sneak me a piece of dessert."

"She didn't mind paying the gang?"

He shook his head. "There was nothing to mind when there wasn't a problem. She got a huge loan from the boss to open her restaurant after the bank turned her down. Even with the high interest, she was grateful to them. But loan sharks aren't your friends and if you didn't have the payment for Dad, his brother was next to drop by for a visit."

"What happened?" I whispered.

Hiro fisted his pants. Up and down his throat bobbed as he swallowed hard. "I'd say you could guess, but no one could have seen this coming," he rasped. "Business got slow for Mrs. Abe. She missed one payment. Then two. Then three. Dad had no choice but to tell Uncle Kenzo who was coming up short.

"Kenzo went over there with two guys and a couple of bats, and they tore the place up. The noise and his mother's screaming brought her son from the upstairs apartment... with a gun. It instantly went bad. He started shooting and killed one of them before they knew what was happening. Kenzo pulled his piece, dropped him, and then they beat him into a coma while his mother watched, screaming for them to stop. He died from internal injuries a few days later."

"Oh my gosh," I breathed.

"I was seven," he said, eyes glazed as he fell into a memory far from me and this room. "No one told me what happened. No one said if Mrs. Abe knocked on our door, I shouldn't open it."

I covered my mouth, eyes widening in horror—because I couldn't ask what happened next. Everything in me shrieked to stop him. He shouldn't say and it was certain I did not want to know.

"Hiro, don't—"

"She was the nice lady who smiled at Dad and gave me two scoops of ice cream. She wasn't the woman who blamed my father for sending the men who killed her son."

"Hiro." I was pleading. My heart had broken one too many times that day. I couldn't take any more.

"When she asked if my parents were home, I said yes. When she asked if she could come inside... I said yes."

I grasped his hand, holding so tightly that my nails pierced his skin. *No more! Please, don't say any—*

"She shot my mother twice in the kitchen and my father as he came running."

A sob ripped from deep inside of me. I wept loud and sloppily, clutching Hiro's hand, and unable to stop as I pictured that innocent child witnessing an act that would change him forever. I saw him standing beside a little girl reflecting the petrifying shock as her only sister was mowed down.

Hiro's eyes were clear—his cheeks dry. He said nothing as I cried, but stood and rescued tissues from his drawer, handing the box to me and using one to wipe the blood from his mouth and chin.

"She turned herself—"

"Hiro," I cried, clamping down on his hand.

He stopped, allowing me more time. As my tears slowed, he unfurled his fist under my death grip. His palm lay flat underneath and I laced our fingers together. I could be mad at him. I could hate him. I could want to beat him into dust. But none of that would stop me understanding him better than anyone else ever would. Hiro didn't tell me this sooner because it wasn't fair to bring me closer. It still wasn't fair, but it was done. Far down where I couldn't reach, tenuous tethers connected with Hiro and refused to let go.

"Okay," I said. "I'm ready."

"She turned herself in to the police immediately after," Hiro continued. "They put her in prison and picked up Kenzo too. My mom's parents had passed away by then, so in one afternoon, I lost my entire family.

"It was foster care afterward. Bouncing around from one shit home to the next. Half of those people beat the mess out of me because they could. The other half didn't notice I was in the house. I ran away from all of them. Eventually, I'd get found and sent somewhere worse. It kept up until middle school and meeting Cassius and Clay."

"What?" My voice passed for a croak. "What did they do?"

"They could tell things weren't good in my foster home, and by then, Rio had stepped into their lives like a fairy godfather and made it all better." Bitterness seeped in. "The triplets thought he could do the same for me, so they told him what was going on. The next day, Rio took me."

"He took you?" I repeated. "What does that mean?"

"He and his men walked into my foster home, sent me outside, and I don't know the rest. A half an hour later, they came out with my stuff and drove me to the Martins. I lived with them until I came to the academy."

"But— But you can't just take a kid."

"You can if you're Rio Cruz. He arranged for my file to disappear and I just slipped through the cracks. I wasn't screaming kidnapping though. Ryan Martin was a Horseman. Worked for Rio and owed him a favor. Had to be a big one. Either way, they took me in, didn't lay a hand on me, and fed me three meals a day. I haven't spoken to them since they dropped me off freshman year, but I'm grateful to them. Gratitude I was wise enough to know Rio would one day cash in on."

I stroked his knuckles. "So, this is how you became Angry Boy."

He dropped his chin, gazing at me. "I was angry. I *am* angry. Everything that happened was because of me. My dad joined the Eastside Crew to give me a better life. They wanted me to make something of myself and I tried, Ember. I worked hard at school, I got into the academy, and I saved every cent I got from Rio. I tried to give myself the future my parents died for and in one night, yours took it away."

I lowered my gaze, eyes stinging.

"Blackmailing you wasn't really about the money," he forced out. "I wanted you to give me a reason, so I could fuck up your future too. If you had paid everything I asked, I would've done it anyway. That was until—"

"Eli."

He nodded slowly. "I don't think my parents would like the man I've become." Hiro let out a harsh laugh. "And that's saying something seeing as they were a gangster and a gangster's wife. It doesn't matter that I didn't do the hitting. Eli got hurt because of me. You got in deeper with the Horsemen—because of me.

"I don't live with that, Ember. I became a piece of shit worse than all of my foster parents and Rio combined. At least I deserve it! I opened the door and fucking invited my parents' murderer inside. I deserve a shit life in this shit town and your folks stealing my money only put things right."

"Hiro," I whispered. "Please, don't say that."

"Why not? It's true. The worst part is"—the barest touch brushed my cheek—"I finally realized what I truly wanted, and I ruined that too. This is what I do, Ember. I destroy everything I love."

I blinked and tears spilled from my eyes, dripping onto his finger. "You haven't."

"Yes, I have. Cassius, Clay, and Royal won't look at me the same after this. And those messages you left me said with great detail how you feel about me now."

"Hiro, that was... before." My question to Royal came back to me. *"What did you tell Eli that has him believing Hiro deserves forgiveness?"*

"The truth."

Hiro vaulted to his feet. I jerked at his sudden move. "I'm going to Hart. I kept silent for this long first to not get expelled and then because I knew we'd be done the second you found out."

"Wait." I scrambled up.

"I was a coward and he got away with jumping Eli and blackmailing you for all of this time." He threw open the door. "I won't apologize again, Ember. But I will make this right."

I shot in front of him, pushing him back inside. "Will you please just stop? I just— I don't want—" I scrunched his shirt in my grip. "I don't know what I want, but just wait!" Burying my face in his chest, I hung on as every range of conflicting feelings ravaged me apart.

Tentatively, Hiro's arms came up. He hugged me, soft at first, and then so tight I thought I'd break.

The door swung shut, enclosing us in our own world.

I TRACED SHAPES IN the ceiling, reminiscent of the night I lay on the floor next to Eli. Hiro's hair tickled my temple and I burrowed closer rather than brush it away. It was a mystery how we started this with me punching his face in and ended with us in his bed.

"I just need to think," I said, picking up our conversation.

"What is there to think about?"

"I don't understand why you let Nolan dangle you over my head. You went along with the plan knowing he was going to tell me the truth after Royal was arrested."

"I thought he was lying," Hiro burst out. "It wasn't possible that he knew I was involved unless..."

"Unless," I prompted.

He sighed. "Unless Mallory told him. Makes sense Ives would be in with her. I'm not the only one who needed to sneak contraband on campus or a heads-up on room searches. She told me she didn't know anything about the drugs or the dealer, but she did know I had plans for you. The only way Ives could've known about me and not the other guy, is if Mallory spilled."

"Mallory," I hissed. "I'm done with this woman, Hiro. Helping a drug dealer get their stuff into a high school? Agreeing to fuck up an innocent student's transcripts? Forget fired. She needs a cell, not an office chair."

"Em, if she goes, so does the store. I won't be able to pay the pot." He shook his head. "But it doesn't matter now. I'm screwed either way. Rio can do what he has to do."

I frowned. "I don't like this, Hiro. The things you're saying. The way you're acting. You earned a punch in the face—or twenty—for writing those notes and running up on my brother with that psychopath. But you don't deserve the Horsemen, a life of abuse, a dead-end future, or to see everything you've worked for gone.

"It feels like you're desperate to punish yourself for more than Eli, and I understand that, I really do. I picked fights with people because I wanted them to hurt as much as I did all the time. I know a bit about hating myself and it didn't lead anywhere good."

"You're the strongest person I know." Hiro's arm was secure around my waist. "Your method of coping didn't hurt you."

"My method of coping pushed me onto a ledge."

Hiro tensed beneath me.

"I tried to kill myself, Hiro. It was Royal who talked me down. Saved my life. So, this is me talking you down." I rested my hand over his heart. "Your parents chose the right name for you. It's not a symbol of what you can't do. It's a hope for what you must choose to do every day. Forgive them. Forgive the mistakes and wrong turns. And to forgive yourself because you were seven years old and that innocent little boy didn't know ugliness like that existed in the world. You couldn't have recognized it to not have invited it inside.

"If you don't believe you're the man your parents wanted you to be, you can still do something about it. But if you ask me, you're closer to that man than you think."

Hiro's jaw was clenched and ticcing. He stared straight up, hanging on my words.

"They wanted you to be smart and you got into one of the best academies in the state. They must've hoped you'd be strong and resilient, and you've survived things that would break most people, Hiro, and you're still going. They wanted you to be happy." I poked his side. "And you are when you think no one is looking. Reading your manga or hiding a laugh at something Cassius said. It's not too late to turn things around."

Hiro was quiet for so long I thought the conversation over.

"It is too late," he said. "I can't get out of Raven River or the Horsemen without money, Ember. I invested everything I had in the lodge and the money I've saved since isn't enough to start over when

Hart expels me. No academy. No academy rich kids buying my products. I'll need a new way to make money and the next job Rio gives me won't be as harmless. It's over, Em."

"It's not," I said firmly. "Look, I'm not saying everything is okay between us now. You have a long way to go to earn my trust back and there's a real possibility you've got another beating coming your way."

The corner of his lips tugged up.

"I'm still angry. He's my brother, Hiro. No one messes with my little brother." I took a deep breath. "But in this case, I'll let Eli decide what he wants to do about you. I'm more interested in the one who has taken over—pocketing his ransom with filthy hands that hurt Eli."

I propped myself on my elbow, looking down at him. "It's time you told me his name."

"I know." Hiro's fingers left a burning path on my cheek. "I just didn't want this to end. Not yet."

Swallowing, I replied, "This was a blip. A pocket of reality outside of normal space and time. But now it's time to wake up. I won't deny I have feelings for you, Hiro. I pictured a future with me, you, Royal, Cassius, and Clay. But I'll let those fantasies die a quick death before I get involved with someone I can't trust." I drew out of his arms, sitting up straight. "Trust is everything to me. My parents abandoned me. My friends turned on me. I won't spend a life side-eyeing a man and wondering what he'll do to hurt me next."

Hiro flinched. "I wouldn't want you to live that life, Ember, but..." He sat up, arm draped over his knee, and eyes boring a hole in mine that brought color to my cheeks. "Does this mean I still have a chance?"

I pressed my lips together tight lest something foolish pop out.

A grin spread across his lips. "Huh."

"What?" I snapped.

"I do have a chance," he said. A full-blown smile lit his face and just about knocked me sideways.

My cheeks heated to a blaze. "I didn't say that."

"I'm going to earn it." Hiro kissed the back of my fingers. "Consider me off the ledge. From this point and every single day for the rest of my life, I'll be the man *you* want me to be. I promise."

If there was something to be said in response to that, my brain fiendishly decided not to supply it.

"You— I—" *Shut up, Ember.*

Smile fading, Hiro clasped my hand between his. "I'll start with this... It was Brandon, Em."

The fog he induced cleared under a chilling bucket of icy truth to the face. I heard him speak as if behind glass—muted and removed.

"He beat up Eli. He's been demanding the money."

"He couldn't," I said through numb lips. "His family wasn't one of the victims."

"His father died and his mother kept her maiden name. It would have been under Mori, not Lacroix."

I barely heard him. Tipping off the bed, I scraped my knee hitting the floor and didn't stop.

"Ember? Ember, wait!"

I shot out the door, my mind supplying me with exactly what to do next.

Chapter Two

Bang! Bang! Bang!

I pounded Brandon's door like a madwoman.

"Open up! Brandon, let me in!"

Hiro ran out of his room. "Ember, wait."

Whipping around, I snapped, "Wait for what?"

Royal stepped out of the triplets' room, alerted by my noise.

"I'm not telling you what to do, but I thought I knew what this guy was capable of until I didn't. Skip confronting him and go straight to Hart. She'll call the police and this all ends"—he moved in closer—"without you getting hurt."

"I'm not the one who'll get hurt." I spun on my heels. "If he's not here yet, I'll get him coming through the gates."

Cassius, Royal, and Hiro tried to follow me. Clay grabbed Hiro, pulling him up short.

"We need to talk."

I escaped from the boys' hall and jabbed the button for the elevator. My mind ran so fast, I couldn't hold on to a thought long enough to follow it to a conclusion. The only thing that felt real was the heavy weight of violation dragging down every memory of my "friendship" with Brandon. The first day in the hall when he said he didn't have a problem with me or my parents. Him holding me as I cried. Teaching me to play tennis. Laughing with each other at our reject table like everyone else didn't matter. Brandon swearing he'd earn my trust and friendship.

All of it lies. Every grin and wink a play put on by a master manipulator. Brandon lied. Hiro lied. Nolan lied. My parents lied. Was anyone in this godforsaken town real?!

A scream ripping out of me, I punched the button panel. Pain blossomed from my knuckles and spread through my hand.

Cassius took hold of me. "Ember, hold on."

"No!" I roughly shook him off. "I'm not holding on or calming down! Stop—"

"No, listen," Royal broke in. He cocked his head, face scrunching up. "What's that noise?"

Beneath the roaring in my ears, another persistent sound pulsed low and steady.

"Isn't that... the alarm?"

Three pairs of eyes snapped to the girls' side.

Royal rushed to punch in the code. Throwing it open, the piercing beeps poured out of the door, originating from one place.

"Is it Camila?" I cried, racing down the hall.

"Cam's not here," Cassius said. "She's driving Dad's car up later."

"Who's in there?!" I jammed my key in the knob.

Nolan, Brandon, Rio. Every horrid possibility ran through my head as I burst inside and—

Eli glanced up from my computer, blinking at me. *Em? What's wrong?*

Relief weakened my knees and I fell against my desk. "What's wrong? What are *you* doing? Why are you in my room?"

Cassius snatched up the door wedge and brought a blessed end to the noise.

"Sorry," Eli signed, noticing the alarm. *"I didn't mean to freak you out. I forgot about it."*

"Why are you in here?"

Eli held up a piece of paper. Cassius plucked it from his fingertips too quick for me to stop him.

"What's this?" he asked, scanning the hidden note from my parents.

"Eli, you can't—"

"*I figured it out,*" he interrupted me. "*I know what the note means.*"

My lecture died in my throat. "*You do?*"

He beamed, nodding.

I looked to Royal, whose shock reminded me he knew sign language, and then Cassius's cutely clueless face.

"Guys, can you give us a minute?" I rescued the note from Cassius. "All's fine here. I just need to talk to my brother."

Cassius ducked out with a shrug while Royal followed at a slower pace, asking me questions with his eyes that I couldn't answer.

But apparently Eli can.

I locked the door and yanked over Camila's desk chair. Brandon was not forgotten, but pushed into a stewing corner of my mind to be dealt with later.

"What do you mean you figured it out? And how did you get in here?" I demanded. "Followed by the obvious question, who said you could pop into my room whenever you want?"

As expected, Eli rolled his eyes. "*I had to. You keep the note in your desk and won't let me see it. And getting in was easy.*" He jerked a chin at the door. "*Cassius has been teaching me to pick locks.*"

I groaned, throwing an exasperated look through the wood. If we had children, I'd have to watch that man around every one of them.

Eli shook my hand, getting my attention. "*I know what it means, Em. I'm sure of it.*" He took the paper and pointed at the letters. "*I was thinking about CMB. We've been looking at it like initials for the place they're hiding, but then I thought, what if it's about money instead?*"

"Money?"

"It was obvious when I realized it. The B is Bank, Em." He twisted my laptop around. *"I searched for all the banks named CM and came up with three. Two are in China and the last is Charles Magallon Bank."* Eli pointed to the address below the logo.

"Easthaven," I whispered. "They have a branch three hours away."

"Plus, look at this." Eli got a pen from my drawer. He made a slash through the long string of numbers. *"These numbers aren't a code, sis. The site says all US bank routing numbers are nine digits and personal account numbers are ten to twelve."* He presented it proudly. *"Nine and twelve."*

My eyes widened, running through his logic and not finding a flaw. *"Could it be that easy?"*

"It seems obvious, but it's like I said. No one was going to search Mrs. Henderson's mail. They could tell us what we needed to know." Eli bounced in his seat. *"The bank is open on the weekend. Call them now."*

"Wait. Can we slow down for a minute?" I signed. *"What does it mean that they've left us an account number? Why that of all things and not an apology for freaking disappearing in the middle of the night?"*

"Their information could be attached to the account. New names. Address," he offered. *"Or maybe it's money to take care of us."* Eli brightened, latching on to his own idea. *"They knew the FBI would freeze our accounts. They stashed some away so we wouldn't be left with nothing. You wouldn't have to ask Uncle to release your trust fund, we could leave on our own."*

"We can't keep money they stole from innocent people."

"But we can keep money from Dad's trust fund," he returned. *"It could've come from there."*

Eli felt around my pockets and took out my phone. *"Call the bank."*

"Ember?" There was a knock on the door. "What's going on?"

I bit my lip. Royal had been there for me every step of the way. I couldn't keep him out of this.

Or Cassius. Or Clay. They love me. There's no question they wouldn't tell Rio.

"Come in."

I unlocked the door. Royal and Cassius came inside each bearing questioning looks for different reasons.

Taking a deep breath, I said, "Cassius, there's something I need to tell you..."

I launched into the entire tale from finding the key in the vase to the search of Raven River's lockers and then finally our trip to the lake house.

"So, the message had a double meaning the whole time. You two have been hiding it from us, and your parents led you to a bank and an account number," Cassius summed up in a voice too flat for me to tell his mood—which meant he wasn't happy.

"Cas, I'm sorry," I said. "I love you and I trust you."

"Then why didn't you tell me?"

"I didn't want to put you in the position of having to lie to Rio." Standing up, I rested my forehead on his chin. "Not again. You'll never be hurt because of me again."

Cassius blew out a breath. "You just had to have a good reason, didn't you?"

A smile tugged at my lips as I rose up and kissed him. "All that matters is I'm telling you now."

Eli tugged on my shirt.

"My brother was not raised on patience," I said with a sigh. "I'm going to call the bank and see if I can find out anything about this account."

"How much information will they give over the phone?"

I gestured at the note. "I have the account and routing number. We'll see how far it gets me."

"It can't be under your parents' names," Royal put in. "Feds would've found that."

"That's true," I said while I dialed. "For all I know, they did find it and I'm about to call up for information on a frozen account." I pressed the phone to my ear and sat across from Eli, making it easier for him to read my lips. "We have nothing to lose at this point, and if it is the remains of Dad's trust fund, it'll go a long way to funding my future as your sugar mama."

Eli screwed up his face, giving the boys a funny look.

Okay, maybe I didn't need to let him read that.

Charming music filled my ear. I drew the card closer, readying for the robotic voice to ask for my details.

"Good afternoon and thank you for calling Charles Magallon Bank. My name is Savannah. How may I assist you?"

"Oh, um..."

That was not a robot.

I cleared my throat. "Hi, I'm calling to check on my account."

"Of course, ma'am," said the cheerful woman. "May I have your account number, please?"

I read the second part of the numbers, hoping Eli was correct about the split.

"—six four five," she repeated. "Thank you for that. Now may I have your name and date of birth?"

"It's..." I stalled. Name and date of birth? Whose? Mom's or Dad's?

But wait. Royal is right. They wouldn't use their names, so what do I tell this woman? My name?

"Ma'am?"

"Ember Bancroft," I blurted. What else could I do? Run through every name in the baby book and hope I hit on the right one?

"Thank you, ma'am," Savannah replied, not skipping a beat. "And date of birth."

If that was right, then... I relayed the day I was born.

"Excellent," Savannah said. "Now, if I may have your passphrase, and then I'll be happy to assist you with your business."

"Passphrase?"

"Yes, ma'am."

"Phrase," I repeated. As in not a password. As in a bunch of words I had to string together into the right sentence to get access to the account.

I threw a panicked look at Eli. What the hell was the passphrase?!

"It's— Uh— Just a second."

"Is everything all right, ma'am?"

"Yes, fine."

"*They're asking for a passphrase,*" I quickly signed. "*You've got me this far. What do I say?*"

Eli bugged out, tossing me the patented, "Why is this on me?" look.

"Hmm. If you cannot remember your phrase, why don't you call back another time?" She sounded decidedly less cheerful.

"No," I cried. "I know it. It's..."

I flapped my hands at Eli.

"*It has to be something you'd know. Think, Em.*"

"Thank you, ma'am. Have a nice—"

"Surrender," I rushed out. "Surrender an offering onto the goddess."

The other end went quiet.

"Sorry about that," I added, forcing a laugh. "I keep it written down in a notepad and couldn't remember where I put the damn thing."

"We advise memorizing the passphrase instead of writing it down. For your security."

I goggled at Eli. *It worked,* I mouthed. *It actually worked.*

"You're right. I should," I said aloud.

"For your protection," she repeated. "Now, what can I assist you with?"

I cast a look at the boys. "What name is the account under?"

"Ma'am?"

"This account was set up for me," I tried, injecting some honesty. "I'd like to know all the details if this is now mine."

"Of course, I understand. One moment, please."

Faint tip-tappings on a keyboard floated over the phone.

"Here we are," she said. "The name on your account is Aurora Fiscal Holdings. Established June seventh of last year."

"Aurora." Her name escaped me on a soft whisper and left the biting pain inside.

"Two people are authorized to access and withdraw from the account, provided they have the proper information."

"Who are the two people?" *Frank and Lenora.*

"Why, you of course," she said with a laugh. "And an Eli Bancroft."

Me and Eli. Looks like my brother's theory was correct. Our parents did stash away some funds for us.

"Is there an address connected to the account?" I asked. "For the... fiscal company."

"Yes, it's 543 Rosehip Lane..."

I wrote down the address and passed it off to Eli. His fingers blurred looking it up on my computer.

"You said it was opened June of last year." That was shortly before my parents took off.

"That's correct," she confirmed.

Eli showed me the results, shaking his head. On the screen were the details of a company that allowed the use of their physical address to those who wanted to maintain their privacy and not put down their own. Our parents were not at 543 Rosehip Lane.

A gripping hollowness seeped into my gut. Mom and Dad hadn't led me to their location, an explanation, or the last several months of my life back. It was a slush fund, so at least they'd feel a tad less guilty for leaving us completely on our own in a town full of people that hate us. Including the people forced to take us in.

I should feel lucky they left us anything. They wanted out of this town and away from me. At least I can give Eli and myself a new life.

"Okay," I said, slouching in the seat. Eli lost his smile reading my mood. "Thank you. Can I request two debit cards? One for me and Eli."

"Yes, ma'am. I'll get those sent over to you right away. Just so you're aware, we have withdrawal limits in place for debit cards, but none for checks. Would you like me to send a pack of personal checks as well? The first pack of one hundred are of no extra cost to you."

"Sure." I reached over and ruffled Eli's hair, trying to put the smile back on his face and my own. Having our own money and not relying on Uncle Harrison was a good thing. As long as this money wasn't stolen, it could further my dream of raising a teenager and shacking up with a couple of gangbangers. I was a simple girl with simple goals.

"What's the balance on the account?"

"Let's see... The total balance is..." The tip-tip-tappings filled my ear. "Twenty-five million, four hundred thousand, three hundred and eighty-two dollars."

I dropped the phone.

Tipping over, I scrambled to pick it up, narrowly bashing my head on Eli's knee. "What did you say?" I shouted at her.

"The balance is twenty-five million—"

I smacked *end call* in a panic. "Oh no," I breathed. "Oh no, oh no, oh no."

"Ember," Royal said. "What's wrong?"

I hardly registered him, hurrying to my nightstand and taking out the list of victims. Flipping to the back, I read the final total of monies stolen.

"Twenty-five million, four hundred thousand, three hundred and eighty-two dollars."

The boys were fuzzy shapes converging on me.

All of the money to the exact cent was in the account they led me to. What does that mean?

"What does what mean?" Royal asked. I had spoken aloud.

I handed him the papers. "All of the money they stole is in that account, Royal. They set up a fake company and put it in our names. Why?"

"All of the money?" Cassius spoke up. "Are you sure?"

Eli slipped between the boys. "*What's going on?*"

"Mom and Dad put the lodge money in the account, Eli," I said and signed. "Over twenty-five million dollars."

"All of it," Cassius repeated, stuck on that point.

"*What about Mom and Dad?*" Eli's agitation shook his hands. "*Was there another clue? How do we find them?*"

It killed me to shake my head. "I don't know."

Eli shrunk—shoulders slumping and hands falling to his sides. I wrapped him up in a hug, hearing his heart break all over again.

"They gave you both access to it," Royal said. "What did they think you were going to do? Become millionaires overnight and hope no one noticed."

I suddenly felt ill. "Maybe that's exactly what they thought. There's more than enough money to start a new life. I could take off with Eli and set up in the Maldives, and they wouldn't torment themselves with guilt for leaving us with nothing. Ugh! How could they believe I would do that?" I scoffed. "They told Mrs. Henderson I would know what to do with the account and I do. I'm giving the money back."

"Guys." Cassius took the victim list off me. "All of the money is there? Are you sure?" There was an odd, insistent note in his questions.

"Yes," I said. "According to the feds and Savannah."

Cassius tossed his head, brows furrowing. "But if all of your accounts were frozen and they haven't touched this... What have they been living on? How did they buy that mansion in a nonextradition country? What paid for the private jet out of the States?"

"They..." I trailed off.

Eli lifted his head, sensing the rolling rigidity of my body and gazing at me confusedly. Then he looked to Cassius.

"It takes money to start a new life," Cassius said, "and they've used none. Doesn't make sense considering how much trouble they went through to steal it."

"But they..." My head was spinning. I kept trying to speak but nothing that made sense would come out.

"Plus, they gave you access to all of it." Cassius was on a runaway train that would not be stopped. "Do they not know you? You wouldn't hide the account. Once the feds knew, they'd be out all of their cash."

"*What is he talking about?*" Eli asked.

Cassius looked to Royal. "Am I the only one thinking there's something wrong?"

"No, you're not," Royal said. "It's not right."

"*What's not right?*" Eli tugged Cassius's arm and repeated his question. Royal interpreted for him.

"Guys." My voice sounded strange. Too soft. Too small. "Wait."

"It's been months and they haven't touched this money. More than that, they made sure Ember found it to do what they had to know she would do." I think he took my hand, but nothing was real except for Eli's eyes growing wide. "I have a bad feeling, baby. Your parents... something must have happened to them. Something bad."

I couldn't stop it. His claim was out. It was said. And Eli took one horrified look at me and broke down.

TWENTY MINUTES LATER, Royal and Cassius were out of the room and it was just me and Eli. I pushed them out, eyes stinging, as Eli cried and the boys wore masks of such guilt, begging to stay and make it right.

But how could they do that?

Eli sobbed into a pillow on my lap. I stroked his hair, soothing him as I thought of something—anything—I could say to erase Cassius's chilling conclusions and come up with another explanation.

My parents hadn't touched a cent of the money. Why steal it, run away, and then leave me clues to get to it? Why haven't they spent it? What have they been living on? What did they use to get away?

I reached the end of my trail of thought, and instead of insight, I had questions I couldn't answer... and a hollow ache that I didn't want to.

I bent over and kissed Eli's damp cheek. Gently, I lifted his head and wiped his face with a tissue. I wasn't crying. Eli didn't need that from me. He needed me to be strong and tell him everything would be okay. So, I did.

"Don't cry," I crooned. "Everything's going to be fine."

Eli's hands shook. *"But Cassius—"*

Grasping them with both hands, I held them to my chest, drawing him closer and pressing a kiss to his forehead. He buried his face in my chest, tears slowing. Only when he was calm did I continue.

"Cassius doesn't know any more than we do what happened to Mom and Dad. It's too soon for tears."

"But why haven't they spent the money?" he asked. *"It's been months."*

I cast my mind for an explanation. "*They haven't spent the lodge money, but that doesn't mean they don't have money at all. The feds didn't find this account. Who's to say they didn't have another they hid under a fake company.*" My mind hit on a notion and I seized it. "*Plus, the bank lady said only two people were given access to the account—me and you. What if they... never planned on... spending it?*"

My hands fell in my lap, scrunching up as the random thought spread and took root.

"Ember will know what to do," I whispered.

"*Never planned on spending it?*" Eli repeated. "*Then why steal it in the first place? That doesn't make sense.*"

"*Why give us access to it?*" I came back. "*That doesn't make sense. Our friends, family, and neighbors lost everything. They had to know I wouldn't keep quiet about it.*"

"*Mom and Dad could've given the bank our names because they couldn't use their own,*" Eli replied.

"*If that's true, we come back to the same point. Why let me know the account existed?*" I trapped his gaze. "There is something more going on here, but it is *not* what Cassius is suggesting," I said and signed to get my point across. "I promised you I would follow this through to the end and nothing has changed. I will find Mom and Dad, Eli. I'll bring them home."

Hesitation etched in the grooves of his forehead. I sensed he wanted to believe me, but the barriers before me were too big to climb.

He was wrong.

I committed a felony, faced the most dangerous man in town, and held on to a secret that would blow Raven River apart—all for Eli. There was very little I could not do for my younger brother.

"Hey." I flicked his chin. "Have I ever lied to you before?"

He smiled—the barest twitch of the lips, but a smile. "No," he said aloud.

I held out my arms. "I'll take my hug now."

We stayed in my room talking for hours. Long past our rumbling stomachs liked, and when Camila arrived, she kindly offered to bring up our food. We went back and forth on our parents. Where could they be? What was my next step in tracking them down? What do we do with the twenty-five million dollars in our names? And, of course, how would we handle Eli's attack?

"Brandon jumped me?" He pushed his tray to the side, suddenly uninterested in dinner. *"But he's always been so nice to me. And you? He's just been pretending to be our friend all of this time! Why?"*

"So we wouldn't suspect him. And I didn't. I looked at every boy in this school but never once glanced at him. He's the right height and size. He sidled up to me on the first day of school and went out of his way to be my friend. I didn't know what to think of him at first, but with him swearing our parents didn't steal from his, I had no reason to believe he wasn't sincere." I tapped his forehead with mine. "I was stupid. I'm sorry, Eli."

"Don't apologize. It was him, not you. He played you like Nolan and even Hiro."

I dropped my head. "That's why I'm an idiot. How many people am I going to let fool me? I freaking dated Nolan and didn't see what a psychopath he was. I went after Hiro and he was lying to me the whole time. I was friends with Brandon for months and didn't suspect a thing. My judgment is screwed up and you've paid for it."

Eli lifted my chin. *"You don't have to be perfect, Em. If it was me beating myself up, you'd say trusting people isn't a character flaw, and it's those assholes who should be ashamed of themselves. So, that's what I'm saying to you. Don't waste time feeling guilty. Make them feel bad instead."*

"I couldn't agree more, little brother. Where do you want to start?"

It was a long night. So long Eli ended up crashing in my room and pushing me onto the floor. As he slept, my mind whirled in a kaleidoscope of shifting faces. Mom, Dad, Brandon, Rio, Nolan, and shadowed figures we've yet to identify.

I twisted around, gazing up at him. All I wanted was to keep him safe, but my life was more dangerous than ever. Rio crept into my world, spreading like ivy and destroying all that he touched. My boys wouldn't be in deep with the Horsemen if not for him. Nolan would not be after them. All that couldn't be laid at my parents' feet could be laid at his.

Their actions were theirs to be ashamed of and theirs to face, but mine in the months ahead were just as important. I held the town of Raven River's future in my hands.

I'll have to play this much smarter.

Rio's warm breath ghosted over my fingers. Empty eyes beheld me, reflecting neither warmth nor kindness as his smile shone both. His promise to see me again after his search of the lake house inevitably didn't pan out rang in my ears.

One wrong move will get me killed.

Chapter Three

"**A**re you okay, Em?"

Brandon studied me rubbing my temples. My head was pounding and his proximity wasn't helping.

"I'm fine," I said in a measured tone. "Just a headache."

"I've got ibuprofen." Brandon shrugged off his bag, digging inside. "Here."

"Thanks." He brushed my palm handing over the pills. Disgust shivered up my spine.

Monday morning and the first day of the new semester. Brandon jogged up to me coming out of the dorm building, falling in step beside me like so many times before, and it took all of my willpower to not kick his teeth in.

Stay cool, I reminded. *One wrong move...*

"Winter break," Brandon began. "I heard about what happened. Nolan and the Christmas Eve party. How are you?"

"I'm fine. I walked away with a few bruises but it could have been worse."

"I'm glad it wasn't." He squeezed my shoulder, pressing his cheek to my forehead.

Did he always touch me this much or was my repulsion sending out the wrong signals and making him paw me more than usual?

"It's insane," he continued. "Nolan selling drugs. Trying to kill Royal. Shooting his best friend and attacking you. He was always so quiet. I mean, he wasn't any nicer than the rest of the Raveners, but he didn't go out of his way to come for us. The whole time, he was the worst out of all of them."

"It just goes to show you don't truly know anybody."

He sighed. "Yeah, you're right."

Cassius loitered in front of the cafeteria, speaking to Camila. I picked up the pace. "I've got to talk to Cas about something," I threw over my shoulder. "I'll see you inside."

I ran up to them.

"—with Dad," Camila said. "We have to do something."

"Clay and I will figure it out."

She folded her arms, adopting a stance I knew well. "They're my parents too. You're not taking on everything by yourselves."

"You got into university, Cam. Mom and Dad are both proud of you. You know they want you to go."

"I know but—" Camila spotted me and then flicked over my shoulder to Brandon. "We'll talk about this later."

Camila broke off and went inside with Brandon. I watched them go with a churning stomach.

"Maybe I should tell Camila," I said under my breath. "I get the feeling Brandon is into her."

"You don't have to worry about that. Cam's serious about not dating. It doesn't make sense when she leaves for Florida in seven months and she *is leaving.*"

My forehead scrunched. "What's wrong? Everything okay with your mom and dad?"

"Of course not," he scoffed. "But lately it's even worse. Cam told Dad about her acceptance and then followed it up with the list of schools that would be perfect for me and Clay. Ones with the majors we want, scholarships, grants, and potential part-time jobs that will cover tuition for the three of us. The girl is a planner."

I leaned against him, placing my hand on his chest. "Why does that sound like a bad thing?"

"It's bad because ever since, Dad has gotten worse. He hasn't said anything. Instead, he drinks himself into a stupor every night. It's gotta be hitting him that he'll be alone, and because of it, Cam's gone from happy to guilty. She doesn't want to leave him like this and she even suggested turning down her acceptance, going to a state school, and working to help pay for Dad's rehab and a living facility for Mom."

"Oh." I dropped a kiss under his collarbone. "I'm sorry she has to make that decision—"

"It's not a decision. She's going to Florida. Clay and I found a place for Mom. We don't have enough yet, but we will. As for Dad, we're not abandoning the guy. We'll stick around, make sure the bills are paid, and that he's got what he needs. Once he sees that, he'll be fine. Cam tossing away everything she worked for isn't the answer."

Chewing my lip, I chose my words carefully. "Cas, she's not giving up on college. She's finding a way to have both. Go to school and be there for her family. You and Clay don't have to carry it all on your shoulders."

"Someone in this fucked-up family should have the life they want," he forced out. "Why is that too much to ask for?"

I threaded my fingers through his. "It's not, baby," I whispered. "But... maybe the three of you could build that life together."

Cassius kissed the bridge of my nose. I noticed he didn't agree.

"Are you okay?" he asked. "I saw the look on your face as you walked up with him. I don't like you having to deal with that shit."

"That shit" was well-named.

"I don't like it either." I clutched my twisting stomach. "I literally feel sick."

We drifted further away from the door, seeking privacy behind the building.

"I still don't understand why you're going through this instead of turning him in?" he asked. "Hart will have him thrown out and arrested."

"Hart knows there were two of them. Once she's got her hands on Brandon, she'll ask who the other guy was and he'll give up Hiro because why wouldn't he? I want Hiro to face what he did, but I don't want him expelled and trapped under the Horsemen for the rest of his life. Neither does Eli. For now, I have to act like everything is fine, but trust me, Brandon will not get away with this."

Cassius looked away. "I can't believe he blackmailed you. Royal, Clay, and I did horrible things to you too, so I've got no room to talk. I just never would have thought Hiro could be involved in something like this. I'm amazed you even care if he's expelled."

"I understand him much better now. It doesn't excuse what he's done, but..."

From this point and every single day for the rest of my life, I'll be the man you want me to be. I promise.

"I'm willing to see what he does with a second chance." I poked his chest. "I gave you guys one and it worked out."

Cassius clasped his hands behind my back and pulled me in for a kiss that banished the last traces of my headache. "I don't know how you do it, baby. You're way stronger than I'll ever be."

"That's what I think whenever I'm with you."

"What are you doing during lunch?" he asked, grinning.

"Hmm... You?"

"The lady's smart too."

I went inside with Cassius, giggling and snatching kisses through the food line and up to the loft. The smile dimmed as I landed on Brandon, yukking it up with Camila and Gabriel. My declining mood was also helped along by Royal, Clay, and Hiro.

The three of them were back at the Angel table, eating and talking like they never left.

"What's up? You're not sitting with me anymore?"

"We're not sitting at that table anymore," he corrected. "We don't have your self-control, baby. Lacroix can't expect to eat his pancakes next to us and keep his teeth." He moved away, walking backward to his table. "You should sit with us. You are our girl."

That statement sent a thrill through me the first time Royal said it and this time was no different.

I glanced at my table. "I can't now. I'll take you up on that later."

Cassius shrugged, waving me off to my emptier-looking table.

"I guess we're not the cool table anymore," Brandon said as I sat down.

"Julian, Nolan, and Leo are gone," said Gabriel. "*Gone* gone in Leo's case. His parents transferred him to another school."

"What?" Camila, Brandon, and I said at once.

Gabriel nodded. "I heard most of the colleges he applied to amended their decision after Camila's letter. That plus what went down over winter break. His folks transferred him to a boarding school overseas and I'll bet money they're going to donate a wing or something to a university over there to get him in."

I threw my fork down. "This is why I say karma is bullshit. Leonardo 'Rich Boy' Tremaine gets to coast through his last semester in a fancy Swiss school and then skip to Oxford. He'll return in four years to take over Tremaine Lumber and he won't have learned a fudge-fucking thing."

"I'll never have to see him again," Camila said. "Plus, the letter is out there. It'll follow him around for the rest of his life. I've gotta believe karma will do something with that."

I squeezed her arm under the table, sending waves of support.

"Two of the king Raveners aren't coming back," Brandon said. "Life is going back to normal."

"What's normal?" I mumbled.

"TAKE A LOOK AT YOUR schedules." Geske walked up and down the row, handing out slips of paper. "You'll notice a new addition."

Geske placed the schedule on my desk.

Monday-Wednesday: AP English Lit II, Calculus, PE, AP Biology, Communication & Problem-Solving.

Tuesday-Thursday: Spanish, AP Psychology, AP Statistics, AP Comparative Government, Communication and Problem-Solving.

Friday: All classes.

Whispers went up around me. Communication and Problem-Solving? This couldn't be what we thought it was.

"That's right," Geske said. "Our illustrious headmistress has decided to continue the workshops in an official capacity."

Groans drowned out the rest of his speech. I smothered a laugh. Headmistress Hart just had a son shot, then her community twisted themselves into pretzels trying to blame her nephew—the intended victim. Raven River's problems were real to her in an entirely new way.

"All right, all right," Geske said. "Believe it or not, the tools you learn in this class will help you throughout life. You need to find better ways of relating to each other that don't include throwing pudding cups and denigrating people you've been told you're better than, because—and this better not be news to you—none of you are better than anyone else."

The groans and whispers quieted under the stern set to his chin. "All of your teachers here want the same thing. For you all to grow into happy, successful adults, achieving your goals and putting just as much good into the world as you receive. To show our support, we've all agreed to shorten our class time by ten minutes, so you'll have forty minutes in Mrs. Seeger's class every day."

Beau raised his hand. "Who is Mrs. Seeger?"

"Headmistress Hart understandably has her hands full running the school. She's enjoyed the work she's done with you thus far, but is now handing the reins over to Mrs. Seeger. She is a licensed therapist with experience in the classroom, and working with teenagers and young adults. I'm sure you'll all make her feel welcome."

With that, Geske told us to sit quietly and prepare for the day. I spent the rest of class organizing my binder according to my schedule.

After homeroom, I hung back while Royal put away his notebook and gathered his things. "Seriously. How do you maintain your grades when all you do is draw and sleep with me?"

He chuckled. His thick, raven strands fell over his eyes—a crime punishable by shaving. "Clearly that's not all I do."

"I'll need proof of that."

He bent over me, filling my space with the sweet smoky scent of Royal. "You want to watch me study when you could be riding my dick instead?" He nipped the tip of my nose and I seriously considered how much trouble I'd get in for letting him bend me over my desk.

"It's not an either-or proposition. The dick-riding will come after the studying."

"Bet. Your room or mine?"

"Yours. I believe we're due a conversation."

He shook his head, rolling his eyes up. "There's always a catch."

"There is not," I cried, swatting his arm. "You and the Angels have unfettered access, my friend, and lucky you. Where would you be if I decided to trade up?"

He shrugged. "Sleeping with some other girl."

My foot shot out but Royal was fast. He caught my leg, laughing as he tipped me over and trapped me between the metal bar and his body.

"I'm kidding, princess." His kiss was soft, sweet, and unrestrained. My irritation melted under its heat. "I'd be the same fucked-up mess that wasn't worth your time. I am lucky you chose me anyway."

"Miss Bancroft." Geske glared hard at us both, but addressed me. Standing before his desk was Hiro. "Get to class, please."

I picked up my things to follow Royal out. As we passed, Geske continued his conversation.

"I think that's a great idea, Mr. Saito. See me after class and we'll discuss it..."

"What's that about?" I asked out in the hall.

"Don't know." He popped a quick kiss on my mouth. "Hopefully it takes a while. You've been slacking on your duties as muse."

I grabbed his collar, bringing him down for a real kiss. "I don't think there are any more positions I can twist myself into," I said against his lips. "But feel free to prove me wrong."

He made a low, husky noise deep in his throat that went straight to my core. "I will."

My morning classes passed in a tense blur. I had English and calculus with Brandon. There was no room for conversation, but just being in the same room with him grated on my resolve.

Ramadi should be marching him out in cuffs.

He'll deny everything, the rational part of my brain said. *And when that doesn't work, he'll take Hiro down with him. I'll deal with this another way. If I can handle the Angels, I can handle Brandon Lacroix.*

The lunch bell brought a blessed end to calculus. Cassius's text intercepted me in the hall and changed my course.

Cassius: I've got your food. Skip the cafeteria.

I walked a little faster across the lawn to the dorm building. It wasn't easy seeing the triplets over the break. Aunt and Uncle refused to put them on the "approved visitors" list. They were even weirder about Royal coming to the mansion. I felt their eyes on me every time he came to visit. And forget letting him enter past the living room.

Alone time with my boys had been seriously lacking, and after everything we experienced over break, I needed to be wrapped up in their warmth and reassurance more than ever.

I rode the elevator up and punched in the code under the watchful eyes of the new cameras. There wasn't an official rule that girls couldn't know the code or go over to the boys' hall. And I'd tramp in and out of this door every day until there was.

Cassius opened the door on my first knock. He growled deep in his chest and the noise turned my desire up to maximum.

"What took you so long?" He snapped me to his chest, his mouth on mine and swallowing my answer. We collapsed on the edge of the bed and fell off in a tangle of limbs.

Cassius had his way with me twice on the carpet, and after, I stretched out, coming down from chain orgasms, grinning like an escaped loon that got away clean.

"I'll have that for lunch every day, please."

Chuckling, Cassius scooped me up and placed me on the bed. I sat up as he picked our trays off a stack of textbooks.

"Tacos, coleslaw, and cucumber salad," he said. "Good news is it'll still taste good cold."

I let him put the tray on my lap. He reclined at my feet, grasped my ankle, and dropped little kisses on the soft flesh that sent ripples up my leg.

"Maybe next time we eat first," I offered.

He crooked a brow. "Next time I'll be the dumbass gorging on tacos when your pussy is for the taking? Nah, baby. I have my priorities straight."

I simultaneously giggled and rolled my eyes the way only Cassius Walker could make me do.

"I thought about you all morning," I said, nibbling on a cucumber.

Cassius cupped his package. "Fantasize no more. Here I am."

"Behave." I poked him with my toe. "I thought about what you said. At least one person in your family should have the life they want. Why does it have to be just one of you? What life do you want, Cas?"

He expelled a rough breath, dropping onto his back. "Em, let's not."

"Not what? Not talk about the future?"

Cassius stared up at the ceiling saying nothing.

I allowed the silence to stretch, eating my taco as I chose my words. "We're not hooking up anymore, Cas," I began. "This is a real relationship, and you can put this down to the insane number of romantic comedies I've watched, but it has to be more than just the physical stuff when you love someone. We have to talk. Share in everything." I poked his side. "Including our dreams."

"Is that right?" he asked lightly.

"Like I said, I've got hours upon hours of viewing to back me up."

He twisted his head, letting me see his half grin. "How can I argue with that?"

"Come here." I patted the spot next to me. "Eat with me."

Cassius moved to my side. He rested his head on my shoulder and opened his mouth for me to feed him bits of taco.

"The place you talked about for your mom. Is it here in Raven River?"

He shook his head. "Easthaven is the closest place that has facilities like that. I've talked to her about going. She said once that she will, but... you know."

I nuzzled his temple. "Yeah, I know, baby."

"Then there's Dad. He wouldn't take it well if she was sent away. The only time the guy stays sober for more than a weekend is when

I bring Mom home. It helps him—in some small way—just being wherever she is."

"So, if your mom leaves Raven River, your dad has to go with her," I said. Something the triplet said came back to me. "And it costs a lot of money to buy three people a new life."

He gave me a smile without mirth. "If Clay and I take off, we put taking care of Mom and Dad on Cam's shoulders. If all three of us leave, we know exactly what we're abandoning them to. The only option is for Clay and me to stay because we have to do that anyway. Rio will move us up in the Horsemen. We'll make more money and, eventually, we'll have enough to get our parents out of here. You see, baby, that's why there's no point thinking of another future. I don't have options. This is the way it has to be."

"If you did have options," I said. "What would you want? Where would you go to school? Florida like Cam?"

"Em." He made my name into a sigh.

"Do I need to reference the rom-coms again?" I teased. "Just for fun. Tell me."

He leaned back, parting his lips. I dutifully placed a tomato on his tongue.

"Definitely not Florida," he said, giving in. "Nothing against the place, I'd just miss the seasons."

"Soooo..." I laced our fingers together. "Up north. Maybe a particular northern city that's pretty popular."

"I wouldn't mind New York, baby." Cassius's voice was laced with amusement. "Columbia has a good mechanical engineering program."

"Oooh. Mechanical engineering. You would look so hot with a blowtorch."

"Oh yeah? I'll keep that in mind. You know, anytime you want to add props to this"—he gestured to our naked bodies—"I'm down with that."

I rubbed his nose with mine. "Usually, you don't give a girl a chance to get her socks off, let alone reach for the toys. If we're moving up to props, I'm down with that too."

"What can I say?" His husky voice quickened my pulse. "I give my girl what she wants when she wants it. I haven't heard any complaints."

"And you never will."

Cassius drew me in for a kiss that plumped my lips and curled my toes.

"What were we talking about again?" I asked, breaking away with a gasp.

"Sex." Cassius pulled me back.

I wiggled free, laughing. "You're not distracting me with your sexy blowtorch, Cassius Walker. I didn't know you were interested in engineering. That would be perfect for you." I snuggled into his chest. "You're smart, creative, and talented. You should do something that lets you express all that you are."

He scoffed. "Rio says once I'm past the gates, he'll have me lifting diamonds and rubies off Raveners' necks. That's smart and creative."

"Hey," I said softly. "Stay with me, baby. Stay in New York."

Cassius's pale eyes held the agony of dreams he wouldn't let himself have.

"Tell me about our loft and how you want our bedroom. Tell me about the home your parents have in upstate New York and the trips we take on the weekends to visit them. And don't forget the Thanksgiving dinners when your sister comes to visit with the sweet, handsome boyfriend that you and Clay approve of."

He relaxed slowly, sinking onto my chest. "No guy will ever be good enough for Cam," he muttered. "But if he's not a total tool, I'll let him come in and leave with his wallet still in his pocket."

"Also tell me about our children that you will *not* be gifting knives and teaching how to pick locks."

"It was a multitool, not a knife," he protested. "And picking locks is a valuable skill, Em. Do you want our son to be *that kid* on the playground who doesn't know how to pick a lock? He'll get his ass kicked."

I howled, nearly knocking my food to the floor. "What playgrounds have you been going to? He or she will also not be getting lessons in lifting wallets and phones from unsuspecting innocents."

"Em, this is the bad boy stuff that ladies love." He patted my thigh. "It's how I got you out of your panties. You'd ask me to deny our son these methods?"

"Our son?" I repeated. "What if we have a daughter?"

"She'll get an actual knife to fuck up anyone who tries to mess with her."

"Oh my gosh, Cas. I definitely have to watch you with our kids."

"No, you won't." His grin tinged with something else. "You'll be far from Raven River living the life you deserve in New York. You and Eli. I'll be here and there won't be any kids, loft, Columbia, or weekend trips." He stroked my cheek. "I want that life with you, Em, but a fantasy is still a fantasy."

Tears pooled in my eyes. Why couldn't he let me hold on to our perfect picture for a little longer?

"Cassius, all I hear when you say things like that is you believe we have an expiration date."

"You can't stay here and I can't go. I'd do long-distance with you, Em. I'd do anything. But how long until you decide to move on with your life with guys who can actually share it with you?"

I bent, resting my forehead on his. "You are the guys who will share your lives with me. I believe that even if you can't right now. I have faith enough for all of us."

Cassius tangled his hand in my hair, smiling softly. "That's why I love you."

He brought me down for a kiss and swallowed all the things I wanted to say.

I will save you. I don't know how, but I will.

COMMUNICATIONS AND Problem-Solving was held in a disused classroom on the first floor. A faintly stuffy smell of a room rarely opened hung in the air. Thin layers of dust covered the bookcase and window ledge. And Mrs. Seeger puttered around, opening and closing drawers as she familiarized herself with the space. I drew lines under the blinds, mind far away as the classroom filled with students.

The man I loved didn't believe he had a future with me. Do they all feel that way?

You know they do, my thoughts whispered. *Why else does Royal change the subject when you talk about life after the academy and Clay just smiles and kisses you? What are you going to do to get us all out of here and free from the Horsemen? Uncle Harrison may agree to a stipend to raise Eli, but releasing enough of the trust fund to live with the guys he wouldn't let through the gates? It's not going to happen.*

I winced, abandoning my dust stick people to clutch my stomach. Whether it was our cold lunch or the conversation we had while eating it, my stomach had been rebelling since I left his room.

"You okay?"

My head snapped up in time for Clay to drop a kiss on my lips.

"I'm fine," I said. He sat down behind me—back row as unwritten rules commanded. "Just thinking about some things. Serious things," I said as I twisted to face him. "That you and I should talk about as well."

"Yeah?" His brows scrunched up in that cute way that made his grin mischievous. "Am I in trouble?"

"Always, I suspect. But this time not with me."

Chuckling, he leaned in and kissed me so thoroughly a blush warmed my cheeks. Despite the insults Pomona whispered to me in the halls, I wasn't quite so adventurous that I didn't mind people's eyes on me. Which they were as we broke apart—Hiro especially.

He passed by us, holding my gaze as he claimed the seat on Clay's left. A vibe welled up in me as we looked at each other. Our attraction couldn't be denied. It was a living, breathing force that charged the air and affected everyone in a fifteen-foot radius. But there was more to a relationship than sex as I had to remind Cassius. Hiro had to prove he would be the man I needed.

"Good afternoon, seniors."

Mrs. Seeger was a welcome excuse to break free of his invisible hold. I turned to the short, freckle-faced, auburn-haired woman. She was younger than I pictured, early thirties, but seemed to be overcoming that by dressing older than her years. Her hair was pulled in a tight bun and her pantsuit was a better fit for the boardroom. All the same her smile was bright and the touch of chalk on her nose endeared her.

"Good afternoon, Mrs. Seeger," we chorused.

"Ah," she said, chuckling. "I see news of my arrival has gotten around. Should I bother with the introduction, or have you already researched the nefarious woman who's going to make you talk about your feelings five times a week?"

That set off the flood of interrogation.

"Are you from Raven River?"

"What exactly are we doing in your class?"

"Why do we have to be here?" Destiny asked. She laced that question heavy with scorn. "We don't have an issue with communication or problem-solving."

Mrs. Seeger lifted her hand for silence. "I see I do need to give my spiel. If you'll indulge me, I'll cover all your questions voiced and unvoiced."

We fell silent.

"All right." Mrs. Seeger came around and leaned on her desk. "To begin, my name is Harper Seeger. I am Mrs. Seeger ninety-nine percent of the time, and Harper when we are in the sharing circle."

Groans went up through the room.

"Yes, yes," she said, smile playing on her lips. "The sharing circle is everything you're dreading. We're going to get real."

I stifled a smile. The class was looking at the windows and door planning an escape, but I kind of liked Seeger. She had the easygoing air necessary for dealing with the people in this asylum.

"As for me, I married my college sweetheart and we recently moved back into town on the acceptance of this job with our son. My husband was born in Raven River and lived until he was five in, what you call, the outskirts. Hearing from my in-laws what life is like in Raven River and what drove them to move, fascinated me."

She waved her hands, encompassing our entire town. "This place is truly one of the most unique little ecosystems. Incredibly diverse in ethnicity but almost entirely without a middle class. You are either among the wealthy or the low income and it seems that this very school is the only place in town where members of both socioeconomic classes interact in any meaningful way.

"I'm told that this has without a doubt created tensions in your school and that is why I'm here." Her gaze slid to Destiny. "To help you navigate those inclinations to reject instead of accepting each other," she said.

"So, in this class we'll go through exercises, play out scenarios, and generally discuss how you feel about your community and your place within it." She beamed. "This does count as a grade and participation in all activities is mandatory. How did I do?" she asked. "Did I answer all of your questions?"

She did and the class did not look happy about it.

"Perfect. Shall we jump in?" she asked. "Everybody, up. Move your desks out of the way and grab a cushion from the back. We're giving our first sharing circle a test spin."

Moans and scraped tile drowned the room. I stood and got my cushion without complaint, tossing it down next to Clay and leaning on his shoulder. A whoosh of air hit my thigh as another cushion fell next to me. Hiro sat down, his knee brushing against me and not moving.

I zeroed in on that knee as goose pimples dotted the sensitive skin. *Do I move? Do I tell him to move? Why is he sitting next to me anyway? I never said he had* that *kind of second chance and nothing was written on my face despite the Angels' love of pulling that line. We understand each other now, but nothing romantic is going to happen between us. Nothing, nothing, not—*

Hiro squeezed my thigh.

I jerked, jumping out of my skin and startling Clay. "What are you doing?" I hissed. I grabbed his hand and he held on, pointing with his free finger at the woman staring at me.

"Everything all right?" asked Mrs. Seeger. She had that look on her face like she'd been trying to get my attention.

"Oh, yes, I'm fine." I loosened my hold on Hiro. He didn't. The boy held tight to my fingers, his touch firm but gentle. "I'm sorry. Did you ask me something?"

"I'd like you to start the introductions. Let's get the ball rolling on me learning your names. Introduce yourself and tell me one thing you love about your town."

"Okay." I tried tugging free. "My name is Ember Bancroft and I—"

Hiro slid through my fingers, spreading them apart. Achingly slow he brought my hand to his lips, giving me what would have been time to stop him if my brain wasn't screaming too loud for me to give it directions. His mouth brushed a kiss so light it was barely there, and then he let go just like that.

I shoved my hand under my thigh, face burning fire-engine red. Short of having sex right there on the cushion, that was possibly the most intimate act to share in front of an audience. And the asshole just leaned back and stared at me with the rest of the class.

"Yes, Ember?" Seeger prompted.

"The— I—" I tore my eyes off of Hiro. "One thing I love about this place is the river. I grew up swimming in it."

"My husband and I took our son just last weekend," she said. "Truly a beautiful slice of heaven you all have here." She smiled at Clay. "What about you?"

On and on we went around the room. Students introduced themselves and Seeger responded to everyone, making a few kids laugh and wiping away annoyed frowns. I wasn't the only one warming up to her.

Seeger reached the last in the circle, turning her smile on Hiro.

"My name is Hiro Saito and the only thing good about this place is it's where she lives."

I flushed from the top of my head to my pinkie toes. He didn't look at me or say my name, but I knew who "she" was.

"Surely not the only good thing," Seeger replied. "What about a favorite restaurant? A place connected to a happy childhood memory? Or the beautiful forest surrounding us?"

Hiro let his blank-faced silence be the answer.

Seeger's smile twitched but didn't fade. "All right, thank you, Hiro. And thank you, class, for sharing. I find it's better to begin from a place of positivity before we get candid. Hold on to the things you love as you consider my next question," she said. "What would you change about Raven River? One thing that would make life better for the people who live here? Ember?"

"One thing?" I repeated. "There are two million and three things. But the place I'd start with is… tearing down the gates."

The blowback was immediate.

"Hell no."

"Why should we do that?"

"Fucking terrible idea."

"That's not going to fix anything, Backwater," Pomona threw in. "Where do you get this shit?"

Seeger put her hands up. "First rule of the sharing circle: disagreement is fine, disrespect is not. You do not have to agree with Ember, but you will not disrespect her by interrupting and putting her down. The same courtesy you will be afforded when it's your turn to speak. Understood?"

"Yes, Mrs. Seeger," they mumbled.

"Harper, please," she lightly corrected. "Now, Ember. Please, continue. Why should the gates be taken down?"

"It's the reason for everything from the economic divide to the imaginary one that has us calling each other Raveners, OB kids, and backwater brats. We don't act like we're one town and one community because we're not. And we never will be as long as that gate keeps us apart."

"Interesting," she said. "Thank you, Ember. A show of hands only, who agrees with Ember's statement?"

Every OB kid put their hand up—Clay and Hiro included.

"And who disagrees?"

All the Raveners raised their hands except for Gabriel. His hands stayed by his side.

Seeger pointed to Major. "Why do you agree with taking down the gates?"

"Because everything Bancroft said is right," he replied. "I heard we're both the poorest and the richest town in the country. It's all because people from the OB can't even get through the gates to look for a better job. People end up moving to Easthaven or somewhere else like my brother did. And it becomes a— a—" He snapped his fingers. "Mr. Jennings said it was a... brain drain," he recalled. "Smart and talented people get the hell out of here and the OB doesn't get any better."

A few kids nodded, murmuring their agreement.

"Great points, Major," said Seeger. "Many communities experience the 'brain drain' effect as well. And you, Pomona, why do you disagree?"

I tensed up before she turned her narrowed eyes on me.

"Raven River Estate is a private community. It has a gate around it like thousands of other private communities all over the world, but here everyone acts like the Raveners are being mean and prejudiced. Tell me, *Ember*, did you have a fence on your property? Did you let whoever the hell tramp through your backyard?"

A slow smirk spread across my lips. "No, Pomona, I didn't let anyone in my backyard. But I also didn't call the people on the other side of my fence trash and then went out of my way to treat them like it. Why do you keep calling me Backwater if that gate is nothing more than iron?"

"Yeah," someone whooped. A couple of kids clapped as splotches stained Pomona's cheeks.

"It's not just iron," she returned. "It's there to keep us safe. The OB is dangerous and it's only gotten worse in the last few years. The gangs have taken over and someone is murdered every other day. If we open the gates, that shit will spill into our home." She motioned to us. "You and your boyfriends crashed one party and mine was *shot*! You can keep your asses on the other side of the gate where they belong."

"Pomona," Seeger began.

"How many times do I have to say it was Nolan?! Your Ravener best friend, the drug-dealing attempted murderer!"

"Ember!" cried Seeger.

"He wasn't aiming for Julian! It never would've happened if the Angels—"

"Are you seriously blaming them?!"

"Enough!"

Pomona and I snapped our mouths shut. Seeger's patient smile was gone and replaced by a hard set to her chin that came from someone who truly had years of experience dealing with young adults. It cooled our rising tempers. I'd get nowhere arguing with Pomona Winchester.

"Thank you, ladies, for sharing your thoughts. Next time, let's remember the rules of respect and disagree in even tones." She gestured to the guy next to Pomona. "I noticed you didn't raise your hand, Gabriel. Care to share your thoughts?"

Gabriel glanced to his right, gazing at Pomona. She met his eyes and they both flicked away like pinging ball bearings.

What is up with those two? The overheard conversation from that night outside of the party floated to my ears. *The vibe between them has been strange for a while.*

"They're both right," Gabriel said. "Separating the town has caused problems that are obvious to anyone paying attention. I've seen the way Raveners treat the OB kids and it's messed up. But the OB is a dangerous place and that's obvious too. The gate isn't coming down while Raveners have to worry about the Horsemen making them afraid to leave their houses, like they've made them afraid to leave the gates. Once the issue of gang violence is addressed, there could be a discussion about both communities opening up."

"Can the issue be addressed while the Raveners act as though it's not their problem?" I asked. I thought of Rio and the empire he built in a few short years. "If the people of the Outer Borough could force the gangs out themselves, they would've. As it is, they can't even rely on the police to protect them. If anything is going to change, we need the entire community to come together, but how can that happen when we refuse to see ourselves as one community?"

Gabriel inclined his head. "That's true. We—"

"It's not true," Destiny piped up. "Why is it the Raveners' responsibility to clean up the Outer Borough? We didn't screw it up in the first place."

"What could we do anyway?" Pomona asked. "It seems to me that your boyfriends are the obvious people to take them down." She pointed at Clay and Hiro—who was very much not my boyfriend. "They could walk into a police station at any time and turn their fellow gangbangers in. Why don't they?"

"Pomona," Seeger gasped. "What a terrible accusation. If you cannot be civil to your classmates, I will ask you to sit out this discussion."

"But it's true! They're Horsemen. They've got the tattoo to prove it."

"They..." Seeger trailed off, sliding a surprised look to Clay and Hiro whose expressions gave nothing away. "I'm sure that's not true," she finally said. "Let's move on. Destiny, what is one thing that would make life better for the people who live here?"

Class continued on in a tense, but calmer vein from there. Seeger likely thought she was tossing us in the shallow end on our first day but even a simple question of how to make life better in Raven River was polarizing. All I knew was I was in for an interesting final semester.

The bell rang, cutting off Vera's impassioned speech for more guards at the gates and restricting the rules for who can come in.

"All right, class, great discussion." Seeger waved us up. "I'm excited for the months to come and the work we'll do together. Hopefully by the end of the year, you'll graduate with the tools to make the changes you seek in your community."

I stood and turned to find Hiro picking up my and his cushions. "I've got it." I got up in his face and tugged it free. "And just so you know, kissing my hand and being all sweet is not going to work," I hissed.

"You think I'm sweet?"

"Grasp the main point of that sentence," I snapped.

He grinned. "What you're saying is admitting that meeting you made every single day I've lived in this shit town worth it is not going to work. It won't work to say you're the most beautiful, kind, forgiving person and I want to spend the rest of my life proving I deserve you, even though I never will. And this—"

Hiro took my hand, pinning me with his gaze as he brought my palm to his mouth. Hot breath ghosted over me as Hiro licked a scorching trail and then pressed a light kiss on my hand.

"—this won't work either," he finished. Hiro whispered in my ear, "Good to know. I'll try harder."

"Y-you just— You just can't—"

Hiro took my cushion and walked off as I stood there a stuttering, big-eyed mess. Clay walked in front of me, smirking like the hot asshole he was, and I spun on my heels and got out of there.

I went to the dorm and up to Royal's room. The guy let me in and I blew past him roaring my frustration. "I fucking swear! Hiro is so— so— ugh!"

"You have every right to be pissed at him."

"Like where does he get off? I don't have those feelings for him anymore." The damp patch on my underwear taunted me. "I'll give him a chance to put this right, but that's it. A relationship is *not* on the table."

"Who are you trying to convince?" Royal snaked an arm around my waist and kissed my temple. "Hiro's not here."

"Shut up." I flopped onto his bed, shedding my clothes as I crawled up to the pillows. "I'm owed a big, fat, soul-baring talk from you, Royal Cruz."

"There won't be any soul baring," he deadpanned.

"And I'm going to get it," I continued. "I want to know everything about the Horsemen and Rio. All that you've been keeping from me and I want to know it now."

"Then why are you taking off your clothes?"

"Because." I settled on his pillows in nothing but my panties. "I'll reward you by letting you give me that touch-up you promised."

"Yeah? Mind if I don't draw an angel?"

I laughed. "I'm completely okay with that."

A few minutes later, I was relaxed on his bed, playing with his locks as he bent over my chest with his marker. "I'm listening," I said.

"Where do you want me to start?" The cool ink stained my skin. "And what do you plan to do after you hear this?"

"I'm going to steal you, Cassius, and Clay from this life. I'm taking you all to New York where you'll worship my body all night and spend every day living the lives you truly want."

Royal shook his head, a grin tugging at the corner of his mouth. He acted like I was kidding whenever I brought this up. I'd never been more serious in my life.

"Sounds good, princess."

I sighed. "You can start by explaining what you meant when you said Rio needed big money for big moves. What is he planning? What does he have you, the triplets, Hiro and the rest of the Horsemen paying for?"

Royal did not answer right away. His forehead scrunched up—whether from concentrating on his design or thinking of a way to dodge my question.

"You tell me. What do Rio and the leaders want?" he asked.

My brows came together. "What do they want?"

"What have they been after for the last few years?"

"They… want the Outer Borough. To rule the entire community unchallenged."

"No."

"No? What do you mean no?"

"Rio didn't leave everything behind to move here, ruthlessly take over the Horsemen, and convince the other gangs to join him, just to rule the OB. Rio wants Raven River, Ember. He wants all of it."

Understanding stole my breath. "You mean… the Estate?"

Royal nodded.

"But he can't," I burst out. "It's impossible. How would he—"

"How did any of the Raveners get full access to the Estate, Em? They bought a house there and that was it. They can come and go as they please. They can give out visitor passes to whoever they like. Flooding the Estate with Horsemen is as simple as buying that sweet little fifteen bedroom on the end."

Royal paused to lick his finger and rub away a mistake above my navel.

"I say simple," he continued, "but we're talking about a freaking mansion and those aren't cheap. It's taken five years, four gangs, and over a hundred guys like me working their rackets and throwing money in the pot to get Rio close. And he is. He started talks with the realtor over winter break."

"Royal." I stayed his hand, propping myself up. "You're telling me that man is shopping right now for the house that will let him and the Horsemen have free rein over the Estate and the entire town? What is he going to do?"

Pulling out of my grasp, he traced a line down my forehead, smoothing my brow. "Don't look so scared. He's not going to raid and pillage the place, rounding up the virgins and putting the men's heads on a spike."

"Don't joke with me right now, Royal."

"I'm serious. This is an expansion of business, not a plot for more violence. Rio, Donny, and I are the only Horsemen that can get into the Estate. It's why I have to steal the cars and not too often or I'll risk getting caught. Once we're in, he can turn that over to his other guys and focus on training me to take over for him. He's planning a trip for us after graduation to introduce me to his contacts and teach me the fine art of grifting." A thick layer of bitterness covered his words. "Cassius is coming too."

"Cassius? Why?"

"Rio sees his talent... and his looks. He can charm his way into some lonely old Ravener's life and then take her for all she's got. The other leaders have taken their picks too. Noble wants Clay. He ran the Southside Crew and they were a one-stop shop for fake IDs, forged passports, documents, and counterfeit money. Clay's got a knack for picking pockets and opening accounts in people's names. Noble is going to take him to the next level.

"Hiro's going to the Eastside Crew. His father and uncle used to work for Endo and he wants him back. Endo needs a new enforcer."

"Enforcer?" I cried. "He wants Hiro to terrorize old ladies when they're late with a payment? This is some inherited honor?!"

"Ember, calm down."

"Don't tell me to calm down!"

A chill prickled my naked body. All of a sudden, it was as far from sexy as it could be. I snatched my shirt off the pillow and shoved it on.

"This is not happening. None of it!"

"You can't stop it," Royal said. His touch was gentle as he cupped my cheek but a hard glint darkened his eyes. "Rio Cruz has done a lot of terrible shit, but nothing that he was arrested for under that name or his real one."

I barked a humorless laugh. "Rio's not his real name? I don't even know the name of the man who's been making my life hell for months."

"Rio is short for his middle name, Antario. But it doesn't matter," he added as I opened my mouth. "The point is they won't have reason to deny him a home in the Estate. He's going to do it, Em, and the leaders he promised a nice life living in the community that's always turned them away, have a vested interest in making sure nothing goes wrong. You can't stop it. I can't stop it. No one can."

I sucked in deep, slow breaths. My stomach was twisting more than ever under the assault of my whirling thoughts. My sweet, naughty, devilish Cassius playing some rich widow's pet to milk her for money to line Rio's pocket. Clay in some dark, dirty back room stashing fake money. Hiro forced into the life that killed his family. And then a vision of Royal formed in my mind.

Slicked-back and gorgeous—a smile twisted his lips that didn't reach his cold eyes. Glaringly expensive clothes clung to Royal's frame and concealed the gun in the folds of his coat.

Rio.

I leaped off the bed. Royal shouted after me as I burst into the bathroom and emptied my stomach into the toilet.

Footsteps sounded behind me. A soothing hand pulled back my hair and stroked my neck as I heaved. Royal didn't speak. After too long, I sat back, falling onto his chest. Royal held me as rough breaths wracked my chest.

"I'm not letting this happen," I rasped. "I don't care what I have to do. The Horsemen won't have you."

Royal lifted me and carried me to the sink. I watched him as he set me on the counter, got a washcloth, and ran it under cool water.

"Do you believe me?" My voice was small.

"I want to." The truth was ripped from the depths of his soul. The tiny part of him where he allowed himself to hope. "I really do, princess. Any life with you is better than the one Rio has planned for me."

My heart slowed, mind cleared, while Royal cleaned me up and draped the cool cloth around my neck. I rested my head on his shoulder, soaking in his warmth.

"Will you help me?"

Royal rubbed my back, slow, caressing circles that quieted my flipping stomach better than I could.

"Help you take Rio down," he stated. "There are lots of things I'm willing to do, princess, but putting my own father in jail isn't one of them. I won't stop you. I don't have the right after what he's done to you. But I can't help."

"I understand. Honestly, I do. If I found my parents tomorrow, despite everything they've done, I couldn't be the one to turn them in." I sighed, holding him closer. "If the jail cell he so desperately belongs in is off the table, then I'll think of something else. I just need to know you, Cassius, Clay, and Hiro are on my side."

"You've got them under the same spell. All of them would drown themselves in the river if you told them to."

A tiny giggle escaped me. "That's one magical pussy."

"That's what I'm saying."

We laughed and for one perfect second it felt like everything would be okay.

Just one second.

I straightened, clearing my throat. "Sorry I freaked on you. I wanted to have this conversation, so let's have it." I held up my fingers. "We have Noble, Endo, and Rio. Who's the fourth leader of the Horsemen?"

"The fourth, and arguably the most dangerous, is Cavanaugh. He's a gunrunner."

"A... gunrunner?" My brain fritzed out trying to comprehend.

"He's a cold son of a bitch. He works for a guy who has a private airstrip just outside of Easthaven. Cavanaugh smuggles in weapons and keeps the gang fully armed. You want to know why it's been so easy for the Horsemen to take over the OB? Because Rio brought Cavanaugh to his side first and everyone else fell in line quick. Or they died." He grasped my chin between two fingers and raised me to meet his eyes. "Do you see why these are not the kind of guys you piss off?"

I made a choked noise. "Um, yes! And you're saying Rio and his *colleagues* are going to roll into the Estate and sip tea and crumpets? I'm terrified to think of what they have planned."

"Expansion of business, Em. That's all they have planned. I promise your aunt and uncle aren't in danger."

I pressed my lips together. Royal got straight to the heart of my fears.

"Raveners want guns, fake passports, stolen goods, and off-the-record loans just as much as the next guy," he said. "But they have a lot more money to get their hands on them."

"I don't care what they want or why, they have to be stopped. For all their claims of helping and protecting the OB, the Horsemen have killed people that stood in their way. If a bunch of angel-tatted guys rolled into the Estate, the residents will do something about it and it'll get bloody."

Royal picked me up. Cradling me to his chest, he carried me to the bed, laid me down, and reclaimed his marker. We didn't speak for a while as he resumed his drawing and I sank into my thoughts.

"If the people of the Outer Borough could force the gangs out themselves, they would've."

How would I do what an entire town full of people couldn't?

Chapter Four

I woke up in Clay's bed the next morning. After our talk and the activities that naturally followed my nakedness, I went to dinner and then joined the triplets in their room to talk about the Horsemen's plans for them. Their faces were identical down to the grim expressions as they admitted they knew the whole time. They didn't tell me because they couldn't bear to drive home that a future between us was impossible. I broke my promise not to break down and cried myself to sleep in their arms.

Bear. Starfish. Grinning man with one eye.

The many nights I spent in their room, I knew the shapes in the popcorn ceiling better than my own. One of the boys would be pressed against me, lulling me in comfort, and my imagination conjured tales of the bear, starfish, and one-eyed man to preoccupy my racing mind.

That morning, I couldn't be distracted by Cornelius wearing his starfish friend as a seeing-eyepatch and them fighting the bear together. My thoughts kept drifting back to the seasoned criminals spreading their influence throughout my town like miasma.

A fence. A forger. A loan shark. And a fucking arms dealer.

It was hard to believe there was someone more dangerous than Rio Cruz, the guy who tried to put a bullet in my head, but every molecule of self-preservation and common sense in my body said I did not want to meet the man who gave Rio that gun.

Royal was most likely correct that the Horsemen weren't going to storm the Estate and cause a bloodbath. This was a desire for increased net worth, not a long prison stay followed by a short sit in the electric chair.

They'd keep low and quiet, and their presence would be felt if not heard. The pervasive mist of fear that clung to the OB would overcome the Estate and those that can't take it will move. Those that refuse to leave will fight. And those that need their services will feed them until they grow stronger and deadlier. The Horsemen will have Raven River and Rio's long game that began with his own son will be achieved—

—unless one teenage girl stopped them all.

"How in the hell do I do that?"

Clay stirred beneath the sheets. "Em?"

"Sorry," I whispered. "I didn't mean to wake you."

"It's okay."

Cornelius and his friends disappeared. Clay pulled the blanket over my head and tugged me closer, laying his head on my temple.

"Still upset?"

"Of course." Burrowing deeper, I pulled his arms tighter around me. "Aren't you upset?"

"I wasn't... until you."

"You always deserved more than the Horsemen, Clay."

"I see that now because it means losing you."

"You're not going to lose me. We're getting out of here together. Are you applying to Columbia too?"

"I'm not applying anywhere."

"Clay." A thick note of warning layered his name.

"For now," he finished. "If my brother's going to Columbia and my sister to UF, one of us bums has to work to pay for it. I'll get a job and take some classes part-time or online. NYU isn't going any-where."

I relaxed. "All three of you bums could work to cover school. It doesn't have to all be on you. Besides, your rent will be cheap split between us."

"What do you picture when you see the four of us living with you? Rooms separated by sheets? One bathroom for all of us?" He laughed. "And that's more than we could afford."

"The four of you?" I repeated, freezing. "You mean Hiro?"

"I meant Eli. Did *you* mean Hiro?"

I flushed down to my chest. "No," I said too quickly.

"Sure you didn't."

Twisting, I nipped his cheek. "Just for that, your bedroom will be three sheets and an air mattress."

He laughed out loud, pulling a groan out of a waking Cassius. "I'll love it if you're sharing it with me."

My nips were replaced by kisses on his cheek and down his jaw. This is what I loved about Clay. He wanted me smiling so badly, he'd live in my fantasy for as long as I wanted. I'd keep him there until I made it reality.

IT WAS A SLOW START to my morning. The boys employed various methods to hold me up. Eventually, I made it to my dorm to shower and get dressed for class. Camila was long gone. I snagged my backpack and psychology textbook and hoofed it downstairs.

I rounded the building and came to a jerking halt.

Hiro bent over the trash bag, holding it open while he jabbed at an elusive candy wrapper stuck beneath the hedges. I watched him, brain attempting to understand what it was seeing.

The trash-picker finally caught the wrapper and he shoved it in the bag. Turning around, he spotted me.

"Ember."

"Hiro." I cautiously approached as though I feared the hallucination would dissipate. "What are you doing?"

"Picking up trash."

"I can see that," I said slowly. "Why?"

He looked down at his blue coveralls, gloves, and garbage bag. "I believe they call it penance. Community service is what I would be doing if you turned me in. I have to pay for what I did and I won't dodge that punishment. I went to Geske saying I wanted service hours to put on applications. I'll do this for the rest of the semester."

I crossed my arms. "You think it's penance if you decide your punishment?" For some reason, irritation crept up on my good mood. "You want to make it up to me and my brother, and fishing wrappers out from under bushes doesn't begin to cover it."

"Kicking my ass is still on the table." He put his arms out, grin playing on his lips. "Should I put up a fight this time?"

"Asshole." I stalked off.

Hiro grabbed my hand. My heart shot into my throat as he pulled me back, securing his arm around my middle, and shrugging off his gloves. Darkly tempting pools of obsidian encompassed my vision until they were all I could see.

Hiro's fingers burned a trail up my forearm, over my shoulder, and then to my chin as he tilted my head up.

My shrinking, softening internal voice said to pull away, tell him off, swear up, down, and sideways that the kiss we shared in the elevator was the first and last. Hiro Saito could have my forgiveness, but never my love.

My lips parted and nothing came out.

Hiro caressed my mouth—his touch like a gentle breeze skimming the cupid's bow, and he left it wanting to cut a path over my nose to my forehead. He brushed a teasing lock of gold from my eyes and pushed it behind my ear.

"There," he gruffed. "You're perfect."

And then he was gone.

I stumbled, surprised to find myself suddenly out of his arms and expected to stay upright on shaky knees. Hot, steaming embarrassment tinged with something else forced my mouth to work.

"Ass!"

Laughing, Hiro resumed his trash picking, leisurely striding to the back of the building.

I stomped off, more mixed up than ever.

Dammit, fine! I'm attracted to the guy and I can't pretend otherwise. The long-haired fucker keeps calling my bluff. His efforts to prove he's become a better man are appreciated, but it'll take more than picking up trash.

The fact is that any guy that comes into my life becomes a part of Eli's life too. If it was just me, it'd be a different story, but it's not. What he honestly had to prove to me was that I could trust him with Eli, and he had quite a lot of work ahead of him to get there.

After breakfast, I took the long way up to my locker. One of the many ways I avoided Brandon. I don't think he noticed since he was busy with tennis practice most mornings. A good thing since I didn't want to give myself away too soon. It made my skin crawl to be near him, but be near I must.

I threw open my locker and there on my English textbook was a single folded note. The lock dug painfully into my palm as my grip tightened.

I have a plan. I have a plan. I have a plan.

I repeated that to myself as the urge to track Brandon down and beat him with a racket overwhelmed me. I unfolded the paper.

You've been so good. I'm sure it won't be a problem if we up the price to two thousand dollars. Next Monday. Locker 487.

If it is a problem, you know what will happen.

I tucked the note in my backpack and took out my phone. It rang as I ducked into the bathroom and checked beneath the stalls for feet.

"Good morning and thank you for calling Charles Magallon Bank. My name is David. How may I assist you?"

"Hi," I said, hopping on the bathroom counter. I was going to be late but Geske would get over it. "Can I speak to Savannah, please?"

"I'd be happy to assist you with anything you need, ma'am."

"For sure, but Savannah and I have built up a rapport. She wouldn't stand it if I cheated on her with another customer service rep."

"Certainly, ma'am." I picked up the barest chuckle. "I'll see if she's available."

"Hello." A bright cheery voice took over the call. "This is Savannah. How may I help you?"

"Hi, Savannah. I spoke to you the other day and the call dropped. About those checks and debit cards. Can we put a rush delivery on those?"

"Of course, ma'am. If I could have your information first..."

GESKE DID NOT GET OVER my tardiness. He gave me detention after school and I accepted my fate without complaint. After homeroom let out, I risked another afternoon in detention by sliding past Spanish class and heading to Blanchett's office.

The kind woman lit up at seeing me—a reaction that still threw me.

"Ember, dear. I know what brings you by." She beckoned for me to follow her. I walked past the pillar and spotted someone on a cot. "Gabriel?"

He stretched out on the white blankets, nursing a fat lip. I forgot all about Blanchett and ran up to him.

"Are you okay? Who did that to you?"

"I'm fine," he said. "It happened in class, so Seeger forced me to come here. Julian's back." He scoffed, putting the ice pack in his lap. "And if you were wondering, the bad shoulder isn't slowing him down."

"Julian?" I took the pack and pressed it to his lip. "Why would he hit you?"

"Probably has something to do with me sleeping with his girlfriend."

My eyes popped. "Sleeping with who now? Does he have another girlfriend I don't know about?"

He cracked a smile. "Pomona felt guilty after he was shot and she told him the truth. You won't tell anyone?"

"No," I swore. "They wouldn't believe me if I did. I guess this explains why you two were so weird with each other."

Gabriel sighed, dropping his head onto the pillow. "She loves me, Em. The problem is she loves him too."

"Is sharing not an option?"

That got a real laugh out of him. Good. That was my intent. Anyone trying to get between Julian Hart and Pomona Winchester needed a brighter outlook on life.

He motioned to his lip. "Obviously not."

"What are you going to do?" I asked gently.

"Convince her to run away to Dartmouth with me. She got in too. She also got into Stanford where Julian is going."

"Can I just put this out there? Pomona is the spawn of Satan," I stated, blunt as a truck. "She's never let me close enough to find the mark of the beast on her scalp, but it's gotta be there. Whereas you are a genuinely decent guy. You're hot. Smart. And rich." I reached for his hand, softening my tone. "You could be with anyone, Gabriel. Someone who'll see what they have in you, and know you're the right choice every time."

Despite what I said, he smiled. "You've got looks, smarts, and strength working for you too, Ember. People would say you can do better than a couple of Horsemen. But we love who we love, right?"

I smiled back. "Right."

"Ember?" Blanchett broke in. "You should hurry, dear. You have to get to class."

"Good luck," I told Gabriel.

Blanchett held the door open for me and closed it firmly behind. She went to her cabinet, dug around, and emerged with my delivery from the pharmacy.

"Here you are. Do you need anything else?"

I held the bag, gazing down at it. Blanchett's urging for me to get to class didn't move me. "Can I ask you something?"

"Of course, dear."

"If your parents had done what mine did, could you forgive them? Would you give them another chance to make it right?"

Blanchett gripped my shoulder. "Where is this coming from, Ember?"

"Nowhere." I stepped out of her grasp. "Forget I said anything."

"No." Blanchett walked into my path and diverted me from the door to a chair. "I promised you could come and speak to me when you needed. I'll write you a note for first period. We'll say it's cramps or something."

I laughed. "We're really lucky to have you, Mrs. Blanchett. I hope everyone knows it."

"You lovelies are very sweet to me. I know I'm appreciated." She sat next to me, patting my hand. "Tell me what's bothering you?"

"I think there's more going on with my parents and their disappearance. But who cares to listen to me after what they've done?"

"You knew them best," she replied. "If you believe there's more to the story, then you're most likely right. But forgiveness is another question. I believe a child can forgive their parents almost anything... which is often a tragedy."

"My life is a tragedy and forgiveness was always in short supply. I'm not deluding myself into believing they are something that they're not. I know who they are and what they're capable of. But all of that said, it doesn't change that they might need my help."

As I spoke, I accepted what I had to do.

"Thank you, Mrs. Blanchett." I got to my feet. "This really helped."

"Any time. Though I'm not sure what I did," she said with a laugh.

I stuffed my birth control in my bag, received my late pass, and left for Spanish.

My morning classes passed in a blur. Clay shared psychology with me, and at the bell, he walked me out of class, arm around my waist in a standard possessive move, but I wasn't mad about it.

"What do you think about sneaking off campus tonight?"

"Nolan's ruined our spot for me," I admitted.

"We can find another spot."

I shook my head. "I can't be out there without thinking of him kneeling in the dirt, spouting lie after lie. Plus, it's too cold for swimming and getting naked in any form," I said.

Clay kissed my crown. "I want to spend time with you. Just us."

My skin tightened. It might've been my own anxiety, but I swore I sensed *"before our time runs out,"* added to his declaration.

"I'll think of a place for us," he said.

"Options are limited. I'm excited to see what you come up with."

"Me too." He laughed. "Can I think outside the fence?"

A groan beat my grin away. "We can't. My uncle and aunt are under some affliction. Not sure what, but I'm hoping it's not contagious. The result is I'm not allowed to leave campus without their permission and driver."

Clay shrugged with one shoulder and held open the door to the cafeteria with the other. "They only find out if you go through the office. We want to leave, we'll just leave. Security's not that tight."

"Hmm. He has a point." We strode up to the food line. "Punishment if we're caught?"

He whistled. "Steep."

I rose on tiptoe and stole a kiss. "I'll risk it."

We slid down the line and loaded our trays with pizza, salad, and tomato soup. Sitting at our regular table was Brandon, Gabriel, and Camila. I shot Camila a wave and then veered off, joining Clay at the Angel table. It was not a good idea for me to be near Brandon with his latest ransom note weighing down my backpack.

Cassius and Royal were seated. Cassius paid his food little mind while he messed with his phone. Royal was buried in a sketch as usual.

"Clay," said Cassius. He didn't look up from the screen. "What's Sheridan Oakes's visiting policy?"

"Why? Who are you talking to?"

"Mom."

Clay paused with his pizza halfway to his mouth. "Who?"

"Our mother. Remember? She carried the three of us around in the same hot tub for eight months," he said. "What's the policy? She wants to know if we can visit her every weekend."

"How the fuck are you texting Mom?" Clay hissed. "She doesn't have a phone."

"I bought five and left it with her friends and the workers at the shelter. But she's home with Dad right now. On her meds."

"She's with Dad? And she's asking about the home? Which means Dad knows about it."

Like Royal, I pointed my eyes down at my own business. I cared about the triplets and wanted to help however I could. When the time came, they would tell me how. Until then, I was the silent supportive girlfriend.

"Yeah." Cassius's tone said it all. "He knows."

"Shit!" Clay shoved away his food.

I put my hand on his thigh, sending waves of comfort.

"He's going to talk her out of going." Clay was careful to keep his voice low, but his frustration came through loud.

"She's talking *him* into going, Clay. Mom's excited. She thinks they'll live there together."

"It's not a rehab facility. Once Dad looks the place up for himself, it's over."

"What do you want me to do? She's lucid and she remembers us talking to her about the place. How was I supposed to stop her telling Dad?"

"Cas. Clay."

I jumped. Camila appeared out of nowhere. It must have been triplet telepathy because she picked up on a problem from three tables over and was at their side with a matching frown.

"What's wrong?" she asked.

"We can't do this here." Clay pushed away from the table. "Let's go."

The three filed off, food untouched. I glanced at Royal after they were gone. "I hope they work all of this stuff out. I can't imagine how hard it's been having to take care of their parents." I moved around the table and edged onto his lap, pushing his sketch—of me—aside. I draped my arms around his shoulders, teasing the soft hairs at the nape of his neck. "That's better. The real-life version deserves all of your love and attention now."

"All right, but we'll get kicked out of school if we do that here."

"Shut up," I laughed. "And thank you. I needed that."

"Any time."

"I heard Julian's back."

He nodded.

"Have you seen him? How is he?"

"Hart wouldn't have let him come back if he wasn't good."

"That's true." I nuzzled his cheek, marveling that I got to touch this man. Kiss him. Listen to his heart beat beneath my ear as he slept. Receive the rare I love yous that fell from his lips. "How are you? I've been thinking about nothing but Nolan, Rio, Brandon, and my parents. A nonstop loop that's stripping away my sanity. How do you deal with all of this?"

"I'm not scared. If Nolan comes for me again, I'll be ready for him."

"He's got a gun and you have a switchblade," I whispered.

"You're right. I should lose the knife. Make it a fair fight."

I heaved a sigh. "Can you just not be your confusing brand of sexy and reckless right now?"

Royal smirked. "Not if keeping it up gets you out of here and in my room."

"You can't distract me with sex. We're going to talk. A lot. Long, deep, open conversations about our future and our plan to make it happen. Get ready, baby."

His laugh was deep and rich. "I'm ready."

"Good. Then we can go back to your room. Is Hiro there?"

"No." Royal took that cue to pack up his things and tossed his notebook in his bag. "He's with Eli."

"Excuse me?"

"He's eating lunch with Eli," he repeated like it was no big deal.

"No, he's not," I said.

"See for yourself."

I hopped off Royal's lap, rushing to the edge of the loft to peer down at the crowded cafeteria. Sitting in his regular seat with his pizza-eating best friend, Tatum, was my brother. The odd sight was Hiro Saito sitting across from him and the empty seats around them cleared by the Angel's presence.

In a blink I was off the loft and racing down the steps. Eli appeared perfectly fine. He smiled as he signed something to Hiro. That grin twitched as he noticed me barreling across the lunchroom, scattering students like bowling pins.

"*Hi, Em.*"

"What is this? What are you doing?"

"Ember." Hiro's fingers skated down my palm and tried to link through mine. I snatched my hand away like he caught fire.

"Don't even think about it," I snapped.

Hiro grinned, far from shamed, and his smile ignited the usual flutter in my stomach.

Eli tugged my blazer sleeve. "*It's okay, Em. I'm teaching Hiro sign language.*"

"Teaching him sign language?" It didn't make sense saying it out loud either.

"*Then he's walking with me to class and telling Dylan Manzoni if he doesn't stop copying off my paper, the Horsemen are paying him a visit.*"

I repeated that to Hiro who, of all things, nodded. "I won't scare the freshman that badly, but yeah, I'll handle that cheater."

"Why in the world would you do that?"

Hiro looked me in the eye and said, "I'm his bitch."

"*Yep,*" Eli signed, beaming. "*He's my bitch.*"

My eyes ping-ponged between the two of them. Then I gazed around to check I was actually in the cafeteria of Raven River Academy and not Bizarroland.

"Run that by me again," I said. "You're his what?"

"I can't be with you until things are right between me and Eli. Whatever he wants for the foreseeable future, I'll do it."

I gaped at him. *What he honestly had to prove to me was that I could trust him with Eli.* Was this guy reading my mind?

"But you… can't."

"Why not?"

"*Yeah,*" Eli asked. "*Why not?*"

"I'm your sister. If someone is bothering you in class, I'll take care of it."

"*Hiro had to make it right with me on his own. And he's doing it. It's cool, sis. You're not being replaced.*"

"Can I talk to you?" I grabbed Hiro's arm and drew him off to the side. "You need to earn Eli's forgiveness, but if this isn't about that, and you're just trying to get with me—"

"I'm not." He shook his head. "Actually, I *am* trying to get with you, but I'm not using Eli to do it. He was beaten up because of me. I don't deserve forgiveness but I have to work to earn it anyway. You know my history, Ember. This is bigger than my feelings for you."

My indignation leeched away. In spite of everything, I believed him.

"Okay. But seriously, don't let Eli get it into his head that you're his muscle or something. Just tell that cheater to change seats."

"I've got this." Hiro laced our fingers together. I didn't pull away. "What about you? And Brandon?"

"He left me another ransom note. This time for two thousand dollars."

A furious hiss leaked through his teeth. "He's getting fucking bold."

"That he is," I agreed, "and that's what is going to hang him."

Chapter Five

The first week of classes passed with aching slowness. Friday afternoon and the expected call from Mallory was a welcome relief.

Finally, I thought as I hurried out of PE. *Express shipping doesn't mean what it used to.*

Mallory hunched over her keyboard. The twenty-six-year-old looked older scrunched up like that. Eyes squinted at the screen and lips pursed in concentration. I approached her desk, studying her with the same scrutiny. Even if Hiro wasn't lying about when their sexual relationship started, she should be fired if not jailed for letting alcohol and drugs into the school. Not to mention she was perfectly happy to mess up my transcripts.

Just sitting there so fucking innocent. My lips twitched into a sneer. *Any revenge plan that doesn't have her in it is incomplete.*

"Hello," I said brightly. "You called about a package?"

"Yes."

Mallory doubled over and fished a box out from under her desk.

She didn't ask me to open it, and a mix of relief and nausea accompanied the thought that being the Angels' girl earned me a pass on that rule. I breathed a sigh of relief that Savannah followed my instructions and put the checks and debit card in a plain box. She allowed me to take it unchecked, but Mallory was still a treacherous bitch and for all I knew she was the one passing Royal's and my movements to Rio and my aunt and uncle. Better to lean on the safe side.

Mallory handed me the box and sign-out sheet, then she returned to her work, dismissing me.

"Thank you." I stuck it under my arm. "So, how crazy is it what happened with Nolan Ives?"

"What?" She lifted her head, turning squinty eyes on me. "Excuse me?"

"Nolan Ives," I repeated. "I was there, you know. The night he lost it and shot his best friend while trying to kill my boyfriend."

"Oh, I'm sorry." She fixed her face in an expression that mimicked sympathy. "That must have been awful."

"It was. He was saying all kinds of horrible things. That everything he'd done was to avenge his sister. Dealing drugs on campus and funding a dangerous man. I can't let myself think about what would've happened if Julian hadn't stopped him."

"Don't think about it." Mallory laid her hand over mine and revulsion crawled up my skin. "Just be thankful they're both okay and trust the police will find Mr. Ives."

"I hope they're doing everything to look for him... and the person who helped him sell drugs on campus." I raised my gaze to a poster over her head that boasted about the spring book fair. Didn't want her reading the contempt in my eyes. "Because when you think about it, he couldn't have gotten away with it for so long without help."

"Well, I don't know about that. Dealers are getting smarter these days about hiding and moving their product. I've suggested more than once to the headmistress that we need more random searches and harsher consequences for this kind of thing."

I had to give it to her. She gave a great impression of a responsible, concerned adult.

"No, he had help," I stated. "He practically bragged about it while he had a gun to my head. I made sure the police knew that their search doesn't stop with him. There's more than one person responsible for what happened that night, and I'll make sure they get theirs.

"Anyway." I walked backward, waving goodbye. "Thank you. Enjoy your weekend."

"You as well, Miss Bancroft." Mallory's face was disturbingly unreadable. "Goodbye."

I had two minutes to get to my next class. It pained me to stuff the box in my locker, but this was too important to be held up by detention.

I shut the door and came face to face with Brandon.

"Hey."

"Whoa," I cried. "Have you added apparating to your list of skills?"

He laughed. "No, but I dig the Harry Potter reference. What are you doing after class?"

"Can we walk and talk?" I asked, sidestepping him. "I have a minute to get to communications."

"Sure. I've got psych. It's the same way."

We walked side by side through the hall like so many times before. So why did I feel like I didn't know how to do this?

I sucked in a deep breath, trapping and holding it.

"It feels like we haven't hung out in forever," he said. "With all that shit over break, you know I'm here for you right?"

"I know."

"How about tonight we do a movie marathon? All your favorites but I reserve the right to make snide comments."

I forced a laugh. "Sounds good. After dinner?"

"Let's do it."

He hugged me in front of Seeger's class and kept walking as my smile disappeared. *I'll need three showers to wash his stench off of me.*

Seeger had the desks pushed to the side and out of the way. It possibly meant a sharing circle, but in the short time I've known the woman, she's proven herself unpredictable. The day before she took us outside to a mini obstacle course, paired me with Gabriel, blindfolded me, and then made him shout directions at me to get me through. I fell on my face twice.

Hiro and Clay posted up in the back, talking. My talk with Brandon must have shown on my face because both stopped and asked me what was wrong.

"Back-to-back conversations with two people I despise most in the world," I replied. "How was your day?"

The guys shared a look but didn't ask for more details with people listening in. "Cas and I have to go home tomorrow," Clay said. "Take care of this situation with our parents before it goes south."

"Oh." I chewed my lip. "I was about to ask you for a ride tomorrow, but that's more important. I'll ask Royal instead."

"Nah, it's fine. Why do you need a ride?"

"Bank," I said simply.

"We'll take you. We can drop by the house after."

"Don't let me get in the way, Clay."

"You're never in the way. Besides, you have to meet them sometime. It's better we do this while Mom's... home."

I got the subtext clearly. "I'd love to meet them. I hope they like me."

"Of course they will."

"Everyone in this town hates me, so it's a fair worry."

He chuckled. "They're not the types to judge a person for the sins of their parents. Trust me, they'll love you."

"All right, class." Seeger clapped. "Let's form two lines down the middle of the room, please. Today we're playing out a scenario where you've gotten into an argument with your friend and now your peer group is choosing sides. How do we navigate this situation?"

Class passed in typical fashion. Pomona disagreed with everything I said and made sure to let me know as rudely as possible.

Seeger sent us to opposite sides of the room and I spotted Pomona in the corner speaking to Gabriel in low tones, arms clasped like she was hugging herself. It didn't take a genius to figure out she was upset about Julian—who I still hadn't seen since he'd been taking all of his meals in his room and we didn't have classes together. Pomona's torment had to go somewhere and I was her favorite punching bag because I punched back.

"Good work, everyone," Seeger called at the end of the lesson. "Enjoy your weekend."

I was first out of the door, thinking of the box waiting for me in the locker. Hiro caught up to me quickly.

"Hey. We couldn't get into it in class, but are you okay?"

"I might have done something stupid." I didn't know when we graduated to talking normally but there we were. "I went to the office to get a package from Mallory and I couldn't hold myself back."

"What did you say?"

"To sum it up: that the police were onto her ass."

"Yeah, I agree," Hiro deadpanned. "Not the best idea."

Hiro was a strong, towering presence beside me. The sharp, pleasing scent of vanilla and eucalyptus suffused the air around us. Hiro Saito was always perfect. Even decked out in bandages to cover his tats. His hair was washed, shiny, and intoxicating. His uniform was neat. No part of him was out of place.

"I couldn't help it. She can't just sit there banging on her keyboard after everything she's done. That woman doesn't belong anywhere near students. I will see her fired before I get out of this place."

"If it makes you feel better, my arrangement with her is over. She's getting a cut of my profits instead of my dick."

"She is?!" That was too astonished and high-pitched and I regretted it as soon as it was out of my mouth. I cleared my throat and tried again. "I mean, she is? Why? And why would that make me feel better?"

"I can't sleep with her when I want someone else. She wasn't happy about it, but she agreed."

"What about your payments?"

"I'll make enough to cover it."

"And save up for school?"

Hiro looked straight ahead, letting the question pass without an answer.

"I feel like I should say you don't have to do this for me," I whispered.

"But you won't." Hiro hooked his pinkie through mine. "Because you're glad I can be all yours now."

I could've denied it. Probably should have.

I could've pulled away. Probably should have done that too.

But I didn't do either of those things.

My heart thrummed a wild, erratic beat, telling of all the things right about this, while my head reminded that they were trumped by all the things wrong. I swore I heard his saying the same.

He attacked me. Blackmailed me. Threatened my future. Took a bullet for me. Made it up to my brother. Traded his dreams for the tiniest chance I'd fall in love with him again. I think Mom was right about love.

I turned my palm, taking his hand properly.

It's not any good unless it's a mess.

THAT NIGHT THE KNOB jiggled a warning. I hurriedly closed my laptop as Camila pushed into the room.

"Hey," she said. "You scarfed your food and ran out of dinner so fast. Is everything okay?"

"Fine." I flapped a hand at my computer. "I just had to finish up some homework before the movie."

Camila flopped on her bed. "Oh, yeah. Brandon told me about that. Is it cool if I join you guys or is it a best-friends-only thing?"

"Umm. You're one of my best friends, so that's an automatic invite."

She laughed. "Thanks. We can torture him with the cheesiest, sappiest romance movies in cinematic history."

"See? This is why we're close."

Camila bounced off the bed and hugged me from behind, propping her chin on my head. I liked her so much better when she wasn't blackening my eyes.

"I heard you're coming with us to see Mom and Dad," she said.

"I didn't know you were going too."

"Yep." She released me and pulled up her desk chair. "I was worried about Dad and his drinking, so I took the car. Now that he's doing better, I have to drive it back so they can get around. Also, I haven't seen Mom in weeks."

"I swear you guys can just leave me in the car. Crack the window and I'll be fine."

Laughing, she waved that away. "You're dating my brothers. Even got an 'I love you' out of them. Meeting the parents was the next step, and the best time is when Dad's sober and Mom's lucid," she said, echoing her brother. "You can see where I grew up."

"I'm excited. I really want to meet them. Be a part of your lives."

"You already are." Camila got up. "I'm going to take a quick shower before we go to the boys' dorm. Raid the stash under my bed for the chocolate and two bags of popcorn."

"Ooooh. I might've raided that stash already."

Rolling her eyes, she chuckled her way to the bathroom. "No one ferrets out sweets quite like you, Ember Bancroft."

The door closed behind her with a soft click. I snapped my chair around and opened the laptop. Two apps were up. The one with the letter typed and ready for me to send. And the email app showcasing the message I received.

Aurora Fiscal Holdings was formed with an address of a warehouse company that accepted mail on behalf of people looking to protect their privacy. The act was perfectly legal. I checked to be sure in my search to know everything about Good Samaritan Mail Services. Another bit of information I learned was to set up an account, you had to give a real address for them to forward your mail.

543 Rosehip Lane was nothing but a warehouse, but my parents could've given Good Samaritan a real address to be contacted, especially since Aurora Holdings was sitting on over twenty-five million dollars. It was solid thinking that ran into a predictable roadblock.

Hello,

I'm sorry but we do not give out client information. In the event the account owner is unable to access the account due to death or tragic circumstance, please contact the legal department.

If you're the account owner and you've been locked out of your account, you may follow the steps to create a new password or username.

I stopped reading and clicked out of the email. Of course they weren't going to send me the information. I wasn't stupid enough to say the account owners were the infamous Frank and Lenora Bancroft, but even an honest plea for help saying that my parents were missing was a no go. As was contacting the legal department because the minute I said their names, the feds would get involved.

"It was worth a try," I mumbled. Moving on, I brought up the letter, finished it off, and printed it out. I placed it in my drawer on top of my freshly minted checks from Charles Magallon Bank.

Camila poked her head out of the bathroom. "Em, can you pass me my lotion? I left it on the dresser."

"Sure."

I closed the lid, feeling an inch closer to in control than I did that morning.

Camila finished up in the bathroom and came out wearing a sweater dress and ankle-high boots. She applied her makeup with a light hand and then spritzed peachy perfume on her neck. I couldn't tease her for dressing up for movie night because the girl looked this great all the time.

"I'm ready," she sang. "Do you have our movies picked out?"

"The cheesiest and sappiest."

"Then let's go."

Words couldn't describe how happy I was that Camila would act as a buffer. I was even happier that movie-viewing didn't require talking. I'd sit on the floor with Camila between us, stuff my mouth with popcorn, and get out of there as the credits rolled up.

He can't expect more than three movies out of me, right? I thought as we crossed to the boys' hall. *I'll be out of there around midnight.*

Brandon answered on Camila's second knock. "Ladies, come on in." He hugged me on my way inside.

Yep. This guy is definitely overdoing it on the pawing.

"Craig's here but he's heading out soon. He's crashing with his girlfriend."

Craig glanced up from his desk, nodded at Camila, glared at me, and went back to his laptop. If I was wondering if things were still frosty between us; the answer was yes.

Brandon swept out his arm showing off the chips, popcorn, candy corn, and bottles of cream soda. "Feast. I'll set up the TV."

One reason the movie marathons were in Brandon's room was he had a television that he used to stream his movies. We didn't have to huddle around his laptop. Televisions were allowed in the dorm. Some kids lived here all year. Hart did her best to make it comfortable for them.

"What are we watching?" he asked.

"We've got three movies picked out and don't even try to say *DoubleFeature* doesn't have them because we checked," warned Camila.

"Oh no. That means this isn't good for me."

She grinned around a bite of popcorn. "We'll take *Pretty Woman, To All The Boys I Loved Before,* and *Definitely, Maybe.*"

"Ugh," Brandon cried. "Why, Ember? I thought we were friends?"

Wrong, motherfucker.

"You said you'd watch all of my favorites," I replied.

He leveled a finger at me. "I also said I reserve the right to make snide comments."

"I expect nothing less."

Brandon returned to fiddling with the cords while I got to work stuffing my mouth. Camila laid out pillows and a blanket for us on the floor. If our friendship was what I once believed it was, these would have been the senior-year memories you collected in the mental scrapbook of your life. Recalling the time you were young, irresponsible, and looking forward to a future where anything could happen.

My scrapbook had rips, spilled ink, browning edges, and those wrinkly pages you get from dropping a book in a puddle. And now, I couldn't even have my senior year. It would always be tinged by the boy who came up to me on my first day and pretended to be my friend.

"Can we do *Definitely, Maybe* first?" Brandon spoke up. "Ryan Reynolds is my famous alter ego."

Camila snorted into her drink. "Who told you that?"

"Are you kidding?" Brandon did a spin. "Just look at me."

"I'm looking, and again I ask, who told you that?"

I smothered a laugh. I hated every second of being here with him, but I'd enjoy Camila riding him all I wanted.

"For real. We've all got one. Yours is Margot Robbie. Ember is Mena Suvari. It's obvious."

"Huh." Camila squinted at me. "I see it."

"Told you. So, admit I'm Ry—"

"Guys."

The single word drew our eyes to Craig. Shifting colors shone on his face. Whatever he was looking at stole his affable smile—and this time it wasn't me. "You need to see this."

"What is it?"

He motioned to the TV. "Brandon, channel four. It's broadcasting live."

Brandon switched over to regular TV, flipping to the news station as his roommate requested.

"—here on Marshall Street where the bodies of three men were recovered from a dumpster behind Kilkenny Pub." Reds and blues flashed behind the reporter. We made out a bar, a small crowd of people, and the police.

The four of us gathered before the screen, overtaken by a grim darkness that preceded the rest of her report.

"The victims have yet to be identified but police have confirmed they each bear matching tattoos of an angel on their arms."

Camila flashed out, seizing me in a tight grip.

"Angel wings were graffitied above the heads of the victim. This mark has been present at more than a few crime scenes over the years, but never at the scene of a triple homicide. At this time, police are unsure if this horrific crime is an act of retribution or a sign of more violence to come. We'll keep you informed as the investigation unfolds. I'm Amy Kouris with Channel Four news."

Brandon shut off the TV late. Much too late.

The four of us traded looks.

Bodies dumped in the garbage was a horrifying reality of the Horsemen, though those bodies never had an angel inked on their skin.

What did this mean? Had another gang retaliated and sent a brutal message? Or did the Horsemen send their own message? They would take out anyone who crossed them. Even their own.

Did Rio find his traitor?

"Excuse me, guys." I made for the door. "Start the movie without me. I'll be back soon."

I was out before they could say anything.

Ten steps brought me to Royal's door. Three knocks got him to open it.

"Em?" Royal stood there in nothing but black sweatpants and that after-shower citrus smell.

"Have you seen the news?" I pushed him inside. My sudden arrival interrupted Hiro reclining on his bed reading manga. "The police found three bodies with angel tattoos in a dumpster behind Kilkenny Pub."

Royal flicked to Hiro.

"What?" I demanded. "What's that look?"

"Kilkenny Pub is Cavanaugh's bar."

Hiro bugged out. "Royal, what are you doing?"

"It's fine. She knows."

"Not enough," I said. "Why would someone kill those men and put their bodies behind his bar? Was the news right about it being a revenge killing? Or did Rio find the men working against him?"

Royal shook his head, freshly washed locks swinging. "Rio wouldn't have put their bodies on Cavanaugh's doorstep if he did."

"Unless Cavanaugh is the traitor," I said. "Nolan said he got the gun from the man he's working with."

"Still no, Em," Hiro replied. "You don't provoke a guy like Cavanaugh and then give him time to strike back. Rio's too smart for that. If Cavanaugh is the traitor, Rio would have him over for dinner and shoot him under the table while he's sucking on the oysters. It'd be a strike he never saw coming." Hiro looked to Royal. "No offense."

"I know what kind of man my father is." Royal was hard and matter-of-fact. "Hiro's right, Em. This isn't Rio's style." He backed toward the bed. "I don't know anything about this. Wait here."

Royal grabbed his phone and blew out of the room.

"Em." Hiro swung his feet to the floor. I moved in as he patted the spot next to him. "You don't need to be worried about this. A traitor gunning for Rio is not your problem."

"How can you say that when a few weeks ago it was our problem? Royal was almost a casualty of this war, and three more were taken today. Have you seen the tattoo on your arm lately? If someone is killing Horsemen, I'm worried."

Inexplicably, he smiled. "We're safe here, Em. No one is going to storm the gates to put us in a dumpster."

"What happens after school? I know the plans Endo has for you."

Hiro cursed under his breath. "Royal didn't have to fucking tell you everything."

"Yes, he did." I put my hand over his. They were oddly cold and I squeezed to impart my warmth. "I'm done with secrets. You don't keep them from someone you love."

He laughed—a rough, wry sound. "Then here's the truth. It doesn't matter what happens to me after graduation because you'll be far away from here, living with Eli and the guys."

I dropped my gaze. "Who's to say you won't be there too? You said every day for the rest of your life you'd be the man I need. The rest of your life isn't five months, Hiro."

"Maybe this is my gift to you, Em." He stared at our hands with a strange kind of intensity. "This is how I become that man."

"What does that—"

Royal walked in the room.

"That was fast," Hiro said. He stood, dropping my hand.

"It was a quick conversation. The Horsemen didn't do this and Rio found out about it along with everyone else. On the news," he confirmed. "It's a message."

"What message?" I cried. "'Please, please, please, find me and put a bullet in my head. I have a death wish the size of Europe.' What kind of psychotic maniac would pick this fight with the leader you said was the *most dangerous* Horseman?"

"If this was another gang, it's going to get bad in the OB," Hiro said. "It'll get bad either way."

My phone buzzed in my pocket.

Camila: You okay? Are you coming back?

"I should go," I said. "We'll talk about this later. Both of you," I told Hiro.

I returned to Brandon's room, plastering on a smile for hours of watching movies that would be labeled in my scrapbook under the awful night I sat quietly next to Eli's attacker, realizing deep inside that Royal's warning was a prediction. The Horsemen were at war.

THE NEXT DAY, I SLIPPED through the gap in the fence and left shining Raven River Academy behind.

They really need to fix that fence, I thought as I began the long trek through the forest for the road leading to town. Cassius and Clay's car idled next to a large sequoia tree. Through the window they stopped mid-conversation and Cassius hopped out to open my door.

"This was overkill, baby. No one was going to catch you sneaking out."

"Better safe than sorry. Do I look okay?"

I did a little spin, flaring out the hem. Aunt Violet would never know I voluntarily wore one of the dresses she bought me. Long, belted, and made of warm teal cashmere. I didn't hate it as much as her other picks, and to meet my boyfriends' parents, the standard jeans and cropped tee wouldn't do.

"Beautiful."

I climbed into the back seat and pulled Cassius in with me. I draped his arm around me and got comfy. "Driver, the bank, please."

"So, I'm the chauffeur and Cassius's the one you feel up in the back seat? What did I do to get downgraded?"

I laughed. "Don't feel bad. I'm tipping you *handsomely* after this."

"That's more like it." Clay set off down the road. "Because there will be an after this. Cas and Cam are taking the car back and you and I are going to that place we talked about."

"We are?" I was grinning like a goof and the rearview mirror confirmed it. "Where?"

"You'll find out."

"Isn't it too risky to be out all night? We've got cameras in the dorm now."

"They won't notice we didn't come back."

"That disturbs and reassures me."

Clay turned up the music. We belted along to a classic rock station in between my intense make-out sessions with Cassius. For a single Saturday, everything was perfect. I was a normal girl messing around with her boyfriends and on her way to have lunch with their parents. Minus the detour to withdraw two thousand dollars' worth of ransom money.

"We have to go to two ATMs," I said. "They have withdrawal limits."

"We'll hit up some closer to the gates," Clay replied. "It's the middle of the day, but you don't want to be carrying that kind of cash deep in the OB."

"Are you paying Lacroix with the lodge money?" Cassius asked.

"Have to. My car thieving days are over."

"When can we know this plan? Because I'm good to handle our Lacroix problem my way."

I stroked his stubbly chin. "You already know more than you should. This is bigger than Rio. I should have reported the account the minute I found it. The feds were eager to charge me with obstruction the first time. I'm not letting you guys get deeper in this than you already have."

They argued with me, of course, but my lips stayed sealed.

Clay brought me to three separate ATMs when the first refused to give me more than five hundred dollars.

"Done." I slid into the front seat and popped a kiss on Clay's cheek. "Thank you, driver. On to your parents' house. Or should we stop and get something? Flowers?"

"Mom doesn't like fresh flowers," said Cassius.

"Chocolates?"

"Dad's allergic to chocolate," Clay added.

"Wanna help me out here?"

"There's a place that makes good shortbread cookies," Cassius said with a laugh. "They love those."

"Shortbread cookies it is."

Clay turned the car around, heading deep into the OB. "We should warn you of a few things before we get there."

"I won't say anything about the stuff you've told me," I said. "That goes without saying."

"Don't talk about the Horsemen either, or how we make our money. Mom will try to get you alone and ask about your life and plans for the future. Don't tell her you want to leave Raven River and take us with you. Actually, don't let her get you alone."

"Dad's quiet," Cassius threw in. "He won't say much, so don't feel bad if he doesn't talk to you."

Their warnings took up most of the car ride to the bakery. I purchased my treat with more than the right amount of nerves. I could pretend this was a normal lunch, but those didn't include talks of rehab and institutions while cleverly avoiding that those measures would be paid with gang money.

I should just speak when I'm spoken to. Never pulled that off before but there's a first time for everything.

Outside of my window, the Outer Borough revealed under the blazing sun. The entire OB could be classified as low income, but that didn't make all areas the same. North, south, east, and west reflected the culture and diversity of the people who lived there. East OB had the best Japanese restaurants this side of the coast.

The north was denser. The homes more spread out and bleeding into the forest. It was quieter over there. You got the feeling neighbors could run into each other and not have a clue who they were looking at. The area directly circling the Estate was the most well-off by Outer Borough standards. Those that worked in the Estate but couldn't afford to live there, set up their homes on the perimeter. Two police stations resided there and they patrolled frequently.

The southside I knew better as it was closer to my home on the outskirts. One day, my friends and I snuck out to a photo gallery—thrilling for the express warnings our parents gave us to never go into the OB alone. Then there was the westside.

The location of Royal's apartment. Home of Clay, Cassius, and Camila. Arguably the most dangerous part of the OB for one simple fact. It was the birthplace of the Horsemen.

If every neighborhood has a feel, then west OB was tired. Plaster and paint couldn't be bothered to cling to their buildings. Efforts were made to decorate for the holidays, but none to remove them. Lights lined the roofs and Christmas greetings cheered me from the windows weeks later. Overflowing trash cans dotted the sidewalk, and faded graffiti garnished the cracked pavement. People passed each other on the street without speaking or making eye contact with the other.

Clay turned off the main road onto a street I'd never been to, but often heard about.

"Rainer."

I reached over and squeezed Clay's thigh. My boys grew up on one of the most dangerous streets in town. A meth lab was busted a few doors down. Four years ago, a raging man was hauled out of his house after a standoff with the police. He shot and killed his girlfriend, and then fired on the cops when they came to arrest him. I watched this on the news from the safety of my big house with the pool in the back and three cars out front, my father's stern directive to stay out of the OB finally making sense.

But my boys lived it. They became the ones responsible for taking care of their parents and they turned to the smiling shadow man when he extended the hand of help. Thinking over all I've come to know about Rio Cruz, it still didn't make sense to me the lengths he went to in order to rescue Cassius, Clay, and Hiro.

The obvious reason being that he was creating men that would one day be indebted to him, didn't sit comfortably in my mind. A care for life? The man tried to kill me without a second thought. Concern for the welfare of children? He bulldozed into Royal's life and transformed his happy son into a thief and future leader of a merciless street gang.

Was there a long game at play? How could there be when he met the boys as twelve-year-olds? He couldn't have known they'd grow into the smart, resourceful men they were, poised to be trained by the leader of the Horsemen themselves?

Or maybe the simple fact was Rio Cruz was a collector. Like an enthusiast collects coins, stamps, or comic books, secure in the knowledge they'd one day be valuable. Rio collected people. Hardened, dangerous men to fund his upward mobility. Check.

A son. Rare. Only one of his kind. Perfect as a future successor. Check.

Clever little pickpockets. Desperate. Willing to do whatever they had to for their family. Check.

An angry, tough little boy. Heir to the Eastside Crew. Check.

A girl with no options. And twenty-five million dollars in a bank account. Check.

He collected us all expecting we'd one day be useful to him. If that day never came, we'd be gotten rid of just like that.

Maybe that's the key to getting us out from under him, I thought as we parked in front of a house. *Prove that we're an investment that's more trouble than it's worth.*

"Ready?" Cassius asked.

"I'm ready."

Clay took the hand off his thigh and kissed it. "Keep your money in your purse and your purse on you at all times. Mom's an even better pickpocket than us."

I choked. "You saved that info for the last second!"

They laughed. "It'll be fine."

Cassius came around and opened my door. He held out his hand, helping me out to the full view of his childhood home.

A chain-link fence penned in a lawn that was dead grass and dirt. A spare tire nestled next to a collection of empty flowerpots by the porch. Their home was, of all colors, pink, and light-green-painted bars covered the windows.

A horn beeped as we stepped through the fence. Camila waved through the window. She parked behind the boys and bounded up the sidewalk to take Cassius's place by my side.

"I'm so happy we're all here. Mom and Dad are going to love you, Em. Just in case you were worrying about that."

"You know I am. It's not every day parents meet the person dating both of their sons."

She tossed her head. "They won't care about that."

Clay climbed the porch and opened the door with his key. "Mom? Dad?"

A voice reached us from the depths of the house. "Son? Come in, come in."

The inside of the Walker home was and wasn't what I expected at the same time. We stopped on the welcome mat, toeing off our shoes, and dozens upon dozens of pictures greeted me. It was a gallery featuring the photographer's favorite models: Cassius, Clay, and Camila.

The three of them in diapers all facing different directions and making different faces. The triplets in the tub. The triplets sharing a crib. The triplets as toddlers—boys in matching shirts and Camila in a frilly pink dress. The triplets as bright-faced, scabby-kneed kids. And even the photo Clay told me about where a scared Camila tipped her father into the river.

I passed slowly, scanning each one. "Look at you, Clay." I pointed to a photo of them around one year old, using a coffee table to stand. "Cutest little chubby cheeks."

"How do you know that's me?"

"I don't. I took a fifty-fifty shot with the babies not wearing a dress."

"And you were right. You should take those odds to Vegas."

I spun on the woman who could only be their mom.

"Mom," Camila cried, erasing all doubt. She threw her arms around her, burying her face in her neck like she wanted to soak her up and never let go.

"There's my beautiful girl."

Camila was a beauty, and as I gazed at her mother, I saw she came by it honest. Gray prematurely streaked her blonde, stressed hair. Dark bags hitched a ride under her eyes and wrinkles dabbed her temples. Threadbare clothes hung off her thin frame, and in spite of all of this, her smile struck me sideways. The perfectly formed button nose she passed to Camila. The wickedly teasing grin she gave her sons. The hauntingly beautiful eyes she gifted the world by passing to all three.

"Boys?" their mother prompted.

Clay and Cassius moved in on the hug, encasing them both and kissing her cheeks.

"Em, this is our mom, Virginia Walker."

"Ember." She slipped out of their hold and came for me, arms wide. "So happy to meet you."

"Hello, Mrs. Walker. I brought you these—"

She crushed me to her chest, cookies and all. I grunted into her collarbone, inhaling her mix of flowery soap and fresh laundry.

"You are gorgeous." Virginia stroked my hair. "Lovely color. Is it real?"

"Au naturel," I said into her neck.

"So thin. And you smell great." She squeezed me even tighter in the longest hug I'd ever received. "I see why my boys are taken with you."

"Mom." Gentle hands extracted me from her hold. "Where's Dad?"

"Right where I left him, Clay. We're making lunch. Sausage, peppers and onions, and salad." Virginia didn't let them lead her too far from me. She snagged my hand, taking me along. "Ember can help us. You make the salad."

"Okay."

"I'll make the salad," said Cassius. "Then we can talk."

Virginia cocked her head. "Talk about what?"

"We'll get into it later."

Our group passed through the living room—a space of worn, mismatched furniture and more photos of the family. A proper look confessed none of them showed the triplets older than twelve.

A swinging saloon-style door beckoned us into the kitchen. Cramped from the dining table taking up most of the floor, it held a full-sized fridge, small countertop, sink, and stove.

Seated at the table was a hefty man, obviously tall even sitting down. He cut the peppers with careful precision, transferring them to a bowl and then reaching for another one. The flexing of his movements hinted his heft was of muscle. Taking him in, I noted the broken capillaries around his nose and the yellow tinge to his skin. They told their story without detracting from the strong jaw and full head of wavy, blond hair.

In that moment, I saw the beautiful young couple with their three babies, whole and happy and looking forward to the future. Until illness, poverty, and addiction ate away at the happy scene.

Virginia plopped me next to him. "This is my husband, Glen. Say hi to Ember, sweetie."

He nodded to me, not pausing in his task. "Hello."

"Look at what she brought us." Virginia took the cookies out of my hands. "Our favorite. Wasn't that nice?"

"Thank you."

"How are those peppers coming?" She grasped his shoulders, bending down to kiss him. He tilted his head up like a sunflower seeks the sun. The tiniest smile graced his lips as she nuzzled his nose.

"Almost done."

"Do a good job. This is the first time the boys have brought a girl home to meet us." Virginia went to the fridge, humming to herself as she rifled inside.

Camila took the seat on my other side. "Hi, Daddy."

"Baby girl. Boys."

The boys were right about their father being a man of few words. I went back and forth between starting a conversation and keeping my promise to wait until I was spoken to.

"Here we are." Virginia emerged with a bag of salad and bottle of balsamic. She set both in front of me and Cassius immediately slid it across the table. He grabbed a bowl out of the cabinet and set to prepare the salad himself. "Clay, start cooking the sausage."

"Sure, Mom." Clay slid a look to his sister. "Cam, give Ember a tour of the house."

"I'll do that." Virginia was around the table and lifting me out of my seat before I could blink. "Cammy, help Daddy."

Clay smoothly blocked our path. His mentioning that I shouldn't let his mom get me alone rang in my ears. "Dad can handle it himself. Mom, I bet Camila wants to show Ember her room."

"Yeah, Mom. I'll take her."

Cam and I were up and off. She threw me a wry smile as we ducked into the living room. "Sorry. Mom loves it when we're all together. She can go overboard. And you are the first girl my brothers have introduced them to."

"I like her. She's got this energy that you can't help but gravitate toward."

"That's Mom."

Camila led me down a short hallway with three doors.

"Bathroom. Back door. And this is my room." She pushed through into a K-pop paradise. Dozens of posing Korean men and women smiled, smirked, or seduced me from the posters on her wall. Camila made use of the tiny space by putting her twin bed in the corner and letting the desk, dresser, and television take up the rest.

Camila propped herself on the desk. "There's only two bedrooms. My brothers sleep in the other room and Dad takes the pull-out couch. But we shared this room until we were ten." She laughed. "Cassius is going to kill me for telling you he used to be massively afraid of the dark. We had to sleep with two nightlights. After our parents put us to bed, he climbed in next to me because I wasn't afraid. It's like he thought it'd rub off on him."

I smiled, crossing the length of the tiny room. "Yeah. My sis—"

My throat closed and cut the confession off. *What the hell just happened? I almost told her about Rory.*

It felt so natural to speak about her and that had never happened. Years had passed and I did not utter her name on purpose or by accident. Even when she was all I was thinking about. Why could I say it now?

"What?" Camila prompted.

"That's so cute," I finished. "I love that you guys were always close."

"They were my best friends back before people told me it was strange for your siblings to be your best friends."

"People are stupid. Never listen to a word they say."

She chuckled. "I hear that. Come on. I'll show you the boys' room."

Camila led me out past the kitchen to the front hallway. I overheard them as we walked by.

"—talk to us about something, sweetie."

"I know what they want to talk about," replied a deep, gruff voice. "Sheridan Oakes."

"Oh yes. Beautiful place. Lots of trees."

"No, Ginny," said their dad. "We don't like that place, remember? It's too far."

Their conversation cut off as we went into the next room and Camila shut the door. The boys' room was nothing like their dorm at the academy. I was missing the stacks upon stacks of books, the messy beds, and the band posters. Two simple twin beds, two dressers, and one desk with a broken leg took up the slightly bigger space.

I stretched out on one of the beds, gazing up at the ceiling and imagining little Cassius and Clay doing the same. Camila lay down by my side.

"Would you really turn down your acceptance to UF?" I murmured. "You were so excited to go."

Camila rested her head in the crook of my neck. "I do want to go. Sunshine. Beaches. Theme parks. The opposite of this place in every way."

"Can't blame you for wanting out of Raven River. Look what it's become in the last few years."

"Of course I want away from here, but I never wanted to get away from my family. I made myself feel better thinking they'd be okay while I was gone. Mom would go to Sheridan Oakes. Dad would get into rehab. And Cas and Clay would go to New York with you. It sounds so easy, but life never is. Only when it's reality can I go knowing I didn't abandon them to all the shit I'm running away from."

"I understand."

"I know you do. You'd sacrifice anything for Eli."

We chilled for a while, talking about the reality we wished for.

"Cammy," Virginia called. "Ember. Where did you get to?"

"Coming!" Camila heaved herself off the bed. "Let's go. It's the simplest of simple meals, but the Walkers make seriously good sausage and peppers."

We walked into a tense atmosphere in the kitchen. Their father sautéed the food with more vigor than needed while the boys sat at the table wearing matching masks that did little to hide their frustration. Virginia, on the other hand, puttered around the table pouring drinks and humming a song that sounded eerily similar to one we belted out in the car.

"No long faces." She stuck her head between the boys and smooched both their cheeks. "Sheridan Oakes won't work but you'll find another place. One for me and your father."

I halted at the threshold, good manners preventing me going any further. This was one of those things I shouldn't be a part of. I knew I was getting in the way.

"It doesn't really work like that, Mom," Cassius said.

"Of course it does," she replied, completely self-assured. Virginia snuck up behind her husband, wrapping her arms around his waist. "How does that sound, Big Bear?"

I backed up as Glen turned to hold his wife. The look in his eyes as he gazed at her stirred a feeling I'd only just begun to understand. If I had been through the life Virginia had and my boys still looked at me the way Glen did—like his love had cracked the seal and would shower her until he died—I'd be the luckiest woman who ever lived.

"Perfect," he said. "For both of us, or you stay."

I turned around. My instinct said to give the moment privacy. I took my chance to give the family photos a closer look. Another one of the five enjoying a day at the river hung over the mantle. I got in close, grinning to match the wide ones of the kids.

"Ember."

Jumping, I spun on my heels and came face to face with Virginia. She put a finger over her mouth. "Shh. Finally, I have you to myself." She glanced over her shoulder to make sure we were alone and then motioned for me to come closer. A mischievous glint lit her crystal blue eyes, like she was on the verge of sharing her biggest secret.

"I know," she said under her breath.

"You know? Know what?"

Virginia placed her arm on my shoulder and whispered in my ear.

My mouth fell open, shock forcing a reply to my lips and just as quickly stealing it away. Eyes wide, I gaped at her trickster's grin as Clay called out for me.

"Em?" He appeared above the saloon doors. "Em, what's wrong? What are you guys talking about?"

"Nothing, sweetie." Virginia winked at me. "Sit down, sit down. We're all starving. Let's get some food in our bellies."

Virginia hooked my arm and marched me after her. Clay intercepted at the door and tugged me out of her grasp.

"What happened?" he asked, drawing me to the side. "What did she say to you?"

"She said..." I drifted to the spot where she disappeared. "We have her blessing. She can't wait to have a daughter-in-law."

"She said that? Well, that's good, right?" Clay cupped my cheek and kissed me sweetly. "I told you she'd like you."

"You were right. She honestly does."

LUNCH HAD A ROCKY START but ended better than I hoped. Virginia was a bundle of happiness, asking her kids about their lives at the academy and teasing smiles out of her husband. In the middle of the best sausage and peppers I ever tasted, Camila put forth the idea of going to school close to home.

"But I thought Florida was your dream?" Virginia said. "You go, baby girl. Don't worry about us. Cassius and Clay will take good care of me and your father."

It amazed me that even to Virginia, the boys were the ones responsible for their welfare.

After lunch, I helped their mom clean up. We stood at the sink together while I silently prayed she wouldn't repeat what she said in the living room.

She didn't, and we made it through tidying up the kitchen and eating my shortbread cookie dessert in the living room while making small talk about school and bigger talk about the events of winter break and the search for Nolan Ives.

The sun was beating a retreat across the horizon when we packed up to leave.

"Visit us any time, Ember." Virginia squeezed me hard enough to rip my seams. The warm smooch she popped on my forehead made me laugh. "If you need anything, call me."

"Thank you, Mrs. Walker. This was great. I'm glad I got to meet you both."

Glen came up behind his wife, putting one arm around her and extending the other to me. "It was nice to meet you too, Ember."

I shook, marveling at receiving a full sentence.

"Son." Glen drew Cassius a ways down the hall. "Stay out of the neighborhood for a while." He made an effort to whisper. He wasn't low enough. "It's getting bad around here. Dangerous. There's even talk of a traitor. Just don't leave that school."

I frowned, concern growing as they softened their voice too low for me to hear.

"Bye, Mom. Daddy," said Camila.

I left as the triplets traded hugs with their parents. They tromped out one by one, meeting me at the car.

"I'm driving," said Cassius. "What time am I picking you up tomorrow?"

"We'll call you," Clay replied.

I forgot for a second that Clay and I had separate plans.

"Are you okay?" I asked as he reached around to open my door. "I know that didn't go the way you hoped."

He blew out a breath. "Sheridan Oakes was perfect. We could afford it and it was closest to Raven River. But it is what it is. We have to find somewhere else that Dad will sign off on."

Clay and I climbed in the back and Camila sat up front with Cassius. I rested my head on his shoulder, eyes falling shut as he stroked the nape of my neck. The perfect mix of Clay, the triplets' soft conversation, and the rocking car put me to sleep.

"Em? Ember?"

I peeled my eyes open. I was curled up on Clay's lap. He brushed the hair from my face, smiling down at me. "We're almost there."

"Where's there?"

"The forest was out. My house is out. And I wasn't bringing you to a dirty OB motel. That left the next best thing."

"Intriguing." I pushed myself up, looked out the window, and saw...

Nothing.

I sat up properly, making out through the gloom a porch light and the modest home to go with it. A fair distance away we passed by another house. It appeared we were in the northern borough. A place I rarely had a reason to visit.

"What's out here?"

"No other word for it but a safe house," Cassius spoke up. "Rio keeps it for when one of us needs to lie low. It's empty right now."

I gave Clay a look. "I'm all for some time alone with you, but *our place* is not going to be a gangster's hideaway. What if Rio or someone else stumbled in on us?"

"Just this once. It'll be you and me, Em. Like that night by the river."

The shred of my willpower evaporated. "You and me." I kissed him—a playful, explosive kiss of battling tongues and hushed moans. "I love you."

"I love you too."

Cassius turned onto a long driveway. At its end was what I expected of a smart man like Rio. A simple white single-story house with a screened-in porch and nothing living on the lawn that would need to be tended. Nothing about this house made it look out of place.

Cassius parked and let us out. I leaned through the driver's window to kiss him goodbye. "See you tomorrow."

"Bye. Love you."

He honked down the drive, leaving the two of us alone. A profound quiet swept over the night. This wasn't like the forest—alive with skittering critters and the babble of the river. The murmurs of the town didn't reach the northern borough. Neighbors were too far to share their noise. It was like Clay promised.

Just us.

"I know what you're thinking," he said.

"You do?"

Nodding, he held my hand. "It's much better on the inside."

"All it needs is a bed and food."

"It's got both."

Clay walked backward, guiding me up two steps onto the porch. He reached for the door and I saw that one thing made it stand out. The lock opened by touchpad, not by key.

A soft chime signaled we were in and Clay gestured for me to go in first. Cautiously I stepped over the threshold, part of me worried Rio would emerge from the shadows.

I flicked up the panel of switches and light flooded the living room. It was better on the inside.

We weren't talking big-screen televisions, antique vases, or Van Goghs on the walls. The living room was done up with a comfortable brown sofa, a plush rug, and a modest television hanging over the fireplace. I went further inside, poking my head into the small bathroom, the kitchen stocked with canned food and utensils, and then the bedroom.

It wasn't a holiday retreat, so the twin-sized bed and a single trunk made sense. This place had everything you needed to stash away for a few days, and I wished we could. I didn't want to go back to school. Pay my supposed best friend his ransom money. Or pretend like we were problem-solving our way to a better Raven River when Nolan was on the loose, Rio got closer to taking over the entire town every day, people still looked at me like I was walking, talking, scum, and my parents were who-knew-where.

Clay slipped his arms under mine. He captured my hands and folded them under my breasts, holding me secure to his chest.

Yes. Gangster's hideaway or not. There with Clay was where I wanted to be.

I dropped my head back, happy sigh escaping my lips. "The bed is kinda small," I pointed out.

"We have another option."

"We do?"

"Mm-hmm. Scope out the kitchen for something to eat. I'll take care of it."

I did as he asked, searching the cabinets until I found two cans of potato soup and a package of pasta at the bottom of the pantry. "Score. Are you hungry now? I can... make it... for us."

Clay pulled his shirt over his head and let it pool on top of a bed of pillows, couch cushions, and blankets. A soft glow emanated over his makeshift creation, lit up by the electric fireplace. Clay's answer was to hold out his hands. I forgot all about canned potatoes and ran to him, jumping in his arms.

We were kissing before his knees hit the floor, bringing me onto the cushions and the pleasing heat of the fireplace.

"Are you sure we won't be interrupted?" I asked.

"Just us." Clay traced the outline of my lips, then he satisfied their need by giving me a scorching kiss. "I swear."

"In that case." I flipped him over, straddling him, and meeting his surprise with a grin. "I don't have to hold back."

"You should never do that."

"Remember our first date?" I asked. "An article of clothing for every honest answer. Want to play again?"

"Nope. Just take those clothes off."

He tried to flip me over. Giggling, I darted away, skipping to the fireplace, and planting myself before him. "Uh-uh. Not so fast. I gotta make you work for it every now and then. Keeps it interesting."

Clay propped up on his elbows. The position contracted his arms and abs, and dropped golden hair over darkening, piercing eyes. Like this he was a masterpiece. The duality of light and dark. Peace and brutality. Sex and… sex.

"I think we're keeping it plenty fucking interesting," he growled.

"Come on, baby." I lifted my hem slightly, wiggling my hips. "They'll be easy questions."

"Fine. First one."

"What is eight minus three divided by one over six plus two?"

"That's it!"

I shrieked, running away as he dove for me. I made it three steps and was scooped up and tossed laughing on our bed. Clay jumped on me and made short work of my dress.

Splaying my hands on his stomach, I took my time moving up to his shoulders and pushing him down. On top of him where I belonged, he gripped my hips, rocking me on his hardness, and I arched my back, moaning unreservedly.

I reached for my bra hook and he took over. My straps were slid down my arms, freeing my breasts to his hungry gaze. My bra fell on his chest and then I did, kissing his collarbone and continuing the trail over the bumps and dips of his sculpted, inked body.

Clay hissed as I drew the fabric over his length. He sprang free and heat surged in my lower belly like desire turned on the tap.

"No teasing," I promised, "but tonight I want to take it slow."

"Whatever you want. Just come back here." I lay on his chest and our lips met in a kiss unlike the many we shared before. His tongue caressed my bottom lip, parting it to play with mine. Goose bumps rippled over my flesh, riding waves of shivers. A million Clay kisses over a thousand years, and each time would feel like the first.

Clay reached for my panties.

"You rip those," I whispered, "and you'll be in so much trouble."

I tasted his laugh on my lips. "Slow, baby." He moved down, holding my gaze in his ocean blues as his nose skimmed over my stomach. "No ripping necessary." Clay drew my underwear down with his teeth and flung it away.

"I want to play that game," he said.

"But my clothes are already off."

Clay draped my legs over his shoulders. "Just have to play for something else."

My brows shot up my forehead. I liked where this was going. "Okay. First question. How do you feel about me?"

He hissed. "Ooh. If I've got to be completely honest..."

I smacked his thigh, getting a guffaw out of him.

"I love you, Ember Bancroft. I love that you blush even while you're getting on your knees to do the dirtiest, hottest shit I can think of. I love that you're crazy competitive. And I love that you treat everyone the same. In this entire town, you're the only one who would look past"—he swept his hand over his angel—"this."

"There's so much more to you, Clay, and I'll admit, I'm happy I'm the only one who sees it. Or else I'd be fighting bitches every day defending what's mine."

"I am yours," he replied, grinning as he lowered his head. "I should get a tattoo of the true woman who owns me." Clay's tongue darted out, licking my lower lips. "Where should I put it, baby?"

My legs fell open, welcoming every part of what was to come. "Right across here." I traced a line on his forehead. "That way no one will miss it."

He was laughing as he put his mouth to me. Sweet vibrations curled my toes and his expert tongue curled the rest. I fisted his hair, soft moans filling the room while Clay kept his word, taking it slow, drawing out the languid swipes and gentle probing of his tongue. He wound me muscle by muscle, and then when I thought I couldn't take anymore, he pushed one, then two fingers past my folds. I rocked on the squashy cushions, meeting him as he pushed in, drawing back as he pulled out.

I loved the sounds of sex. The moans, the grunts, the smack of skin on skin, the filthy things my boys whispered in my ears, and my screams that spurred them on. And I loved the imagined cries of my clit fighting the relentless ministrations of Clay, sending waves and waves of pleasure to let me know its battle was failing, and then breaking under the final thrust. My orgasm wracked my body, claiming Clay as the victor of my heart and soul, and I fell back pleased and purring.

"Oh yeah, right on the forehead. You're mine for good, Clay. Get used to it."

"I've accepted my fate," he said, grinning. That grin found my lips and we kissed slow and sweet while our hands freely roamed. "Next question," he whispered, nipping his way along my jaw to my neck.

"Do you think we'll have it all? The home? The family? Careers we love with bosses we hate and lives where the biggest thing we worry about is who's making dinner?"

"I never believed I could until I met you, Ember. If I could make that life happen with anyone, it'll be you."

I hummed. "I'll accept that answer. Your prize: a blow job."

Clay pumped his fist. "Yes."

We cracked up. What was more perfect than this? Being with a man I could have fun with. Completely comfortable in and out of my clothes with him. It's how I was with Clay, Cassius, Royal, and with every passing day, Hiro.

I do have men who look at me the way Glen does Virginia, and that was why—

"I'm never letting you go."

We traded places, rolling to the edge of our bed, and soaking in the heat of the fireplace. Beads of sweat prickled my skin, but I loved that too. Everything about this was delicious. The raw masculine taste of his cock and the salty cum sliding down my throat. I grasped him eagerly, swallowing his head and cupping the base of his cock.

"Shit, Em," he hissed. Clay tangled his fingers in my hair, bobbing me up and down, up and down to the perfect rhythm. My moans competed with the hum of the fireplace.

Releasing my hair, Clay drew a path up the sweat on my back. His finger glided over my skin and it took me a bit to realize he wrote a message.

I love you.

Smiling around my mouthful, I reached up and wrote a message of my own on his chest.

Fuck me.

"Beautiful sentiment, baby."

I snorted, heart cracking with so much love for him that I popped up and stole a kiss before returning to my job. Picking up the pace, my cheeks caved in sucking like the expert I'd become. Three guys with healthy sex drives will teach a girl everything she needs to know.

Clay's grunts filled my ear—rough, raspy sounds that tightened my lower belly and slicked my sex with arousal. I sensed him getting close and went faster. Clay fisted my hair and lifted me up just as he exploded, covering my chin and chest. He arched my neck, pulling a cry out of me, and wrote another message in the sticky wetness.

Yours.

"Next question."

"The only one that matters right now," I said. "Top or bottom?"

He sank onto the pillow, arms folded behind his head. "I'll have to go with both."

"Oooh. Interesting answer. So, judges, what does he win?" I swung my leg over him. Grasping his length, I positioned him at my entrance and swallowed him without preamble, stretching to my limit. Now that was a prize.

I rose on the balls of my feet, gasping as I rocked back. The wanton sex demon that inhabited my body begged for a punishing pace. Clay gripped my hips, slowing me, and leisurely pulled out to the tip.

I choked on a moan as a hard jerk of his hips thrust him in. Clay kept up the mind-bending, delightfully hot take on slow sex. Gentle retreat. Hard thrust. Gentle retreat. Hard fucking thrust.

I gasped with every strike of that spot. I wasn't driving this train. Clay may have been mine, but at that moment, he owned my body. Its shakes. Its moans and its orgasm. He would be the winner of this game. "Shit, Clay. Yes to both."

Thrust.

Thrust.

Thrust.

I clamped down on his wrists, eyes rolling up in my head as I came hard. Tipping sideways, I collapsed next to him, riding the orgasm down.

"Wow," I breathed. "We definitely keep it interesting."

Clay slid his arm under my neck, bringing my forehead to his lips. We lay there for a while, not saying anything and not needing to. I fell into a half doze watching the flickering molten red of the fireplace.

"Hungry?" Clay asked.

"I could eat. In the mood for soup or pasta?"

"Pasta. I'll make it."

Clay heaved himself up and went into the kitchen. I sat up, pulled his shirt over my head, and arranged the cushions for us to eat comfortably. While Clay cooked, I flipped through the channels for a movie we could put on low.

Clay returned carrying two bowls with mismatched utensils. He handed me mine and then went back for the drinks. A simple meal, on a sorta bed, in the place the most dangerous men in the city hide away, but none of that mattered because Clay.

"You were amazing today," he said. Clay squeezed in between me and the couch. "The way you were with Mom and Dad."

"I like them. It's obvious how much they love each other."

"They do." He changed the subject. "We can't make coming here a habit. We're back to searching for a place. Got any ideas?"

"I'll hide you in the trunk, sneak you through the gates, and we'll rendezvous at an Estate motel. They call them motels but they are on another level."

"A level we can afford?" he asked, laced with amusement.

"Hmm... no."

We cracked up, but Clay soon sobered. "It's getting rough in the OB. It might be better for us to stay on campus anyway."

It was on the tip of my tongue to ask about the murders, the traitor, Rio, and the Horsemen. I bit it back and pushed it down. They were a problem for the next day. That night was completely about me and Clay.

I took his spoon and fed him a bite of creamy pasta. "You did magic with those sausage and peppers today. Where did you learn how to cook?"

"My mom. Her dad was a short-order cook that messed around after hours coming up with his own recipes. Mom was his taste tester and sous chef."

"I'm a terrible cook. Eli picked up that skill. You should try his blueberry pancakes."

"I can't stand blueberries."

I gasped. "What?! You think you know someone."

He laughed. "Hey, you wanted me. This is the full package."

"No chance of return?" I teased.

"None."

I relaxed, settling into our night and allowing the rest to fall away.

"So, I looked it up," I began. "A five-bedroom Manhattan loft is totally doable if we've got a spare eight million lying around. Think we can swing it?"

He laughed. "One of us can."

"Oh yeah," I drew out. "What is a girl to do with twenty-five million dollars?"

Chapter Six

Monday morning, I placed the envelope in locker 487. It held the two thousand dollars as demanded and the note I typed up the other night. It was time for this shit to end.

Enjoy this money because it's the last cent you'll get out of me. You can save your threats about what will happen next. We both know nothing is going to happen.

I underestimated you before and you hurt Eli. I won't make that mistake again, but neither will you. My brother is protected now. You can't get to him, which means you'll have to come after me, and I hope you do.

I'm more than ready to fuck you up, see you led away in cuffs, and end this once and for all.

I had more to say. Paragraphs upon paragraphs that would've turned into a novel. But I kept it short and sweet, secure that the note would get my point across just fine.

Seven days later, my blackmailer dropped another note through my locker's vent.

Your brother is not as safe as you think. I've proven that once, I can do it again. But in case you're right, think about the many people I can get to before you.

Camila. Brandon. Gabriel.

Is an oversized interpreter following them wherever they go?

Don't threaten me again. Now you're up to 2,500.

You have one week.

Calmly, I folded the note and put it in my backpack.

"It's time."

THE LUNCH LADY HANDED me a burrito bowl with a side of salsa and sour cream. I thanked her and carried it up to the loft, spotting Hiro, Eli, and Tatum at the freshman table. I kept waiting for Angry Boy to reappear. Go back to glaring, snapping, and ignoring me. Reclaim his fearsome reputation by dropping his freshman master. Decide that his future was more important than a girl he had to share with his friends.

I kept waiting… but day after day, Hiro sat with Eli.

Upstairs, I bypassed the Angel table and sat at my old one. Camila, Gabriel, and Brandon weren't there yet. Neither one would remark at seeing me. I mixed it up sitting with them and the boys. Partly because I wanted to hang with Camila and Gabriel who had done nothing wrong, and because I had to play like everything was fine with me and Brandon for a little bit longer.

Almost there.

I plopped down and dug into my burrito bowl. The food at this school was uncharacteristically good. Wesley High was about healthy eating too, but they lived up to the stereotype that everything good for you tasted like baked rubber. Here in this rich kid paradise, they discovered spices, seasonings, and a generous use of honey. I bit into my honey and walnut banana bread and moaned. A thud snapped me out of my trance.

Julian dropped his tray on the table. My mouth hung open, food half chewed, as he sat across from me and picked up his fork. This was the first I'd seen him since he'd been back. If you wanted to know if being shot by his best friend and finding out his girlfriend cheated on him made Julian any less the breathtaking sunset of a man, the answer was no.

His silver halo caught the sunlight and made the unnatural hair color perfectly natural on him. Eyes so blue they hurt, held mine across the table, staring without blinking.

"Hi, Julian," I said. "How are you?"

He didn't speak. He didn't move. I wasn't entirely certain that he was breathing.

"I wanted to visit you again," I continued. "But I think your mom was worried I'd smack around more of her family members. I should feel bad but—"

Julian cut through my chatter like a blade through soft butter. "Did you know?"

It would have been insulting to pretend I didn't know what he was talking about. "No," I said. "I didn't."

He nodded slowly, almost to himself. I waited for him to leave. Then I waited for him to say something. Julian did neither of those things, opting to resume his staring contest. I went back to chattering.

"I heard you got into Stanford. You must be excited to get out of this place. Live in California. Meet new people. Go from being Julian Hart, Ravener and son of the headmistress, to just Julian. That's what I'm excited about. Being lost in a big city where people don't instantly recognize me as—"

"My best friend shot me."

I lowered my fork, growing serious. "I know."

"He shot me while trying to kill my cousin and then he left me bleeding on the floor. My girlfriend has been cheating on me almost the entire time we've been dating. My father is marrying his child mistress." He leaned forward, getting as close as the table would allow. "That's a lot of shitty luck for one person, don't you think?"

"I—"

"'Cause you know what I think?" The intensity in his gaze clashed with the monotone. "I think it's karma. It's gotta be, right?

Life can't shit on a person this much when they don't deserve it. And I do. For the way I treated you. For not taking the first, second, or twelfth no. For using your best friend. For making the bet in the first place.

"I've put my mom through a lot of shit," he said. "I treated every OB kid that came through here like garbage because I was pissed Mom changed the rules for Royal." He scoffed. "I know what you're thinking. How fucking petty is that? The guy who has everything angry because Mom tried to keep Royal off the streets. It's worse than petty, and it's why I deserve this."

"No one deserves to be shot, Julian," I said gently. "Or cheated on. You've made mistakes and you've been an asshole to more than a few people in your life, but that bullet didn't kill you. You can make things right. Apologize. Leave Pomona, or forgive her and move on. The point is that you have choices. People who waste their time blaming karma believe that they don't, but you do."

Julian looked away. "You're nicer to me than you should be, Em."

"I'm not nice," I said with a wry smile. "I've been unfiltered and uncensored about how I feel about you through the years. Plus, I punched you in the throat after you slept with and ghosted my best friend. I'll give back what you give me."

He looked at me then. "Sure, but it won't change anything between us. Or what Pomona did."

"You don't change for other people. You do it for yourself."

Julian inclined his head, seeming to agree, though his face was unreadable. His gaze flicked over my shoulder. Just like that, he shoved away from the table. I twisted around and saw what he did. Pomona and Gabriel coming up the stairs together, chatting like nothing happened.

Pomona noticed Julian and dropped her smile immediately. "Julian, I— Wait! Let me explain!"

He blew past them, stomping down the stairs with Pomona hot on his tail. Shaking my head, I returned to my food. I felt for Julian and what he was going through. Life had piled a lot on him, and for his sake, I hoped he worked it out and emerged from the other side a better person.

My friends—and Brandon—soon joined me at our table and we wrapped up lunch discussing the latest exercise in communications class. We split apart at the bottom of the staircase and continued our day.

That night, I sat down at my computer to do what I'd been waiting forever to tackle. One message from my blackmailer and it was finally time.

"What are you working on over there?" Camila asked. She reclined on her mattress browsing through the brochure for Easthaven College.

I paused to lick the envelope, then said, "Taking down Eli's attacker."

"In that case, let me help."

"Thanks, but I got it." I jerked my chin at her book. "What do you think of Easthaven?"

"It's a great school. It has my major and it's one-third the cost of UF. I can get a job on campus to pay for tuition and my dorm."

"Would you still want to go there if your brothers find another facility that your mom is willing to go to? They said Sheridan Oakes is the only one close by. If everyone moves out of state, you'll be stuck here and you wanted to leave more than anyone."

"True," she mumbled. Sighing, she tossed the brochure in the direction of the nightstand and ignored it when it missed. "I guess I could always transfer if that happens. I won't really be stuck. Plus, my parents aren't packing up the house and leaving tomorrow or even in the next month. I'll focus on picking the best school for now, and when my folks are in a good place, I'll figure out the next step."

A grin spread across my lips. "Can I make a suggestion...?"

"Ugh." Camila threw herself back. "I knew it was only a matter of time before you put me in your suitcase too. I'm tired of being cold, Em, and you want me to look at schools even farther north?"

"You'll be close to your brothers," I tried.

"I don't like them *that* much."

"Liar." I laughed. "You'll have friends, family, theaters, concerts, art, culture, and great food in one of the most amazing cities on the planet. No pressure but I'd love it if we took this friendship into the college years. Clubs, shopping, meeting up for brunch."

"Well, don't tell me that," she cried. "Now I'm picturing it."

"We might end up in the same classes too." I dropped the envelope and reached into my bottom drawer. I held it up for Camila to see. "I'm applying to NYU and Columbia."

"You are? But I thought everything was on hold until you knew if your aunt and uncle would grant you guardianship of Eli."

"They will," I said firmly. "They've got zero reasons to say no and every reason to say yes. They don't want kids and they drove that message home by throwing us in the academy the minute enrollment opened. That's okay. It really is. It can't be easy losing your brother, sister-in-law, money, and family respect the same day you're forced to take in two teenagers.

"I understand why they felt this was the best option for all of us, but once I graduate, they can't honestly believe Eli would be better off alone in this school every single day for three years than he would be with me. There's a better option now and I'll make my uncle see that."

I stroked the face of the brochure. "I got on the boys for not believing in our future which is ironic because neither did I. I don't need to wait on my college applications. I'm applying to absolutely every college in New York that might take me. On top of that, I'm searching out places to live near the Chapman School for the Deaf where Eli will be attending, so when I go to my uncle, I can tell him exactly how much of my trust fund I'll need for us to live on.

"Speaking of Chapman School"—I pulled another brochure out of my desk—"I've got Eli working on the application."

"Wow. You don't mess around."

"Nope," I said. "If I want this, I have to make it happen."

"You know..." Camila riffled in her bag and pulled out a second glossy catalog. New York University emblazoned proudly on the front. "Shopping, brunch, and concerts does sound fun."

I clutched my chest, eyes widening. "Don't do this to me, Cam. Don't toy with my emotions."

"I'll apply. No guarantees I'll get in or go if I do, but being in New York with you guys sounds ten times better than being in Easthaven by myself. Even if it's cold as balls."

Squealing, I launched across the room and leaped on top of her. She howled into my hair as I attacked her with kisses. "I promise we'll bundle up next to three heaters while we sip hot cocoa in our onesie pajamas."

"Oh my gosh. Is that supposed to sweeten the deal?" she asked. "Because it totally does. If you got Cas and Clay into those pajamas too, I'd for sure move to New York to see that."

We stayed up for half the night talking about after graduation with much brighter adjectives than we did a week ago. The other half of the night I worked under a single lamplight to complete my project.

I finished at 5:14 a.m. and dragged myself to bed fully clothed to catch about an hour of sleep.

My alarm clock blared much too soon. I tipped out of bed, trudged to the shower, dressed, and grabbed my stuff. I found Hiro after some searching. He was knee-deep in the millennium garden—weeding, pulling, and replanting. He tidied the school in the morning, followed Eli around during the day, and helped teachers reorganize their classrooms after school. Twice I told him he could stop, but eventually I realized it wasn't just my or Eli's forgiveness he was fighting to earn.

"Hiro."

He sought me through his curtain of hair. "Em, you okay?"

"I am but I need a favor. The kind of favor you can't question me about. There's something important I have to do," I said. "It requires your car and an unauthorized trip off campus after school. Just say yes or no."

Hiro dropped his trowel, face twisting in a frown. "Is it dangerous?"

"I just said not to ask me questions."

"I'm asking that one and you're answering if you want my car."

"No, it's not dangerous," I lied.

"Are you lying?"

"No."

"Then I'll drive you."

"You can't be a part of this."

"Why can't I be a part of it if it's not dangerous?"

"You're really struggling with the 'don't ask questions' rule."

He cracked a smile. "Just swear to me you're not going into the OB."

"I know it's getting bad."

"You don't know," he said. "Tensions are high with three of our own killed and dumped on Cavanaugh. He handed out more weapons and ordered the men to put down for good any rival gangs that are still around."

"Holy hell," I breathed.

"Then there's Rio. He's been rounding up the Horsemen and questioning them to find the dealer and traitor. The Horsemen aren't looking at each other as brothers anymore, and they're looking at everyone else as enemies."

Hiro closed the distance between us, threading his fingers through mine in the way that made my pulse race. "Whatever you're doing must be important, but please promise me, Em, you'll stay out of the westside."

"I promise."

That was the truth. I didn't need to go to the westside to handle my business and I was plenty fine with that. A third gun in my face wasn't necessary to realize I was living in dangerous times.

"No chance you'll let me come with you?" he asked.

I shook my head.

"Then be careful." Hiro brushed his lips on my forehead. I held my breath as he lingered. It was a short journey to my lips and I honestly wasn't certain if I'd stop him on the way.

Hiro stepped back and picked up his trowel. I stomped on my disappointment—hard. We weren't together and I wasn't a hundred percent sure changing that fact was a good idea. Better not to throw another kiss in the swirling mix of attraction, anger, and building trust.

I guess that's why I still haven't opened his Christmas present. I couldn't handle it if he gave me something that cracked my heart even wider.

I left him to his work, gearing up for a day of two quizzes, an essay exam, and the wonder that was communications class on an hour of sleep.

I somehow survived my classes and met Hiro by my locker at the end of day. He placed the keys on my palm.

"You made me a promise," he said. "I expect you to keep it."

I gave my hand a slight tug. Hiro didn't let go. "What are you imagining I'm going to do?"

He shrugged. "Track down Rio and kick his ass for starting the crap that led to Ives doing what he did, and throwing the town into a war because of it."

"I very much want to kick Rio's ass, but I won't be doing that to-day."

"Good."

Taking a step back, our clasped hands hung between us. "I should take off. Get it done and have your car back in an hour."

He nodded.

"Don't ask to come with me again," I said. "What I'm doing isn't dangerous and—"

Hiro closed the distance in one move and cupped the back of my neck. I barely got out a squeak before his lips were on mine. The kiss was rough and insistent for the second it lasted.

I ripped away, shoving him off. Opposite we stood, chest heaving, eyes sparking with the boiling cauldron of unchecked emotions that made him Angry Boy and me Backwater Bitch.

My lips peeled into a snarl. Rage balled my fists. A thousand rebukes clogged my throat rushing to hurl at him at once.

And then I was on him. Our mouths clashed in a feverish, almost desperate explosion. Hiro slammed me against the locker, wrapping my legs around his waist. My hands were everywhere—pulling his collar, running through his hair, finding the hem of his shirt and slipping underneath.

This kiss was nothing like the one we shared in the elevator. Hiro's guilt and my ignorance tainted that kiss for both of us. Nothing stood in the way of this one. Hiro laid bare his life, mistakes, wants, and soul and served it up for me to reject. And the many times I convinced myself that I should let him go and be content with the three men who loved me, the part of me that only Hiro truly knew called out to him.

And she devoured him like a roast turkey on Thanksgiving.

I bit Hiro's lip, earning a hiss of pain that was part groan. I swallowed it, claiming his mouth, and our tongues battled in a public display uncaring of who was watching. The lock dug into my back. Hiro's grip would leave little round marks on my thigh for days. I knew why I waited this long to kiss him, but I was cursing myself for doing so all the same.

"Ugh, guys."

A voice shattered our world.

"If you could just scoot down a bit, so I could get in my loc—"

Hiro's neck snapped around. "Fuck off, Lacroix!"

Brandon tripped scurrying away. The retreat was simultaneously hilarious and a cold bucket to the face.

"I have to go," I rasped. "Seriously, I do. The place is going to close."

We extracted ourselves from each other reluctantly. I tried to think of something to say as I got my backpack and dropped the key in the side pocket.

"It'll probably be more like two hours," I said as I hedged toward the stairs. "I'll call when I'm on my way back."

"Okay."

"Bye."

"Bye."

That was the most awkward after-make-out conversation in the history of human intimacy. I wanted to acknowledge what happened but doing so in a crowded hallway wasn't appealing. I left school under the torrent of swirling emotions and puffy lips. I shifted my thoughts to my off-campus task but they naturally drifted back to Hiro.

You'll talk with Hiro after. Focus, Ember. One wrong move and it's very likely you'll end up in jail. Or dead.

That thought knocked Hiro out of my head a little longer. I reached the break in the fence and ducked into the forest.

Raven River Academy wasn't negligent about security. There was a fence surrounding the entire property and the front gate was locked Monday thru Friday. On weekends, they unlocked it for seniors to leave but, otherwise, administration expected us to stay where we're put. The trouble was the student parking lot was on the other side of the fence. Once you made it through, you were free and clear to take off—which I did.

In spite of my promise, I couldn't avoid the OB. It was called the Outer Borough for the exact reason that it surrounded everything. It was the town and the Estate was just living in it.

I drove along the outskirt road all the way up to the northern borough to enter the Estate through the north gate. I'd never been through this gate and the location added another twenty minutes to my driving time. Considering the alternative was going deep into Horsemen territory to reach my usual gate, I got over it.

Two unfamiliar faces peered through the window as I pulled up to the gates. Both were decidedly hostile at seeing an unknown in a less-than-luxury car roll up.

"No," one of them said before I opened my mouth. "The Estate is closed to visitors. Leave."

"I'm not—"

"It doesn't matter if you're on the list," he snapped. "Residents only."

"Slow up, Interrupty. I'm Ember Bancroft and I live with my uncle, Harrison Bancroft. Check your list."

The men shared a narrow-eyed look.

"Take my ID and let me in," I said. "I'm running late."

It took more time than it should've for the guy to step out of the security hut and take my license. Undoubtedly, they'd been given reason to be suspicious. The pristine community experienced its first shooting and the OB was spiraling out of control. They wouldn't have us unwanted riffraff inviting more violence.

The guy spent about five minutes examining my face and photo. *I wonder if anyone remembers it was a Ravener that invited violence into the Estate in the first place.*

"Alright," the man gruffed. "You can go through."

I tucked my ID in my bag as the gates rumbled open. A glance at the dash clued me in to how much of my time the scrutiny ate up. I had thirty minutes to get there before it closed and at least a twenty-minute drive winding around mansions.

I pushed the boundaries of the speed limit rushing to get there on time. I summoned patience I didn't know I possessed to make it this far, I wasn't waiting another day.

Crossing the final light, I turned into the post office parking lot with eight minutes to spare. The clerk waved to me as the doorbell chimed overhead.

"Good afternoon." The guy was tall and cute, sporting a wider smile than you usually saw for someone working customer service. "How can I help you?"

"I need these"—I dumped the contents of my bag on the counter—"to go out in the first bag. Priority, overnight, one-day delivery if we can swing it."

The smile faded under goggle-eyed shock. "You want all of these letters to go out overnight?" He picked up a handful and perused the addresses. "They look to be local, but I'm afraid it will still be expensive."

"That's fine. They just have to get there as soon as possible."

"Of course. I'll take care of this for you."

It took longer than eight minutes to sort through and ring up my charges. I cleaned out my wallet handing over all the Christmas money from Uncle Harrison.

"Throwing a party," guessed Bexton—according to the name tag. "A physical invitation is a nice touch over an e-vite. A party would certainly brighten things up around here."

"I'm not throwing a party," I replied, "but I'll deserve one after these go out."

Bexton's brows said he didn't know what I meant, but his smile was pleasant as he handed over my receipts. "These letters will be delivered tomorrow, Miss Bancroft. You're all set."

"Thank you," I said. "You have no idea but... thank you."

I was confusing this man left and right. All the same, he happily waved me out of the door.

My drive to campus was a lot less eventful. I made one stop along the way that broke my promise to be back in two hours, but I wrapped things up as quickly as I could and arrived at the academy. I parked in the student drive and made my way through the forest without an issue. Walking into the dorm, I rode the elevator up, veered left, entered the boys' hall and went straight to Royal and Hiro's room. Hiro opened the door.

"We need to talk—"

"Come inside," Hiro broke in. "You have to see this."

Just then I heard the soft murmurs of a female voice. Hiro stepped aside to let me in. Royal stood behind the desk chair, arms folded and handsome face chipped out of stone as he beheld the laptop. I shifted around to see what he was watching.

"—police are asking those with any information to come forward." The six o'clock news streamed live on the Channel Four website. A familiar reporter stood in front of a small corner store I didn't recognize. Looking past her, I saw the police and a crowd of onlookers.

"The bodies recovered have not been identified but authorities have confirmed they also bear an angel tattoo. If these killings are gang related, it will be the fourth and fifth murder just this week connected to gang violence."

"This week?" I cried.

Hiro nodded gravely. "We didn't tell you the Roadhouse Club took credit for the first three killings behind Cavanaugh's bar. Cavanaugh responded by killing three of their guys... and not quickly."

I clutched my stomach, gasping on the bile burning its way up. "Oh my gosh. That's terrible. Who are they? Why did they do this?"

"Motorcycle gang in the southside," Royal replied, gaze fixed on the screen. "Small. About twenty-five members. They stayed out of the way until now."

"Until they shot their mouths off. The worst part is after Cavanaugh's *questioning*," Hiro added, "he doesn't believe they killed our guys. They took credit for it to up their reputation. Get loud about taking the southside back. That was a mistake."

"If they didn't do it"—I motioned to the screen—"then who did this?"

"—in the Outer Borough," the reporter continued. "The rise of drug- and gang-related deaths in the last few years has rocked these tight-knit communities. Many are asking when will enough be enough? Tonight, I spoke to—"

Pop!

Pop! Pop! Pop!

The young woman whipped around, dropping her microphone. The camera shook, blurring the scene, and through the confusion I made out figures running.

A rough voice shouted, "The Horsemen ride!"

The cameraman righted his equipment as the young reporter faced the lens.

Pop! Pop!

She jerked—a hard spasm of her body. I looked directly into her widening, shocked eyes as she fell out of frame.

A scream tore from my throat.

"Holy shit!" Hiro sprung forward, snapping the laptop shut, though the broadcast had already shut off.

I clapped my hand over my mouth, ragged breaths leaking through my fingers, tears running down my cheeks. My mind stalled.

A woman was murdered right in front of my eyes.

I barely registered Royal putting his arm around me or whispering in my ear.

That night, I slept in their room, secure in Royal's arms. Though I say slept. A proper description would be that I lay there for hours begging sleep to give me relief and eventually gave up. All I could see was the horrifying surprise on that innocent woman's face.

A creak of the mattress opened my eyes. Turning my head up, I read 3:00 a.m. on the clockface.

What has Hiro up this early? I thought as our eyes met in the dark. *Is he seeing her face like me?*

For a while, we simply gazed at each other. Memories of our kiss floated through the others fighting for dominance. We never did have that talk. What would we say to each other?

I have feelings for you? We both knew that we did.

I want to be with you? We both knew what we wanted on that topic too.

I can trust you now?

Okay. It's possible we didn't have everything decided. Maybe we didn't have to either. Not that night. Or the next.

I reached out and sought him through the gloom. Hiro found me, holding my hand tight.

Maybe a kiss could be a kiss and my feelings could be what they were without deciphering. I was simply grateful that Hiro was becoming the man he wanted to be, and that man was there for me. Holding my hand. Making me feel safe. For the time being, that could be enough.

Chapter Seven

The next morning, I ate breakfast with Eli.

News travels fast in a small town and going to school forty-five minutes outside of the center didn't slow it down a bit. The cafeteria was buzzing with talk of the drive-by and I preferred Eli got the truth from me.

"*Is that lady okay?*"

"*She's in the hospital,*" I signed. "*The last update said she was in stable condition.*"

"*I'm glad she's okay. I saw the video. It was so awful.*"

"*Eli, why would you look at that?*"

"*I didn't know what I was looking at,*" he explained. "*Tatum just put the laptop on my bed and said to watch. Was it the Horsemen?*"

I shook my head. "*Royal is sure they're not behind it. The shooter yelled out 'the Horsemen ride' and that's not a thing they say or ever have. Also, they're technically the victims since two more of their own were killed. They have nothing to gain by shooting at innocent people and making the police hunt them down instead of the killers.*"

"*If they didn't do it, someone wants people to believe they did.*"

Eli came to that conclusion as quickly as I did. It was the only explanation.

Retaliation from the Roadhouse Club? A strike from another gang?

For a brief second, I considered Nolan. I dismissed the thought soon after it crossed my mind.

It had become soberingly clear to me how little I knew my ex-boyfriend. He was a cold bastard and he proved that he didn't give a shit about people or their lives if it served his revenge. Still, this level of getting your hands dirty wasn't his style and it wasn't smart. If Nolan Ives was anything, he was smart.

"Finish up," I signed. *"We'll talk about this outside."*

Eli scarfed down the last bites of his oatmeal and we took the conversation outside to the tennis courts. We weren't practicing that morning but usually we could count on the court for privacy. Another group had the same idea as the bleachers were taken up by kids eating breakfast and talking most likely about what happened the night before.

Eli and I veered off and sat in the pavilion instead.

"Did you get to the post office in time?" Eli asked.

"Yep. All of the checks have been mailed out. You and I are no longer multimillionaires, my brother."

"No, but at least we won't be the most-hated siblings in the history of Raven River."

"I like to think giving everyone's money back will earn us some points."

"I still don't understand why you had to wait this long."

"All will become clear," I replied. *"Trust me."*

"Are you sure this is the only way to find Mom and Dad?"

"It's our last option. I don't have anything else to go on or know where to find another clue. Aurora Fiscal Holdings and Rosehip Lane are a dead end."

"How long before the checks arrive?"

"Around noon. People will get back from work near four or five. They'll call their friends, families, and kids by seven. The entire school will know by dinner—or the latest tomorrow at breakfast. Then it's Brandon's move."

"What do you think he'll do?"

"Can't say, but I know what I'm going to do." A smile curled my lips. *"And I'm looking forward to it."*

I SAID NEWS TRAVELS fast in a small town, but rarely do you get to see it happen. To be there at the start of a rumor—the spark.

Watch it grow—the flame.

See it spread from person to person, raging out of control like wildfire until the minds of an entire group of people are engulfed by one face and one name. In this case, mine.

Beau and I were in the middle of a trust exercise that afternoon in communications class. Seeger had us put our desks facing each other. Beau described a picture for me to draw without telling me exactly what it was.

"First, a square," he said. "Then draw two circles on the bottom corners."

I pressed down on the colored pencil and the tip snapped. "One sec. I have to sharpen this."

I stood just as Destiny's head snapped up. She was seated next to us with the photo on her lap and her phone on top of it. Destiny watched me pass in openmouthed shock, speechless for the first time in her life.

I thought she might say something, but I returned to my desk—colored pencil freshly sharpened—and all she did was sneak glances at me through the exercise.

After class, Clay and I walked through the hall, me tucked under his arm. A few students stopped their packing, walking, conversing, everything the minute they saw me. One kid finally ran up to me.

"Ember," Amir Blake huffed, out of breath. "My dad just called. Is it true? Is it real?"

"Yes, Blake. The check is real. The money is real. It won't bounce."

A grin so transforming broke out on his face, I thought I blinked and the snarling guy who hissed *bitch* at me in the halls disappeared.

"Thank you!" He launched at me.

Clay pulled him up short, fisting his collar and pushing him back. "Verbal appreciation will do, Blake. Keep your hands to yourself."

"R-right, sorry." Amir looked at me, smile fading. "And also... sorry, Ember. For everything."

"It's in the past, Amir. Let's forget about it."

He inclined his head and sidestepped me to leave. We hadn't made it two steps before we heard him on the phone with his dad. "Dad? Yes. It's real, Dad. Tell Mom. Everything's going to be okay..."

I glanced up at Clay. "Normally, I'm not up for strangers touching me, but in this case, I've earned my accolades. Bring on the hugs."

"I'll take my accolades first."

"Oh, yeah? Did you just single-handedly save a town?"

"No, but I give insanely good head."

Pressure built in my middle. "Yep. You get your accolades first."

Spending the afternoon in Clay and Cassius's room saved me the drop-ins from girls and guys knocking on my door to question me the same as Amir. But news spread fast in my little ecosystem, and when Camila and I walked into dinner that night, the entire cafeteria fell silent. I should've put money on my prediction to Eli. Everyone knew by dinner.

Fiona clambered down the loft's steps and charged me. Instinct threw my fists up. Fiona crushed them to my chest as she threw her arms around me.

"Thank you," she cried. "Thank you so much."

I was more than a little surprised by this reaction and who could blame me? Fiona never believed I didn't know where the money was and assumed like many did that I was the smug bitch counting the days until graduation when I'd take off to the Bahamas with their life savings. I thought it was a long shot that she and her family would trust my letter. Apparently, they did.

Included with every check for the full amount of what was taken from them, was a letter I typed up explaining as best I could.

Dear Mr. and Mrs. Blake,

Despite what the media insinuated, I did not know the location of my parents or the stolen money. I wish I did know from the start, so I could have eased the town's suffering sooner. All this time, I've been searching as hard as everyone and I finally found it. I've recovered the entire amount investors gave to the lodge. My parents did not spend a single cent.

Enclosed is a check for the full amount of money taken from you along with the deepest apologies on behalf of the Bancroft family.

If by this point I've earned enough goodwill, I'd like to ask a favor.

In my search for the money, I've discovered there's more to my parents' disappearance. Months on the run and they did not spend any of it. Instead they kept it safe so I could one day return it to you. I don't know yet what this means, but I'm desperate to find them.

If you have any information about the time leading up to their disappearance, please contact me.

Thank you.

"I can't believe you found the money." Fiona wiped her tears on the heel of her hand. "How? And what are you going to do about your parents?"

Fiona set off the floodgates. The student body converged on me, food forgotten.

"Where was the money?"

"How'd you get it back?"

"Why did it take so long?" That came from Pomona.

"Are the checks real?"

"Why did your parents steal it if they weren't going to spend it?"

I put my hands up. "Guys, hold on. Give me a chance." I pushed through them to climb the stairs. Brandon was at our table talking on the phone. He saw me and quickly ended the call. Sliding past him, I grabbed a chair and brought it to the edge of the loft. I climbed up and the whole of the cafeteria lay before me.

"Here it is," I began. "My parents are not thieves. Using everything I know about them, I figured out where they put the money and I gave it all back. I was able to do that because in all this time, they did not spend your money.

"Are the checks real? Yes. Why did it take so long? Because if the money was easy to find, none of us would be in this mess. And why did they take the money and not spend it?" I took a deep breath. "I don't know. I wish I had more to say about that but the truth is I don't understand it either. All I can say is I won't give up looking for them."

I felt gentle pressure on my leg. Camila came up next to me, taking my hand.

"One last thing." My voice carried through the silent space. "All the checks have been mailed. Everyone who invested in the lodge was paid back. So, the cowardly, violent, shit-brained waste of blood and skin that attacked my brother and has been blackmailing me, can pack up their ransom notes.

"If this was honestly about getting back what your family lost, mission achieved. I better not hear from you again, and if I do, I'm getting the police on your ass. I'm done playing around."

With that, I hopped off the chair and into Camila's hug.

"I can't believe that was what you were doing. You found twenty-five million dollars and you gave it back. I don't think I'm being pessimistic when I say most people wouldn't do that."

"You would."

"Nooo," she drew out, tossing her head with a laugh. "I'd be sailing international waters in my ten-story yacht. Y'all would never find me."

We cracked up.

Together we went down to get our food. I collected thanks, praise, and pats on the back on the way down and up. Cresting the stairs a second time, I caught Brandon hurriedly ending a call again. I'd bet twenty-five million dollars that I knew who he was frantically speaking to.

I sent checks to everyone on the list except Ellen Mori. I relied on word spreading fast, and by then, Mrs. Brandon's Mom realized everyone had gotten their money back except for her and she called her son to find out what was going on.

I'd love to know the excuse he's giving her for why she can't speak to me directly, I thought as I plopped my tray down. I wasn't nauseous at having to eat with him that night. On the contrary, I was fighting my facial muscles to not grin.

"Ember," he greeted.

"Hey, B. About the stats homework, did you understand question four because—"

"You found the money." Beads of sweat dotted his brows and upper lip. I had the boy sweating literally and figuratively. "That's incredible. Where was it?"

"Bank account," I said simply. "Everyone wants the dirty details but that's really it. I stumbled on the account number while retracing my parents' footsteps."

"And you paid back everyone?"

"Yep." I scooped a bite of my shepherd's pie. Watching him struggle to be casual was bringing me too much joy. Chewing would stop me from smirking. "All the money was there," I said around my mouthful. "Can you believe it? The town got back everything they lost."

"But how can you be sure you paid everyone?" he pressed. "There were a lot of investors."

"I found a list and tracked down the addresses."

"Ember stayed up all night writing checks and addressing envelopes," Camila spoke up. "I just didn't realize that's what she was doing."

"Oh gosh." Brandon laughed. "Half asleep and writing under a desk lamp? What if you messed up an address?"

I frowned. "Messed up an address?"

"I'm just saying." He shrugged. "You should call or check your tracking numbers. Make sure everything got where it should be and this is finally over."

"I'm sure it's fine. If a check gets there late or doesn't arrive at all, that person can call me. Everyone knows I'm here."

Brandon smiled. "True." He picked up his fork. Topic dropped.

Camila and I fell into conversation about the statistics homework. Halfway through, a faint buzzing sounded from Brandon's pocket. After a minute it stopped. Two seconds later it started back up again. I peeked at him through my lashes.

He played it cool, eating his dinner like nothing was wrong. On the third buzz, he finally fished out his phone. "It's my mom," he said. "I've got to take this. See you guys later."

"Bye," we said.

Brandon got up with his tray, hurrying off the loft. I got up to watch him leave. He flung the plastic tray and all in the garbage and stormed out, phone already to his ear. As the door swung shut, I took out my cell and dialed a number I saved months ago but never thought I'd use.

A soothing, masculine voice answered on the first ring. "Hello. You've contacted the FBI Sandoval Field Office, desk of Agent Lee Underhill."

"Hello. This is Ember Bancroft, daughter of Lenora and Frank Bancroft. I'm sure Agent Underhill remembers me fondly. Is he there? I need to speak to him."

"I'm afraid he's left for the evening. If you're in immediate danger, please hang up and call the local authorities. Otherwise, if you've information about a crime, I will see it passed on to the proper persons."

"I do have information. I need Underhill to call me or he can drop by Raven River Academy for a chat. If he doesn't know why, he will very soon. Thank you."

It was an abrupt end to the call, but I had no choice.

Royal topped the landing, and through the sea of flitting faces and students waiting to get my attention, our eyes met. Royal tilted his head, gesturing for me to follow him.

I met him at the bottom of the stairs and we silently walked out together.

Night crept over Raven River, pushing the sun over the horizon. Royal didn't head toward the dorm like I expected. We ambled to the soccer field. To anyone watching we looked like an attractive couple bathing in the blues, purples, and oranges of a sunset walk.

"You gave all the money back," he said.

"You can't be surprised."

"I'm not. I knew you would and I knew I'd have to say this when you did." Royal swung around, stopping in front of me and bringing me to a halt. "Rio will find out about this—if he hasn't already. Twenty-five million dollars, Em. You found it and you didn't hand it over. He won't let that go." Royal's eyes bore into me. "Ever. You can't leave this campus, and after you graduate, you can't stay in this town."

"I'm ready for the fallout, Royal. I planned for every part of this—"

"No, you didn't."

"I can handle Rio—"

"No, you can't!" Royal gripped my forearms. "He will kill you, Em. He's lost his chance at the money. You've gone from a payday to a liability. I can protect you here, but if you go into his territory, the Horsemen will find you and he will put a bullet in your head. I don't know how much more serious I can be."

Cupping his jaw, I stroked his cheek. "He's not going to kill me because I still have something he wants. I'm not blind to the danger I'm in," I added when he made to argue. "Rio is a ruthless man and I accepted, as I put those letters in Bexton's hands, that I was buying my one-way ticket out of Raven River. The Horsemen and I can't live in the same place after this, but I have a plan to stay my execution long enough to get on the bus."

"What plan?"

"I can't tell you."

"Ember!"

His anger passed right through me. "This is for you, Royal. You asked that you not be a part of taking your father down, and I respect that. I honestly do. But that means I have to do this alone and you have to trust me."

"Unless this plan includes giving him a spare twenty-five mill you have lying around, it won't end the way you think." His grip on me tightened. "Promise you'll stay on campus. With me."

"I promise."

He bared his teeth. "Ember…"

"The plan doesn't include strutting through the OB with a target on my back, Royal. I'll stay on campus, and if for some reason I have to leave, I'll make sure I'm protected."

"You're staying close to me until this is over."

"Okay."

"I'm not messing around," he growled.

I couldn't help my chuckle. "Why are you angry with me? I'm agreeing with you."

"You're never fucking agreeable. It's suspicious as hell." Royal grasped my chin, trapping me in his chestnut eyes and yanking me below the depths. "I will lose my shit if you disappear on me, Ember. You can run your plans on everyone else, but don't play me."

"That's fair. No games." I rose and kissed a jaw as hard as granite. "Come on, baby. You're tense. Let's take our dinner to your room and then have a bath."

My sweet suggestion did little to temper his mood. He ate dinner in his infamous silence though I chattered away the whole time, content curled up in bed and resting on his chest. After I drew us a sudsy bath and put him between my legs. He tried questioning me as I rubbed his shoulders, but got vague answers in response. I've never gotten head from a guy while he was pissed at me, but it was a surprisingly enjoyable experience—as was the hard pounding I took on the bathroom floor.

I fell asleep that night safe in his arms. Why would Royal think I'd want to be anywhere else? The final confrontation with Rio Cruz was coming. It was as inevitable as the rising sun, taxes, that thousands of babies will be born the next day, and around the world, thousands will die. I would not share that day with them. Or the next. Or the many after that.

I had a plan for Rio Cruz. He wouldn't have this town. My boys. Or me.

THE NEXT MORNING, I slipped out of Royal's room and returned to my dorm to shower and dress. I kept my phone close to me—impatiently awaiting two particular calls.

Stepping out of the bathroom, I found Camila talking with the person waiting for me.

"—put in my application yesterday," Camila said. "Next step is sending my transcripts. Have you?"

"I'm holding off until we figure out this stuff with the folks. There are a few institutions around the country that offer rehab too, but Dad would have to leave after he finished the program—if he agreed to do it in the first place. He wants to stay close to Mom, so we have to set him up in a place nearby and pay his way until he finds work."

"Between the three of us, we can manage. Just pick a home that Mom will like while she's capable of being a part of the decision. We'll handle the rest after."

Cassius nodded. Amazingly, the boys were done fighting her. They had each other's backs through everything. This would be no different.

"Baby," Cassius greeted. "Ready for breakfast?"

I checked my phone's ringer for the fiftieth time. Still on. Still turned up loud. "Ready."

Cassius walked me down. We got outside and Royal emerged from behind the building with uncanny timing. He silently fell in next to me. He said I was safe here but he had the look of someone not taking chances.

We joined the breakfast line. I had my phone in one hand and my tray in the other.

The ringer trilled.

I shoved the tray on Cassius. "I'll be right back."

Rushing outside, I didn't recognize the number on my screen. That eliminated the federal agent I was waiting to hear from.

I hope it's her.

"Hello?"

"Yes, hi. Am I speaking with Ember Bancroft? This is Ellen Mori."

I quickly tapped *record*. "Ellen Mori?" I repeated.

"Yes, Brandon's mom. I hope you don't mind. I got your number from a friend who also invested in the lodge."

Ellen Mori had a surprisingly kind, gentle voice. Though her trash bag of a son fooled me for months, I sensed instantly in that first five seconds that she wasn't involved in his blackmailing. Brandon would've told her not to call me to protect the lie that my parents didn't steal from her. That she tracked down my number and called anyway showed she didn't know there was a secret to keep.

"I don't mind," I said. I turned around and started. Royal was right behind me, propped against the wall. I gave him a hard look, gesturing for him to go inside. The jerk lifted a brow like I was adorable and didn't budge.

"Is something wrong?" I continued.

I drifted a bit away to give us privacy. A beep sounded in my ear, alerting me to a text.

"Well, I..." Hesitation crept in. "I truly feel uncomfortable asking this. I certainly don't want this to come across accusing or threatening. It's just that I also invested in the lodge and my check hasn't arrived. I wanted to make sure you knew about me."

"Of course, Mrs. Mori. I'm so sorry. I remember your name. If your check hasn't arrived, it may have gotten lost in the mail."

Her breath of relief whooshed through the phone. "I was certain it was something like that."

"I'll get a new check to you right away. Should I mail it?" I offered. "Or I could hand it right to Brandon?"

"You can give it to Brandon," she said brightly. "I'll drive over on my lunch break to pick it up. Thank you so much, Ember. Again, I'm sorry to bother you."

"No, thank you for giving me a chance to make this right. I apologize for all the trouble my family has caused yours."

I ended the call and spun on Royal. "Are you going to follow me around everywhere? 'Cause I'm happy to say again that I'm not going anywhere and you need to trust me."

"I know you're not. And I do."

Eyes narrowing, I folded my arms. "So go inside. I'll meet you in there."

He lifted his shoulders. "I'm cool here."

"Right. If I go back to the dorms, are you suddenly going to decide you're cool there too?"

The asshole had the gall to smirk. "Possibly."

"Is this your version of trust?"

"I want to be with you. What's wrong with that?"

"Don't get cute with me," I snapped.

Royal threw his head back laughing. "Alright, I'll go inside," he said as he backed away. "Because they're serving crème brûlée French toast and your sweet tooth will only hold out for three more minutes."

He strolled inside. Just to be obnoxious I waited four minutes and then followed him. The French toast was my favorite breakfast. Brandon could wait for a little longer. Standing in line, I pulled up the text. An unknown number flashed across my screen. I tapped it.

034-637-7652: Tgiving 14 years send help. Dont reply!

I screwed up my face. *What the hell is this? Tgiving? Send help?*

Was this a spam text? It didn't make sense. It also didn't want a reply.

I turned off my phone and put it away.

The cafeteria ladies handed me my sweet treat and I carried it up to the loft. The Angels were seated at their table. I claimed the spot between Hiro and Cassius. Cassius scooted my chair closer to see what he was watching on his phone.

"Check this out." A live stream news report sounded over the speakers.

I pulled back. "I can't take another one of those, Cas."

"This is good news, baby. Look."

"—the line is around the block." Another young reporter stood in front of another crowd. Again there were police behind her and again she reported from the Outer Borough, but this scene was nothing like the horrific murders that brought the news crew into town.

"Raven River Bank was supposed to open thirty minutes ago." Sasha Lane, as the screen read, was sharply dressed, attractive, and hungry for her big break if her willingness to take this assignment after the last woman was shot proved anything. "The bank manager arrived to work today and received quite a shock to find nearly the entire town waiting for him. Like Santa Claus on his yearly mission, the people of Raven River woke yesterday to a present."

It wasn't quite like that but some artistic license can be forgiven.

"The daughter of Frank and Lenora Bancroft alleges to have found the money her parents stole. As you know, the infamous couple sold investors on a plan to build a forest retreat. That plan was never to become reality. They fled with the hope of this town riding in the back seat."

Laying it on strong, lady.

"But the brave young girl they left behind worked tirelessly to right their wrong. The victims I've spoken to today all confirm they've been written a check for the full amount of monies stolen, and as you can see, these people will see that money returned to where it belongs.

"The manager called the police for crowd control and safe escort from the bank to their cars, but he assures everyone in this line will be seen today and those checks processed. After seven long months, the nightmare is finally over."

"If the world didn't know before," Clay said, "they know now."

Cassius brushed a finger over my cheek. "Do you think your parents will see this?"

"I hope so," I whispered. "I trust that this was what they wanted me to do."

"Hey." He kissed my temple. "We'll find them."

It warmed me that he said we. Even though it felt like it some-times, I wasn't in this alone.

I looked to Hiro. "I didn't know the name of your proxy, but all of the checks were sent. They would've received it."

"He did," Hiro confirmed. "He's actually in that line right now. Once the deposit goes through, he's transferring it to my bank ac-count."

"You'll get your college fund back. This will finally be over and... we can talk."

He nodded. "I want that."

We ate our breakfast but not in peace. The unseen barrier around the Angel table prevented people approaching me. It did nothing to stop them calling to me from their tables. I wasn't entirely used to people shouting praise at me instead of all the things I could do to myself that weren't anatomically possible. All the same, I kinda liked it.

I walked to homeroom between Royal and Hiro. We were tech-nically going to the same place. I gave them side-eye anyway. Did they think I would skip first period to rush off and confront Rio?

Inside the classroom I dropped my stuff on the desk and made to sit down.

"Don't get comfortable, Miss Bancroft," Geske announced. "The headmistress wants to see you in her office."

No need to ask why.

"Take your things with you," he said.

I did as ordered. Walking past the nurse's office, I remembered that I owed Miss Blanchett a visit. She should have another package for me.

My phone went off in my bag. I paused to check and stopped dead.

"Agent Underhill," I greeted.

"Am I speaking to Ember Bancroft?" There was a roaring sound coming from his end—like he was driving with the windows down.

"Yes."

"I received your message this morning and it seems it was too late." I pictured he said that through clenched teeth because it sure sounded like it. "The news is claiming you found the stolen money and *gave it all away*!"

"Paid everyone back is a more accurate description. Look, you and I are past due a chat and I'm more than ready to have it, but I can't talk now, I've got a date with the headmistress. Just grab your partner, get in the car, and be here no later than tomorrow."

"We're on our way now. What you've done is extremely serious—"

"I'm a guppy in this pond, Underhill. We've got bigger fish to catch. Just get here. Bye."

"Hold on. Don't hang—"

I hung up. Continuing on, I headed into administration. Mallory saw me over her desk and waved me on. "They're waiting for you."

They?

Thinking back, I shouldn't have been so surprised to walk in and discover who *they* were. My shock at their reaction, on the other hand, was warranted.

"There she is!" Uncle Harrison jumped to his feet. "Ember, what on earth were you thinking?!"

I blinked. "You're mad?" I asked, screwing up my face. "You just got a check for five million dollars. What's to be angry about?"

"We thought that check was a joke," Violet cried. "Federal agencies and countless private investigators have been searching for that money. We're supposed to believe you succeeded where they failed?"

"You can't write twenty-five million dollars' worth of checks and that be the end of it!" bellowed Harrison.

"We woke to our phones ringing off the hook," Violet said. "Our friends were in knots asking if these checks were real and what we knew about this. Do you know how embarrassing it was to say we had no idea what our niece was up to?"

"This is stolen money!"

My head snapped to Harrison. They were doing an incredible job ping-ponging their lectures.

"You should have come to me immediately!"

Hart had enough. "Mr. and Mrs. Bancroft, please. Let's sit down and—"

Harrison whirled on her. "Excuse us," he barked. "We need to speak to our niece alone."

She held his gaze unflinchingly. "This is my office," she said evenly. "If you'd like to speak in private, you may use the conference room. I will insist you refrain from shouting in there as well. This is a workplace."

I'd never seen anyone put my uncle in his place so smoothly. He was positively steaming as the three of us followed her out and moved the short distance to the teachers' conference room, and lucky me, she left me alone with them.

Harrison walked around the table apparently so he could slam his knuckles down and bore over it. "That was stolen money in a federal investigation, Ember. The minute you found it and didn't report it, you committed a crime."

"We don't honestly believe this is real, do we, darling?" Violet asked him. "She can't have found it."

"I did find it," I said. "I had something the feds and private investigators didn't have."

"And what is that?" asked Harrison.

"A bank name, account number, passphrase, and a helpful lady named Savannah with my address."

They exchanged incredulous looks. "Explain," he said.

I did. Starting from the middle, I left out the stuff about Rory. They knew about her, of course they did, but my dad and his brother weren't close at the time of her death and Frank didn't feel the need to say more than she was hit by a car. They didn't know the full story and I had no desire to tell them.

"I visited the lake house and found a key to a mailbox that wasn't ours. Inside it was a message for me with the bank and account number. I called, learned the money was here, and she sent me a bunch of free checks."

Harrison looked at me like I said I found the vault housing his millions and set it on fire.

"Why didn't you come to us, Ember?" Violet asked, echoing her husband. "What were you thinking?"

"I was thinking that my parents ran off and left me and my brother with nothing— Strike that. They did leave us with something. A town full of people who want to burn us at the stake. We've been bullied, attacked, and threatened—all things I came to you about and you did nothing."

Harrison's mouth disappeared in a thin line.

"I was thinking that I had to find them for Eli's sake at the very least. I wasn't expecting to find the money instead, but I did and I gave it to the people who've been waiting more than half a year for it. That's a long fucking time to cry about losing your future."

"Language," Harrison barked.

I scoffed under my breath. *Because my language is the issue here.*

"You may have believed your intentions were good, but your duty was to report the account, not slip a check under everyone's pillow like the money fairy." He waved his phone at me. "I had to call our family lawyer on the way over here. Do you know that holds are placed on deposited checks to verify the money is there on the other end? All those people who rushed to the bank this morning will be disappointed in a week's time when the authorities freeze that account. They will not get their money today or even soon. This should have been done the right way."

"I agree."

"And another thing— Excuse me? You agree?"

"It should have been done the right way," I repeated. "But for many reasons, I couldn't. The main reason was Mom and Dad. Uncle, don't you see?" I closed the distance between us. "The feds were after my parents to recover over twenty-five million dollars. If I just called up some field office and handed over the account number, Agent Underhill would've patted himself on the back, returned the money, and moved on to hunting serial killers and kidnappers. The search for the thieves-who-didn't-spend-the-money would go way down on the list."

Harrison's brows morphed from anger to consternation.

"Doing it this way was technically against the law. Whatever. I did what I had to do to force the feds to come back here. They have to interview me, listen to my story, and come to the same conclusion that something is wrong.

"Right now, the whole world is watching us. We're a trending news story and people are paying attention. They're asking what happened to Frank and Lenora Bancroft and why didn't they spend the money?"

I shook my hands, voice rising. "They didn't spend any of the money, Uncle! Why steal it in the first place? Why lead me to the bank account? You have to agree there's more to this."

Harrison stepped back. I watched a thousand emotions cross his face before he turned his back on me. In his fit of rage, he didn't think of what it meant that I was able to give all of the money back. He thought about it then.

"Darling? Harry?" Violet grasped his shoulders. "Whatever you're thinking, remember that we do not have all of the facts yet. Let's tackle the problem in front of us."

"Yes." His reply came from far away. "Yes, of course, you're right." Clearing his throat, he twisted on me. "The authorities will be on their way as you said. When they arrive, you, me, and the lawyer will sit down with them and take care of the possible charges against you. He assures me he can get you off without a blemish to your record and that's our first priority. We'll look into the rest after that."

"All right," I said, surprising them with my agreeableness. "Sounds like a plan."

He gave a sharp nod. "I'm late for work and your aunt has a meeting. From this point forward, you're to speak to no one. Do not answer calls from reporters. Ignore people asking you to explain how you found the money. Do you understand?"

"Understood."

Harrison made for the door. Violet was slower to leave.

"You just happened to find the key at the lake house, did you?"

"Yep."

"What would make you look there?" she asked. "And who drove you?"

I lifted my shoulders. "I held out hope that the feds missed something when they searched and it turned out they did. Lucky, right?"

She looked me up and down. "Yes. Lucky. As for my second question?"

"I got a ride from my boyfriend."

What Violet thought of that, I didn't find out. Uncle Harrison called for her and she left without another word to me.

I waited until they were well and truly gone and then hit redial on one of my four missed calls.

"Agent Underhill?"

"Bancroft," he growled. "Do not hang up."

"Sorry, but I'll have to. I've got first period. I just called to tell you we have to speak privately—before my uncle and the lawyers get involved. The police station is no good because some of the cops are dirty."

"Dirty? What are you basing that accusation on?"

"I'll tell you when you get here. Gotta go. Bye."

"Ban—"

I hung up on the poor man again and left for class. The hard fact was that things had to play out a certain way. You don't knock over a trail of dominoes by toppling the one in the middle. Harrison, Underhill, the fancy-pants lawyer, and I needed to have a talk. But before all of that, I had to talk to someone else.

MY MORNING CLASSES passed in a blur. My teachers might as well have spoken the six thousand five hundred languages I didn't know in a thrown-together jumbled mash for all the sense they made to me. My mind was on one thing and one thing only.

The bell rang for lunch and I was the first out of my seat. Brandon had PE that period. His routine was to shower and change in the dorm after the Raveners filmed and shared his public groping.

Students streamed out of the double doors to the cafeteria. I joined the pack, resisting the urge to bulldoze through them. Who knew when Mrs. Mori and the federal agents would arrive? Brandon and I had to handle our business before then.

I broke away on the path to the lunch hall and rounded the building. My phone went off as I reached the dorm. A glance at the screen revealed an unknown number.

"Hello?"

"Sweet Ember."

I froze in the entrance. The door swung back, smacking me painfully and shoving me inside.

"You and I need to talk," Rio said. "I—"

I jabbed *end call.* Quickly I blocked the number and nearly flung my phone at the wall for good measure.

Royal knew his father wanted to kill me. *I* knew he wanted to kill me. But as his voice came through the speaker, soft and steady like the day he pulled the trigger, I knew as surely as I knew my name that he would.

Shaken, I got into the elevator. *You're fine. Rio is not here and he's not coming here. Focus on Brandon.*

Taking a deep breath, I held it until my lungs ached. Thoughts of Rio blew out on my expelled breath. Time to deal with Brandon.

As I crossed into the boys' hall, I tapped *record* on my phone, slipped it into my pocket, and lingered on the check brushing my fingers. I'd been carrying it all day in anticipation of Mrs. Mori finding a way around her son. She asked me to give Brandon the check. That's exactly what I would do.

The distance to Brandon's door doubled, then tripled as I approached. It was the only explanation for the eternity it took to stand level with the dry-erase board proclaiming Brandon and Craig's room.

I rapped twice on the door.

"Who is it?"

"It's me."

Pause.

"Coming."

Footsteps sounded on the other side of the wood and then he was in front of me. A rush of sweet, woodsy steam billowed out of the room. Brandon slung a towel around his shoulder. It collected the gentle *drip, drip, drips* traveling down his wavy hair. I followed the path of one droplet to avoid looking him in the eyes. He couldn't read the disgust in them until I completed one final performance.

"Hey, B," I began. "Your mom—"

"Before you say anything, let me explain." Brandon gripped my wrist, pulling me inside. "My mom told me she called you and said she was an investor. It looks bad—like I lied to you. But I only did it because the first day we met you were ready to blow me off believing I was like everyone else looking to hurt you."

Brandon lowered himself on his desk chair. His hand slid down to hold mine. "If I admitted my mom was ripped off too, you would've told me to fuck off. I didn't hold what your parents did against you, so why should it come between us?"

His deep, flinty green eyes were filled with so much sincerity... I wanted to smash the laptop in his face.

"I understand," I heard myself say. "The fact is I would've avoided you if you told me the truth. Why take the chance that you were playing me?"

"See?" He squeezed my fingers. "So, you're not mad?"

"No," I replied, smiling. "I'm not mad about that."

He blew out a breath. "Great. You're fucking amazing, Ember. You better know that."

"I do."

His gaze flicked to my pockets. "So, my mom is on her way. Do you have the check?"

"Yep." I slipped it out as his grasping fingers came up. "It's minus two thousand dollars obviously. You'll have to hand her the cash from the last ransom drop."

Brandon stilled. Likely the first honest emotion he displayed in his empty life blew apart his charming grin.

Pure, unadulterated shock.

Brandon recovered quickly. "What? Ember, what are you talking—"

"Really?" I yanked out of his grip. "You're gonna waste my time with that when I obviously know? You were counting on a certain someone to keep your secret in exchange for keeping his. Skip the righteous indignation. He told me the truth."

Brandon's face twisted into a mask of confusion. "I don't know who told you what but—"

"Alright, then. How about I rip up this check and explain to your mom why?" Pinching it between four fingers, I lifted it over his head.

"Wait!" Brandon jumped up and swiped at it.

I jerked back. "Uh-uh. Think you can grab it before I rip it, Brandon? Think again. Sit. Down."

He stood his ground. Fists balled. Shoulders shaking. The Brandon I thought I knew came apart in front of my eyes. The guy in his place... I'd never met before.

A look of such stomach-twisting revulsion curled his lips. "How long have you known?"

"Long enough," I replied. "I'm sure you know all the questions I'm going to ask. Let's start with the first one. Why take it as far as you did? You wanted your money back—fine. But why pretend to be my friend?"

He smirked. "I never told you what I'm going to study at Columbia, did I? Acting. I pretended to be your friend so you wouldn't suspect me. It's that simple."

Fury eroded my self-control. "You don't even have the decency to fake being sorry?"

"I'm not sorry," he snapped. "Somehow you convinced yourself that you're special, but you're just like them. A Ravener. You're another spoiled rich bitch who thinks you're better than everyone else."

I reeled back. "I'm sorry. Has your brain been on vacation for the last seven months? Because there was this little thing where my parents disappeared, left me with nothing, and everyone spat on me in the streets."

"Boo-freaking-hoo," he scoffed. "You were sent to live in a mansion in the Estate. And it didn't look like anyone was spitting on you when you ditched me every day to sit with the Raveners and the Angels.

"You think you had it tough because your life wasn't completely perfect for seven months? Try getting it your whole life! A little princess like you has no clue what it's like growing up in the OB. Beaten up every day on the walk to school. Our restaurant held up at gunpoint twice. Working and studying all day to get into the academy only to be called trash every fucking day.

"I kept my head down. Stayed out of their way. And that didn't stop the Raveners holding me down and sharing my junk around the school. Then, because life is never done shitting on you, my mom tries to change things for the better and your parents steal her savings. Can you blame me for deciding enough was enough?"

"Um, yes, you twisted fuck. I *can* blame you. You beat up my brother!"

"I didn't want to do that. You weren't taking the notes seriously. I saw you throw them away. You forced me to take it that far, Ember."

My voice was low, soft, tightly controlled. "Are you blaming me for attacking Eli?"

"What more do you want me to say? Your family stole from mine and I did what I had to do to make you pay up." He stepped closer. "We're done with that now. The whole world knows you found the money. You can rip that check up into confetti, but you'll just have to write another one. You can't keep what you stole."

"I wasn't going to try," I said. "Your mom and sisters are innocent. I don't have a problem returning what my parents took from them." Just like that, I placed the check in his hand.

Brandon brought it to his face, examining it.

I turned my back to him and ended the recording. Slipping the phone in my pocket, I said, "My problem is only with you."

"We don't have a problem. You and I don't have anything anymore. As long as you keep your mouth shut, I won't tell Hart your boyfriend and I were in it together."

Crossing the room, I moved to Craig's desk.

"You'll go back to your life and I'll go back to mine," he continued. "Everybody's happy."

Grabbing Craig's chair, I wheeled it closer.

"Considering what your parents did to mine, I could've done a lot wor—"

I hefted the chair up and flung. It smashed into Brandon, knocking him into his desk and dragging him to the floor. I pounced with a roar.

Dazed and groaning, he couldn't stop me fisting his wet hair, yanking his head back, and punching him once.

Twice.

Three times in the face.

Pain wracked my knuckles and I didn't stop.

"You beat up my fucking brother!?" I screamed. "Left him alone and bleeding in the dirt! And you think you get to walk out of here?! How's this for a princess?!"

I grabbed his neck and slammed his head on the floor.

"Argh!" Brandon blindly swiped and struck me across the cheek, snapping my head to the side.

The second try I caught his wrist and twisted, crunching bone until he screamed. Brandon wasn't a fighter. He went for Eli as the easy target and he'd regret that every day for the rest of his pathetic life.

Brandon bucked and the chair toppled onto me. Pained grunts bordering on tearful wheezed through his bloody lips as he tried to get up.

I shoved the chair off. Jumping up, I seized his laptop and swung. The collision of plastic and metal on cartilage made the most satisfying sound. Brandon dropped, laid out like a mewling animal and crying even louder.

"S-stop! Please!" he bawled.

I landed a brutal kick to his stomach. He choked on a gasp, eyes bugging out and mouth open in a silent scream.

"Say!"

Kick.

"You're!"

Kick.

"Sorry!"

Kick.

"I-I'm sorry!" he rasped. Tears soaked his face, mixing with the snot and blood. "I'm sorry I hurt Eli! I'm sorry for blackmailing you! Please, stop!"

Stumbling away, my chest heaved with ragged pants. Adrenaline surged through my bloodstream, kicking my pulse into overdrive and sparking my nerve endings to prickle my skin.

"Good," I huffed.

Straightening, I smoothed down my uniform and fixed my hair. Brandon moaned on the floor while I checked myself out in the mirror.

"This is what's going to happen. You'll tell people you busted yourself up slipping as you came out of the shower. Got it?"

He nodded with difficulty.

"Also, your partner was Nolan Ives. That fucker is in a mass of trouble. A little more won't hurt. You keep Hiro's name out of it, and we really won't have a problem anymore." I crouched next to him. "Say you understand."

"I understand," he croaked.

"Let's go, *friend.*" I lifted him around the middle and draped his arm around my shoulder. His body weight collapsed on me and carefully I arranged him to bear him out. "I think you need a nurse."

It was a long trek from the dorm to the nurse's office. Brandon was practically dead weight. With everyone at lunch, we didn't run into witnesses in the hall.

I pushed into the office and called for Nurse Blanchett.

"Ember?"

She emerged from her office, took one look at us, and rushed to help me with Brandon.

"Heavens," she cried. "What happened to him?"

"He slipped coming out of the shower," I said. "Smashed his face on the toilet."

"Oh my gosh, you poor thing." She lifted him easily onto a cot, fussing and clucking over him.

Brandon caught my eyes over her shoulder and I glared fit to burst his head.

"Y-yes," he forced out. "I fell."

"You're going to be all right, dear. You just rest."

Blanchett flitted about the room grabbing gauze, bandages, and showering him with more kindness than he deserved.

"When you have a minute, Nurse Blanchett," I began, "I'd love to grab that package from the pharmacy."

"Of course, dear." She dabbed Brandon's bloody nose while he sobbed like a bitch. "Wait for me in my office and I'll be right in. Thank goodness you found him and brought the poor love here."

"Yes," I said. "Thank goodness."

Chapter Eight

Blanchett handed over my goods and I blew out of there. I had no desire to stick around until Brandon's mom showed up.

I went to lunch like nothing happened. I set my tray down between Cassius and Royal and the boys immediately zeroed in on the pinking bruise on my cheek.

Royal toppled his chair jumping up. "Who the fuck did that to you?"

"Relax." I righted his chair and eased him down, sitting on his lap. "Brandon and I had an open and frank discussion about his actions. Things got a bit heated in the middle, but by the end of our talk, he saw the error of his ways."

Beaming, I pulled my tray toward me and dug in to a host of incredulous, disturbed looks.

"Did you kill him?" Cassius asked bluntly.

I tossed my head back laughing. That did not have a reassuring effect.

"He's alive."

"Is he walking?" asked Clay.

"Of course not."

He smirked. "That's our girl."

We finished eating and went to class. I didn't see Brandon for the rest of the day, and by communications class, Major told me his mom took him home. I was less than concerned about him at that point.

Mrs. Seeger stood in front of the class explaining the theories of nonviolent problem-solving while I cycled between writing notes and checking my phone. The field office was only four hours away. What was taking Underhill so long?

"What are some ways we resolve an issue nonviolently?" Seeger asked. "Including a physical altercation. Destiny?"

"You can tell the other person how you feel and—"

Seeger's desk phone rang.

"I'm sorry, Destiny. One moment." She picked up the phone. "Mrs. Seeger's class. Yes? No, it's fine. She can get the notes later. Okay. Thank you."

Seeger looked to me. "Ember, the headmistress would like to see you in her office."

I was up and grabbing my things before she finished her sentence. I walked into administration and found Mallory had escaped her desk. She hovered outside of Hart's door.

"Miss Keene?"

She jerked.

"Are the federal agents in there?"

Mallory looked from me to the door and then to me. "Yes," she said slowly. "What is this about?"

"I can only discuss that with them. Excuse me."

I walked around her, knocked on the door, and went inside at Hart's permission. The agents rose from their seats. Underhill was exactly as I remembered—unsurprisingly as it had only been a few months. Dark circles under his eyes told of long nights and hard days. His suit too nice but ill-fitting. Like he treated himself to one outside of his price range but couldn't take the expense of having it tailored. He had the height, build, and scowl of a hardened agent while his short, slim partner bucked the stereotypes.

Agent Forbis was barely taller than me and that included the full head of wavy, brown hair. He had a smooth face that was younger than his years. It lessened the effect of the stern look he gave me, but it still did the job.

"Thank you, Headmistress," said Underhill. "We'll take over from here."

"Hold on a minute," she said. "You can't just barge into my school and pull my students out of class. Ember isn't speaking to you without her uncle and lawyer present."

"It's okay, Headmistress," I cut in as Underhill opened his mouth. "I asked them to come. I need to speak to them alone."

Hart got up and drew me aside. "Are you sure, Ember? You're eighteen, so I can't stop you, but you should remember that although returning the money was noble, it entered into a legal gray area. Don't face them defenseless."

"Thank you for looking out for me. I am in a sticky situation but I asked them here because they're going to leave with bigger problems to tackle."

I sensed she wanted to argue, but what she said was, "Okay. You can use the conference room."

I thanked her and then motioned for the men to follow me. We made it into the room and they started in on the click of the lock.

"Would you like to explain to me how you happened to find the money and why you did not report it immediately?" Underhill demanded. "Saying you couldn't reach me won't work as you had no trouble doing so yesterday."

The conference room was a bland space boasting one long oval table and a screen for presentations. I pulled out the seat in front of the projector and sat down.

"Gentlemen, please sit." I gestured to the chairs on my sides. "We have a lot to talk about."

They threw each other disbelieving looks that screamed "what is up with this girl?"

"I'm done with these games, Miss Bancroft," said Underhill. "You start talking here or you can do it at the station."

"I'm not the one holding us up. Sit down and I'll tell you every-thing."

Forbis was first to approach. He edged in and slowly pulled out the chair like I rigged it to explode. Underhill remained stand-ing—arms folded and staring me down.

I rolled my eyes. *Men and their power plays.*

"Do you swear you'll let me tell the full story?" I asked. "No in-terruptions."

"I wouldn't dream of it," Underhill sniped.

Forbis nodded. "Go on."

"All right." I took a deep breath and let it go. "The note my par-ents left me was a secret message."

"I knew it!" Underhill burst out. "You—"

"What happened to not interrupting?"

Forbis held up a hand to silence his partner. "Continue, Miss Bancroft."

"I lied when I said I didn't know what it meant but I honestly thought it had nothing to do with the investigation. They were telling me to go to the cemetery, I assumed it was to pay respects to my dad's parents on their behalf."

I would be honest but only about ninety-five percent of it. Auro-ra and what I did to her wasn't going down in a federal report.

"Your grandparents?"

"Yes. It was a while before I finally got to the cemetery, but when I did, that's when I found the key and realized there was more to the note."

"What key?" Underhill surged forward. "Why didn't you tell someone about it?"

"Tell them what? I found a key in the cemetery and I have no clue what it opens? What were you supposed to do with that?"

"It's not for you to decide what's relevant in my investigation," he said through gritted teeth.

I turned away from him and focused on Forbis. "Like I was saying, I found the key but didn't know what to do with it. I searched all over town and eventually ended up at my lake house where I discovered it opened an old mailbox. Inside was this note."

I reached into my backpack. Both men gripped their holsters, training kicking in. They eased up as I slid the paper to Forbis.

"What is this?"

"Charles Magallon Bank. Account and routing number."

Forbis whipped an evidence bag out of his pocket and claimed my parents' final message.

"I figured they put away some money to take care of us. I never thought when I called the bank that I'd found the missing money," I said. "This was at the start of school. After I got the checks, I mailed them out and now we're here."

I put my bag on my lap. "Your next question was why didn't I tell you right away? I'm more than happy to explain that to you, Underhill." I leveled a mirthless smile on him. "You see, when you decided to tell the world that note had a hidden message and I knew what it was, you royally fucked up my life."

The man frowned, looking around like I couldn't be speaking about him.

"You basically announced to the town that I knew where the money was and refused to say. People have tortured me trying to get it back. I've been attacked, filmed in the shower, threatened, blackmailed and almost killed."

"Killed?" Forbis cried.

"It's twenty-five million dollars." The pain and rage of the last few months bubbled over and heated my gaze. "Did you think they'd ask nicely, Underhill?"

He had the decency to look away. "Miss Bancroft, if this is true, I can assure you it wasn't my intention—"

"It's true," I said firmly. "And it's the reason I didn't call you. First, you need to know about my so-called friend, Brandon. Since the beginning of school, someone has been leaving ransom notes in my locker."

More digging in my backpack. I retrieved the notes I hung on to and gave them to Forbis.

"I ignored them at first and my little brother was beaten. You can check with Officer Ramadi," I added. "Her police report will back up everything. Anyway, I couldn't let it happen again. He kept asking for more and more money I didn't have."

I plucked the papers from Forbis's hands and showed him the one where Brandon asked for two thousand dollars.

"I used the money from the account to pay him. Afterward, I told him I wasn't giving him any more and he sent me this saying he'd go after my other friends. Then there are the two recordings I'm sending you. One is his mom proving she's one of the investors, and the other is him confessing to what he did. There you have it," I said. "Everything you need to prosecute him for blackmailing."

Underhill shook his head. "Hold on. Are we to understand that you kept quiet about the account so the withdrawal of the ransom payment could be used as evidence?"

"Pretty much. I believe this is what they call an ironclad case. You have proof that threat of harm was real, that I was forced to make a payment, and the blackmailer gave himself up."

This was the only way for me to do it. I couldn't prove he blackmailed me by sharing my adventures as a car thief. I had to wait for Brandon to demand another payment and then withdraw from funds they could track.

"It was either this or I beat his ass into a coma," I went on. "Thankfully for him, Mrs. Seeger has been teaching us nonviolent methods for solving problems."

All right. The lesson didn't take in the end and I beat him anyway. But what can I say? I've only been in her class for a few weeks.

I gave them a hard look. "I want him arrested."

"He will be." Fissures of displeasure crumpled Forbis's brows as he read through the ransom notes. "These letters more than prove malicious intent. For heaven's sake, your brother is just a kid. We'll have this Brandon boy picked up right away."

The tight ball of frustration and helplessness nursed in my chest since Eli's attack finally loosened. "Thank you. But I'm not done. Brandon's not the only one threatening me. He's not even the most dangerous. You've heard of the Horsemen, haven't you?"

Underhill's folded arms flopped to his sides. Power play over, he sat down, leaning over the table. "Yes, we have. You have no idea the interest your sleepy little town has garnered over in the Bureau. The Horsemen have grown quickly in the last five years. We've been looking into them for possible ties to smuggling, arms trafficking, and more than thirty open murder cases. We've picked up a few low-level thugs but all refused to roll over on the leaders or reveal the structure of the gang. Are you saying you've had run-ins with them?"

"I'm saying they've had run-ins with me," I corrected. "A few months back, men grabbed me, knocked me out, and I woke up in some back room. They tied me to a chair and pulled a gun on me to force me to tell them the secret message. I refused to and they made threats against my friends. In the end, they let me go with the understanding that I was to find the money and give it to the Horsemen... or they'd kill me."

"Did you report this?" Forbis demanded.

"No, and this is why." Another root around in my bag. Another sheaf of papers handed to Forbis. "The Horsemen got the cop or cops in their pocket to get this out of evidence for me."

"This... is the complete list of the victims," he said for Underhill's benefit. "I gave this list to your chief myself. You should not have this."

"He got it for me when I asked. Took him about a week. Make no mistake, the Horsemen own the Outer Borough. I wasn't about to shoot my mouth off in the station about Horsemen when any one of them could be working for him. I wouldn't have survived the walk from the door to the car."

"Who is him?" asked Forbis.

I shook my head. "I don't know. Never met him. I just have a name that's probably fake."

The lie fell easily from my lips. I could've told them about Rio. Shared the history of the troubled boy who fashioned himself into a clever fence, terrible father, and leader of the Horsemen. I could have and I would have—if not for Royal.

He didn't ask this of me. On the contrary, he said he wouldn't dare get in the way of my revenge against Rio. Royal refused to be a part of sending his own father to prison, but over time, I realized I couldn't be responsible for it either. Deep down I knew it would change things between us. The same way it would affect me if Royal tracked down my parents and gave them up to the cops. I would understand. I'd recognize he was justified. But in the back of my mind, he and that act would forever be connected. I wanted Royal to look at me and see only me.

Not Rio Cruz.

Underhill took out his notepad. "What's the name?"

"Dante."

"Can you describe the men who grabbed and threatened you?"

"Two of them are named Damien and Jay. Unless those are fake too." I described Damien and the two brutes as best I could. My silence did not extend to the men who beat my boys. As soon as I was finished, Underhill was on his phone and across the room, feeding the description to the person on the other end. I waited till he came back.

"I was ordered to find the money," I continued, "and since then his men have stalked me, trapped me, and came within an inch of putting a bullet in my skull. I found the money but a call to the police was a call to the Horsemen. I held out long enough to trap Brandon and then I emptied that account so they couldn't get their hands on it.

"You can tell me about the law, look disappointed, and ask why I didn't call this person at that time, but my life was threatened by a gang that not even the FBI can pin down, and still I did the right thing. I returned the money to the people who've been waiting long enough for it. I think any jury in the world would cut me some slack."

Forbis and Underhill shared a private communication honed by years of working together.

"There won't be charges, Miss Bancroft," Underhill said, "and for the part I played in this, I'm truly sorry. You will need a protective detail. Obviously, the local force can't be involved. I volunteer myself until we can get a couple agents down from Sandoval."

"No," I said. "Thank you, but that's not necessary. I'm safe on campus and in my uncle's home. I'm not planning on going anywhere else until graduation sees me running off with my diploma and my bags to the bus station. What I really need is the final reason I brought you here."

"You believe there's more to your parents' disappearance," Forbis stated. The badge was not wasted on him.

"Yes. You do too?"

Forbis's expression was grave. "It crossed our minds on the way over here that if you were able to return all of the money, your parents went months without spending it. Why steal it and let it sit there?"

"Exactly!" I cried. "I don't want to think that something's wrong but... I just have to find them and I don't know where to go from here. If you agree something else is going on, don't let go of this case."

"Though the money's been located, I can assure you finding the people who made off with over twenty-five million is a top priority," said Forbis. "You don't have to fear that your parents will be shuffled off into a cold case bin. We're actively searching for them. Especially in light of these red flags."

The men got to their feet. "Thank you for speaking candidly, Ember. Also, because it must be said, thank you for finding the money and not doing what even the most honest of people would be tempted to do. Even so, a freeze is being put on the account and all of the checks will be canceled."

"But—"

Underhill held up a hand. "It has to be done this way. We must confirm the right amount goes to the right people. New checks will be issued from the government."

"Will you let everyone know the person standing in the way of their money is the government this time? It was a nice feeling seeing everyone toss their needle-ridden Ember voodoo dolls in the trash."

Underhill chuckled. "I'm more than happy to take the blame. I believe we'll see each other again tomorrow. See you then."

I let them go.

For a long time I sat there asking myself if after all I've done, was I any closer to finding my parents and what would be at the end of this path. I stayed until Hart found me and sent me on.

CASSIUS WAS A WARM blanket of comfort and safety. I tangled up in his bed that night, happily playing the part of little spoon. Clay sat up in his bed reading.

"Today was the longest day of my life," I announced. "From Brandon to FBI agents. I'm glad to be horizontal right now."

Cassius nuzzled my neck. "I know what will make you feel better."

"I'm always down to pound, Cas, but tonight I'm exhausted."

He laughed. "I'm not always after sex, Em."

"Really? Since when?"

He nipped my ear. "Trying to lose your present?"

I giggled. "Nope. Present, please."

Cassius vaulted off the bed, opened his minifridge, and held up a bottle of cream soda and Nerds.

"Aww. You do love me."

I accepted my treats, not wasting time downing half the bottle on the spot. The sweet, fizzy drink eased my tension.

"We saw Brandon as they carried him out of the nurse's office. Nicely done, baby," said Cassius. "What's going to happen to him?"

"They're going to arrest him. I'll tell Eli the good news in the morning." Cassius placed a pillow on my lap and stretched out on me. I ran my fingers through his hair, mind drifting to something else we needed to talk about. "How are your folks?"

"Mom is still at home," Clay spoke up. "We've been sending suggestions to her but now she's saying she can't choose until she visits the place. Most of them are out of state. It won't be easy."

"I'm going to the clinic on Saturday. I'll drop by the house and try convincing her in person," Cassius told me.

Clay dropped his book on the nightstand. "Let's watch a movie. Em's earned a break to eat her weight in sugar and just relax."

"I'm slowing up on the sugar," I said with a laugh. "Just one bottle for me. I'll save the Nerds for later."

The boys got up and pushed the beds together. We went back and forth on movies until we settled on *Now You See Me*. Action-packed for the boys but with some lightness and humor for me.

I rested my head on Clay's chest and secured Cassius's arm over my hip. "I love being the filling in a Walker sandwich."

"That sounds crazy dirty," said Cassius. "You trying to get something going because I thought you were too tired?"

I swatted his thigh. Cassius's vengeance was swift. He jumped on top of me and tickled me breathless into the sheets. It took a while to calm down and get into the movie. We laughed, joked, tore apart the tricks, and for a stolen pocket of time I was a normal girl basking in attention from the boys I loved.

The next morning, I dressed in my room and then returned to the boys' hall to knock on Royal's door.

"Morning." I pecked him on the lips. "I figured I'd make your stalking duties easy and invite you to the court with me and Eli. We're getting some tennis practice in."

"It's not stalking when you're mine."

"I should be curbing this possessive streak, but I really like being yours."

Royal grasped my waist. Guiding me back, he pushed me up against the frame and propped his arm over my head, brushing stray strands from my forehead. Royal closed the scant distance agonizingly slow. "Of course you do. I know what else you like."

I bit my lip. "We're meeting Eli, remember?"

Royal kissed me—tempting my puffy lip between his teeth and then plunging inside to battle my tongue into submission. "Be my muse tonight."

"Hmm. How you beg." I let out a gusty sigh. "If you insist, I'll let you ravage me and then sketch your work."

He grinned against my lips. "Give me a minute. Gotta grab my stuff."

I slipped in behind him. Hiro tossed textbooks in his bag while he scanned his candy stock.

"Hey, Hiro. Want to join us on the court?"

"I can't. I have more work to do on the millennium garden."

I crawled up on his bed. "I'm ready to have that talk whenever you are."

"I'm ready too. There's one more thing I need to do and then I'll know what kind of talk it'll be."

Fear gripped my heart. "What does that mean? Have you changed your mind about...?"

"You?" he finished. His smile carried that fear away like dust. "Never."

"Okay. Good." I couldn't resist a grin of my own.

I left with Royal, grabbing Eli on the way. On the court I filled my brother in on everything that went down the day before.

"*Uncle's supposed to come by today to take me down to the police station with the lawyer. I wouldn't mind getting Underhill to say on the record that there won't be charges.*"

"*Wild.*" Eli crossed to his side of the court, striding up and down as he ingested what I told him. "*Brandon will be arrested. Do you know if they did it yet?*"

"*I've been avoiding the news since that poor reporter. I'll ask when I see them today.*"

"*What about Mom and Dad?*" he asked. "*They've been looking for months and haven't found them. What's going to change?*"

"*They know about the account now. The feds will get farther with Good Samaritan Mail Services than I did. That's a good place to start.*"

"*That's true.*" Hope brightened his cherub cheeks. "*Make sure you tell them about it.*"

"*I will.*" I gave him a one-armed hug and dropped a kiss on his forehead. Over his head, Royal sat on the bench sketching, and past him, Hiro trekked through the morning dew in his cleanup coveralls. It was crazy that he still looked hot in them.

"*All right, little brother. Chapman School has an award-winning tennis team and we're getting you on it. Show me what you got.*"

"You gonna freak when I beat you again?"

"Watch those sass-hands, gremlin. I don't freak. I'm a graceful, and beautiful, loser."

He rolled his eyes so hard it probably hurt.

We took our positions. Holding the ball aloft, I fixed my stance and drew my racket—

"The Horsemen ride!"

I twisted. "What? What is—"

Pop!

Pop! Pop!

In the tiny gap between heartbeats the world stopped.

The wind died. Birds quieted. The few students milling about froze. An unfamiliar black car rolled to a stop before the gates.

And then my heart beat and screams broke the air.

"Ember!"

Pop! Pop!

I whipped around, sprinting to an oblivious Eli. Royal got to him first. Scooping him up, Eli cried out as Royal grabbed him and then me.

We bolted behind the bleachers. Through the gaps, we saw students run for the main building, the pavilion, or up to their fleeing friends, not knowing what was going on.

It was chaos. Eli clung to me, terrified for the simple reason he didn't understand what everyone was running from. I held him to my chest, fear making me hold him too tight as visions of that reporter's wide eyes haunted me.

Pop!

The black car sped away from the gates, veering a sharp right, I heard the squeal of tires from our hiding spot. It disappeared down the forest road.

Rising up an inch, I scanned the lawn for Hiro.

Where is he? I didn't see him run—

My gaze fell on the millennium garden. Lying prostrate on the zinnias, marigolds, and daffodils was a still blue mass.

"Hiro!"

I released Eli and ran.

"Ember, wait! Stop!" Royal shouted.

I raced past the pavilion and the petrified kids huddled inside. The flowers encircled his form, as if they cradled him in their beauty to offset the horrible reality. Despair reached inside of me and ripped everything out, creating a hollowness that it filled with infinite sorrow.

"Hiro, no!"

Hiro snapped his head up. "Ember? Ember, what are you doing?! Get out of the open!" He scrambled to his feet. "Hid—"

I tackled him. He grunted as we collapsed to the bed in a tangle of limbs.

"You're okay," I cried. "You're okay." I threw my arms around him, attacking him with kisses on his nose, lips, cheeks, everything within my reach. He was wholly warm, alive, and unharmed.

Hiro tried both to get up and flip me over. "Ember, we h-have to get down."

"It's okay. They're gone." I kissed him one, two, three times. Hiro was fighting me a lot less. "I saw them drive away."

I pulled back and punched his arm.

"What the fuck?!"

"What is wrong with you?!" I screamed. "Why would you play dead?! Were you trying to give me a heart attack?!"

"I wasn't playing dead," he grumbled. "I was staying low instead of running around trying to catch a stray bullet. And what happened to kissing me? Go back to that."

Laughter and tears bubbled out of me in a baffling mix. Hiro pressed his forehead to mine, cupping the back of my neck.

"It's okay, Em." His kiss was sweet and gentle. "I'm not going any-where."

Beep! Beep! Beep!

We jerked, breaking apart at the blaring alarm.

"What is that?" I asked.

"Lockdown."

"Attention, students and faculty." Hart's voice rang through the forest. I wasn't aware until that moment the school had an intercom system. "This is not a drill! Full lockdown protocol initiated. I re-peat, full lockdown. Students, wherever you are, lock the doors, stay away from the windows, and do not open the door until a member of staff comes to get you. You must not open the door for anyone else."

"What do we do?"

"They've locked down the school. We're stuck out here." Hiro helped me up. "Did you really see the shooter?"

Nodding, I pointed over his shoulder. "A black car. They drove up to the gates, fired, and sped off."

"Then we can tell everyone waiting out here that they're gone. I'll get them to move somewhere safer. Just in case."

Hiro went to the kids hiding in the pavilion, coaxing them out. I ran into Eli's arms.

"I'm so sorry," I signed. *"I didn't mean to run off and leave you like that. Are you okay?"*

Eli socked me square on the arm.

"Ow!" I was a bad influence on this kid.

Royal stormed up to me and snatched me in for a kiss that rav-aged the last few corners of my being that terror left untouched.

"Don't ever do that to me again," he whispered.

"I'm sorry." I burrowed my face in his neck, breathing him in. "Let's move behind the school to wait. Hiro's right. They're gone, but they could come back."

It was a subdued, silent group that waited behind the school for the end of lockdown. I wished I could go inside and tell them the threat was over, but even though I saw people inside, the school and cafeteria were locked and no one would let me in.

All that time sitting there, Eli secure at my side, I went over every single detail to relay to the police who would inevitably need to speak to me.

Black four-door. License plate too far to see. Windows too dark to make out who was inside. The windows were up on the driver's side, so either they rolled down the passenger window to shoot, or there was more than one person in the car. Either way, that person or those people had to be the same ones who shot the reporter. Their phony Horsemen catchphrase made it obvious they wanted us to know that.

It felt like hours before Coach Sutton found us. Quickly we were shuffled into the gym and made to wait some more.

Class was over for the day, and as I looked around at students clutching each other and crying softly, it wasn't the only thing that was taken from us.

ROYAL, CASSIUS, CLAY, Eli, Gabriel, Camila, Hiro, and I formed a group on the bottom bleachers. A sweep was done by the teachers, freeing students trapped in bathrooms, club rooms, the dorm, and the cafeteria. All were moved to the gym to wait while the police searched again.

I wasn't certain what time it was. The gym clock being taken out by a basketball coupled with Sutton confiscating our phones made it difficult to be sure. That caused an uproar from kids wanting to contact their families. She promised they would be returned after the all clear.

At some point, an officer came in with bags of chips, apples, and a sandwich for the kids who didn't make it to breakfast. We ate and settled in for more waiting.

Eventually, Headmistress Hart stepped into the gym flanked by Ramadi and two other officers.

"Hello, students," she said. "Thank you for your patience while the officers did their work. I can imagine how stressful it's been for you to sit here and wait for news."

A hush fell over the room.

"When I'm finished, Officer Ramadi will speak to witnesses, but let me say before anything else that no one was hurt. All students and faculty are accounted for and unharmed."

Hart paused while hugs and murmurs of joy rippled through the students.

"This is an immense relief to us all. Your safety is my responsibility and I could never forgive myself if something happened to any one of you. This brings me to an important and immediate change in school policy.

"In light of the rising violence plaguing the town and what happened here today, Raven River Academy is now a closed campus." Her eyes swept over the assembled students. "Seniors are no longer allowed to sign themselves off campus. In fact, no one may leave campus unless signed out and driven off by a parent or guardian. The gates will remain locked and guards posted around campus. I'm certain you have questions about this and I'm pleased to answer them. I want complete clarity on this because violators will be punished in the strictest possible manner."

A kid I didn't know raised their hand. "What if you're eighteen and you don't have a parent or guardian?"

"Of course, there are such cases," Hart said. "There are also students who leave campus for standing medical appointments. These are the exceptions and the only exceptions where you are allowed to leave campus on your own power."

Hart went back and forth answering questions. During her explanation of the new lockdown drill schedule, Sutton walked around passing out phones.

"All right, everyone," Hart announced. "Classes are canceled for the rest of the day. The dorm has been cleared. I suggest you all return to your rooms and stay there until mealtime. You all may go except for those who saw anything that could be helpful to Officer Ramadi."

I sent Eli off with the boys and hung back to tell Ramadi what I knew.

She gave me a tired smile. "We meet again, Miss Bancroft. Always under terrible circumstances."

"A hazard in your line of work."

She sighed. "That it is. Today I had the duty of processing Brandon Lacroix for the attack on your brother. Now I'll end the day with a school shooting on my mind. What has this town come to, Ember?"

A question Rio Cruz and the leaders should answer.

"It won't be like this forever. One day, we'll run the gangs out of Raven River. There was a time before the gates, the separate neighborhoods, the poverty, and the violence. We can be that again."

She cracked a smile. "This is what I admire about the young. You see nothing but hope ahead of you."

I told Ramadi the little I knew and she confirmed my report matched the witnesses at the first shooting. The same car drove away.

I walked out of the gym and dialed my uncle.

"Ember, I just received a call from the school. Are you and your brother all right?"

"We're fine. I was calling to ask if we're still going down to the station today."

"In light of today's events, we're rescheduling."

The call-waiting alert chimed in my ear.

"I'm also extending the offer for you and your brother to leave school for a few days."

"Thank you, but we're fine here. Hart is beefing up security."

"If you're certain," he replied. "I have to go. Goodbye."

I said bye and hung up. The man wasn't the warmest soul out there but he was capable of making an effort when he chose.

The call-waiting was an unknown number. Hope swelled in my chest thinking it was someone responding to my plea for information on my parents. I couldn't resist that hope despite many of the calls I'd been receiving coming from journalists, thankful investors, or weirdos.

The ringing ended and I hit redial.

"Hello?" I said.

"Ember," that smooth voice replied. "I would strongly suggest you don't hang up."

Energy wasn't spared thinking about how he found another way to call me. He could get his hands on a thousand phones and call me a thousand times. Ignoring Rio Cruz would not make him go away.

"I'm not going to hang up," I said. "I've had a pretty terrifying day, so why not pile on? I found the money, Rio, and I gave it back. In every version of reality where I had that money and a choice, my choice always would have been to give it back. That should give you some comfort to know you're not slacking on your scary thug menacing. I'm just too hard to break."

His soft laugh trickled through the speakers and ran down my spine. "I have a feeling that very soon we'll both discover that is untrue."

I stopped in the empty hallway, knuckles whitening under my grip.

"You're not going to kill me, Rio. You won't hurt me at all."

"Oh? Is that so?"

"It is. The money is lost to you. Accept it. But there is something else you want just as bad and I can give it to you."

"Something I want as badly as twenty-five million dollars? I feel forced to say I don't have a schoolgirl complex either, Ember."

My skin crawled. "No," I said through clenched teeth. "Not me. Nolan Ives."

The silence on the other end was deafening.

I kept talking. "The guy tried to kill your son. Conspired with one of your own men to flood the town with drugs and pin it on the Horsemen. He's gearing to take you down and he's the reason the criminal organization you worked so hard to build is falling apart at the seams. Once you get your hands on Nolan, you can end this threat to yourself and the Horsemen."

"You know where he is?" he asked—sharp and demanding.

"I don't but I can find him. He's my ex-boyfriend. I know his parents, his friends, and his other exes. All who look at me more favorably now that I've returned their money. I doubt he's given up on destroying you. If it was my sister, I wouldn't stop until you or I was dead. Which means he has to be hiding out somewhere close by, preparing his next move. I'll find him and hand him over to you. After what he tried to do to Royal, I can honestly say I don't care what happens to him."

"In exchange for my forgiveness, you propose to track down and deliver my unseen enemy," Rio stated. "Interesting. Finding Nolan Ives is certainly a priority. As is finding the snake among my men. Your delivering him would make my life easier—"

My tautness eased.

"—but not like twenty-five million dollars would have," he finished. "You and I are due that coffee date, Ember. This weekend, we'll discuss what else you will do to get into my good graces."

"I'm not meeting you anywhere and I'm not doing anything else. I'll give you Nolan Ives. Take it or leave it."

"Leave it," he replied without hesitation. "You overestimate your usefulness. From the beginning, you were good for only one thing—getting me that money. You defied me and I'm certain you dragged my son into the betrayal. You must know that cannot stand."

It was unnerving that he didn't sound angry. I wondered if in that cold, dried-up husk where his heart should be, Rio Cruz was capable of feeling anything.

"I will see you, Ember. Very soon."

The dial tone echoed in my ear.

I went ahead and blocked that number too. Pushing Rio out of my mind, I continued to the dorm and the single thing Rio did right in his life.

Royal.

Chapter Nine

The spinning blades cut soft *whomp, whomp, whomps* through the air. I'd never been particularly interested in ceiling fans and nothing had changed on that topic. I stared at the fan to calm my flutters as Hiro did his exploration.

The brief minute I believed he was dead was up there with the worst moments of my life. All those questions I needed to answer came back a resounding yes as I held him in my arms. Yes, he was mine. Yes, I was putting him in my suitcase and taking him to New York. Yes, I could do something just as important as loving him.

I could forgive him.

The day after the shooting, a somber atmosphere seeped into the school. For many kids, the troubles that plagued Raven River were out of the gate and out of mind. A shooting on their doorstep. Trapped in a lockdown. Police crawling all over campus. The shooter still at large.

It was too much for a fair amount of my classmates and they took their parents' offers to go home for a few days. Half the seats in homeroom were empty.

My brain was plagued by the same things, except I also had Rio to deal with. After Royal sketched a gorgeous drawing of me in an upside-down sexual position that was as fun to execute as it was to pose for, we lay face to face in bed and I told him about the conversation with his father. I wanted him to trust me. That required honesty on my part.

"You can't leave campus, Ember," he said. "Rio doesn't risk himself on others' turf, but the second you enter the OB, he'll come for you. Five months and you'll be out of here. You'll be safe."

"We," I corrected. "Five months and we'll be out of here."

He trailed a finger from my temple, popping goose bumps on my skin. "I'm a long way off from getting on that bus, Ember. Maybe one day I'll join you."

"There's no maybe about that, Cruz. We're leaving together, and if you keep making me repeat myself, we're going to have a problem."

Royal smirked. "You and I having a problem doesn't look much different than when we're cool."

He did have a point, but I had to hold out hope that Royal would choose me in the end. Now more than ever I needed him.

I need all of them, I thought as I watched Hiro through the window the next day, replanting the flowers in the millennium garden. *The vision of my future isn't complete without all of them in it. I thought I kept my heart in a music box. Tucked away. Hidden and ashamed. But the whole time it was held by an angry boy, two replicas, and an insane angel.*

"How are you feeling, dear?"

Nurse Blanchett shook me from my reverie.

"I'm doing well." I moved from the window and hopped up on a cot.

Blanchett puttered around the room restocking cotton balls and tongue depressors. "It's been a stressful few days for all of you. I hope you're taking care of yourself. Listening to what your body needs."

"I am. Spending time with my boys is just what the doctor ordered." With that, I slid my gaze to the window in time to see Hiro pack up his gardening tools and say something to the guard standing watch. I gave points to Hart for how quickly she got patrols on the scene.

"Speaking of which," I said, "I should go. I hope you're taking care of yourself too, Mrs. Blanchett. Yesterday was scary for all of us."

"That is true," she murmured. She rubbed the back of her neck, eyes drifting to the same window. "The headmistress has offered to hire a second nurse to give me more time off. My husband travels so much for work, I prefer to be here caring for my students rather than home alone, but a trip to my sister in Cape Cod sounds wonderful about now."

She turned away, smiling at me. "But not until after you graduate. You and I are in this together."

"Thank you."

I hugged her, said goodbye, and escaped the school to intercept Hiro on the path.

The coveralls were unzipped to the waist, freeing his upper body and the sleeveless shirt underneath. His head-to-toe outfit got him around the "no visible tattoos" rule. They were fully displayed, drawing my eyes to the intricate web of ink alive under his skin. Beads of sweat dotted his forehead, sticking to his sable locks. He swiped them with the back of his hand, timing it with a hair flip worthy of a slow-motion leading-man scene.

Be still, my heart.

"Ember." Hiro met me on the path and took my hand like it was the most natural thing in the world. "What are you doing out here?"

"Looking for you."

His smile lit up the far recesses of my soul. "I'm about to head up, shower, and crash. Want to hang o—?"

"Yes." I laughed. "Sorry. Was that too eager? Ask me again."

"Want to—?"

"Yes."

We cracked up.

"Perfect," he said. "Let's go."

Hand in hand, we walked the back stairs up and entered into the boys' hall. Royal and Hiro's room was sans Royal. I still didn't know how he spent his alone time. My guess was secluded in a private spot sketching.

Hiro closed the door, shutting us in our own world. "Feel free to raid my candy stash. I won't take long."

"This sweet tooth is giving me a reputation," I mumbled.

I skipped the candy and browsed his manga collection instead. While he showered, I hopped on his bed and lost myself in a story about a young dragon slayer and his wizard friends.

Against the odds, the story sucked me in. I got lost in Natsu, Happy, and Lucy's battle with an undefeated enemy.

Hiro came out of the shower with the towel slung around his waist.

"This is the book you gave Eli for Christmas," I piped up. "It's better than I thought. I may have to rethink my stance on mangas."

"Like it? I've got the entire collection."

"Natsu and Lucy are so cute. I've got to find out if they end up together"—Hiro dropped his towel—"some other time."

I flung the book aside, openly feasting on him as he crossed the room bare-assed and rifled in his closet for clothes. Water dripped off his hair, running down his back. The water droplets and I traced a tattoo between his shoulder blades.

"What do your tattoos mean?"

"I'll show you." Hiro drew up his boxers and left the rest of his clothes on the hanger. I swallowed as he approached, sharply reminded of the first time we were alone in his room. He lifted me, cradling my body to his chest while behaving like a raging jackass. I was ready for the part of the relationship that was all sweetness and no hatred.

He lay crossways on the bed, stretched out at my feet, and held out his hand for mine. "This one here." He used my finger to trace the kanji characters above his heart. "It spells Kimiko. My mother's name."

"Beautiful," I whispered.

Hiro drew my finger down, skating over his skin but mine was the one prickling with goose bumps. Reclined as he was, perfect, long flowing hair, muscled body, and beauty that wouldn't diminish with age, I imagined I knelt before a feudal lord, offering myself up for a taste of all a life with him could give me.

"This one." Another collection of kanji inked his abdomen. "It's my father's name, Yuno. It's not common in Japanese families to give your child the same name as yours. Instead, Dad took the first character in his name and gave it to me." He placed my hand over the character. "This is Hiro."

"From Yuno comes Hiro. I like that."

Hiro released me and gestured to his arm. "You know what this means," he said to the angel. "I don't mind it, to be honest. Ours are different from the other Horsemen."

"They are?"

He nodded. "The other men just have the wings. The angel herself was Royal's addition. Marked us as his crew. From the beginning, he's stood out from his father. Refused to let Rio drag him all the way down." Hiro lifted my chin. "Ember... Royal's not going to make it out of here."

Stiffening, my nails scraped his skin balling into a fist.

"You know Rio will never let him go. But one thing I'm sure of is he won't be like his father. When he takes over, Royal will change the Horsemen. He'll make them what they pretend to be—protectors of the OB. I hope that makes you feel better."

"It doesn't," I snapped. "Rio can't have Royal. He's mine. Rio can't have you either—in case you were wondering. Neither will Endo."

Hiro caressed a path up my chin, smoothing the curve of my tight lips. "I don't see an outcome where you get to keep all four of us, Ember. Some of us, but not all."

"I'm sorry. Did you not hear what I said? I don't give up on the people I love—ever. Want to bet against me?"

"No," he said, grinning. "Definitely not."

I flopped back onto the pillows. "Good."

Hiro moved up next to me, resting by my side. He pointed out a stretch of barbed wire disappearing over his shoulder. "This I got as a reminder."

"Of what?"

"That life is short for life sentence. And there's only one way out."

"Dark." I rubbed his shoulder like I could erase the ink.

Hiro captured my hand and kissed it. He didn't let go. "I was in a dark place when I got it."

"And now?"

"I'm not," he said simply.

Our eyes met and locked, held in place by a tangible force. Endless obsidian lakes called me into their depths of pain, fury, and anguish. They invited me down to discover what was underneath. The true Hiro Saito.

Hiro was first to break away. Laying your soul bare was difficult for anyone.

He looked to the hand on his shoulder. "I don't have a story for the rest of my tats. I got them because I like them." He turned a grin on me. "Your turn."

"My turn? But I don't have tattoos."

"Why should that stop me from getting to know your body? You've seen me naked how many times now? My count is still zero."

Heat steamed my cheeks. It was wild that I could blush that hard considering the frequency and creativity of my sex life, but there it was. "That's different. You just like to strip."

He laughed. "And you're shy?"

"I didn't say that," I murmured.

"Then just shy with me?"

I shook my head, amusement tugging at my lips. Wiggling down, I undid the buttons of my top and shrugged it off. Hiro stopped me as I reached for my skirt.

"I've got it," he said softly.

Hiro drew the skirt down my thighs, over my knees, and kissed my ankle as he pulled it off. Hiro licked a strip from my calf to my knee. My breath caught and held behind my bitten lip. I thought he'd reach for my panties, and my mouth parted to tell him to wait.

"We shouldn't have sex yet." Hiro moved like a stalking leopard, crawling up my body, his nose skimming my stomach as he breathed me in. "Not until we have that talk."

"We could have it now." The urge to tangle in his hair overwhelmed me. I fanned my fingers through his locks, basking in the fragrant, woodsy smell of his shampoo.

"We will. Soon." He dropped a kiss on my lips. "But not yet. By the end of that talk, I want us both to know where we stand."

I stopped him as he drew back. Cupping his cheek, I kissed him slow. "Do you not know where you stand with me? Because you can let that be a clue."

"I know how I feel about you. That's a different thing."

"Not to me," I said. "All the same, I agree. It's been rocky between me and you. We shouldn't go too far until we both know where we stand." My eyes flicked to my bag. "Would your Christmas present be a clue?"

"Christmas present?"

"I haven't opened it yet. At first I was too upset, and then I wouldn't because I wanted to stay angry. I think it's time. Don't you?"

"Yes."

Seeing where I was looking, Hiro climbed off and rescued my bag. He placed it on my lap and then returned to his spot crouched over me. I felt his eyes on me as I grabbed the still perfectly wrapped gift.

Shaky fingers peeled back the paper revealing a small blue box.

"Is it jewelry?" I asked.

"Open it and find out."

I hesitated only a second longer. Pushing the cover off, I saw it was indeed jewelry.

A shining silver chain glinted at me on a satin cushion. Hanging from the chain was a single charm. I squinted at it and then at Hiro, eyes falling on the tattoo on his stomach.

"It's Hiro," I said as I fingered the tiny kanji charm. "You're giving me a necklace with your name?"

He nodded. "My parents gave this to me when I was five. I haven't worn it since they died. I just... couldn't for a long time." Hiro brushed my hair back, popping goose bumps on my neck. "Now I see it's truly meant for you. Forgive is you, Ember. It was always meant to be you and I was always meant to be yours. Will you wear it?"

I bit hard on my lip, curbing the serious danger that I'd cry. "Of course I'll wear it."

Hiro lifted the chain and secured it for me, leaving a kiss just below my collarbone as he did.

I placed my hand over the charm, eyes falling shut. I wanted to capture that exact moment. The cool chain on my skin. Hiro above me. His bed—soft, warm, and smelling of him—below me.

Hiro pulled me from my reverie with a deep kiss that said everything he claimed must wait until our talk. Slipping out of my hands, Hiro kissed his way through the valley of my breasts. "Turn over."

I complied and scrunched the pillow under my chest, propping myself up while my scanty thong left little to the imagination.

"You ever thought about getting a tattoo?"

"I've been asked that question about a dozen times since I got tangled up with you guys," I said. "Cassius, Clay, and Royal have given me plenty of suggestions, all of them denote me as theirs in some way."

"I was just about to say inking the character for Hiro right here"—he kissed my lower back—"would look perfect on you."

I giggled. "Or maybe my name in Japanese."

"Yeah. You could put that next to it."

Laughing, I landed a swift kick to his backside. "Tattoos aren't my thing, and I say this as someone who thinks they look ridiculously sexy on you."

"I'll just have to change your mind." I felt his presence hovering over me and tilted my head back to capture his lips.

Humming, I replied, "I'm a stubborn girl. It might take a while."

Our noses brushed. "I'm up for the challenge."

"You sound like a guy who knows where he stands."

Nothing existed outside the curtain of his hair. I was safe in this world with him. Loved though he said it in every way but one.

"There's only one thing I know for sure." His words poured out, washing over me. "I love you."

No, I was loved by Hiro in every way, and whatever barriers he thought were in our way, I'd bring them down. It's a mistake to bet against me.

THE WEEKEND WAS A MERCIFUL end to a stressful week. Many students didn't come back to school, and from Gabriel's texts, more than a few Raveners were thinking of extending their time off. They no longer felt safe outside of the gates.

Friday night, Cassius, Clay, Royal, Hiro, Camila, Eli, and I took up various spots in my room. I convinced the boys to join us for a movie night. Something normal to take their mind off things before

I sat them down to talk. Camila popped in early from getting her hair done and then Eli dropped by. The night morphed out of a date night to a relaxed hangout.

Royal sketched on my bed. Cassius and Clay researched homes on Camila's laptop. Hiro and Eli practiced sign language at my desk—he was getting pretty good. Camila and I were the only ones giving the movie any attention.

We passed a bowl of caramel popcorn back and forth—both eyes on the laptop but our conversation going strong.

"How'd it go down at the station?" she asked.

Harrison and the lawyer picked me up earlier that day to give my official statement about tracking down the money. The Bancroft family lawyer—Kenneth Gunderson—was the slicked-back, well-dressed, quick-witted vision of a lawyer most held in their heads. He coached me on what to say on the drive over and warned me not to veer off-script. I did, and said, exactly what he told me, picturing the face of Rio's pet cop on the other side of the two-way mirror.

"It was fine," I replied. "I got in and out and the agents assured me there won't be charges."

"That's a relief. I just heard from my friend that the announcement went out about the checks being canceled. A lot of pissed-off people. Thankfully not at you."

"As long as it's not directed at me. But I do understand why the feds aren't leaving it up to an eighteen-year-old girl to dole out twenty-five million dollars." I switched topics. "How's it going with the search for your mom's new home?"

"Ooh." Camila forgot about the movie, spinning to face me. "I found the greatest place in upstate New York."

"New York?"

"Yep." Her eyes shone with excitement. "It's beautiful. Everything Mom will like. Surrounded by forest and even a waterfall that she can visit. It's a permanent living facility and a rehabilitation center. Both are on one property with tighter security on Mom's side. Dad can do his rehab right next to her. After his treatment, he can live with her since he's her husband, but we'd have to pay for them both and it's crazy expensive. My brothers are looking it over now and tomorrow Cassius is going to try selling Dad on the home, rehab, and buying a place nearby." She scoffed. "I don't envy him."

"Sounds like it has everything they wanted. It might go well."

"It will," Cassius spoke up. "That's why they're sending me. I'm the favorite."

Camila rolled her eyes. "Is that why Mom and Dad mix you two up all the time?"

"They loved me so much, they made two of me."

Camila nailed him square on the back of the head with a pillow. She gave me a look while he howled. "Are you sure about that guy? Honestly, if you want out, blink twice."

I tipped onto the nightstand guffawing. "Sorry, Cam, Cas isn't underselling his awesomeness. He's mine for good."

She heaved a sigh. "There's just no accounting for taste."

"Hey!"

What followed was the pillow fight of the millennium. Eventually the boys filed out, kissing me goodbye one by one and leaving us to our roommate time. I never got my chance to talk with them. The conversation would keep until the next day.

ELI WAS NOT PLAYING tennis for the foreseeable future. It crushed me. How could it not that my brother was afraid to go outside. The drive-by was fresh on everyone's mind. I'd give him some time before I pushed him to beat me on the court again.

Saturday after lunch, I let Tatum and Eli teach me to play a video game they'd gotten into. Between battles, I texted Cassius.

Me: How'd it go at the clinic?

Cassius: Still in remission. Your boy's got a clean bill of health.

Me: Yay. Come back soon and we'll celebrate.

Cassius: I'm at the house. I'm selling them on Folkstone Center and then celebrating is exactly what we're going to do. Call you on the way back.

Me: Alright. Love you.

The boys beat me in their fifth consecutive superhero-against-superhero battle and I called it quits. Heading up to my room, I checked my phone for the time and a response from Cassius.

Almost four.

The talk with his parents must be running long. Of course, they'd have a lot of questions, and if his dad's not on board, Cassius would have a lot of arguments.

Me: Good luck, baby.

I messed around in my room until dinner. Eli and I walked to the cafeteria together. We grabbed our bowls of Italian wedding soup and sides of garlic bread and salad. Eli went off to his table and I climbed the stairs.

Hiro and Royal sat at the Angel table. Ghost fingers caressed my skin as I thought of my afternoon rendezvous with Hiro. After he explored my body to his heart's content, he lay on top of me and read manga to me over my shoulder, teaching me what the different characters meant.

I put my tray down between him and Royal. "Where are the triplets?" I asked. "Are they holed up talking about Folkstone? Cassius was supposed to call me on his way back."

Royal gestured with his chin. "There's Clay."

Clay jogged up the stairs. He was devoid of his food and his brother. "Ember, have you talked to Cassius?"

"No, and don't think I'm not mad about it," I joked. "I'm still waiting for my 'love you too' text."

"Shit," he swore. Clay twisted, scanning the room. "Where's Camila?"

"Why? What's wrong?"

"It's nothing," he said mostly to himself. "He probably stopped to get something."

"Clay." I rose, unease pushing me to my feet. "What is it?"

"Cassius should have been back by now. I called Mom and Dad, they said he left three hours ago."

"What?" I cried. "What are you saying?"

Clay finally looked at me and the distress darkening his blues crushed my chest. I'd seen a lot of emotions in the eyes of my always-strong and always-in-charge love, but I'd never seen them hold true worry.

"I've called him three times, Em. He's not answering."

"His phone could've died," Hiro said.

"It doesn't explain why he's not here yet. Ember, when's the last time he texted you?"

My phone was already out. I scrolled up and tapped on his name. "He texted me when he got to your house. Nothing since and he said he'd call me."

I put the phone to my ear. It rang and rang until the voicemail picked up. Taking a deep breath, I pushed it deep into my lungs and trapped it.

Cassius is fine. Cassius is fine. Cassius has to be fine.

The breath tore out of me and I said, "Maybe he stopped for something like you said. It's too soon to be worried."

"Baby, I don't want to scare you, but we should be worried. The OB is hell right now. Some crazy fuck is *killing* Horsemen and putting them in dumpsters."

I trembled, panic welling up in my throat. Clay came around and gathered me in his arms. "I'm sorry. Everything's going to be fine, Em. Let's just find Cam."

We went off in search and ran into Camila coming out of the dorm.

"He hasn't called me either," she said. "When did he leave the house?"

"A few hours ago."

Her eyes widened. "Hours?! What are we still doing here? We have to tell Hart." She rushed off to the faculty building where the teachers and staff slept and ate. Clay hung back.

"Keep calling him, Em. Tell me when he picks up."

"I will," I rasped.

Hiro left with Clay. Royal and I stood in the glow of the entry light—a worried look on my face and a tight, stiff-jawed expression on his.

"Em, go upstairs to my room. I'll be there in a minute."

"What are you going to do?"

"Call around. Find out if any of the guys from the neighborhood have seen him."

"Okay." I kissed him, drawing some comfort. "Tell me everything is going to be okay."

"Everything will be okay."

I hung on to his reassurance, cradling it to my chest as I did my phone, and sent Cassius another text.

Me: Please call me. I'm getting worried. Let me know you're okay.

I stepped inside the elevator. It dinged in time with my ringer. Cassius's name flashed on the screen.

"Finally, baby," I said. "Are you okay? Where are you?"

"I'm doing very well. Thank you for asking."

Reeling back, the phone slipped through stiff fingers. From the floor, Rio's voice came through loud and clear.

"You'll forgive me if I don't tell you where I am. That would ruin the purpose of this call."

I dove for the phone. "What the fuck is going on?! Why do you have Cassius's phone?"

Rio's honeyed baritone didn't inflect above relaxed. "Naturally because I have Cassius."

Icy horror gripped me and emptied my lungs. Complete silence echoed on the other end. Rio waited me out, content to let the terrible realization sink in.

"What does that mean?" My voice sounded like it came from someone else.

"You and I have a date, sweet Ember. I would hate for you to stand me up, so Cassius is here to ensure you keep the appointment."

The elevator opened on the fourth floor. I froze to the spot. Unable to move. Unable to breathe. Unable to scream. The metal slid closed, trapping me inside.

"What have you done to him?"

"Nothing," he said lightly. "Cassius hasn't been harmed, and he won't be as long as you come to 3872 Becker Street tomorrow at eight. You should recognize the address. You and Clay Walker enjoyed my hospitality here several nights ago."

My eyes flared. *Rio knew we were at the safe house? How?*

"Come alone goes without saying, but I'll say it anyway. If I see the police, Cassius dies. If you send my son believing he will stay my hand, Cassius dies in front of him. If anyone but you and you alone approaches the house... Well, I believe I've made my point."

A million fire ants raced beneath my skin. They were the only proof I was real and breathing as my world crashed around me. Rio would kill Cassius... if I didn't let him kill me.

No, that's not going to happen! Get ahold of yourself. Think.

I took that deep breath and held it until my heart slowed.

"If I do, Rio, what happens?" I began. "You're asking me to skip to my death with no proof Cassius is okay or that you even have him."

"If you want to speak with him, you only had to ask."

"I want to speak to him. Put him—"

"Ember?" A rough, unmistakable voice filled my ear.

"Cassius! Are you okay? Where are you?"

"Don't come, Ember! Don't—"

A grunt followed by a roar burst through the other end. Then there was silence.

"There you are," said Rio. "Eight o'clock tomorrow night, Ember. Do not be late."

"What is the point of this, Rio?!" I shouted. "The money is gone and killing me won't get your hands on it!"

"You elected to sour our relationship. Now it must end a certain way. It was your choice, not mine."

"You have a choice, Rio. A choice not to do something that will make your son hate you for the rest of your short, empty life. And if you want the truth, you'll hate yourself for it too."

"Are you attempting to appeal to my paternal side?" He tsked. "A move that reeks of desperation. It's beneath you, Ember."

I clenched my teeth so hard my jaw popped. "Maybe I can appeal to your practical side. The academy is closed. No one goes in or out. Plus, I don't have a car. I can't get to you, alone or otherwise."

"A little gate and lack of transportation is going to stop you from saving Cassius's life? It seems I was wrong about your feelings for him."

The elevator came to life and rumbled its way down.

"Don't do this, Rio. Please." I hated myself for pleading, but I would've hated myself more if I didn't do it for Cassius's life.

"Until tomorrow."

Click.

And then I did scream. Just as the doors opened for Royal.

"CALL HIM."

"I did."

"Call him again!"

I flinched at Clay's shout. I leaned against Royal's headboard, hugging my knees and trying to understand how twenty-four hours earlier, I was happy and laughing with my boys. How could so much change in a day?

"I've called Rio five times," Royal said. "He knows my number and he's not picking it up. He's not answering from Ember's phone either."

Clay stalked up and down the room, fists balled and eyes alight with another emotion I'd never seen. "Call Damien or Jay."

"They won't go against him."

"We have to do something!" He snapped around, advancing on Royal. "Ember's not going to that house. You've got to convince Rio—"

"I'll find him," Royal said, "and I'll bring him back." Royal knelt beside the bed. "You have to stay here, Em. Whatever you're thinking of doing, stop. Trading your life for his isn't a fucking option. You can't go to that house." He pried my fingers off and clasped my hand. "Trust me."

"Isn't that my choice?" My voice was barely above a whisper.

"What?"

"To go is my choice and I'd never forgive myself if I cowered here and left Cassius to die."

"You're not going, Ember."

"No, you're not going!" I ripped out of his grasp. "Rio swore to kill him in front of you if you interfered. We don't have options, Royal. Doesn't Rio know all the places you'd search and the people you'd call? You'd waste the day going down dead ends while Cassius's time runs out. I have to go and we all know it."

Hiro had been quiet up to that point. He rose from his chair. "You can't go, Ember. You're crazy if you think we'd let you. We can get Cassius back safe and protect you from Rio. Why won't you trust us?"

My lips trembled. "Stop talking to me about trust. This has nothing to do with how I feel about you and everything to do with Cassius. I will not let Rio hurt him."

"We won't let Rio hurt you," Clay said. "Cassius wouldn't want you to do this and he told you as much."

"Rio is not going to kill me."

Royal tossed his head, biting off a curse. "Why do you keep saying that when you know it's not true?!"

"He won't," I insisted. "I'm not useless to him yet."

"Because you think you can find Nolan?"

"Because I can either make his problems go away or give him dozens more. When he gets over his pride at being outsmarted, he'll see that." I looked hard into his eyes. "It's time for you to show that you trust me."

"This has nothing to do with trust and everything to do with protecting you," Royal flung back at me. "You're not going."

Vaulting off the bed, I blew out of the room to angry shouts—a few of them mine.

I didn't make it far. Swinging back around, I grabbed Clay and dragged him to his room. They weren't about to sit around plotting without me and, even in the midst of my anger, I wouldn't let Clay sleep alone.

We fell asleep that night stiff, silent, and weighted down by the clock's relentless ticking toward the worst day of our lives.

ROYAL LEFT EARLY THE next morning to search for Cassius. That left Hiro and Clay in charge of watching me.

"What do you think I'm going to do?" I snapped when my third request for space was denied. I needed to be there for Clay and Camila, but twenty minutes to break down and cry alone wasn't too much to ask. "I don't have permission to leave or a car if I did. I'm not going anywhere, so give me a few minutes."

Clay gripped my waist, guiding me onto the bed and his lap. "I'm going out to look for him too. The only way I can be out there focused on Cas is if I know you're safe here. Please, baby. We'll bring him back. I promise."

Shoulders slumping, the fight went out of me. My boys weren't the enemies. They were trying to protect me from Rio. From the beginning, he's been the true threat. The real obstacle to the life we want together. Rio deserved every ounce of my hatred and wrath. I wouldn't deny him the full pleasure by aiming it at Hiro and Clay.

"I'm not going," I said. "I'll stay here. Just bring him back to me."

"I will."

Clay left soon after, picked up by his father. There were more safe houses and hideaways. Clay would try every one he knew.

Hiro and I stretched out on my bed. He held me under the crook of his neck, rubbing slow circles on my arm.

"I'm going to take a shower," I said. "It will help me feel better."

"Okay. Want me to join you?" Hiro didn't say that sexually. He genuinely sought to stay by my side and comfort me.

"No, thank you. I need some time."

He nodded. "I'll be right here."

I bent and kissed him. "I love you."

"I love you too."

Collecting my clothes and towel, I carefully tucked my phone in the folds. I stepped into the bathroom, closing and locking myself in. The shower turned on with a groan of the pipes, and hot steamy water beat on the porcelain tub.

I dialed his number right away, hoping against hope that the offer still stood.

"Hello?"

"Uncle," I said, careful not to let my voice carry. "I said that we were fine, but we're not. The shooting scared Eli, and we can't go near the tennis courts anymore. Is it okay if we come home for a couple of days? We need to be somewhere we feel safe."

"I'll send Monroe with the car in a couple of hours."

"Thank you, Uncle." I met my reflection in the fogged mirror. Seeing her pale, drawn face made me flinch. "You have no idea what this means to me."

Two hours later, Monroe was downstairs and Hiro was wrapped around me, reading to me from his manga and being as perfectly soothing and attentive as I needed him to be. I loved him, and the last thing I wanted to do was deceive him, but nothing would stop me from being at that northside hideaway because that's where Cassius needed me to be.

"Hiro?"

"Yeah?"

"I love you, but these attempts to distract me just remind me of what I'm being distracted from. Let's watch a movie instead. Something I can really get lost in."

"Sure, Em. Whatever you want."

"You pick the movie," I said as I slid off the bed. "I'll get Eli."

Hiro caught my hand. I stilled, facing straight ahead and holding my breath. "We will get him back. You're not the only one who has something Rio wants. He'll let Cassius go."

"I know he will." I slipped out of his grasp and left.

Eli was packed and waiting for me at the entrance. *"I don't understand why we're going to Uncle's house all of a sudden."*

"I needed a break and I wasn't leaving you here by yourself. It's just for a few days. You'll read, watch movies, miss out on homework, and we won't have to worry about crazed gunmen."

"*I'm cool with that.*"

I hustled Eli outside and through the gates like Hiro would appear any moment. Of course, he'd realize I was gone and where I went. And in his case, he could come after me. Hiro, Royal, and Clay could track me down and blockade the road to 3872 Becker Street. It wouldn't stop me being at that house at eight o'clock.

Monroe didn't chat much on the way to the Estate. I got the feeling he wasn't a fan of being chauffeur to a couple of teenagers. I couldn't be sure of course—because of the not-speaking-to-me thing.

Monroe stuck to the back streets, keeping out of the Outer Borough until we turned for the road that led through the northside and the back entrance to the Estate.

I scanned the horizon picturing the house that Clay and I made ours for just one night. That perfect picture crumpled in Rio's fist.

We arrived at the house and found ourselves alone except for the staff. My uncle was at work and Aunt Violet was attending one of her many society meetings. I took Eli upstairs and left him in his room watching a movie. I stepped into mine, gazing around the impersonal, albeit luxurious space. A chaise was placed beneath the window, looking out over the pool and the fabulous job the landscapers did with the gardens.

I sat down as my phone went off. Swiping ignore on Hiro's call, I put my feet up, stretched out, and pulled the throw blanket over me. It was a long wait to eight o'clock.

"PASS THE SALT, PLEASE, Ember."

I slid it over. My uncle accepted the salt shaker with a thank-you and we resumed our silent dinner. Our presence at the dining table was required for every meal. Even if we spent that meal only opening our mouths to put food in it.

The small dining room was an intimate space with a four-person table, photos of my aunt and uncle, and a small wet bar in the corner. The opposite of the grand dining room complete with five crystal chandeliers, a grandfather clock, silver dining sets displayed in a case, and a table for fifty that sat empty almost every night.

"Have you given any thought to where you're going to college?" asked Harrison.

Seems we're going for conversation tonight. I glanced at the clock. *Glad he's in the mood to talk. Maybe he'll also be in the mood to lend me the car.*

"I've applied to a couple of schools in New York," I said. "I should hear back any week now."

"Excellent. I feared you'd let the search for your parents derail your college plans."

"We'll find Mom and Dad long before I leave for college."

Eli nodded having read my lips.

"I gave my number to half the town and the media's broadcasted it. Someone somewhere knows something about their disappearance and they will call."

"The authorities have it in hand," he replied. "Your days of sleuthing are over, Ember. Let them do their work."

I didn't bother pointing out they'd been doing their work for months and were no closer to tracking them down than anyone else.

"Uncle," I began, switching topics. "Now that we're talking about college, I'm guessing that discussion about my finances is coming up too."

He frowned. "What do you mean?"

"I'm assuming I'll have to pay for tuition and my apartment out of my trust fund. I'll need to know how much is in there and work out a stipend situation. Unless you're giving me access to the whole thing."

"I most certainly will not give an eighteen-year-old full access to that amount of money. Why on earth would you assume you're paying for college? I intend to cover your tuition, books, and dorm."

I blinked. "You do?"

"Excuse me?" Violet's spoon clanged in the bowl. "Harry, we didn't discuss this."

"My father's intent behind the trust fund was clear. It's to give Ember and Eli options when they're old enough to make the decisions about what they want in life. We'll pay for their schooling." He turned to me. "Any extras you can pay for with a part-time job."

"That... sounds fair." Shock colored my reply. "Thank you, Uncle."

There'd be another talk about my plans to take Eli with me, and by the look on Aunt Violet's face, she had a few words for Harrison too. All of that would have to wait.

"Can I borrow the car tonight? My friend Gabriel invited me over to hang out and watch a movie."

"You're not leaving the Estate," said my uncle.

"He lives here. Gabriel Lighthouse."

"I know the Lighthouses, darling," Violet said. "They're a good family. Much better company than the kind you've been keeping lately."

I bit back a retort. Arguing with her would not get me the car. "So, can I go?"

"Yes, but don't stay out too late," Harrison said.

"Thank you," I said. *You have no idea how grateful I am.*

I cleaned my first, second, and third course quickly, feigning that Gabriel expected me by seven thirty. Uncle Harrison excused me early. I hurried upstairs, grabbed the phone I left on the nightstand and cleared the seventeen missed calls.

Tonight will not go the way Rio believes, I thought as I started the car. *I will get Cassius back and both of us will drive away from that psychopath—whole and safe.*

I set on the path for the safe house. Driving out of the gate, I turned onto the main road, knuckles paling under my constricting grip the closer the drive brought me to the house. A left onto a side street and my surroundings began to look familiar.

My phone went off in my pocket. I pulled it out, ready to hit ignore on the boys, and stopped. It wasn't Royal, Hiro, or Clay.

"Rio," I answered.

"Hello, Ember. There's been a change of plan. Pull the car over. Right now."

I twisted, surveying the empty stretch of road. "But I'm almost there."

"Do it."

Hitting the brakes, I pulled off beside a mailbox.

"Get out of the car."

"What's going on?"

"We're changing locations," he replied. "From the twenty calls I've gotten from my son in the past day, you told him about our meeting and no doubt where it is. We wouldn't want him interrupting us."

While he spoke, headlights lit up my rearview mirror.

"Is your license plate one, three, two, X, K, nine?"

I swallowed as the car stopped behind me. "Yes."

"Good."

The driver's door opened and Damien stepped out. If Royal, Clay, and Hiro were waiting at the house for me, I'd never make it.

I turned off the car and got out. There was no choice.

Damien was a silent, hulking mass at my side, walking me to the sleek, silver Lexus and shutting me in. Jay twisted around in the passenger seat. The gun served as his greeting. He leveled it at my head. Damien climbed in, threw the car in drive, and pulled a U-turn.

I put the phone to my ear. "Are you still there?"

"I am."

"Where are they taking me?"

"You'll find out soon enough."

I eyed Jay. "Want to tell your dog to put away his toy? I don't like guns in my face."

"He's ensuring you don't do anything foolish."

"I want Cassius back. I won't do anything foolish."

"Give him the phone."

I passed it over. Jay listened for a beat and then dropped his gun. Just like that.

"Any more requests?" Rio asked, sounding amused.

"None for now, but I'll get back to you."

He ended the call mid-laugh.

I sank into the leather, still and quiet like my captors. We pulled onto the main road and drove away.

Away from Becker Street.

Away from the Estate entrance.

Away from town.

Damien took the outer road all the way down until pavement became dirt. We disappeared into the trees, swallowed by Raven River forest. Absolute darkness ate at the headlight beams. There were cabins dotted about the forest. Remote and secluded as was the draw of our patch of nature. A single gunshot and a shallow grave and I'd never be found.

That's not going to happen. I'll have this chat with Rio and tell him how things are going to be from now on.

The car rattled over the uneven, earthen path, bouncing me in my seat. Motion sickness churned a stomach gnawed by worry. I breathed slow, fighting to keep my dinner as light peeked through the trees.

We rolled to a stop in front of a modest cabin with a single car out front. Damien opened my door. He reached in, pulling me out with an ironclad grip on my forearm.

My eyes swept the property. Darkness surrounded us. No lights to signal another cabin nearby. The one I was brought to had a wraparound porch with nothing on it and overgrown bushes serving as a garden. Nothing about this place would make a curious trekker look twice.

Damien dragged me up the porch and threw open the door. I was shoved unceremoniously inside.

Rio didn't look up though I nearly fell on top of him, tripping on the carpet and dropping on the leather sofa. I recoiled from him, scooting to the edge of the couch.

I glanced around, taking our new meeting place in. The inside of this place was nothing like the outside. The couch was plush. The rug Persian. A big-screen television played a soccer game on mute. This wasn't just any cabin. It was Rio's.

"Ember." Rio set his mug aside on the coffee table. A form-fitting white sweater and black pants wrapped around his body, obviously expensive from the little I knew about these things. A thick silver band poked out of the sleeve as he shifted to me, draping his arm over the couch. The smile on his face was completely relaxed. Pleasant. Bordering on kind. "Thank you for joining me."

"Where's Cassius?"

Rio made a show of looking around. Sitting at the dining table, silent and watchful, was the other brute that served as his bodyguard. But no Cassius.

"I'm afraid he's not here, but feel free to check yourself."

I was off the couch before the end of the sentence. Shouting Cassius's name, I burst into the bathroom, lone bedroom, and out to the back porch where another brute I'd never met waited. He advanced on me, forcing me back inside. It didn't matter because Cassius wasn't out there either.

I stormed past the kitchen. "Where is he?"

Rio was on his feet. He stepped around the couch, meeting me toe to toe.

"You said if I came, you'd give him back!"

"And I will," he replied. "Once our business here is concluded."

I scoffed. "You mean once you killed me and buried me in the backyard with the other bodies? Let me wake you up from that dream. You're not going to hurt me, Rio. In fact, you're going to walk me out of here, put me in the car, and wave goodbye as you grow small in my rearview."

Rio cocked his head. "Is that so?"

"Yes," I gritted out.

"Why is that?" Folding his arms, Rio leaned on the back of the sofa, legs crossing at the ankles. "Please. Enlighten me."

"Because killing me will make your life extremely complicated. There—"

"Hey!"

A muffled shout came from outside, turning both of us to the door. Rio's thug pushed through us, his gun up and leveled at the wood.

"Get the fuck out of my way! Ember? Ember!"

"Royal?" I bolted. "Royal!"

"Grab her!"

His man fisted my shirt, wrenching me off my feet. I fell on the carpet, crying out.

"Ember!"

"I'm here!"

Thuds and grunting sounded from the other side of the wood—obvious sounds of a struggle.

"What are you doing?!" Rio barked. "Bring him inside!"

The door kicked open. Royal fought in Damien and Jay's hold. Both guys had him under the arms and the blood weeping from Jay's nose proved they paid for it. They dragged him inside, slammed the door, and shoved him against it.

"How?" Rio snapped. The shit-eating, this-is-all-so-amusing grin was nowhere to be seen.

"I know how you work, Dad," his son replied. "The address you gave Ember was exactly where you and Cassius would not be. I followed Damien and he led me right to you. Your security is shit."

Damien whipped from Royal to his boss, jaw slack like he wanted to deny the accusation when the proof bucked in his grip.

"Clearly, it is," Rio hissed. "A shame for both of us. I would've preferred you not see this."

I pushed myself up and backed into Rio's guard. He gripped my arm and put me in a choke hold. I stomped the bastard's foot. His grip loosened and he let out a howl. Swiftly, I slipped out, brought my hand up, and backhanded him across the face. "Don't touch me."

The guy scrambled for his gun.

"That's enough," Rio said. "I grow tired of this. You've far outlived your usefulness, Ember Bancroft. Twenty-five million dollars on the line and you were still more trouble than you were worth. Now that the money is gone, you're worth nothing at all."

"You have no clue the kind of trouble I can cause when I'm dead." I smiled to match his. "I keep telling you you're not going to kill me, and here's why. I made a big splash handing out those envelopes and forced the FBI back here for a chat. We had a nice long talk about the last few months and a certain gang that's been threatening me, forcing me to empty the account quickly before they discovered I found it."

Rio's eyes narrowed to slits. "I know what you said to the agents and you didn't speak of the Horsemen once."

"Thank you for confirming your pet cops were listening in. That's why Forbis, Underhill, and I took our conversation off the books. I told them the Horsemen have kidnapped, cornered, and tried to kill me all for this money, and here's the funny thing, they knew about you guys."

I tapped my chin, grin curling my lips as his peeled back from his teeth. "They're investigating the Horsemen for arms trafficking, smuggling, and more than a few open murder cases. Did you know they picked up a few of your guys or that they're sniffing around your organization?"

Rio didn't answer. Neither did his tight expression.

"So, if I go missing shortly after I rip millions of dollars away from the Horsemen, don't you think they'll put two and two together? I'm America's sweetheart right now. Everyone will be on that story and the feds will be up the Horsemen's ass with a magnifying glass. They'll ask around about Jay and Damien"—I looked to the guys holding Royal—"yeah, I gave them your names.

"Plus, my uncle, who I recently discovered doesn't despise me as much as I thought, will put his considerable wealth to making sure the Horsemen, and you, regret that one death too many."

Rio's nostrils flared. Fists balled and dark brown pools alight with seething, destructive fury that begged to escape its confines and reduce me to my namesake. I glimpsed a peek that day in Caesar's Garage, but I'd never seen Rio get real and truly angry. He was angry then.

"What have you done, girl?!" He ate the distance between us, towering over me, and snapping my head back to meet those burning eyes.

"Dad, don't touch her!" Royal thumped against the wood, fighting harder to get free.

"I haven't done anything yet," I said calmly. "But here's what I will do because losing over twenty million dollars has got to sting. My offer to find Nolan still stands. I'll hunt him down and make him give up the traitor. I didn't give the feds your name, but I'm willing to give them the traitor's. I'll say he's Dante Gallo, shadowed leader of the Horsemen. He blackmailed and tried to have me killed. He flooded Raven River with drugs."

I moved closer still. His ragged pants skated over my cheeks. "Think about what I'm offering you, Rio. Your biggest enemies taken out. A federal investigation led the wrong way. Doesn't that sound a lot better than the FBI making Raven River and the Horsemen their number one priority?"

Rio's chest heaved, thudding on mine. "For this, I assume you want more than the Walker boy."

"I want *both* of the Walker boys. And Hiro. And *your* boy," I said. "Cassius, Clay, Hiro, and Royal are leaving. They're leaving the Horsemen. They're leaving Raven River. And they're leaving you."

"Is that right?" Rio pivoted, tossing me aside with a thrust of his shoulder. "You want out, son?! Cooked up this little plan to blackmail me!?"

Royal stood defiant in his glare.

"He had nothing to do with this," I shouted. "Neither did Hiro nor the triplets. This was me and me only because—fucking news flash—I hate your ass. The only thing I want more than seeing you rot in prison is getting my boys out from under your thumb. Let the five of us go, Rio, and you get all of Raven River in exchange."

It burned my lips to say that. For all the pain I'd been through, this was my home. But the truth was I knew only one way to free the town from the Horsemen and it was a long shot. In the end, freeing us may be the best I could hope for.

"That's the deal," I said. "Take it or— No, Rio. Just take it."

"Let you go?" he repeated. "You think that's how it works? You betray me. Snitch to the feds. Turn my men—my own son—against me, and then you just get to walk out of here?"

"I—"

Rio moved too fast for me to react. His backhand smashed my face, sending me sailing over the arm and crashing onto the couch.

"No!" Royal roared. "Stop!"

Blinded by pain, I scrambled to push myself up. Rio leaped on top of me, shoving my face in the cushion. I freed an arm and punched him in the neck, earning a satisfying grunt and knocking him back. I rolled and we both went down on his priceless Persian carpet.

Royal's shouts were a backdrop to our struggle. My fists and feet flailed, desperate to get his mass of muscles and brutality off of me. My nails raked across his face. He roared as he caught my wrist and slammed it to the floor. The other hand encircled my throat.

I gasped, eyes bulging under the tightening, unforgiving grip.

"I regret the day I heard your name, Ember Bancroft. You're a plague. A disease!" Spittle showered my cheek. "I welcome the feds and your uncle. My only mistake would be letting you live."

The hand suddenly disappeared from my throat and I sucked in deep lungfuls.

"Don!"

The third guard came to life. He towered over us... and put a gun in Rio's outstretched hand.

"No!" Royal and I screamed. "Don't do this!" I cried.

Rio jammed the muzzle to my temple. He would do this. Rio would kill me without a moment's pause or guilt and the naked hatred etched into the lines of his face promised he'd enjoy it.

"You can't kill me!" The click of the safety echoed in my ear. "I'm pregnant!"

The admission penetrated instantly. Shock knocked the snarl from his lips. He snapped back, looking at me like I'd gone from Ember to a strange, unknown creature.

"Pregnant?" Rio said. Suddenly, the sneer twisted his visage. "You're lying!"

"I'm not." I grabbed his hand. He fought me, but I forced him down, splaying his palm over the slight, but undeniable bulge. The tiny firm mound revealed the secret I'd been keeping all this time.

And Royal. My Royal. He stopped shouting.

Openmouthed, his wide eyes gaped at me as he deciphered what I said from every angle and the answer kept coming up the same.

And then he went insane.

"Get off her!" Royal threw Jay off, hurling him across the room. Jay tripped over a dining chair and fell hard. Royal rushed us and Damien moved quick, tackling him to the floor and restraining him until Jay crawled over, pressing down on his face. "If you hurt her, you're dead, Rio! I'll kill you! I'll kill you!"

Rio snapped from me to his son, growls leaking through his teeth. "Get him out of here!"

Jay and Damien hauled Royal up, dragging him outside. The door slammed on his vicious promises.

"Leave," Rio snapped at Don. The ever-quiet guard left through the back door. Rio and I were alone.

His hand was still on my stomach. I shoved it off, and then him. Rio let me escape him. His eyes tracked me as I scurried around the couch, putting it between us. He rose to his feet, his gun hanging by his side, and the helplessness of my situation closed my throat. The stupid damn couch wouldn't stop his bullet.

"Pregnant." He tried out the word, seeing how it felt on his tongue. "You expect me to believe that child"—he waved his weapon at my stomach—"is my son's."

I covered my belly protectively. "Yes. Royal is the father."

"Really?" Rio moved with me, stepping left as I stepped right, circling the sofa. "No chance the Walker boys slipped their DNA in there?"

I gritted my teeth. "You're going to be a granddaddy, Rio. Get used to it."

"Hmm." Rio looked me up and down. It was hard to explain the expression on his face. "This is how you do it. This is how you spread your *infection*," he hissed. "In a few months, you've taken my most promising men—all who owe me everything. Their life, their education, the clothes on their backs, and the money in their pockets. Cassius, Clay, and Hiro Saito would be nothing without me. They know that and still... they choose you."

Another step and we were on the same side.

"Saito came to me," he said. "He offered me everything he invested in the lodge if I'd let Cassius and Clay leave with you."

Surprise held me still as Rio closed more of the distance between us. "He did what?"

"Said he'd step up in their place. Enforcer, grifter, and forger. He'd do whatever I asked if I let you have two of your angels."

I swallowed, tears blurring my vision. *Oh, Hiro. You stupid, amazing, wonderful idiot.*

Rio shook his head. "Frankly, I don't see the appeal. What is it about you that has stolen my Horsemen and turned my son against me?"

"Of course you don't understand it, Rio. Loving another person isn't something the busted gears and wires housed in your chest are capable of doing, and that fact pushed Royal away long before he met me."

"You're wrong, girl." Rio stopped before me—so close the heady scent of sweat and cedarwood invaded me. "You're counting on me being capable of loving my son." A single finger lifted my shirt. Rio pressed his cold hand to my stomach. "At least enough that I wouldn't harm his child and therefore you. Which I cannot do if there is even the slightest chance this is my grandchild."

A smile spread across his lips but didn't reach as far as his eyes. "Congratulations. You've claimed me too. Another in a long line of men who will do anything to protect Ember Bancroft."

Pop! Pop!

We spun, springing apart. "Royal!?" I screamed.

"Damien! What's going on—"

The door flew open, banging against the opposite wall with the force to swing it back. An angel stood in the entrance. Lit by heavenly fire, radiant in avenging fury, and so beautiful he struck me dumb.

Then I blinked and he was Royal.

My angel stalked inside, gun aloft and trained on one person.

Don burst in. He raced into the living room, finger on the trigger and aimed at the threat. Royal spun and squeezed off a single shot.

My scream echoed through the cabin as Don dropped, bellowing and clutching his arm. His gun skittered across the floor and disappeared under the sofa.

"Ember is coming with me," Royal stated.

Rio stood still and assessing. He calmly studied Royal and then glanced at the man groaning on the floor. "What are you going to do, son? Kill your own father?"

Royal's hand and voice were steady. "That's entirely up to you."

Proving that he was a man that couldn't be predicted, Rio burst out laughing. "And here I feared you were too soft to take over for me. Protecting what's yours—even if it means protecting it from me." Smirking, Rio moved within point-blank range and kept going, not stopping until the gun was an inch from his heart. "Well done. But luckily for me, Ember and I have reached a ceasefire. I will not harm her or my grandchild."

My grandchild. Possession laced the moniker. My skin crawled up to my hairline.

"Ember, come here."

I shot between them, throwing myself on Royal. I grabbed his arm, pushing to bring it down. He couldn't kill his father and he certainly couldn't do it for me. If Rio's incarceration could affect our relationship, his murder would destroy it.

Royal gripped my hip and forced me behind him. "Where's Cassius?" he demanded.

"Oh, that's an entirely different matter, which you well know won't be solved by killing me as his location goes with me." It turned my stomach that the man was enjoying this. "For the Walker boy back, I'll take sweet Ember's original deal. She hands over Nolan Ives and the traitor and Cassius goes free."

"Agh," Don moaned. "Boss. Boss, help."

"Shut the fuck up, Don," Royal said. "It's a flesh wound. Doc will stitch you up in an hour. But while you're listening, let me make something clear." Another shot rang out. Don howled, clutching his leg. "I'm the next leader of the Horsemen. You're not only Rio's men, you're mine. If you ever help him strike against me again, when I take over, I'm putting a bullet in your head."

"Boss," Don screamed. Tears soaked his face. "Boss!"

"We'll get you Ives and his friend," Royal told his father. "And then you and I are done, Rio."

I clung to Royal's back, crying as much as the gangster on the floor. The night had spun wildly out of control. I didn't mean for my love to find out about the baby this way. Nor did I mean for it to be his final push into darkness.

"Think carefully, son." Rio was soft and controlled. "You want me as your father, not your enemy."

"I've never known the difference."

A thick silence spread between them, broken only by our cries.

"You're upset," Rio finally said. "In shock. You've just found out you're going to be a father. We both know how I panicked when I received that news." Rio gripped his son's shoulder. "We'll forget everything that was said and done here. You take Ember and get started on finding me my traitor. The sooner, the better for Walker. I doubt he's enjoying the accommodations."

"Baby," I whispered. "Please, let's go." I tugged on his arm again, forcing the gun down. "I want to get out of here."

Royal allowed me to pull him over the threshold. I firmly shut the door on his father, breaking their stare.

Royal came to life. He scooped me up, cradling me to his chest, and stepped over a moaning Jay lying at the bottom of the porch steps. Damien sat on the ground, propped against his car and clutching his arm. From the running engine, I guessed the guys tried to shove him in and drive away, leaving me alone with his father. Royal didn't let that happen.

He carried me to his car, gently placed me inside, and climbed in. My tears didn't slow as we drove away.

"It's going to be okay, Em." Royal swiped a finger up my cheek, catching my tears. "No one is going to hurt you."

"This isn't about me!" I shrieked. "I thought you hated guns!"

"I do." Royal rolled down the window and fired into the sky. My scream ripped through the car. Emptied, Royal flung the gun into the forest.

"You gotta calm down, Em," he said. "All this stress can't be good for you."

My heart squeezed. "I'm sorry. You shouldn't have found out about the baby like this."

"We'll talk about it at home."

"But I can't. You have to take me to my uncle's car. They're expecting—"

"No."

It seemed pointless to argue, so I didn't.

It was a quiet ride to Royal's apartment. The man did the silent treatment like no one else. I couldn't guess if he was angry, happy, excited, or disappointed. He parked behind his building and rounded the car to help me out. I clung to his hand as he led me up the stairs.

Royal's apartment was how I remembered. Nothing new or out of place. Royal set me on the couch.

"Are you hungry?" he asked. "I don't have much, but I can come up with something." He made for the kitchen.

"I was going to tell you the other night." Royal halted. "All of you."

"So why didn't you, Ember?"

"Because." Appealing to his back, I rose, moving to him. "All of a sudden Camila and Eli were there and I couldn't."

"How long have you known?"

I pressed my lips together, wishing I could keep the answer inside. "Since... the day I visited the triplets' parents. Virginia cornered me to say she knew why my hair was so dry. I didn't know what she was talking about and she explained the same thing happened to her when she was pregnant with the triplets. Virginia gushed about meeting her grandbaby. It hit me then that I'd been nauseous and achy a lot lately. A pregnancy test confirmed it."

"Since Virginia," he repeated. "How long ago was that, Em? Friday night was really the only time you could've told us?"

Wetness collected on my lids, spilling down my cheeks as I closed my eyes on his stiff back. *Why won't he look at me?*

"I wanted to tell you so many times," I admitted. "But I was afraid."

"Of what?"

"Of this! Of you being angry! Of you thinking she was another eighteen-year-old's mistake!"

Royal didn't reply.

"Tell me I'm wrong." I swallowed the gap between us. Slowly. One step. Then another. "Tell me that you love me and our baby." I raised my hand, reaching for him. "Please."

I closed on air.

Royal walked into his room and shut the door.

Sobs wracked my chest. I covered my face, muffling the sound of my heart breaking. How could I expect a better reaction from Cassius and Clay? They're crushed under the weight of caring for their parents. Why would they want a baby too? And Hiro. No teenager wants to be saddled with a girl carrying a kid that can't be his.

Cracks appeared on my being. Spreading and splintering into chips that fell to my feet, crumbling into dust. The Ember I'd become fell to pieces. The girl who was happy. Who discovered what it meant to love and be loved by someone other than her brother.

Four someones. And now it's over.

A warm hand rested on my head. Gently, Royal lifted me up and placed something on my hands. My tears seeped into the sketch, dotting little spots as translucent.

It was the mother and her baby. The drawing Royal took from me all those months ago. The only one I couldn't have.

Sniffling, I gazed up at him through blurry eyes. "I d-don't know what this means."

He smiled—a beautiful, radiant smile, and he was my angel again. "Yes, you do."

I did.

I threw my arms around him, kissing him until I couldn't breathe. Royal laid a trail down my chin, peppering kisses on my neck, chest, and stomach. He dropped to his knees, lifting my shirt, hugging my waist, and pressing his cheek to the little bulge. "I love you and I love our baby."

I was blubbering like a faucet. Royal picked me up around the legs and put me over his shoulder. He carried me into the bedroom and made love to me as Ember reformed—whole and perfect once again.

"IT'S LATE," I SAID. "I'm going to crash here and I'll be back before breakfast."

"What do his parents think of this?" asked my uncle. "There's no need for you to be an inconvenience. You're no more than twenty minutes away."

"It's hardly an inconvenience." I ran my fingers through Royal's hair. "They have more rooms than the White House."

Harrison sniffed. "Fine. First thing in the morning."

I said bye and tossed my phone on the nightstand. We were lying on his bed, cozy and comfortable. Royal's head rested on my stomach. "I don't think she's meant to be your pillow," I teased.

"You both can get used to it."

I rolled my eyes, though I definitely could.

"Also, she?" he asked.

"When I picture the baby, I see a girl. Just a feeling."

"Do you see a girl with black hair or blonde?"

I knew what he was asking. "Both," I admitted. "Cassius, Clay, and I were similarly irresponsible with the condoms, Royal. I can't be sure which one of you is the father. We can get a test when she's born."

His head shook on my belly. "There's no need. If she's yours, she's mine."

My heart swelled to bursting. I bit my lip to stop myself cheesing too hard.

"And either way, we're naming her after me."

"After you? What kind of name can we get out of Royal?"

"Anything to do with royalty. Princess is good. Or Reigna. Tiara works too."

I gave him a look. "We're leaving the naming to me."

He laughed.

"Do you think the other guys will be mad I didn't tell them sooner?" I asked.

"No, Em. They won't."

"It's not like I could've hidden her for much longer," I mused aloud. "Now that she's showing herself. Actually, I'm surprised you guys didn't notice with how often you have me out of my clothes."

"Honestly, I did notice. I'm always sketching you. No one studies your body harder than me."

I blinked. "You did? Why didn't you say something?"

"I didn't think you were pregnant. I thought... Em, you eat a lot of sugary shit."

My jaw dropped. I snatched a pillow and beamed him in the face. "Asshole!" I shouted over his guffawing. "You thought I was getting a gut!?"

"It looked cute on you." Royal pressed his lips to my stomach. "But the truth is even better."

I grumbled under my breath. *Seriously. What in the hell am I going to do with this guy?*

"You'll have everything you need, princess. Both of you." He stroked our little bulge. "I promise."

"Will I?" I whispered. "It feels like we're in this perfect bubble right now, and I don't want to burst it, but we have to talk about tonight. You shot three men and held a gun on your father. Why do I feel he's not truly going to forgive and forget?"

Royal propped up on his arm, gazing down at me. "Em, this may be hard for you to hear, but I'm fine. I didn't kill those guys. I gave them a few weeks in bed thinking hard about whether they ever want to fuck with you. And that's a lesson I'm happy to give again."

My skin tightened. That was hard for me to hear. I wished to wash away the darkness in my love's soul. Take it from him, so he could be the person he was meant to be before Rio came into his life. But love doesn't work that way. I had to take him—all of him—for the man he is, not the man he would've been.

"You also said you were going to be the next leader." I placed my hand over his. "You can't give us everything we need as one of the four. You have to choose. Us or the Horsemen."

"You." His answer was instant. He didn't pause to breathe.

Relaxing, I rubbed his hand along my stomach. "What about Rio?" I asked.

"You heard him. He's proud of me. I've proven I'm not soft." Royal brushed his thumb along my cheekbone. "There won't be consequences for what I did tonight, but there will be if we don't deliver Nolan."

"Consequences for Cassius," I said through numb lips. "Do you know where he could be?"

"Rio's got holes even I don't know about. Tonight was the first I've been to that cabin. Clay and Hiro will keep checking everywhere we can think of. You and I will focus on Nolan. Any idea where he could be?"

"His family has homes all over the world," I said. "But I'm sure he's nearby. After everything he did to take Rio down, he won't stop with the job half done. The obvious place to start is with Julian. They've been friends since they were four. Also, Camila dated him for a long time. He might've mentioned a place he likes to go. If all that fails, I'll talk to his parents."

"*We* will talk to his parents. Seeing the guy their son tried to kill could open them up."

I released a long breath. "We'll find him. We have to. I need Cassius back."

"We'll get him back." Royal crawled up next to me, drawing me secure to his chest, and draping his arm over my stomach. "I promise you one way or another, my father will let him go."

Chapter Ten

"Thanks, Monroe."

The man inclined his head through the window. Eli and I watched him peel out of the parking lot and take off.

Our break in the Estate was over. Uncle Harrison gave us a few days, which in the end Eli and I did need, and then returned us to school first thing Wednesday morning.

"*It's weird being back,*" Eli signed. "*When we were driving over the bridge, all I could think was how much I didn't want to be here. I'll miss Tatum and everything but Raven River hasn't felt like home for a long time.*"

I hugged him tight, dropping a kiss on his forehead.

"*When are you going to talk to Uncle about New York? My application for Chapman is finished.*"

"Soon. Possibly this weekend. There are a lot of important conversations I need to have." I flicked his nose. "First of all with you."

"*Me?*"

I nodded. It was strange keeping a secret as big as my pregnancy from Eli. Especially because I told him almost everything. In this case, it didn't seem right to tell my brother before I told the fathers.

"Tonight or tomorrow, okay?"

"*Okay.*"

"Excuse me, sir. Ma'am?" A guard waved from the other side of the gate. "I need you to step inside now."

Security was a growing presence on campus. I counted more guards on my way through the gates and passed underneath the ladder of the man installing new cameras over the entrance. The concern was understandable considering the shooter was still on the loose.

Eli and I broke apart at the bottom of the stairs. I continued on, my mind turning to Clay and Hiro. It was time they knew about the baby. I wasn't willing to do it over the phone though we did talk over the last few days and I reassured them that I was okay and wasn't planning to meet Rio alone again anytime soon.

Walking into homeroom, Cassius's empty chair was a pang through my chest. Every minute was tinged sour for him not with me.

Clay stood and enfolded me, warm and forgiving. "I love you," he whispered into my neck.

"I love you too. Later can we talk?"

"Of course."

I sat down, sliding a smile to Hiro. I hadn't told him that I knew about his proposition to Rio. That was another conversation you didn't have over the phone.

Classes were beginning to return to normal as students came back to school. The remaining absences were noticeable, but what mattered was who was there. Like Julian.

As morning classes let out, I caught him on his way out of the cafeteria, carrying his tray up to his dorm for lunch. I shot a quick text to Clay and ran up to him.

"Hey, Julian."

"Ember, what's up?"

"Do you have a minute? We could go up to your room and talk."

"About?"

I looked him in those otherworldly eyes. "Nolan."

"You want to know where I think he is," he said, cutting straight to the point.

"Got it in one."

"Yeah, we can talk in my room." Julian held the door for me to go in ahead of him. "I'm surprised you didn't ask sooner."

"I thought I shouldn't tempt myself. If I got my hands on him before the police, there wouldn't be enough of him left to handcuff."

Julian raised a brow. "What changed?"

"He's been free long enough. It's time he paid for what he did."

Julian didn't reply. He said nothing as we entered the elevator. I cut eyes to him, wondering what he was thinking.

"Are you okay with helping me?"

"Nolan's not the guy I knew. If he's out there planning to hurt people, one of them my cousin, he has to be stopped."

"Thank you."

Together we crossed to the boys' hall, heading to his room. "What do you know?" I asked. "Has he tried to contact you?"

"Nothing. Not even an 'I'm sorry for shooting you' text." Julian shoved open the door to his now single room. "I can tell you the same thing I told the police. I can show you too." He set his tray on the desk and woke up his laptop. "His family has a boat they keep out on the river. It's got a bed, toilet, and a fridge."

Julian pulled up photos of little Julian, Leo, and Nolan. They beamed at the cameras with missing-tooth smiles and waved from the deck of a boat that closer fit a yacht.

"His dad also keeps an apartment in Easthaven for business."

Amazingly, Julian had photos of that place too. The boys were much older in those shots and partying hard with the other Raveners. He flipped through pics of a decadent penthouse loft.

"I can give you the address and tell you where the boat is usually docked. The police checked them both out, but the RRPD doesn't stretch to round-the-clock guards. He could still be hiding there."

"Yes to both," I replied. "Thanks, Julian. This is exactly what I'm looking for."

Julian tore a page out of his notebook and scribbled the information. He folded it but didn't hand it over. I frowned as he gazed unfocused at the paper.

"I broke up with Pomona."

"You did? Wow. Good for you."

He bobbed his head. "Did it on Sunday. Want to know how long it took her to start officially going out with Lighthouse?"

I winced. "Monday?"

"Sunday night."

"Yikes," I hissed. "He's my friend but... that hurts. I'm sorry, Julian."

"Don't be. There's nothing holding me back now. It's like you said, Ember. At Stanford, I won't be the guy whose girlfriend cheated on him. Best friend shot him. Or dad ditched him. I'll just be Julian." He glanced around. "This place feels like everything—the whole world in one town. We forget there's life outside of it. Maybe even a better one."

I caressed my bump. "That's what I'm counting on."

Julian shook himself. "Anyway, here you go. Hope this helps."

"Me too," I whispered.

I said bye and left him to his lunch. I shut the door behind me just as Clay strode into the hall.

"Em? What are you doing in Hart's room?"

"Asking him where to start the search for Nolan."

His gaze sharpened. "What did he say?"

I held up the piece of paper. "Let's go in your room."

Clay followed me back and got the paper from me. We went inside and I dropped on Cassius's bed, burying my nose in his pillow and inhaling his faint scent.

"I'll check these out," he said. "It doesn't make sense going to these places one by one. We'll find him quicker if we split up."

"It doesn't make sense to ambush Nolan alone when we know he has a gun."

"That shit can't take me." Clay picked up my feet and put them in his lap. "Hiro will go to Easthaven. You and Royal hit the Estate and talk to his parents."

I rubbed his arm. "How are you, Clay? You don't have to be strong for me."

"Yes, I do, Em," he said quietly. "If I'm anything else, I'm letting myself believe Rio's going to kill him. I can't go there. Cas has been two feet from me my whole life. That won't change."

"No, it won't." Rising up, I cradled him to my chest and laid us both down. "I have something to tell you."

"That you plan on comforting me sexually in my time of need?" Clay kissed my collarbone. "I approve."

"No," I said. "Well, yes, but no. What I was going to say is... I'm pregnant."

The kissing stopped. "What?"

"I'm pregnant, Clay. I've known since your mom told me."

"My mom?" he sputtered. "How did she know?!"

I calmed him down, telling him everything from the beginning. Clay listened in slack-jawed, big-eyed silence. If I'd never seen worry on his face, I'd certainly never seen that expression either.

"I'm more than two months along," I said. "She'll be born a little while after we graduate. If your plans still include me, we'll start our lives together—the six of us."

Clay frowned. "If my plans still include you? What the hell does that mean?"

I swallowed. "You have to get your parents in a better situation, Clay. It's important. So important, I'd understand if you can't choose me and her. Folkstone is expensive, and you didn't factor a baby into the budget."

"Oh, I see. You've somehow gotten it into your head that you're less important than my family."

Scrunching up, I made myself small, hugging my knees. "I can't ask you to compromise what's best for them for what's best for me."

"It's not either or, Em. And it's not a question of if I'll be there for my kid. I will be. She better get ready because I'll be two feet from her every day of her life."

Tears prickled my eyes. "I swear it's pregnancy hormones. I won't always cry this much."

Chuckling, he gathered me in his arms. "You can cry as much as you want, baby. I'm not going anywhere."

I did cry. A lot. Bawled into his chest as the fear I felt for Cassius and the pain of keeping my secret bubbled over. Clay was solid. He whispered in my ear, soothing and assured, promising me everything would be okay.

AFTER CLAY'S AND ROYAL'S amazing responses, it seemed almost greedy to expect the same from Hiro.

I watched him from the other side of Seeger's class. We were doing an activity that was kind of like twenty questions. I thought up my dream vacation and Major asked me a bunch of questions to narrow down my destination. The point was to teach us to listen—which I was hardly doing because my attention kept drifting to Hiro and Destiny.

"Is it Bermuda?" he asked.

"Close. Bahamas."

"Class, that's it for today," Seeger called. "Mr. Saito, may I speak to you up here?"

The class packed up and filed out. I hung back, waiting for Hiro to wrap up his conversation with Seeger. Our teacher noticed me in the back.

"Ember, do you need something?"

"Uhh, no. Sorry."

I brushed past him walking out.

"If you could stack them up on the counter, that would be great," Seeger told him. "The cushions I'm moving to the front cabinets, and the board games to the back."

"I'll get it done, Mrs. Seeger."

"You're a lifesaver, Hiro. With everything that's happened, my husband is concerned about late evenings in the school by myself."

Escaping into the hall, the door closed on their chat. Hiro was arranging another classroom cleanup. I leaned on the lockers to wait for Seeger to leave.

My phone went off in my backpack. I checked the screen and didn't recognize the number. I'd gotten more than a few calls from reporters. They were nothing if not persistent.

"Hello?"

"Hello. Is this Ember Bancroft?" A deep, masculine voice filled my ear.

"Yes, I'm Ember."

"I'm glad to have reached you, Ember. I have information about your parents' disappearance."

I snapped up straight. Every stray thought fled from my head. "What? How? Who is this?"

"I will answer all of your questions, but not over the phone. We have to speak face to face."

My eyes closed to slits. "Yeah, right, we can't talk over the phone. Would a secluded alley on the corner of 'Murder Me Lane' and 'I'm An Idiot Street' be better for you?"

This was the risk of handing out my number to the world. The kooks and creeps were first to pick up the phone.

"Don't you have anything better to do than mess—"

"Ember, please. This is not a crank call and I wasn't suggesting an in-person meeting."

I quieted.

"You're absolutely right to be cautious," he continued. "As am I which is why I can't risk the chance of this talk being overheard or recorded. After I hang up, I will send you a link for a secure video call."

The man certainly didn't sound like a kook. *Is this for real? Should I trust him?*

"Tonight. Nine o'clock. I'll tell you everything I know."

He hung up.

A few seconds later, the trill of a new message announced his link. I almost didn't notice Seeger leaving while I examined it.

It looks legit. Should I go on this call?

So far this man is the only one to contact me with information, another voice spoke up. *If there's even a chance he knows something, I have to listen.*

Putting away the phone, I went into the classroom. Hiro was at the back, pulling cushions out of the cabinet and setting them on the floor. I stood for a bit just taking him in. Hiro Saito was the kind of guy you savored.

"Just going to stand there?" he spoke up, his back to me. "Or are you going to help me?"

"Neither. I came to talk to you about something." I ran my hands up his back, gripped his shoulders and turned him to face me. Hiro locked his arms behind my waist, fitting our bodies together like two corner puzzle pieces.

"Talk to me about what?"

Nerves quickened my pulse and tightened my grip till Hiro's brows drew together. "I feel like I should build up to it," I said. "Start off with how much I love you and that we can still make it work.

Then tell you that it may be difficult but we'll have the lives we wanted and we'll have them together. What could be better than that?"

"Ember, what are you talking about?"

I met those confused eyes, hoping he saw everything I felt and more. "Hiro, I'm pregnant."

"Oh, that?" His expression cleared. "I know."

I gaped at him. "What the hell do you mean you know?!"

He shrugged. "My mom ran a daycare, remember? I was always around young moms and babies. I picked up the signs. You've been eating healthier, taking vitamins, and on my last tour of your body, I hit on a bump." Hiro put his hand between us, covering said bump. "You should've said you were shy."

"Why didn't you say something?"

"Because you'd tell me when you were ready."

Moaning, I dropped my head on his shoulder. I didn't know whether to laugh or cry. I think I did both. "I've been shitting myself and the whole time you knew."

"You thought I'd run out because the baby isn't mine," he stated.

"It crossed my mind." My eyes fluttered shut. "But you were planning to run out on me for an entirely different reason."

Hiro stilled. "Rio told you."

"In the middle of calling me a parasite that's destroying the Horsemen and stealing his men. I can't believe you tried to trade yourself and your college fund to free Cassius and Clay from the gang. You fucking idiot." My blunt, winning personality always won out.

His laugh rumbled against my cheek. "I thought you'd see it as a romantic, self-sacrificial gesture."

"What were you thinking? You're the last one in, so you have to be the first one out? I love you—all of you—the same and there's no version of reality where I'd survive leaving one of you behind." I propped my chin on his chest. "Don't tell me that's what you were waiting on? You had to know Rio's answer before you could decide where we stand."

"He strung me along, playing like he was considering it. After he took Cassius, I offered more money to get him back, and then on Sunday he said none of us were leaving—especially not you. To make up for the insult of trying to get the triplets out, I have to give Rio my college money anyway."

"That guy is a sun-ripened asshole," I grumbled.

Hiro cracked a smile. "He is, but he's an asshole that's made things simple for me. I'm getting my money back and like fuck he'll get his hands on it. I think I'll buy a bus ticket instead. I've always wanted to see New York in the winter."

My lips trembled. *Don't cry. Don't cry.*

"Really?" I glanced down. "You're choosing us?"

"I chose you both a long time ago."

I'm definitely going to cry.

"So... if I ask you where we stand?"

Hiro backed away, letting my arms slip through his hands. "You can let this be your answer." Hiro closed the blinds.

"Oh my gosh," I whispered—no clue why. "Here?"

"You're not getting shy on me, are you?"

I giggled. "Definitely not."

One by one, the blinds shuttered closed on the world. My heart picked up speed as he came for me. I wasn't expecting that end to my day, but you wouldn't see me complaining.

Hiro took my hand the way he'd done so many times before. He held it above us, slowly spinning me like a dancer. His chest pressed to my back, chin resting on my shoulder. "I've waited a long time to be with you." His warm breath washed over my neck, enticing a shiver. "I'm taking my time."

"What if someone catches us?"

"The janitors start on the bottom floor. We've got a couple hours at least until they make it this far."

"Hmm." I reached behind me, tangling my hands in his hair. "A man that knows the janitorial schedule. That's wicked sexy."

Hiro moved down, popping the buttons on my shirt. It fell in a pile at my feet and then my skirt followed.

Suddenly, I was lifted and placed on the cushions. Impossibly tall and inexcusably gorgeous, he towered over me, commanding my gaze as he shed his clothes. I'd seen Hiro naked and each time amended my idea of male beauty. He straddled me and I ran my hands over his chest, stomach, thighs, ass—I couldn't get enough of him.

Hiro busied with his own exploration. Last time, we left my bra and panties on to not tempt ourselves. Hiro unwrapped me like a present, wiggling my straps down and freeing me to his hungry gaze. He stuck his face between my breasts, groaning like a man three days in the desert who just found water. "We're together at last."

"You're so— Ooh."

Hiro licked a stripe up the mound and to the tip. His eyes shone with delicious wickedness as he curled his tongue around the pebble, sucking it to a hardened point, and then going down to do it again.

"Holy hell," I moaned. "This is new."

My breasts were two scoops of ice cream and Hiro had a sweet tooth even fiercer than mine. He pushed them together, squeezing me tender but insistent, and bounced from one nipple to the other, nipping and teasing them mercilessly.

To say this was working for me was an understatement. Wetness soaked my panties. Lip puffy between my teeth, I clenched my legs as waves of tingling arousal clenched my lower belly. I wanted to lie back and take it slow for him, but it's been four whole days since the sex demon was fed. She was demanding more and fast.

"Whenever you feel like taking the party downstairs, don't let me stop you," I gasped.

He grinned with my nipple between his teeth. "We're still getting acquainted up here, but feel free to start the party before me."

I didn't need to be told twice. I slipped my hand through the lining of my underwear and found my center, rolling the nub between my fingers in time with Hiro's expert tongue. The combination of his hot mouth and my heightened sensitivity was undoing my self-control faster than normal. My orgasm was coming quick.

I pushed two fingers past my folds, eager to bring about its arrival, and Hiro was there as the first moan breathed out. He cupped my hand and guided his finger inside of me, setting a slow pace at first and quickening as my moans spurred him on. As one we found that spot and Hiro hit it relentlessly.

"Shit!" I cried, arching my back. His mouth on one breast, his thumb tweaking the other, and fingers showing me how to fuck myself, I came so hard, my body jerked me off the cushion and I bumped my head on the cabinet.

My chest rose and fell like tidal waves as I fought to catch my breath. "Damn," I gasped. "I'm gonna have a lump in the morning." Sweat stuck me to the cushions and Hiro peeled me off with a satisfying sound, kissing me while he fixed them.

He laid me down, licked my fingers clean, and finally slid my panties over my hips.

Raising my legs, I happily pushed them off. "I don't have to ask if you're a virgin," I said.

Hiro cracked a grin over my knees. "Your way of saying I know what I'm doing?"

"You're doing it so well, I'm starting to wonder if *I* know what the hell I'm doing."

"From what I hear, you know what you're doing."

Fire licked at my already heated cheeks. "Please tell me you guys don't sit around discussing our sex life."

"Don't have to. You think I can't hear you and Royal in the bathroom?"

"Oh no."

"If I heard right, I'm supposed to finish this by coming on your chest?"

"Hiro!" Laughing, I swatted his arm. "You'll have to surprise me."

"Oh, I will." Hiro draped my legs over his shoulders. "Mind if I get another party going down here?"

I shook my head so hard it could've popped off. Maybe it was the danger of being caught or the added spice of making love on the sharing circle cushions but the aftershocks of the first orgasm were still humming through my veins as the second one sat up and begged for Hiro.

He licked and tasted my pussy with the same mind-blowing thoroughness that ravaged my nipples. I tried not to scream, mindful of echoing hallways, but my hands were cupping my breast and pulling his hair. Orgasm two ripped a scream out of me so loud, orgasm three was sure to burst my voice box.

"Someone definitely heard that." Hiro laughed.

"Who cares."

Hiro reached for his pants. He dug around and pulled out a condom.

"Dude, get that out of here." I snatched the thing and flung it across the room. "I'm already pregnant."

"I'm starting to see how that happened," he mumbled under his breath.

"Hey," I cried, cracking up. He did have a point.

"Come here." Hiro held out his hand, pulling me up. He changed our positions and leaned on the cabinet. His guiding hands on my hips told me where to go.

Excitement built to a fever pitch as I positioned him at my entrance. Finally after all of this time, my last Angel was mine. I swallowed him, head falling back as he filled me whole. Rising on the balls of my feet, I drew almost all the way out and then impaled myself, crying hoarsely.

Up, down, up, and down. My eyes rolled back in my head as we met a punishing pace bounce for thrust. Hiro gripped my hips, either trying to slow me down or losing control because he couldn't. Overhead, I clung to the door handle, bending over him and moaning as he tasted and indulged the good fortune of breasts bouncing in his face. He came seconds after me, buried to the hilt.

I fell forward and hit my head on the cabinet again. "How long... before the janitor gets here?"

He tugged me down and kissed the crap out of me. "We've got time."

HIRO AND I WALKED HAND in hand to the dorm. Mr. Nixon poked his cleaning cart out of Geske's classroom, waving to us as he moved to tackle the next.

"So, he called me right before we talked," I continued.

After spending another hour having sex on the cushions, a few desks, and the windowsill, we put the classroom to rights, tackling the projects Mrs. Seeger left Hiro to make up for the unspeakable things we did in her classroom. I began telling Hiro about the strange call I received as we left.

"He said he had to be cautious and we couldn't speak over the phone." I passed over my cell. "He gave me this link so we could video chat securely."

"And when you open this link, it'll be a naked guy in a dirty bathrobe dancing and whipping his junk in front of the camera."

I giggled at the image. "That would be a surprise."

"Seriously, Em. Why the secrecy?"

"I don't know but he's the first person to contact me. I've officially approached desperate, Hiro. I'll take Dirty Bathrobe Guy if there's even a chance he can lead me to my parents."

"Don't talk to him alone."

"It's a video chat. I'll be safe in my room. Everything will be fine."

He snaked an arm around me, pulling me closer. "I don't like any of this, Em. It doesn't make sense. Stealing the money but not spending it. Running away in the middle of the night and opening a secret account to give all of the money to you. Unnamed men telling you it's too dangerous to talk about this on the phone. I don't want to scare you, but I have a bad feeling about this."

I leaned my head on his shoulder. "I don't want to admit it, but I do too. I can't get past what Cassius said. What have they been doing all of these months without money or a place to live? I accepted the fact that they took off and abandoned me easier than people assumed. These questions coming up are making me ask if I knew anything about my family at all."

"You knew them, Em." He rubbed my forearm soothingly. "You know them better than anyone. What does your gut say?"

"It says... that they would take off and leave me behind, but they wouldn't do it without Eli and they wouldn't steal from their friends and family. My dad has tried for years to make it up to his brother. Why would he cement his hatred by stealing five million from him and almost wrecking his business? And Eli, he was the baby they poured all of their love into when they stopped loving me.

"I was blinded by their feelings for me, and when the feds laid out the facts, I accepted it with their note burning a hole in my heart. I should have asked these questions from the beginning, Hiro.

There's something not right about this entire situation, and if there's a chance Dirty Bathrobe Guy has the key, I'll be in front of my computer tonight at nine o'clock."

"Okay," he said. "I understand you have to see this through. All I ask is you don't disappear on me again. We're in this together. The five"—he placed a hand on my stomach—"I mean six of us."

I couldn't disagree with Hiro even if I wanted to. The six of us were irrevocably tied, and being in that kind of relationship required honesty. We went into the dorm and tracked down Royal and Clay. I told them about the phone call and my impending video chat.

"This guy sounds like a creep," Clay said.

"You're not talking to him alone," Royal added.

"He's right."

"That's what I said," Hiro threw in.

I heaved a sigh. *Apparently being in this kind of relationship also requires extreme overprotectiveness.*

"Guys, do I need to repeat that it's a video chat held within the gates of the most protected place in Raven River? He's not going to reach through the screen and pull me in. That only happens in the movies."

"Let us be there," Clay said.

"I can't spook him," I replied. "He's the only one who has called with information. Feel free to pace outside my door."

I climbed off Royal's bed, kissed each of them bye, and traded hallways for mine. Camila was in our room doing what she did every night since Cassius was taken, calling their friends from the old neighborhood to ask if anyone had seen something that could help. Between calls I asked if it was okay for me to have the room that night.

"Sure. Clay and I can do this in his room."

She packed up to leave. I intercepted her at the door, hugging her from behind. "We'll get him back."

"In exchange for Nolan." She spat the name. "I've been racking my brain for a place he might have mentioned or somewhere we went together. He didn't like hanging out in the OB, so we spent every date in the Estate. The only possible places he could be holed up in is the country club, the inn where we were together for the first time, and his own house."

"His house?"

"You've visited the place. They have thirteen bedrooms, two kitchens, a basement, and a converted attic. He could be tucked away somewhere in there and who would know?" She slumped. "But he's not and that's why I'm useless. I thought I was in love with that guy and it turned out I didn't know him at all."

"We will find Nolan, Camila, and get Cassius back if I have to search all thirteen of those bedrooms myself."

She hugged me back and said goodnight.

I sat down at my computer, hours early, and failed to distract myself with two movies and a computer game. The whole time I questioned if I should call Eli.

They are his parents, one voice said.

If he intends to flash me his junk, Eli doesn't need to see it too, said another.

And if it's bad news, said my voice of reason. *It should come from me instead of being delivered by a complete stranger.*

By the time the clock struck nine, I was seated, ready, and alone.

The video chat app was one I didn't know. *GenChat* had a sleek, black interface and a tiny notification bubble that told me to wait for the host to initiate the call. I clenched my fists as 9:00 p.m. became 9:01 p.m.

Where are you? Please, this can't be a trick—

The chat bubble winked out. In place of my blank, black screen sat a man.

I took him in. He was older—around my dad's age. Simple but stylish round-framed glasses perched on his nose and brown eyes gazed at me through them. The good news was he was fully clothed in a black blazer, red tie, and white shirt. His coarse hair was shorn close to the scalp and his beard neatly trimmed. If he was a kook, he was a well-groomed kook.

"Hello, Ember." The deep voice of the man from the phone call echoed out of the speakers. "Thank you for speaking with me."

"What's your name?" I asked.

"Andrew."

"Andrew." I tried the name out and it didn't ring any bells. "You say you have information about my parents, but I haven't seen you before. They never even mentioned the name Andrew to me. How do you know them?"

"I knew your father long before you arrived, Ember." He reached for something off camera. Andrew held a photo up.

Squinting, I leaned in closer. Younger, thinner, and sporting more hair, but there was no denying it. The man with his arm around a young Andrew, grinning and tossing a thumbs-up for the picture, was Frank Bancroft. The mass of people serving as their backdrop gave me a hint.

"Is that a college campus?" I asked. "Is that how you know him?"

"Yes." The picture dropped out of frame and present-day Andrew returned. "Your father and I were best friends in college."

"If you were best friends, why have I never heard of you?"

"I will explain all of that, Ember, but it's secondary to the reason I called." He leaned in, piercing me with his wide, serious gaze. "Your fears were justified. Your parents did not steal that money, and that they haven't turned up after its return, proves that they are in serious danger. Possibly dead."

I froze. I think Andrew went on to say more. His lips moved. He tapped the desk with his finger. He held up the picture once again.

A ringing clanged in my ear. Deafening all sound but Andrew's voice saying two words.

Possibly dead.

"—Ember? Ember, are you listening?"

"Why would you say that?" I rasped, lips numb. "They're not dead. Why would you say something so awful?"

He held up a hand. "I can't be sure of course. It's possible they're still hiding."

"Hiding? Hiding from who? The feds?"

"It'd help if I started from the beginning. With the lodge," he said. "Everything you've been told is wrong."

My head spun. "Everything I've been told about the lodge?"

"Yes. Your parents purchased that land legitimately and they had every intention of building that river retreat. But not at any cost. The environmental surveys were completed and the reports handed over to your parents were that they passed with flying colors."

"No, they didn't," I interrupted. "A protected species lives on the land. It's also a floodplain. The reports said this and they paid to have it buried."

"Someone paid to have those reports buried and it was *not* your parents." His eyes grew huge as he bent toward the camera. "This is what I'm trying to explain to you. Someone other than your parents discovered the results of those reports and they bribed the officials not only to bury the truth, but to pass on falsified documents to your parents."

I gaped at him. "Why would someone do that?"

"So that construction would continue. They couldn't risk your parents doing the right thing, so they sought to keep them in ignorance. It might have worked if one of the officials didn't call your father demanding more money," Andrew said. "The man decided to try his luck playing both sides of the aisle. If this mysterious person would pay to keep the report secret, how much more would the wealthy couple leading the project pay?

"This ploy backfired. Your father demanded the real report and said he'd sue him and everyone involved in the cover-up. The man panicked and called the original person who made the bribe. The next day Frank received an email threatening to go public with a secret he thought long-buried if he didn't continue construction."

Bribes? Blackmail? Long-buried secret?

"How do you know this?" I demanded.

"Because after your father received that email, he called me."

"Because he thought you could help?"

He shook his head. "Because he thought I was responsible."

My mouth opened and nothing came out. *Who is this man and why do I have a terrible feeling I'd have been better off with a naked guy in a bathrobe?*

"There's a reason Frank didn't tell you about me," he went on. "We were roommates freshman year and best friends for all four. In our senior year, a few months before graduation, we went to a party."

I went rigid. "No good story starts off that way."

"Ours doesn't either," he said gravely. "I was driving, so I stuck to a couple of beers. Your father on the other hand, had just proposed to your mother and was in the mood to celebrate. He was trashed within an hour and making an ass of himself within an hour and ten minutes. He got a little too wild and knocked over a speaker. We were kicked out of the party after that. I felt fine to drive, so we piled in my car, turned up the music, and kept the party going.

"Frank was messing around. Shoving me. Shaking me. Putting his hand over my eyes. Turning the music up louder. And I was goofing off with him. He covered my eyes and I turned on him, laughing as I scuffled with him. I couldn't have looked away for more than a few seconds and, suddenly, she was there."

"Oh no..."

"I tried to swerve but it was too late." Years later, the wretched pain of that night shown clear on his face. "She died on impact."

"My dad… he never said—"

"Of course not," Andrew cut in. "We panicked. Frank blamed himself. It was an accident, but a breathalyzer would have picked up that I'd been drinking. Her death would've fallen on me and I was the poor kid who fought his way into university while your dad was months away from marrying and living the rest of his life on a tidy trust fund. He couldn't stand for me to go down because he distracted me." Andrew released a long sigh. "So, your dad did what he always did when he got in trouble. He called his older brother."

"Uncle Harrison?"

He nodded. "And your uncle did what he always did. He made the problem go away. Frank told his brother he was the one driving to force his help. Harrison ordered us to leave the scene and then proceeded to pay off the mechanic and a witness. To this day, the hit-and-run death of Kennedy Bryson remains unsolved."

"I can't believe this," I whispered. "And Uncle Harrison?"

My dad and his brother covered up the death of some poor woman. My chest tightened. *What horrible twist of fate was it that years later Dad lost Rory in a car accident.*

"That was the last straw for your uncle," Andrew said. "He was done cleaning up your father's messes and done with your father. And I'm afraid, our relationship wasn't the same after that. Sharing a secret that terrible tore us apart, but it was a secret the three of us swore to carry to our graves.

"Then, your father received that email promising to reveal the truth of that night if the lodge didn't go ahead and the first person Frank thought of was me."

"But it wasn't you," I said.

"No. I don't live in Raven River. I wasn't an investor. I had no stake in whether or not the project went through. In fact, the first I heard about it was during Frank's call. With me out of the picture, he had a serious problem. Neither he, Harrison, nor I told anyone, so somehow this person dug up the truth. He asked me for my help to track them down."

"Why you?"

"We were both mechanical and computer engineering majors. He went the way of domestic bliss while I took a job at Maverick Technologies in the cybersecurity division."

"He wanted you to trace the email."

He nodded. "That's right. Unfortunately, someone with the money to pay tens of thousands in a bribe, also has the money and intelligence to cover their tracks. I hit a dead end."

"There are quite a few people with money like that in my town," I said. "Most of them pushed to see this lodge built and dropped millions to make it happen. Any one of the Raveners could've found out about the reports."

"Raveners?" he questioned.

I waved that away. "It doesn't matter. Keep going. What happened after you hit a dead end?"

"By all appearances, the project went ahead," he said. "But behind the scenes, your parents worked to collect evidence to find the person and pass it on to the police. They got as far as a description from one of the bribed officials."

Lurching at him, I asked, "What did they look like?"

"An older man. Late thirties to early forties. Average height. Dark hair. He dressed well and wore dark shades during their dealings."

"That's it? Average height and dark hair? That describes most of the men in Raven River."

"I agree. That description wasn't enough to go on." Andrew looked away. "But sadly, it was enough to spook him when he discovered your parents were digging. Shortly after, Frank received an email of an entirely different nature. I assumed the blackmailer figured out the house of cards he was trying to build was doomed to fail, and why take that risk if he could have—"

"All the money the investors put into the lodge instead," I finished.

He inclined his head. "He had your father over a barrel... or so he thought. Frank replied immediately. Told him to go straight to hell and that he could do his worst. He received another email a few days later with these photos attached."

Andrew reached out of frame and presented another two photos. I clapped a hand over my mouth.

One photo was of me. I stood on the steps of Wesley High talking to someone who was blurred out. In the other photo, the lens hyper-focused on Eli reading on a bench in the park by our old house. It was obvious neither one of us knew we were being photographed.

"He gave them a deadline and ordered your parents to transfer the money to their account, or you both would be killed. The same went for if they called the police. They swore they would know, just like they knew your parents were trying to get information on them. They were to transfer the money and then disappear. Your parents would be blamed and the investigation wouldn't look further than them.

"Frank let him know what he thought of that. He was going to the police and wouldn't hand over a cent of that money. The next day, someone shot at your mom coming out of her office. Came so close to hitting her they blew out the driver's window as she reached for the handle."

"Who the fuck is this guy?!" I cried. "Why would they do this?!"

"Twenty-five million dollars, Ember. People have done much worse for a lot less."

I pushed away from the desk. Pacing the length of the bed, my scrambled brain worked to make sense of this. *Someone dug up a ter-*

rible secret on Dad, and when that didn't work, they settled on threat-ening his children. It was that piece of shit after the lodge money, not Mom and Dad.

"What did they do after that?" I threw at him.

"It was at that point Frank contacted me again. He explained all that happened and asked me for help that I was happy to give. What happened the night of the party was a hideous shame I'll carry for the rest of my life, but it was also a debt I owed your father.

"Frank came up with the best plan he could think of and I played my part. Risking you or your brother wasn't an option, which meant agreeing to his terms. Meanwhile, I set up Aurora Fiscal Holdings and made it and the paperwork leading to Charles Magallon Bank untraceable.

"The night they were supposed to transfer the money, I moved it into the account under your name. They left you that note and start-ed the trail that would see the money was returned to the investors. Your parents risked the world believing they were criminals, so they could quietly search for the person after them. They assumed with them and the money out of the picture, he wouldn't have a reason to hurt you or Eli."

I sat down hard, legs giving out and narrowly dropping me in the desk chair.

They didn't leave because they hated me. They left to protect us.

"But where are they now?" I croaked. "Keys and letters and ac-count numbers. Why didn't Mom and Dad try to contact me for re-al?"

"I suspect they were trying to protect you. That fool FBI agent put you in enough danger when he announced to the world that the note was a secret message. It's likely that up to this point, the man who threatened your parents has been watching you. Waiting for you to lead him to the money."

I shivered. Disgust crawled beneath my skin at the thought of that man's camera scope focused on me for the last several months.

"And you?" I asked. "You could have told me this months ago. I would've known they needed help. I could've returned the money sooner!"

Andrew had the decency to lower his head. "Believe me, I wish now that I had, but…"

"But what?"

Shaking his head, his gaze drifted over the laptop. "Your father was insistent that my part end after transferring the money. Running away, hiding, and leaving clues was the best and only way to get through the situation and I wasn't to do anything else that could put you two in danger. Looking back, I believe he knew, or suspected, something that drove him this far."

"Suspected something or… someone." I gripped the laptop. "They're in trouble, aren't they, Andrew?"

"They were in trouble when they ran. That they haven't returned following you giving back the money makes me think that trouble caught up with them," he said. "I waited for as long as I could allow myself to respect your father's wishes, but now you need to know."

"A dark-haired man with a connection to the lodge," I said to myself. "I've been over the victim list a hundred times. If he's one of the investors, I'll find him."

"Months have passed," he said. "Ember, you should prepare yourself for—"

"No," I said firmly. "Mom and Dad are out there. They just need my help. I'll go over the… list… and…" I trailed off. A memory jarred loose.

"Why didn't Mom and Dad try to contact me for real?"

"They need my help," I whispered. "Send… help. Send help."

"Ember, are you all right?

"Andrew…" As if moving through water, I slowly reached for my phone and scrolled down, down, down to the single string of nonsense I dismissed.

034-637-7652: Tgiving 14 years send help. Dont reply!

"Andrew, I think my parents sent me this message." It sounded like the admission came from someone else. I was outside of my body, looking down at the phone in my hands as how long I let this text sit ignored struck me.

Andrew shot up straight. "Excuse me? What message?"

"It says Tgiving, fourteen years, send help, and don't reply," I read. "I brushed this off like an idiot, assuming it was spam, but spam messages don't tell you not to reply. They want you to click on their phony-ass links and respond to their bots."

"You're correct, Ember. They warned you not to reply—"

"Because it's *his* phone!" I shot to my feet. "Andrew, can you look up this number? Who is it registered to?"

"I'll find out, but do you know what the message means?"

I resumed my pacing. "This isn't nearly as hard as the other clues they gave me. It's Thanksgiving. Fourteen years ago. And send help doesn't need to be deciphered."

"Thanksgiving fourteen years ago? What's the connection?"

"I don't know," I admitted. "I was only four. But I will find out." I leaned over the desk chair, zooming in on the camera. "Thank you, Andrew. I wish I'd heard from you a lot sooner."

"I do too."

"At least you finally made the call. Tell me the millisecond you find out whose number this is."

"I will."

I closed the laptop and raced for the door. Bursting outside, I skidded into Clay's chest.

"Guys." Hiro, Clay, and Royal posted up against the wall. "I wasn't serious about you waiting out here for me."

"We were," said Hiro.

Clay put his hand on my stomach and wrapped me and Bump in a hug. "Are you okay?"

"No," I said honestly. "Andrew was the real deal, and you're not going to believe what he told me..."

Chapter Eleven

My week officially started in the middle and that didn't stop it from winning the medal for longest week of my life. Thursday morning, Andrew called with information about the phone number. It was registered to a Lila Parker. Deceased five years.

Lila Parker was safely removed from the list of suspects and Andrew didn't have another name to add.

"Mrs. Parker didn't have children or surviving family," he told me. "I'm sorry. You won't find out who is at the other end of that number unless you call it, and I'm certain whoever sent you that text had a strong reason to tell you not to."

It killed me but I had to agree with him. If one of my parents had managed to get their hands on this phone and send me a message, it'd put them in untold danger if that man found out before I was close to finding him.

My parents' situation had turned infinitely desperate overnight. Weeks ago, they sent me that text for help. With every fiber of my being, I knew it was from them, and I'd wasted so much time.

"What can you remember about Thanksgiving fourteen years ago?" Hiro asked me that Wednesday night while we talked in my room following Andrew's call. "Where did you go? Who were you with?"

I held my head in my hands, bent over my folded knees and rocking on my sheets. "I don't know. I was four, Hiro."

"Didn't you spend every Thanksgiving at your lake house?" Royal offered.

"They bought the house when I was seven," I replied. "Fourteen years ago, I'm not sure where we were, but it has to be somewhere in Raven River. The piece of trash that started this must be from here. He invested in the lodge and freaked when he found out the project would be derailed by a few birds and the low likelihood of a flood. Eventually, he decided to end the headache and get his hands on all of the money while he had my parents helpless. From there it spiraled out of control."

Clay put his arm around me, tucking me under his chin. "If this guy is one of the investors, we've got him. Thirties to forties. Dark hair. Average height. Thousands of dollars to hand out bribes. He's a Ravener, Em, and we'll find him."

Their reassurances buoyed my spirits at least enough to make it through telling Eli. I promised I'd be honest with him about what I discovered. He took the truth about as well as can be expected of a worried, stressed-out, fourteen-year-old boy.

I held him as frustrated tears soaked his cheeks and stayed up all night Thursday interpreting while he lobbed question after question at Andrew. He demanded to speak to him and Andrew's guilt rang so clear, he was willing to do whatever we asked.

Friday as I readied for class, the questions were lobbed at me.

"Were we with Grandpa and Grandma that Thanksgiving?" he asked. *"The mansion is sitting empty now."*

It was true. The stately Bancroft Manor sat empty. As Harrison's inheritance, it was his to do what he willed, and he chose to let it collect dust while he lived in another mansion twenty minutes away. We never had the kind of relationship where I could ask him why.

"Maybe, Eli, but I can't remember. My strongest memories of four-year-old Ember were of meeting you and playing with Rory."

"Don't give up."

Bending over my bed, I kissed his crown. "I won't. We're going back to Uncle's house tonight, and that Thanksgiving will be one of the many things we'll talk about."

"*Will you tell him about Andrew?*"

I looked away, remembering the awful secret Andrew, Frank, and Harrison hid. That part of the story I did not share with Eli. I didn't want him seeing his father and uncle differently.

"No," I said and signed. "Uncle has been pretty clear on his feelings about my *sleuthing*. I need his permission to leave campus. If he knows there truly was a plot against our parents and that I'm searching for the Ravener behind it, he'll shut me down and insist the police handle it."

Eli bobbed his head, chin set and determined. "*You're right. We can't tell him.*"

Eli's use of the word "we" had me worried. I was afraid he'd push to join the search and that wasn't happening. This mystery man bribed, cheated, blackmailed, stalked, and committed some act that pushed my parents to send that text. He wasn't getting near my brother.

I finished shoving my notebooks in my bag and hustled us out the door for class. Eli kept up the conversation going down.

"*Are you going to talk to Uncle about New York?*"

"Yes. No use putting it off any longer. Who knows how long this stuff will take in the courts."

"*What if he says no?*"

"I won't take no for an answer."

He grinned. "*You gonna beat him up too?*"

"I can take him."

Eli cracked up laughing. The sound warmed my heart. As long as Eli was laughing, there was hope. Hope we'd find our parents. Hope we'd make a new life together.

With Bump.

Stroking my stomach, I smiled at Eli. "There's something I need to talk to you about also. Tonight."

"*Okay.*"

We stepped out of the elevator and spotted Hiro through the glass doors. He strode across the lawn in his coveralls, heading to another project. Eli took off after him.

I continued on to breakfast. Opting for the healthier option of oatmeal and an egg spinach sandwich, I carried it up to the Angel table. Royal redirected me from an empty seat to his lap.

"You okay?"

"No," I said. "I can't think about anything but Cassius, Mom, and Dad."

"It's going to be okay, Em," Clay said. "You'll speak to your uncle and then Ives's parents tomorrow. Hiro's going to Easthaven tonight. Dad's picking me up to check out the boat, and Royal's been looking up the investors who match the description. We'll get them back."

I told myself that he was right all day. We had a plan and it would lead us to them. I'd never believe it was too late.

The final bell rang ending Seeger's class. I shouldered my bag and walked straight to the main office where Eli waited for me.

On the drive to the mansion, he grilled me on what I would say to convince Uncle Harrison and Aunt Violet. I had a whole speech prepared. Getting him to sit down and listen to it was the difficult part.

"I need to talk to you, Uncle." I trailed him from the living room to his office. "It's important."

"I'm busy, Ember. Speak to your aunt."

"This concerns both of you."

Harrison walked into his office and turned on me. "Then it can wait until dinner."

He shut the door in my face.

Gritting my teeth, I retreated to Eli's room. I waited that long to have the conversation, a few more hours wouldn't hurt. Besides, there was another important talk I needed to have.

Eli glanced up from his book as I lay on his bed. *"Is it time for the super important conversation?"*

"It is." I skipped the preface and fanfare. *"Eli, I'm pregnant."*

His eyes bugged. *"What? Em—"*

He cut off, dropping his hands by his side, and sitting shell-shocked.

"This is huge, I know," I signed. *"I'm still getting used to the idea. I wake up every day and it hits me all over again that this bump is a baby. But she's coming and I'm excited for all of us to make a life with her."*

Eli's face scrunched up, wrinkling his forehead.

"Please, Eli. Tell me what you're thinking."

He flicked off my face, staring hard at my stomach, and then he raised his hands. *"I'm going to be an uncle."* Just like that, a beaming grin burned up his frown. *"Uncle Eli. I like that."*

Laughing, I tipped on top of him. Amazing to be young and things be so uncomplicated. "Uncle Eli" was nothing but great news.

Hours later, Eli and I sat around the dining table eating food I hadn't heard of and being on the outs of a conversation between Violet and Harrison.

"—nice to get away for a bit, Harry," she said. "You've been so stressed with work and now the police are back in our lives raking up the lodge."

"Now isn't a good time to get away, Vi. The firm is getting back on its feet. The community is reaffirming faith in the Bancroft name. This is my opportunity to sway our big clients into coming back to us."

"Just for a week, Harry. Surely you can tear yourself away for that long."

"I'll check my schedule." He squeezed his wife's wrist. "Maybe we can steal away down the coast. Get you on the beach and into a little bikini."

Giggling, Violet swatted him with her napkin. "Stop it, Harry."

Eli wrinkled his nose at me. He read Harrison's lips and was definitely wishing he hadn't.

Perfect time to change the subject.

"Uncle Harrison. Aunt Violet." I dropped my fork, pushing my plate away. "About that talk we had last time on my future and college plans, I thought we should pick that back up."

Violet's smile vanished. "Your uncle and I are still discussing the subject of paying your tuition. Do not push."

"I wasn't going to. It's very generous of Uncle. Whatever he chooses to do, I'm fine."

"What more is there to speak about?" asked Harrison.

"Eli."

All eyes flicked to my brother who innocently ate his sweetbreads and broccoli salad.

"What about Eli?"

I took a deep breath. *Here it goes.* "I want you to give me guardianship of him."

My timing couldn't have been better. Harrison choked on his sip of wine. Coughing up a lung, he wheezed into his napkin while goggling at me. "Excuse me?"

"I can't leave Raven River without Eli," I began. "Him moving to New York with me makes the most sense. I've done my research. I found a great school for him and apartments nearby."

"Whoa. Slow down," Harrison said.

"You two don't want kids," I said. "You didn't plan for us to interrupt your lives, and we both know that when I'm gone, Eli's home will be the academy."

"Just a minute!" Harrison reared up. "Don't you dare insinuate we're neglectful. We enrolled you both in a top institution and granted you the best education money could buy."

"Uncle, I'm not criticizing. Raven River Academy beats out foster care and living on the streets any day. I'm grateful that you both took us in even if I've never said it. But now I'm leaving. If you ask yourselves what's the best thing for all of us, you have to agree this is it.

"You can go back to the way things were. Just you and Aunt Violet. Eli will be happy at Chapman School and have family that's there for him every day."

"Well," said Violet. "We never considered this, but we can certainly discuss it. What will you two do for money?"

"We can—"

"This is ludicrous," Harrison barked. He spun on his wife. "Violet, do not entertain her. There's no way I'm giving an eighteen-year-old girl custody of a child. She's not mature enough to take care of him."

My jaw clenched. "I've been taking care of Eli my whole life. Should I remind you which one of us in this room learned to sign? Spoke to him for hours to teach him to read lips. Arranged his accommodations at the academy. Found the person who attacked him and had him arrested. And, because this should be most important, loves him and is willing to do anything for him. On what planet is boarding school better than what I have and will always offer him."

"The planet where you're a teenager," he retorted.

Eli tugged my sleeve. *"Tell him it's my choice and I want to live with you."*

I did. If possible, Harrison flushed a deeper purple.

"It most certainly is not your choice!"

"Stop yelling at me, dick."

"What?! What was that?" Harrison asked me—no doubt picking up that the reply wasn't respectful from the attitude on Eli's face. "What did he just say?"

"Stop yelling at me," I relayed.

"You—"

"Harry, I agree," Violet cut in. "Calm down and keep an open mind. Let's hear Ember out first."

My aunt was so delightfully transparent. For once it worked in my favor.

"What will you do for money?" Violet repeated.

"A monthly stipend from my trust fund would be enough. I calculated how much we'd need for rent, food, and tuition. Eli and I would be self-sufficient and all it would take is Uncle authorizing the withdrawals."

I left out that my four boyfriends would be kicking some into the house pot. That wouldn't sweeten the deal.

"That sounds reasonable," Violet said. "Harry—"

Harrison banged his fist on the table, rattling me, Violet, and the silverware. "I will not say this again. Your trust fund will be accessed when you are twenty-five and not a second sooner. You can consider the subject of adopting Eli closed as well!"

Shoving away from the table, my uncle stormed out of the room. Face pinched, Violet dabbed the corners of her mouth, set her napkin aside, and slowly rose to her feet. "Go to your rooms. We'll talk about this another time."

Violet strode out the door, likely to have the epic fight with Uncle that she didn't want us to overhear.

"*Think Aunt Violet will convince him?*"

"She better convince him," I snapped. "I'm not above kidnapping."

Eli laughed like I was joking.

I HADN'T COOLED OFF by the next day.

Ives Manor was a thirty-minute walk in the direction of Oak Mall. I skipped asking for the car and acknowledging my uncle's existence by walking straight out the door. I ranted to Royal on the phone the whole way.

"What fucking cheek telling me I'm not mature enough to take care of Eli. This from the guy who still refuses to fit his house with lighted smoke alarms and phone signalers. At least I'd make our house safe for him."

"Can't disagree with you, Em. No one protects your brother like you do. You should have had guardianship of him from the start."

"Exactly. Thank you."

The beautiful morning was at odds with my darkening temper. Towering gates and fences lined both sides of the street, concealing sprawling gardens and courtly manors. My scenery was no less beautiful for their lack. A wrought-iron fence of gold-painted lilies and silver snapdragons stretched as far as I could see, separating the road from the sidewalk.

"I'm almost to the gate," Royal said. "I'll pick you up and we'll stop off for something sweet."

"Aww. I'm almost to Nolan's house, so let's do that after."

"Em, don't go there alone."

"Relax. You'll get there before me. I'm walking."

"What? Why? You shouldn't be walking."

I laughed. "Should I be carried everywhere on the shoulders of my men instead? Bump and I can handle a little half-hour walk."

"Half an hour? Nah. Stay where you are. I'm coming to get you."

Sighing, I said, "Are you going to be like this for the entire pregnancy?"

"And after."

"Thanks for the honesty."

I stopped and waited for him as requested. Truth was I liked my boys fawning over me. Every day I glimpsed what great fathers they'd be to Bump.

Royal picked me up and we drove on to the Iveses' home.

"Think they'll let us in?" Royal asked as their gate loomed ahead.

"I remember his mom was always nice," I replied. "His dad never paid attention to me. Got my name wrong every time. If Mrs. Ives answers, I bet she'll let me in."

"Why are you saying me?"

"For the same reason I'm going to tell you to pull over here and wait outside. You can't talk to them."

Royal cut me a look. "You're not going in there alone."

"Royal, my love, if Nolan knew you were Rio's son, isn't there a possibility his parents do too? Do you think they'll open up to the son of the man they hold responsible for their daughter's death?"

"Ember, my love," he deadpanned. "If Ives Junior has been driven to kill, don't you think his parents could be just as messed up over her death? You don't know what's going to happen if you go in there asking questions."

"They're not going to hurt me."

He cocked a brow. "Why? Because you say so?"

"Yes."

A frustrated groan burst out of him. "I'm not letting you go in there alone, Em."

I kissed him sweetly on his stubbly cheek. "I'm not asking for permission. Pull over and let me out."

He bared his teeth, growling to let me know what he thought of that.

"If it makes you feel better, call me and I'll leave my phone on while I talk to them. Anything happens and you'll know."

Royal argued some more—because he couldn't give in to anything easily—but eventually he finished his second loop around the neighborhood and parked a house down. I stuck my phone and a listening Royal in my back pocket as I reached the call box.

The dial tone ended abruptly. A voice I recognized thrummed out of the speaker. "Hello. This is the Ives residence. How may I help you?"

"Hi, Mags. I don't know if you remember me. It's Ember Bancroft."

"Ember!" The formal tone vanished. "Of course, I remember you, and— Oh. Have you come about that terrible business at Christmas?"

"Yes," I admitted. "I was hoping to talk to Mr. and Mrs. Ives about it. It's been a while but I thought they might like the full story."

"Mrs. Ives isn't available, but I'll see if Mr. Ives is willing to speak to you."

"Thank you."

I rocked back on my heels, content to wait.

One minute. Five minutes. Eight minutes passed.

"Hello, Ember?" Mags clicked on. "Are you still there?"

"I'm here."

"You may come in for a short visit."

"Thanks, Mags."

An electronic buzz signaled the unlocked gate. Mags, short for Magnolia, was there to open the front door and lifted me into a bear hug. During the short time I dated Nolan, Magnolia buzzed me in, brought me into the kitchen, and stuffed me with homemade cookies while I waited for Nolan to come down.

"I'll show you up to the study." Mags tapped her nose. "When you leave, a bag of chocolate chip cookies go with you."

"Bless you, Mags. I missed you most of all."

She laughed. Everything about Mags was pleasant. From her round cheeks to her shining eyes and the way she hugged people like they were on the verge of setting sail around the world.

Mags led the way up the grand staircase. I cast my eyes to the portraits lining our path and shivered like I had many times before. The home of Nolan Ives was not pleasant.

That wasn't to say it wasn't grand, opulent, or reeking of refined class. It was all of those things. But pearl-inlay doors, antique rugs, and priceless artwork didn't make the mansion less... cold.

Neither do those portraits.

Above our heads, four individual paintings of the Ives family tracked my ascent.

The artist's brushwork was impeccable. He captured the curve of Nolan's lips. The arch of Mrs. Ives's nose and the sheen to Mr. Ives's silver locks. But for the life of me, I never understood why he painted them unsmiling. A trip up these stairs subjected you to glares from the entire family. Even Viviana, though her jewel eyes and lovely face weren't diminished by it.

Topping the stairs, we turned down a hallway, leaving the portraits behind.

"It's the room at the end. You may go in."

I thanked Mags and stepped into the study. This wasn't a room I'd been in before but familiarity struck me in the deep brown leather furniture, large oak desk, wall-to-wall bookshelves reaching up to the rafters, and lack of a personal touch. Sweeping the space, I landed on a figure partially concealed by a bookcase.

Mr. Ives stood looking out the window, seemingly unaware of my presence.

"Hello," I called. "Thanks for speaking to me, Mr. Ives."

"Hello, Ember."

My brows rose. *Now he remembers my name.*

"What is the true story that you've come to tell me about my son?" His voice was sandpaper on stone—rough, scratchy, unyielding.

I padded across the carpet. Mr. Ives shifted slightly in my direction, throwing off the cloak of shadows and revealing part of his face. Sharp cheekbones cut beneath cedar brown eyes. Asa Ives was his son thirty years in the future. The resemblance was strong... and unsettling.

"The night Nolan held us at gunpoint, he shared Viviana's story."

Asa turned from me completely. "My own little girl."

"What happened to her was an unspeakable tragedy. She deserved better in so many ways."

"Yes, she did, Ember. Yes, she did."

"I know the man who ultimately led to her death. Dante Gallo."

"Do you?"

My gaze drifted to the arch of the window, growing unfocused. "It's his eyes. They're what get you first. So beautiful you can't believe anything but good is behind them. And when he smiles, like you're the only person worth smiling for, that's when you're lost, and by then it's too late."

Asa shifted during my speech, slowly coming to face me.

"You know him." It wasn't a question.

I nodded. "He's a plague," I said, echoing Rio's bile. "A disease. A pestilence. He enters people's lives and destroys all he touches."

"Yes," Asa whispered. He drew toward me—not entirely of his own volition.

"He came for me too. Spread his infection in my life and it nearly got me killed more than once."

"I'm sorry." And he truly sounded it.

I glanced out of the window. I couldn't see my town through the trees and I didn't have to. I felt her breathing. Felt her pain. Knew the river's desire to swell the banks and wash us clean. "It's what he's done to our town. The violence and ironclad grip of the gangs. People are afraid to leave their homes and students are confined to campus like prisoners. We weren't perfect before but we've gotten worse since he arrived."

"Yes," he hissed. Asa ate the distance between us, advancing on me so fast I almost took a step back. He truly looked like Nolan—especially when his mouth twisted into a snarl. "You know, Ember. You understand."

"I do. Dante Gallo has hurt countless people. It's astounding the damage he's done in just a few years. The first Horseman."

"The Horsemen," Asa spat. "What a fitting title for the men destroying this town. Named for the bringers of the apocalypse. It's why he targeted my Viviana. Gallo needed our money to fund his operation, and when he couldn't get it, he abandoned her in that open sewer they call the Outer Borough."

With that, Asa confirmed he knew exactly who Rio Cruz was.

Nolan discovered the truth about Dante/Rio and passed it on to his father. What else has Nolan shared with him?

"The man is a plague as you say, but infection only becomes plague on the backs of the ignorant and apathetic. The Outer Borough welcomed the Horsemen. They believed they were better protection than the police. Better employment than honest jobs. Better funding than the bank. They didn't force them out and now that they're too strong, they call to us for help."

"The Horsemen need to be stopped," I said.

He bobbed his head, backing away. "Absolutely, they must and they will be." Asa gestured out the window. "My friends and neighbors can't deny it any longer. We thought we were safe behind our walls but the Horsemen have shown they can get to us anywhere. Our children were the final straw."

Inching closer, I chose my words carefully. "Nolan said he was fighting to bring the Horsemen down. Expose Gallo for who he truly is."

"Yes, that's what my son wanted."

Asa was speaking so freely it threw me. The same man didn't have more than two words to say to "Amber" a few years ago.

Never underestimate the power of shared hatred.

"Nolan was misguided in his attempts which resulted in that terrible night and Julian's injury." He shook his head. "To truly get rid of a parasite, you must deny the source of its power. Starve it."

Asa's soft whispers washed over me, eliciting an odd sensation. I touched the back of my neck and the hairs standing on end.

"More violence won't rid us of Dante Gallo and his men. If we're to achieve that goal, we have to cut off and destroy what helped them rise in the first place." Asa looked me in the eyes. "The Outer Borough."

"Cut off and destroy the Outer Borough? What do you mean? How could that even happen?"

"Plans are already set in motion, Ember. You needn't worry anymore. The pestilence that has infected our town will be removed." A smile twisted his lips—and Nolan truly was before me. "And you can tell the same to your *friend* waiting outside for you."

Every muscle in my body turned to lead.

"Ember!" Royal's faint shout reached my ear. "Ember, get out of there!"

"You know, don't you?" I whispered. "The things your son has done... and where he is."

Asa's smirk didn't twitch. "Don't be absurd. I've had no contact with my son since Christmas Eve." Mr. Ives swept out his hand. "I believe it's time for you to go."

It most certainly was.

I hurried out of there rubbing my arms like his smirk crawled over my skin. Royal's shouts were the fire at my heels.

Mags came into the front room holding a Ziploc bag. "Em— Ooh. What's the hurry?"

"I have to get going. My friend is waiting outside." I grabbed the cookies, hugged her, and rushed out.

"Royal, it's okay," I said into the phone. "I'm on my way."

He ran to me as I slipped out of the gates, picking me up, and kissing me breathless. "I told you not to go in there alone."

"And I told you he wouldn't hurt me," I retorted. "Did you hear what he said, Royal? If I didn't know better, I'd say he was proud of his son. I'm betting he knows where Nolan is hiding." I scoffed. "Maybe Camila was right and Nolan's stashed away in his house somewhere."

"He's not going to let you back in there to check." Royal and I got in the car. "That guy was off. What did he mean by destroying the Outer Borough and plans already set in motion?"

"I really don't want to find out. No one wants your father out of the OB more than me, but too many people have gotten hurt in this war against the Horsemen."

Royal's cell vibrated on the dash.

"Yeah, Clay," he answered. "She's here."

Royal pressed *speaker* and put the phone between us.

"I'm on the boat right now. Someone has definitely been living here," Clay said.

I bolted upright. "How can you tell?"

"Soup cans in the trash and the bed's been slept in. This is where he's hiding. I'll take him when he comes back. Call Rio and tell him to give up my fucking brother."

"Slow up, Clay," said Royal. "Unless you found the gun in there, he's probably got it on him. Don't try to do this alone. Call Hiro back from Easthaven. We'll meet at my place. Get tape, rope, and stuff to hold him. Then we'll grab him tonight while he's sleeping."

The surreality of this conversation wasn't lost on me. It was hard to believe a year ago my biggest problem was staying out of fights so Mom and Dad wouldn't ship me to boarding school. Fast-track a few months and I'm plotting kidnappings and making exchanges with gang leaders.

"I'm not waiting," Clay said. "Meet me here or I'll grab him myself."

Royal cursed. "All right, just hang back until I get there. I have to drop off Em."

"You're not dropping me off anywhere," I protested.

"You can't come and you know why."

I grasped his chin between two fingers. "This guy tried to kill you once. I'm not going home to sit by the phone, terrified that I'll call and you won't answer. Not to mention Cassius was taken because of me. I have to be there when we get him back. So, unless you feel comfortable dragging a pregnant woman kicking and screaming from the car, the both of us are going to Clay."

Nostrils flaring, Royal jammed the ignition, peeling away from the curb. "You can't make this easy for me, can you?"

"Everything is going to be fine," I said, easing into the seat. "We found him, Royal, and yes I'm betting Daddy knew Nolan was on the boat. Once we get Cassius back, we can all breathe again. We'll go back to planning our future with Bump."

"Our problems haven't disappeared," he said. "Rio won't let any of us go without a fight. But we can't leave at all until we find your parents."

"No, we can't." I tugged his hand off the wheel and rested it on my stomach. "Your turn. Tell me everything will be okay."

"There's hope, Em. We were thinking the worst when we found out they hadn't touched the money. Now we know they're alive and out there somewhere. As long as they are, we'll find them."

"Thank you. I need to hear these things. Keep them coming."

Royal turned the final corner leading to the gate. We rolled to a stop behind another person waiting to leave.

"Any luck figuring out where you were fourteen years ago?"

"Eli suggested the empty and haunted Bancroft Manor. But what are we assuming at this point? That my parents are being held against their will? If they are, they can't be at the manor."

"Why not? You said it's empty."

"The main house is but the gardener still lives on the grounds. Uncle Harrison's birthright has to look impeccable at all times. With him out there weeding, whacking, and planting all day, I doubt he'd miss a dark-haired man going in and out to check on my parents."

"Good point."

The guard raised the gate to let us through. Passing from the Estate into the OB reminded me of Lucy stepping through the wardrobe. We left the world of clean streets, sports cars, and gilded lily fences for trash cans blowing their contents across the road, graffiti on every wall and bars on the windows.

"Do you have the directions to the dock?" Royal asked.

"It's a private slip off a dirt road that comes out near the cemetery."

"All right." He flipped his blinker, sliding into the right lane. "We'll be there soon and you are staying in the car."

"I'll be your lookout. When he shows up, I'll call you."

"Em." Royal took his eyes off the road to look at me. "Why did you offer up Nolan to Rio? You understand what he's going to do to him, don't you?"

"I do," I clipped.

"And you're okay with that?"

"I'm okay with the guy who tried to frame and kill you being taken off the streets."

"Still trying to save me, princess?"

"Always." I stroked the hand on my stomach. "We need you."

"You've got me."

We left the town center behind, rolling down the long stretch of road that ended at the cemetery.

"Did you come up with anymore names?" I asked.

"I've thought of one for a boy. What do you think of Ransom?"

"Is that a serious question?"

Royal tossed me a grin. "Think about it. You, me, and the Angels got together because of a ransom. That name is perfect for our kid."

"Do we really want to explain that to him when he's older?" I gave in an inch. "I like Rafael or Baron. You guys have strong, kingly names. If he's a boy, he should have one too and be named after all of you."

"I also like—"

A horn blared behind us, startling me out of our talk. A black car grew big in our rearview, gaining on us fast. They beat their horn on the two-way lane and accelerated, closing the gap between us.

"The hell? I'm going fifteen over. Just go around."

My eyes narrowed. "Hold up, Royal. That car..."

As if they heard him, the driver dove into the next lane and zoomed past us. He cut in front of our car like the asshole he was.

"What is it, Em?" Royal asked.

I scooted as far as I could go and squinted through the windshield. "Royal, that's the car! The one I saw outside of the—"

The driver slammed the brakes.

"Ember!" Royal flashed out, holding me back as he stomped his brakes much too late.

We careened into the back of the car, hood crumpling like tissue paper, and the impact throwing me headfirst into the dash as a wall of white rushed to meet me.

The sky winked out. Aimlessly I drifted through darkness, peaceful and consuming, its tethers sought to drag me down. A resounding blare tugged me back.

"Hurry up—"

Who... is that?

I peeled my eyes open, peering through a blurred lens. Colors melded together. White, black, blue, and red.

Red.

"Royal."

Blood soaked Royal's face, speaking to immense pain, but his beautiful face was peaceful in the darkness that claimed him absolute.

"Grab him!"

Royal's door opened. Hands reached in, undoing his buckle and seizing him under the arms.

"No," I croaked.

The fog was clearing quickly. The clamoring car horn battered my eardrums, forcing me into reality. Two figures in black masks formed in my vision as they dragged Royal out of the driver's seat.

Wake up, Ember! Do something!

"Are we taking her?"

"No, leave her."

"Wait. Stop." I scrambled for the door handle.

They lifted Royal, arms and feet, and beat a retreat to their car. I shoved on the door and threw it open. The momentum tipped my battered body out and I collapsed on the ground. "Stop!"

Forcing myself up, I stumbled for the car.

The men loaded Royal in the back seat and raced inside. As the engine revved, one of the captors stuck his head out of the window. I grabbed for the doorknob, screaming Royal's name, and his grin triumphed through the mouth hole.

"The Horsemen ride."

The car peeled away in a shower of gravel. I staggered back and tripped over my feet, falling hard. Panicking terror heaved my chest. Visions of the reporter, fleeing students, and Royal in a dumpster with angel wings above his head flashed in my mind.

My stomach heaved.

No, Em! That is not going to happen. Stop. Take a breath. Think.

I breathed slow, willing my heart to calm. The first thing I did was pull out my phone.

A crack stretched up the screen, but Clay's number dialed without a problem.

"Em, are you guys almost here? We—"

"C-Clay." My voice cracked on his name. "You have to come get me. I'm on Laurel Street. They took him, Clay. They just... took him."

"What? Baby, slow down. Took who?"

"Royal." My resolve to stay calm broke under a sob. "It was Nolan, Clay. That fuck can wear all the masks he wants. I know his voice. He made us crash the car and then he kidnapped Royal."

"Crash the car?!" I heard a thump on his end and the labored pants of him running. "Are you okay?!"

"I'm fine. I hit my head and blacked out for a second, but we're okay." I took in the smashed front of Royal's car. "Please, just get h-here. We have to go after them."

"I'm coming, baby. Stay on the phone with me."

I used up all of my strength to call him. Crawling to the grass, I lay down on the soft earth. Grass tickling my cheek, I clutched Bump as Clay poured sweet assurances in my ear.

"If you're on Laurel Street, which way did they go?" Clay asked. "Were they headed to the dock?"

"No, they drove back toward town."

The crash and capture played on a loop in my mind. The squealing brakes. Blood dripping down Royal's face. Grasping hands seizing him. The pungent scent of burnt rubber hitting the back of my nose. Over and over I watched them take Royal away and a sight I put down to my blurry vision remained as the fog cleared.

"Clay, it wasn't just Nolan. I know who was with him," I said. "I know who the traitor is."

IT FELT LIKE HOURS until Clay's car came into sight. He jerked to a stop and tumbled out, scooping me up and crushing me in a fierce hug. "Are you sure you're okay?"

"I'm sure."

Clay observed the state of the car. Stricken, he said, "I have to get you to a hospital. Let them check you out and I'll go after Royal."

"Clay, listen to me." I cupped his face, making him look me in the eye. "We're both fine. My airbag went off but for some reason, Royal's didn't. Right now, he's hurt and in the hands of a guy who has tried to kill him once. We've already wasted too much time. We have to go now."

That swayed him. He put me on my feet. I stopped only to get my purse out of Royal's car and rushed to Clay's.

"Where are we going?" he called over the hood. "Back to the boat and hope he comes back with Royal?"

"No, we can't wait, Clay." I climbed into the passenger seat and jammed my belt on. "We have no idea what they're planning to do to him. I will not watch another live breaking news of a body found in the OB."

Clay kicked on the car and sped toward town. "I don't understand any of this, Em. How did this happen? Did you notice them following you?"

"It happened because I visited Asa Ives. Either he's working with his son and he tipped him off, or Nolan was nearby watching the house. It's the only explanation for how twenty minutes after speaking to that creepy man, Nolan's in a car following us," I said.

"So, it was Ives who shot the reporter and did a drive-by on the school? What about the bodies in the dumpster?"

"I don't know how much he's responsible for. I just know that Royal was driven off in the same car that sped away from campus."

"What the fuck is he trying to do?"

"Mr. Ives spoke about destroying the OB and cutting off the Horsemen's source. A lot of people think the Horsemen are there to help them, or that they're the lesser of evils. They could be stirring up all this violence to turn people against them."

Clay swerved a corner at breakneck speed. We raced down a garbage-lined street near the Estate gates.

"And the other guy," he asked. "Are you sure it's him?"

I scrolled through my phone, scanning frantically for his number. "I'm sure."

"How are we going to take care of this, Em?" Clay froze the air. His blues chipped from ice and a hard cast set his jaw. "Taking Royal. Almost killing you. They're dead, Em. We're trading Cassius with a corpse."

Putting the phone to my ear, I rubbed his thigh. "It wasn't supposed to happen this way. I had a reason for offering up Nolan because I knew I'd have to search for him anyway. Dangling him in front of Rio was supposed to grant me safety while I searched the town for him and the traitor. I didn't plan on Rio turning me down, snatching Cassius, or Nolan deciding to come to me."

The dial tone echoed in my ear. *Come on. Pick up. I knew I only had one shot to free the town of the Horsemen and this is it. Please pick up.*

"But none of this changes the plan," I said. "We're out of time, but I still have to make this work or Rio will have us, and this town, under his thumb for—"

The call picked up. "Hello, Ember. What can I do for you?"

I clamped on Clay's leg. "It's not about what you can do for me," I said. "It's what I can do for you."

"Excuse me?"

"What if I told you I can hand over a key player in the Horsemen's network who will tell you everything you want to know, and a few things you don't, about the gang and their operation? What if I said this person will turn themselves over to you without a fight and you'll close the kind of career-making case that will have women dropping their panties and men dying of envy?"

"I would say I'm married," he replied, "but extremely interested in seeing those other hypotheticals become reality. What's the catch?"

"At some point, I'm going to call you back, say a bunch of stuff, and then I'll hand over the phone. You will say these seven words: 'do it or the deal is off' and then you'll hang up. That sentence and nothing else. Got it?"

"What deal?"

"I can't tell you that."

His tone sharpened. "Ember, I'm a federal agent. I will not cosign my name and reputation to some shady underhanded deal."

"There's nothing shady about it," I snapped. "Gunrunning, smuggling, and thirty open murder cases, Underhill. You have the opportunity to put dangerous men away and, last I checked, that was your job. All it will take is one sentence."

The silence was deafening on the other end.

"I've earned the benefit of the doubt, Agent Underhill. This sounds like you're doing me a favor but the truth is, I'm doing you one. I'm wrapping up another case in a bow, and I swear to you, I'm not doing anything illegal, so, when I call you, what are you going to say?"

Underhill bit off a curse. "Do it or the deal is off."

"Thank you."

Underhill hung up.

He could sulk all he wanted. The guy would perk up when he got his man.

I dropped my phone in my lap and Clay immediately handed me his—already dialing.

"He'll know why we're calling," Clay said.

"Good. It means his ass will answer."

I said that, but the call rang and rang and then went to voicemail. I hit redial.

Three times that traitorous bastard made me call him, and with every automated request to call back another time, my anger and fear grew. I had to get to him before they did whatever they planned to do to Royal.

I dialed again.

Ring.

Ring.

"Hello?" His deep voice poured out of the speaker. "What's up, Clay?"

"This isn't Clay, it's Ember. Do not hang up, Caesar."

"What do you want?"

"Royal."

"Royal? What are you talking about?" His confused act was good. No wonder he fooled everyone for so long.

"This will be a lot easier if you don't waste my time. You've got that hitch in your step, Caesar, and I saw it as you ran off with my boyfriend. The good news is—"

"Ember, I honestly have no idea—"

"Shut up!" I barked. "If you want to find out how you and I both get what we want, listen up. Whatever you think you're going to do to Royal, you're not. If you hurt him in anyway, there is no deal."

"Deal?"

"I know it's been you all along. You flooded the OB with drugs. You teamed up with Nolan and you framed Royal. I also know why you're doing this. Like I said, I'm going to give you what you want. If you let Royal go unharmed, I'll put the key to taking down Rio right in your hands and you won't have to terrorize any more students or shoot reporters."

Caesar said nothing.

"You and I need to meet face to face," I continued. "You pick the place. Just meet me there now."

"This is a trap," he hissed.

"How could it be a trap? I found out it was you less than an hour ago. When did I have time to set a trap for you?"

"Rio is with you."

"No. It's just me and Clay, and Clay will stay in the car."

"What's your game, Bancroft?"

"Getting my boyfriend back! Where are we meeting, Caesar?"

Caesar was quiet for so long I checked to see if he hung up.

"My garage," he finally said. "Half an hour. If anyone other than you and Walker show up, Royal dies."

"I got it, but you better not touch a hair on his head. Pass that on to your buddy, Nolan."

The line went dead.

"Caesar's Garage," I told Clay.

"You know you're not going in there alone, right? We don't seriously have to have that argument."

"We don't," I soothed. "I just said that to get him to come. The last thing I want is to be alone with that guy."

Clay kissed my palm. "This is going to end with Royal and Cassius free."

"It has to."

I made one more phone call but otherwise didn't say much on the drive to the garage. Over and over I went through what I would say to convince the deceptively harmless little mechanic to give up his plot for revenge, and hand over his opponent's single weakness.

What did Rio do to drive Caesar to this? Rio's sins are endless, but from what Royal described, Caesar's been the dutiful soldier trading car parts for money to throw in the pot. Why turn on him now?

Caesar's Garage loomed in the distance along with a lone man standing by the entrance. Clay parked next to Caesar's car and we climbed out. I rounded the hood and found Caesar gone and the door open.

Clay drew me behind him. "Careful," he said under his breath. "If it goes wrong, you get out of here, Em." He put the keys in my hand. "I'm serious."

"I'm supposed to leave you and end up short three boyfriends in one day?" I hugged his arm to my chest, holding him close as we stepped inside. "Nothing will go wrong."

The common picture of an auto shop was of men and women in greasy coveralls bent over an engine while the sun streamed in, and music played from an old radio. The silent, dank space we entered of long shadows and not a single soul in sight did not fit that description.

I glimpsed a wisp of his jacket disappear into the office. It seemed almost fitting that this would end where it started.

Not much had been done to lessen the sinister vibe of a supposedly innocent mechanic's office. Tarnished hooks stuck in the ceiling suspending the battered ghosts of Cassius and Clay. The darkness was oppressive in the windowless space and the single lamplight on Caesar's desk did little to fight back.

Caesar's only movement was his magnified eyes stalking my approach. He was too still sitting behind the desk in the very chair Rio tied me to.

"Hands on the desk," Clay ordered.

Caesar smirked. "I don't believe you're setting the rules here. Wait outside, Walker. I talk to her alone."

"No."

I put my hand on Clay's chest, holding him back. "It's okay. You'll be on the other side of the door."

"Ember," Clay hissed.

I gave him a hard look. "Royal and Cassius," I said simply.

Clay flicked from me to Caesar, jaw ticcing. He let me move him to the door and close it between us.

"Where's Royal?" I demanded on the click of the latch.

"Nolan is babysitting him while you and I chat. Don't worry. He's in good hands."

"You're enjoying this, aren't you?" I sat across from him, observing the grin that was his answer.

"Why shouldn't I? This has all been a long time coming. Rio will finally get what he deserves."

"He's not getting it through his son." I jabbed my finger on the desk. "I want Royal back by the end of our conversation. As soon as we're done, you get on the phone and order Nolan to hand him over."

The lamp cast odd shadows on his face. They stretched under his eyes like clown paint and were a slash to the side of his mouth. Our first meeting I assigned him role of stout, bespectacled mechanic who cowed in the face of Royal. I was wrong about a lot of people.

"That depends on what you have to say," Caesar replied. "You have the key to bringing Rio down, do you? Let's hear it."

"It's simple." I waved my hand. "You're the key."

He scowled. "Excuse me?"

My attention shifted to the ceiling... and the hooks. "I'm guessing this office has been used for less than illegal activities more than once and you were a witness to it. Not to mention your role in Rio's luxury car chop shop. How much do you know about Cavanaugh's, Endo's, and Noble's operations?"

"Why?"

"Just answer the question," I snapped.

Eyes narrowing, he studied me as if searching for a trap. I waited him out, though not patiently. Nolan was a psychopath with a gun and a mission. I wanted Royal away from him.

"I know quite a bit," Caesar finally said. "What does that have to do with anything?"

"It has everything to do with it. If you're trading your testimony for witness protection, you better have a lot to say."

Surprise cracked a chink in his intimidating mask. "Witness protection?"

"The Horsemen have been under federal investigation for a while. I have an inside with an agent named Underhill who is willing to put you and your family in the witness protection program. All you have to do is testify to everything you know about the leaders—about Rio."

Caesar barked a laugh. "That's it? You want me to testify? Are you joking?"

"Are you?" His response didn't shake me. "I'm betting you weren't counting on me being in the car with Royal when you grabbed him. You knew it was over when Clay's name popped on your caller ID, proving I noticed your limp. Are you imagining you're going to kill both of us and pick up your plan where you left off?" I tsked, tossing my head. "Think again."

He shot forward, beating the shadows back as he surged into the light. "I have Royal Cruz!"

"You have a ticking clock counting down the final *seconds* of your life. Even if you get through me and Clay, you won't get to my friend on the outside who will call and tell Rio everything in"—I checked my phone—"seventeen minutes unless I tell him you and I made the deal."

Caesar's hand shot above the desk. The gun leveled between my eyes. "Call him off now."

Calmly, I met his hard, glinting gaze over the barrel. "No."

He cocked the hammer. "You think I'm bluffing?"

"I think you're wasting my, and your, time. I call him off, turn up dead, and then he tells Rio the truth anyway. You're backed into a corner and I'm offering you a way out. *Put the gun down and take it.*"

"Hooking up with the feds is not my way out. I'm no snitch."

"No, you're a cowardly, sneaking, drug-dealing traitor who shoots innocent women and terrifies children. A much more impressive title than snitch," I mocked. "I'm sure your fellow Horsemen will appreciate your *loyalty* while they're taking stripes out of you."

The gun shook in his grip.

I tried another tactic. "Last time you mentioned having to get up with the baby. Do you have a boy or girl?"

Caesar's jaw ground in its socket. His desire to shoot me came through loud and clear, but the tiniest niggle of self-preservation held him back. I had to reach that voice of reason.

"A boy," he finally said.

"Is this what you want for him, Caesar? To grow up without a dad in a war-torn neighborhood wearing the mark of the grudges your fight will leave in its place? Or do you want to raise him in some cushy suburb living safe and happy while Rio rots in a prison cell? The answer is so incredibly obvious to me that I don't know why we're still having this conversation."

Battle raged on his face. Drawn in the severe lines of his brow and raging in his darting eyes. Sweat beaded his forehead, collecting in wetness that dripped onto his eyebrows. He swiped it away with his gun hand, and then settled it on his lap.

"You can't guarantee witness protection."

I schooled my face lest he read my triumph. *He's listening.*

"I can guarantee it," I said. "This is how they do things. Immunity in exchange for putting men ten times more dangerous away." I raised my phone. "I'll call Underhill right now if you want."

The gun appeared quick. "You're not calling anyone."

"Relax," I said, putting my hands up. "Your time is running out to make a decision. At least let me prove I can hold up my end."

He tracked me as I reached in my purse and pulled out Agent Underhill's card. I slid it across the desk. "He's legit, Caesar. You can watch me dial his number and listen while I tell him exactly what I'm telling you. When Royal's safe, you can negotiate the terms of your protection."

Caesar let it sit there, refusing to touch it like the card might combust. I glanced at the clock.

Twelve minutes.

"Let me call him, Caesar."

"Stop." He dropped his hand on the card, preventing me from picking it up. "It doesn't make sense. Why come to me with offers of protection? You could've called Rio and told him it was me. Or had your agent here to arrest me—testimony be damned." He chuckled. "Are you that afraid of what I'll do to Royal?"

I raised a brow. "I'm sitting here alone with no weapon and do I look like I'm sweating? You are, though. A lot. If one of us is afraid, it's not me."

Caesar snarled. "Careful, Bancroft. I can make a call too. Nolan's chomping at the bit to smash your boyfriend's head into a wall and leave him in the gutter as was done to his sister. Should I tell him to have his fun?"

"You should stop threatening me and use your head. Why do you think I called you and not Rio? If he gets his hands on you first, you're another body in a trash can and Rio gets to continue taking over Raven River with no one to stop him.

"I can't have him arrested or testify against him. *You* can, and I sure as fuck want you to."

"Why can't you?"

"Because my daughter won't be born in witness protection far from her fathers."

Shock split another crack in his mask.

"Let me make the call," I said.

Caesar didn't lift his hand. "So, that's it. If you truly want me to bring an end to Rio, let me continue. Help me." A manic glint lit his eyes. "You have money and access to the Estate. We can work togeth-er."

"You kinda got on my bad side when you crashed our car and took my boyfriend."

"I'll give him back," he replied instantly.

"Will you?"

He bobbed his head. "As soon as I put an end to Rio."

"Wrong answer."

"He's incentive for Rio to stay in line, but he'll be safe." The man had the gall to put his hand over his heart. "I promise I won't harm him."

Another look at the clock.

Eight minutes.

"Will you also promise not to harm anyone else?" I challenged. "You did a drive-by on my school. Shot an innocent reporter. And those bodies in the dumpster? I'm not having any part of your idea of revenge."

"That wasn't me!" he growled. "That was Nolan and I didn't fucking know he was going to do it."

"I'm supposed to believe that?"

"The guy has his own vendetta and always has. It's not like I'm doing this for Viviana Ives."

Seven minutes.

"Your reasons don't matter to me. You know why I'm here. Make the deal with Underhill and hand over Royal."

"Rio had this coming a long time." Caesar went on like I hadn't spoken. "We grew up together, you know. Me, Rio, and Luciano. We were best friends. The only ones looking out for each other in this shit town."

I clenched my teeth to pen in a scream. Royal was hurt and in Nolan's clutches, and this guy wanted to have story time?

"The Horsemen— I mean the *real* Horsemen. The boys that ran the westside before Rio took over and forced us to join with our enemies. They were the protection in this place," he said. "The gang was good to us. Gave us jobs. Respect. We could do whatever we wanted around here. Eventually, Luciano stepped up in his older brother's place to lead the gang and he put us at his side." He slammed his fist on the card. "He trusted us!"

I closed my eyes. "I can guess how this ends."

"Can you?" he flung. "Did you guess the part where Rio got that bitch pregnant and took off at the first sight of the kid? Did you guess that he went off and became that slick-ass bastard and returned thinking he was better than all of us? But Luciano didn't see any of that. The guy only knew loyalty and he welcomed Rio back. Let him have his place in the gang just like that."

"But Rio wasn't happy with second place," I finished.

Caesar grinned mirthlessly. "No, he was not. A couple of weeks after his grand return, Luciano and I drove up to Easthaven to pick up a shipment. The car went off the road at eighty miles per hour. Brake lines cut." Caesar's throat bobbed fighting to keep more than words down. "Luciano was thrown from the car. I had to crawl to him with a busted hip. He couldn't even speak, but I saw in his eyes that he knew.

"Ahh!" Bellowing, Caesar struck the desk with the butt of his gun. "He was my brother! Our brother! Rio pretended to be broken up. Cried at his fucking funeral and swore to catch the guy responsible. A week later he was running the Horsemen."

"I'm sorry." I truly was. "Rio is a ruthless monster. He destroys everything he touches. You can make him pay for it by tearing apart the empire he killed Luciano for. Testify, Caesar. Put them all away."

He didn't seem to have heard me. He stared at a fixed point above my head, tears drying on his cheeks. "It's taken me a long time to get here. Five years I waited and, finally, Luciano will have his justice. Maybe those men they found deserved to be thrown in the trash. Maybe they conspired in Luciano's murder. Cut his brakes, sent him on a fake shipment run, gave Rio an alibi, pushed for him to be next in line, and got rid of anyone who stood up against him."

Caesar stroked the gun barrel. "Maybe there are only three traitors left. Damien, Don, and Jay. Maybe this can't end until they're tossed in a fucking dumpster where they belong. Maybe the money I made dealing could buy my place as leader like money bought Rio's. And it's possible, Rio has to understand the pain he caused by losing the only person he cares about."

Dropping his eyes, he trapped me in his dead, cold gaze. "Just... maybe."

My heart banged on its rib cage like it wanted out of here as badly as I did. It wasn't the first time I looked into the eyes of a murderer, and with everything in me, I prayed it'd be the last. The shudders were a living thing beneath my skin, standing my hair on end, and contracting my muscles. Carefully, I kept the anxiety off of my face.

One minute.

Without breaking eye contact, I tapped the all clear to Hiro, stopping him from calling Rio.

Caesar watched me, expression unreadable, as I forced the card from under his grip and dialed, holding the phone between us so he could see. He let it ring.

"Hello?"

"Agent Underhill," I said clearly. "I'm here with a man named Caesar who's got a choice to make between giving his son a better life and letting Dante Gallo win."

Caesar frowned.

"Because that is what will happen if he doesn't end this here," I continued. "Dante, who cares about people only as far as they're useful to him—won't know his pain. The person who Caesar will be passing his grief on to is his son. An innocent child forced to grow up without his father like he's spent all of these years without the man he called brother."

"Ember, what is going on?" Underhill asked sharply. "Are you in danger?"

"I've explained to Caesar that there can be another ending to this story. You'll arrange witness protection in exchange for everything he knows about the leaders of the Horsemen and their operation."

He sputtered. "You can't make those kinds of promises!"

"A nice house in a safe neighborhood. Every night he'll tuck his son in bed and his little boy won't be awakened by gunshots and sirens. For all of this, he gets to dismantle what Dante truly cares about—the gang he stole from Luciano and the sweet life on the other side of the gate that he used the Horsemen to buy."

I bore into Caesar. "But all of that goes away if my boyfriend isn't standing in front of me in the next *ten fucking minutes*!"

Smiling, I sweetened my tone. "Agent Underhill, if you please, would you explain to him what will happen if he doesn't do what I say."

Underhill cursed. "I said I'd go along with this, but your word better be worth something, Ember."

Silently, I held the phone out to Caesar.

A million emotions warred in Caesar's soul and all reflected in his eyes.

Let someone in this miserable, God-forsaken war love his son enough to do the right thing.

And as the final battle named its victor, Caesar let go of the gun... and took the phone.

"Hello?"

Caesar listened to Underhill's scripted reply and jerked on the beep of the ended call. He looked from the phone to me, smirk gone.

He broke down, sobbing wretched, piercing wails that crumpled my heart into dust. Was Caesar a monster or did Rio Cruz make him one?

Viviana. Nolan. Asa. Caesar. Royal. Ember.

The first Horsemen infected us all.

"You're doing the right thing," I whispered. I don't know what moved me to rise and lean over the desk, resting a gentle hand on the back of his head. "And if you ever question that, look at your son."

His whole body shook with his sobs and still I swore he nodded.

"Tell me where Royal is, Caesar."

"M-my mother's house," he croaked. "It's been empty since she passed. 5387 Galway Street. But you have to get there fast. I told Nolan to stay cool but he laughed about having some fun with him."

I tore out of the office. Clay caught me as I ran out.

"Whoa, Em," he cried. "What happened?"

"5387 Galway Street. We have to get there now!"

Clay didn't waste time asking more questions. We raced to the car, throwing ourselves inside, and speeding away from the broken, crying traitor of the Horsemen.

Fear coursed in my heart and pumped through my veins with every wild, erratic beat. I strained against my seat belt as though I could propel through the window and reach Royal faster.

Clay rounded the final corner, sending a group of kids riding their bikes scattering out of the road. 5387 loomed at the end of the street. Clay careened over the sidewalk and parked the car on the lawn.

Tumbling out, we sprinted to the front door screaming Royal's name.

"Em, get back." Clay kicked the door in. It flew into a coat rack, toppling it in a shower of splinters. If Nolan didn't know we were here, he did now.

"Royal!" I leaped over the busted rack, running to an entrance. "Roy—" His name died on my lips. My abrupt halt knocked me off balance and I stumbled, falling to my knees.

I saw the blood first.

Tiny, perfectly round droplets sprinkled near my body. They led a trail to the growing pool crimson—reminiscent of footsteps seeking the shore.

The body lay still and peaceful at his feet. And him unmoving as he crouched above the prone figure—the bloody knife dangling from his fingers and painting the cheek of the seemingly sleeping boy.

"Holy shit," Clay breathed.

Royal didn't stir at his voice. His shadowed eyes did not leave Nolan.

Slowly, I crawled to him. "Baby," I whispered. "It's okay. I'm here."

I kneeled in front of Royal, blocking him from Nolan's body. Blood wept from his cut lip and his left eye had begun to swell. The injury from the accident left a large, swollen gash on his forehead. I made to hug him and stopped. There was a damp patch on his shirt. Lifting it revealed a deep graze bleeding freely.

"Clay, find me a towel or something."

Clay ducked into the next room. I cupped Royal's jaw, murmuring to him as I pecked his lips, promising everything would be okay.

Clay came back carrying a kitchen towel. He handed it to me and bent over Nolan's body.

"Is he dead?" I asked.

He checked his pulse. "Thready, but it's there. He's unconscious from loss of blood."

"Stop the bleeding as much as you can and then let's get him to the Horsemen Doc. Rio can meet us there to claim his prize. Tell him to bring Cassius."

"Gladly."

It took some time to bind the deep gash up Nolan's chest. I helped Clay as much as I could and left him to carry Nolan to the car. Gently, I coaxed Royal to his feet, keeping pressure on his wound. A glint drew my eye to the gun partially hidden beneath the couch. The scene that unfolded here flashed in my mind.

"Royal, please." He leaned on me as I walked us to the door. "Say something."

"I'm fine, Em. Let's get Cassius back."

I couldn't get any more out of him on the drive. Nolan sat in the front seat, propped up and moaning softly. I rested Royal's head on my lap, stroking his hair, and listening to Clay call the doctor and finally Rio.

"We found out who the traitor is and we've got Nolan. If you want him, you have to grab him from Doc's because the guy is bleeding out. He made the mistake of thinking a gun was enough to take on Royal alone. Yeah. Fine. The deal was we trade him for Cassius. Okay."

"What did he say?" I asked when he ended the call.

"They're on their way now—Cassius included."

I released the breath I'd been holding for a full week. "I can't believe this day started with a leisurely walk through the Estate." I dabbed the cut on Royal's lip. "How did we get here, Clay? Five years ago, a single man comes back to town and all of these lives shatter into a million pieces. How?"

"I wish I knew, Em."

I bent and kissed Royal's forehead. "At least it ends tonight."

The final leg of the drive was made in silence excluding Nolan's groans. The sounds were reassuring. I didn't want him dead and my boyfriend on the hook for it. There were also questions to be answered about the drive-by shootings. If Nolan truly did those things on his own, there had to be a reason.

"We have to cut off and destroy what helped them rise in the first place. The Outer Borough."

What if it has something to do with that? I thought.

I chewed over it until we arrived in front of a modest single-story house. A tall wooden fence reaching higher than my height wrapped around the property. It made sense that if they were carrying wounded and dead men in and out, privacy was key. A fact we appreciated as a lanky, red-haired man pointed us to the side alley and helped us carry Nolan through the fence under cover of trees.

"Help me bring him to the back room," Doc ordered Clay. "Royal, is that serious?"

"No," Royal spoke up. "The bullet just grazed me."

"I'll check it out anyway. As soon as I'm done with him."

Royal said nothing. He drifted into the living room. The firm hand on my arm brought me with him.

The room was minimalist bordering on bare. He had a single white couch, glass coffee table, a thin rug, and a mirror over the mantle where a television usually hung.

I sat next to Royal, burrowing into his uninjured side. "Are you okay?" I asked.

"Yes." Royal tangled his fingers in my hair and continued the path down to Bump. "I am now. I lost it, Em. Thinking they left you on the side of the road."

"They did," I said. "But we weren't hurt. You were. What happened with Nolan?"

"He—"

"Ember." I glanced up as Clay came into the living room holding a first aid kit. "I've got to help Doc stitch Ives up. Take care of Royal."

I accepted the kit, leaned Royal back, and lifted his shirt. Dried blood stuck the fabric to the skin and I peeled it away with an apology. "I'm listening," I said.

"I woke up in that house. Didn't know where you were. It was just me and Ives," Royal began. "The fucker was feeling proud, going on about seeing Rio's face when he found me in a dumpster. He said he'd been running around the OB right under everyone's noses and so much for the Horsemen."

My tender touch was at odds with the temper boiling my blood. All of the terrible things Nolan had done over the last few weeks and the guy was pleased with himself.

"Then he started wailing on me, thinking I was too out of it to fight back. I put my fist through his face and the laughing stopped. He tried to shoot me—"

"He did shoot you," I corrected. Royal was right about it being a graze but all the same that graze was made by a bullet.

"I pulled my knife on him and then you showed up."

"I want to get you to a real hospital," I said. "You may have a concussion."

"There's a doctor in the other room, Em. He'll check me out. Afterward, I'm taking you home. All of this shit isn't good for you."

I kissed his cheek. "Stop worrying about me when you're the one bleeding all over the place."

Royal patiently let me bandage his stomach and forehead. A quick trip into the kitchen and I came back with ice for his eye.

"I'm going to get you home," I said. "Fix you something to eat. Run you a hot bath. Screw the crap out of you. In whichever order you like."

He cracked a smile that must have hurt his lip. "I'm glad you realize you're not going to your uncle's tonight."

"I'll make up some—"

Knuckles pounded on the front door. Our flirty smiles evaporated. We knew who that was.

I shot off the couch.

"Em, wait," Royal called.

Throwing open the door, I clapped eyes on a stranger's broad chest. "Where's Cassius?"

"Em?"

I practically barreled through the man. Striding down the path with two new guards on his side was my slick-tongued, naughty devil. I launched myself at him. Our mouths were clashing furiously before we hit the dirt.

"Enough of that," a smooth voice reproached. "No sampling the goods before the trade."

Suddenly, hands grabbed me under the arms and lifted me free of Cassius. I was carried into the house and dropped on my feet next to Royal.

Royal stood and drew me behind him. A protective move his father more than proved was necessary.

The small minimalist space was dwarfed by Rio, his three new guards, and Cassius bringing up the rear. Under the florescent lights I saw captivity hadn't been kind to him. Dark circles stained under Cassius's eyes and red marks on his wrists proved restraints were used. Still it didn't appear they harmed him and, as he gazed at me, his smile warmed me through.

There'll be a line of guys I'll be screwing the crap out of tonight.

Rio stepped up to his son. A frown marred his otherwise perfect face. "How did this happen?"

"Nolan put up a fight," he said simply.

Humming, Rio cast a look over his shoulder. "He'll soon regret that and more. Where is he?"

"Doc is stitching him up."

"You can tell the doctor not to waste his time. Bring the boy out here."

I ducked into the kitchen, dialing Underhill as I went. There was another person Rio expected delivered.

"Ember," he greeted. "Can I just say my job has become much more interesting since meeting you."

I got straight to the point. "Did he turn himself in?"

"Caesar Ramirez has surrendered himself to the FBI. He's shared with me some of the testimony he'll give in exchange for witness protection and we've already got enough to bring the organization to its knees. And he's just begun. I will be the envy among men, and it appears I have you to thank."

"Remember that the next time I call asking for a blind favor."

Underhill laughed. "I think it's better there not be a next time. But while we're on the subject, is your boyfriend safe?"

"He is," I breathed. "He finally is. Thank you, Underhill. You have no idea what you've done for me and Bump."

"Bump?"

"Goodbye."

The men were facing off in the living room. Cassius had found his way to the other side, standing by Royal.

"—give up who he's been working with?" Rio asked.

"He did." The reply came from me. I strode in front of Rio, resisting Royal's tug on my hand. "It was Caesar Ramirez."

The corner of his eyes twitched. "Caesar? No, that's impossible."

"Why? Because you were childhood friends?" I lifted my shoulders. "The confession came from his own lips. Turns out the friendship soured the day you murdered Luciano."

A muscle ticced in his jaw. What shock didn't break, anger was revealing.

"I did no such thing."

I put my hands up. "Hey, you don't have to convince me. It's not about what I believed but about what Caesar believed. And he's held you responsible for the last five years. He dealt drugs to build capital and cast suspicion on Royal in the process.

"Then he struck out against the men who had helped commit the murder and supported you taking over in his place. They were the bodies that have been popping up in dumpsters all over the OB. The next steps in his plan were to kill Damien, Jay, and Don. Murder your son and rise to leader in your place."

Nostrils flaring, Rio glowered into my steady gaze like he desperately wanted to kill the messenger. "I see," he gritted. "It seems I need to have a talk with my old friend. Devon," he barked. "Bring Ives. We're leaving."

I let Rio get as far as the threshold and said, "If you're running off to confront Caesar, you should know he's gone."

Rio paused. "Gone?"

"He turned himself in to the FBI a short while ago. They're arranging the terms of his immunity in exchange for everything he has on you."

Whipping around, Rio cried, "Excuse me?"

"Ember." Royal grasped me again, pulling me back.

I wriggled out of his hold. I'd been waiting for this moment for too long. I'd face Rio as his world came crashing down around him. "It's all coming out, Rio. I bet the warrants are being written up right now."

Rio advanced on me, a snarl ripping apart his handsome face, and Royal gripped me around the waist. All of a sudden, Rio pulled up and his expression cleared.

"I see what you're doing," said Rio. "This is a trick. You think you can scare me. Fool me into running from phantoms so you can get your wish. Living free of me with my son."

"You are a smart man, Rio, and that would be a good plan, but this is no trick. Caesar is going to testify against you and the leaders. It's all going away. The Horsemen are over."

"No!" He turned on one of his men. "Call Caesar! Now!"

The guy fumbled to do as he said.

I pushed on Royal's arm, trying to get free. He responded by holding me tighter and moving us both back a few inches for good measure.

The guy called once. Twice. Four times.

"Sorry, boss," he said. "He's not picking up."

"Send someone to the garage and his house," Rio barked.

I clicked my tongue as the door slammed behind him. "Should we all sit and sip tea while we wait for him to confirm what I've already told you?"

"With pleasure," Rio growled.

He wasn't kidding. Royal, Cassius, and I stood across from Rio for a whole thirty minutes until his phone rang.

"Where is he?" Rio asked by way of greeting. "What? No. Don't do anything! You did this!" he bellowed, snapping to me. "The police are camped out on Caesar's lawn. He'd never betray the Horsemen. Caesar would rather die than be labeled a snitch. You found him. Said something to him. Did something."

"What I *did* was convince Caesar not to kill your son and gave you a heads-up on a federal indictment. You'd think you'd be thanking me and booking it out of town instead of wasting time yelling at me."

Roaring, Rio flipped the glass table over, shattering it into uncountable shards that struck my leg. "I'm not going anywhere!"

"Think about this, Rio," I said evenly. "You didn't get this far by being impulsive. You know Caesar. Ask yourself if he truly blamed you for Luciano's death, how far would he go? What would he be willing to do? And then ask yourself, how much does he know about your operation and how many years are you looking at if he spills it all? Now tell me if this town is so worth it that ruling it for the next day or so is better than the chance of getting away."

Rio stomped on broken glass to get as close to me as Royal allowed him. "You haven't beaten me, girl. This is my town. It runs on my say-so and stops at my word. Whatever victory you believe you've won will be short-lived. Witnesses rarely make it to trial."

"This isn't my victory," I replied. I broke out of Royal's arm and squared before him. "I set the dominoes and then I washed my hands of you. I couldn't be the one to give your name, have you arrested, or testify against you. I couldn't do it but someone else could and someone else did. And so my conscience is clear, I'm warning you now and giving you the opportunity to get away. If you stay and get caught, don't sit in your cell cursing me. You had your chance."

Rio's fists shook and undoubtedly I knew he desired to kill the messenger. He dropped his gaze, boring a hole in my stomach that made me cover her protectively.

"Pack up the house," Rio ordered. "Tell Endo, Noble, and Cavanaugh to do the same." He spun on his heels, striding to the door. "I'm taking the car. Meet me in Easthaven tonight."

"Yes, boss." The men rushed out ahead of him. "We'll get it done."

Inexplicably, Rio stopped. He turned on his son. "Royal, let's go!"

What? No! I gripped Royal's arm as if I had the physical strength to make him stay.

Royal put his hand over mine. "Dad, I'm not going with you."

Rio charged at Royal. I cried out, reaching to stop what he planned to do, and Royal held me back.

Rio clamped his son's neck. I watched in terror and then confusion as he crushed their foreheads together. Breaths rapid, time running out, he peered into the eyes that were his own and no words passed between them. Just as suddenly, Rio let him go and disappeared out of the door.

"Goodbye, Dad."

Chapter Twelve

"Nolan's going to be fine—the shit-shitting bastard."

Clay, Royal, Cassius, and I left out of the back gate and headed to Clay's car. The sun was beginning to set on the most harrowing day of our lives.

"Doc stitched him up and loaded him with painkillers," Clay continued. "Now that we're not serving him to Rio, Doc will dump him on the hospital. The police will show up quick to handcuff him to the bed."

I rested my head on Cassius's shoulder. "I'm so happy this is over. I missed you like crazy." I peered up at him. "You and I have a lot to talk about."

"Good stuff?"

"I hope so."

"Hungry, Cas?" Clay asked. "Up for Chino's burgers?"

"You know I am."

Clay opened the door for me and Cassius to climb in the back seat. He and Royal took the front.

My raven-haired love hadn't said much since his final goodbye to his father. I couldn't guess what he was feeling but I'd be here for him when he was ready to talk.

Cassius scooted over and pressed me into the door, molding to me as he kissed my forehead, cheek, lips, and every part of me.

I moaned. Cassius Walker was my weakness. His lips on me were what I wanted before, after, and on Christmas.

"Was it awful, baby?" I asked. "Did they hurt you?"

"I put up a fight when Damien and Jay grabbed me. That got ugly. But other than that, they didn't hurt me."

His mouth found my neck. Cassius licked the sensitive flesh, cascading shivers down my spine.

"Royal shot them if that makes you feel better," Clay piped up.

"It does."

"Where were they holding you?" I asked.

Cassius slipped his hand under my shirt and his seeking fingers skimmed the band of my jeans. His kisses became more insistent, finding my mouth and inviting our tongues to dance.

"In a safe house—" Kiss. "—in the southside." Kiss. "Kept me locked in a bedroom—" Kiss. "—and only opened the door to slide me food."

"Oh, I'm so sorry, Cas. I should have gotten you out sooner."

"You did everything you could, Em. We're together now." Cassius slipped his hand beneath my waistband. "That's what matters."

"Cas— Oh," I breathed.

Cassius teased my sex, rolling the nub between his calloused fingers. My nipples hardened to points. The wanton trollops jumped to attention, sensing what was coming next and more than willing to play.

Not in the back of a car with the sun out! Down, girls!

He kissed me again and I tore my lips away with difficulty. "We're almost to Royal's place, Cas. I promise we'll make up for all the sex we missed."

"I can't wait." Cassius popped my seat belt. The next thing I knew I was on my back, blinking up at him.

He covered me with his body. A warm, familiar weight that brought me home. Cassius ground his stiff cock between my middle, washing those fuzzy feelings under a torrent of desire.

"That's cheating."

Cassius chuckled. "I haven't begun to play dirty." He unbuttoned my jeans and tugged them over and off my ankles. He pushed the fabric of my underwear aside and descended like a starving man who'd found his oasis. Cassius swirled his tongue between my folds, yanking a cry out of me that would encourage him when I should hit the pause button until we got to Royal's.

Tell him to slow down, if you can.

I opened my mouth...

...and begged for more.

"Yes, don't stop," I breathed.

Cassius bobbed his head, tongue dipping in and out of my hungry pussy the way he knew drove me insane. This was definitely playing dirty.

Without stopping, he pushed my shirt and bra over my breasts, bunching them up under my chin.

Forget about stopping him. That'd be up there with the worst ideas I ever had.

Cassius pulled my panties off in one fell swoop and spread me bare. I scrabbled at his belt, eagerness striking me clumsy. Finally, his length sprung free. I bit my lip as I palmed him, guiding him where he was supposed to be.

He pushed in with one hard thrust, hitting that spot on the first try like a heat-seeking missile. A week without, I didn't expect him to be shy about it.

Cassius started pumping and my eyes rolled up in my head. He set a punishing pace, feet braced on the door and leveraging him to go deeper, faster, harder. Cassius slid up and down my body, his face buried in my chest and rough, primal groans sounding in time to the wet smacking of our skin on skin.

My toes dug in the side of Royal's seat, rocking him as Cassius pounded the mess out of me. My fevered cries covered the traffic noise. Our body heat fogged the windows. Cassius and I were in our own space of time. Nothing existed but us.

Arching my back, I clenched around him. "Cassius. Same time." Simple sentences were all I could manage.

"Now," he grunted.

I came so hard I cracked my back in half. I shuddered on the seat, nails tearing the leather as Cassius emptied himself inside of me. He collapsed on my chest—both of us spent.

"Mmm," I hummed. "Wow, did I miss you."

Cassius gripped my breasts. "I missed you both too. I swear I'll never leave you again."

Giggling, I whapped his backside with my foot. "Want to direct some of that love to the woman attached?"

"I love you, Em."

"Love you too."

We kissed—playful and unhurried.

"Em," Clay spoke up. "Wasn't there something you had to tell him?"

I broke away. "Oh yeah. Cassius, you should know that... um..." The kisses he was peppering on my collarbone were quite distracting.

"Yeah?"

"I'm pregnant."

He froze, lips puckered. "Wait, what?!"

THE NEXT DAY, ROYAL drove me to the Estate in Hiro's car.

The sky was overcast. Promising the gift of rain to wash away our sins and cast fresh sunlight on a new town free of the Horsemen and their tyranny.

It was a long night with my boys. Hiro drove back from East-haven and the five of us spoke about the baby, Nolan, Caesar, my parents, and what it meant that the leaders of the Horsemen cleared out of town.

Cassius got over his initial shock and took the news of Bump in his usual stride. He boasted that he had been hitting me harder and longer than the other guys, so he had to be the father. By the end of the night, he had named my bump Cassidy.

I let him have his fun. I was happy to argue names and referee who medaled at "Ember's Pussy Olympics" as my triplet had taken to calling it. If these were the biggest worries in our years of living, loving, and raising a baby together, then I'd take it. Out from under the thumb of the Horsemen and the stolen money, we could have any life we want—and they all wanted a life with me.

I cast a look to my left as we neared the gates. Uncle Harrison hadn't been pleased with my taking off without a word. But I wasn't pleased with his denying me guardianship of Eli, so there was plenty of that to go around. I made the dubious choice to throw that reply at him and he ordered me home first thing the next morning.

"Royal," I said. "We didn't get a chance to talk in private last night. How are you doing with your father gone?"

He didn't answer right away. We handed our information to the guard and passed into the pristine community.

"It's strange," he began. "I should hate him. I should wish every day that I pulled the trigger in that cabin after the things he's done to me. But Rio was the one who came back for me, Ember. Sarah dumped me and didn't look back. Rio returned to Raven River to fuck up my life... but I keep thinking at least he wanted to be in it. How screwed up is that?"

I rubbed his forearm. "It's not, Royal. Actually, I think it's painfully normal. Some days my parents would look at me like they wished I'd walk out the door and they'd never see me again. Still, I'm doing everything I can to bring them home."

Taking my hand, Royal kissed my fingertips. "We'll be better parents, won't we?"

"Of course we will. You're already a better father."

We let our conversation hang in the air for a moment—finding our peace.

"I got a text from Doc while you were in the shower this morning," Royal said. "He moved Nolan to the hospital. That information is going to go wide if it hasn't already."

"I wish I understood what his plan was. Caesar killed and dumped the men, but Nolan returned and shot the reporter. He rolled up on the school firing his gun. How was any of that getting him revenge for Viviana?"

"He was counting on delivering his revenge through me—which he tried to do yesterday. The drive-bys. Those were for another reason, and like you said, I don't know what."

"Nolan shouted about the Horsemen as he drove past," I mused. "And his father mentioned cutting the gang from their source. Maybe he did it to turn the OB against them."

"It would've taken a lot more than a reporter who recovered and ruining a school day to get a bunch of townspeople used to keeping their heads down, to suddenly rise up against a heavily armed criminal network."

I blew out a breath. "You're right. The police can get the truth out of him. I have to focus on Mom and Dad."

"I'm narrowing down the guys who could've bribed the officials. Asa Ives is on the list. So is Leo's father. Plenty of dark-haired, middle-aged guys around here."

"If we can find him, we won't have to decipher the message. A good thing because I can't remember where we were that Thanksgiving."

"We'll find them, Ember." Royal rolled to a stop in front of the mansion. "We've got school tomorrow. Take it easy today. Rest. The boys and I will take over."

I leaned across and snagged a kiss. "Thank you. I don't want to be fussed over but I admit Bump and I could use a long, semi-comatose nap."

"Take it. I'll call you later."

I said bye and hopped out of the car. The gloomy Sunday morning brought the gardener to the property. He knelt in the flower garden near the front steps, humming to himself as he transferred a bundle of forget-me-nots to their new home.

"Hi, Mr. Babin."

"Good morning, Miss Bancroft." He tilted his head back. "Looks like it's going to come down today. Better pack that umbrella."

"Is now a good time to plant these? You should come back later."

"Oh, I'm not afraid of a little rain. Neither are these guys." He beamed at the plants like they were old friends. "People think because flowers are small and pretty, that they're delicate. But as rain beats and pours on them, these flowers open their petals and embrace it. There's a lot we can learn from that."

"Hmm. Embrace the rain. I like that." I waved, continuing up the stairs. "Have a good day, Mr. Babin."

"You too, Miss Bancroft."

I let myself into the house and made it five steps up the stairs.

"Ember? Ember, is that you?" My aunt emerged from the living room. "I was just about to call you. Quickly, go upstairs and change into that yellow sundress we bought at Maxfield's. Ruth Slater invited us all out to brunch."

Ruth Slater. One of Aunt Violet's society friends.

"I'm pooped, Auntie V. Mind if I skip brunch?"

"I told you to stop calling me Auntie V," she said. "You can't skip brunch, Ember. She invited us to thank you. She received confirmation from her lawyer that her investment in the lodge will be reimbursed by the end of the week. She feels guilty for the less-than-cordial way she approached you last year."

That's a pleasant way of putting it.

"She wants to apologize and you should be gracious enough to let her."

I bit back a sigh. *This is the part where she pretends its about me when it's really about her. The Bancrofts are loved around here again and she's gotta soak that up.*

"Can't pretend I'm not hungry," I gave in. "Brunch sounds good, but don't get on me if I fall asleep on my croissant."

"Ember." She stopped me as I made to head up. "I spoke to your uncle and he's adamant about retaining guardianship of Eli. Pushing him right now will make him dig his heels in. Give him time."

My grip tightened on the banister. "All right. Just know that I'm not leaving this town without him."

Violet let me go up to change. I stopped at Eli's room. He was sitting on the chaise, messing around on his tablet, and dressed in his coat and dress pants. The grimace he shot me spoke volumes.

"Stop leaving me alone with these people."

I laughed out loud. *"Did Aunt Violet wrangle you into that suit?"*

"She practically barricaded the closet, so I couldn't pick out anything else."

"You look very dapper if that helps."

"It doesn't," he sulked. *"Do we have to go to brunch?"*

"Yes." I shrugged. *"But I might make it interesting. Drop the news I'm pregnant and see how that goes."*

Eli's eyes bugged. *"Uncle would blow through the roof. I definitely want to see that, but* after *he gives you guardianship of me. Don't need him saying you getting pregnant means you're not responsible enough to take care of me."*

"My little brother. The voice of reason."

I skipped over, humming on happiness, and pecked his cheek. Rio was on his way to Nowhere, Colorado. Nolan was chained to a hospital bed. Cassius was safe and sound. Life was pretty close to perfect.

"Any luck figuring out where we had Thanksgiving fourteen years ago?"

Pretty close.

"I have this faint picture in my mind," I said. *"It's not enough to point to a place, and part of me wonders if its more a wish than a memory."*

"What is it?"

"I see myself chasing after Rory. I've been letting her in more now." I glanced out of the window, seeing the flower gardens and how they opened up to the rain. *"Thinking about her doesn't hurt the way it used to. Maybe this is healing."*

"It is," said Eli.

He hugged me. For a while, we just sat there, remembering times both painful and wonderful.

Eventually, I forced myself to change. The yellow sundress tied under the chest and flared at the skirt. It was a cute style and cut. My issue was the garishly bright color that Violet had never seen me in, so why she thought I'd don yellow for her society friends threw me. Instead, I picked out a long, vintage halter dress. The black matched perfectly with a pair of black teardrop earrings I'd been dying to wear.

My finishing touches were a large white belt, flats, and a white hair clip securing my blonde tresses into a tight ponytail.

"I look good if I do say so myself."

A knock sounded at the door.

"Come in."

"Ember, are you read— What are you wearing?"

I glanced down. "One of the Maxfield dresses."

"I told you to wear the yellow one." Her mouth pursed in a thin line. "And you can't wear that belt with those shoes."

She had it off of me before I blinked. Tossing it over her shoulder, she gripped my hips and twisted me to face her. "You're gaining weight," she murmured. "You need a slim black belt with a silver buckle. Black shoes and a red bag," she stated. "What have I told you about pulling your hair back?"

Violet fiddled with my clip, freeing my strands. "You need your hair to cover your ears. They stick out like two car doors. Not to mention ponytails make your head look bigger." Violet shooed me toward the closet. "Now, hurry and change. We leave in ten minutes. Oh, and put some makeup on."

Sighing, I shuffled to the closet. *Apparently I am the only one saying I look good.*

"Makes your head look big."

I froze, smile fading. Violet muted in the background, and then she was gone.

"Girls? Girls, be careful."

Mom's caution didn't slow us down.

Amber and orange leaves crunched beneath our tiny feet. Birds chirped overhead, concealed in their trees and daring us to find them in their expert game of hide-and-seek. In the distance the river called to us, singing her song of wet summer days and leaps off the dock. There'd be none of that today. Mommy said it was too cold to swim.

Rory darted behind a tree trunk. It would have been a good hiding place if her giggling didn't give her away.

I jumped out in front of her, smacking her shoulder. "Gotcha! You're it!"

Twisting on my heels, I sped off running into two strong arms. Daddy swept me off my feet, settling me against his chest.

"You can play later, munchkins. Right now, Daddy needs your help bringing the food inside. Can you two be really, really big girls and carry the bowls in all by yourself?"

"I can do it, Daddy!"

"I'm a big girl!"

Chuckling, Dad put me on my feet and held our hands to the car. Carefully he placed a bowl of green beans on my outstretched hands. Rory took the mashed potatoes like this was her mission in life and her number had finally been called.

Together we followed Mom up the short steps to a pretty purple door. She held the door open for us with one hand and held little Eli with the other.

We stepped inside and the smell of roasted turkey wafted into our nose. Almost instantly Aunt Violet was there to meet us. She took the food off our hands, transferring it to the dining table, and then knelt in front of me.

"Pigtails aren't for you, Ember." She tugged my hair loose of their scrunchies. "They make your head look big."

"Ember? Ember!"

I jerked, snapping fourteen years into the future.

"Why are you just standing there?" Violet asked. "We're going to be late. Hurry up and get changed."

"Okay, Aunt Violet."

I dropped to my knees as the door shut.

"I know where you are," I whispered. "I found you."

The knowledge burrowed deep, expanding into the corners of my mind like the looming purple entrance. My parents were behind that door... and they needed help.

Leaping up, I bolted outside. My heart pounded in my throat, deafening in my ears, and spurring me faster.

How could it have taken me so long? The purple door. That perfect holiday with Rory, Eli, Mom, and Dad. All this time the memory was at the tip of my grasp.

"Uncle Harrison!" I cried. I descended the staircase two steps at a time. "Uncle Harrison?"

The front entrance stood open. I ran past and doubled back, spotting him heading for the car.

"Uncle Harrison."

He paused—hand outstretched to grab the door Monroe held open for him.

"What is it, Ember?"

"I need to talk to you."

My uncle scowled. "If this is about Eli's guardianship, I've warned you the matter is closed."

I flapped my hands, waving that away agitatedly. "This isn't about that. Uncle, do you remember Thanksgiving fourteen years ago? All of us celebrated together. I'm guessing because you and Dad were still trying to pretend you liked each other for Grandpa's sake."

Harrison pinched the bridge of his nose. "Goodness, Ember. The things you say out loud."

"It was a cabin with a purple door," I pushed on. "Do you remember it?"

"What does this have to do with—"

"Just tell me," I half-screamed.

Sighing, Harrison tossed his head like I was his karma for a misspent youth. "Yes, as a matter of fact, I do. Your father and I visited that very cabin last year. We were discussing the décor for the lodge suites and he mentioned modeling them after that old cabin. I didn't remember what it looked like, so we visited the property."

Hope expanded my chest. The cabin was real. The memory was real.

Mom. Dad. I'm coming.

"Where is it, Uncle? What's the address?"

"Why, Ember? What does it matter?"

I cast about for an excuse. "I spent my last Thanksgiving with Rory at that cabin. I've been wanting to go back. See the porch where we played. The room we slept in. Take a few pictures that will last longer than my memory. Just feel connected to her again."

"Ah." An uncomfortable look crossed his face, and he shifted slightly to conceal it. "Ember, I don't believe that's a good idea. It's better not to dwell. Leave the past in the past."

"You can leave behind the past," I said. "But not your family. This isn't about feeling bad or dredging up painful memories. Just the opposite. If I'm leaving Raven River, I want to take a piece of Rory with me."

Harrison stared hard at me. I kept my expression neutral though inside I was bursting to demand the location.

"All right," he gave in. "I don't remember where exactly it is. Somewhere off the Chesil trail."

"Thank you, Uncle. I—"

"Ember!" Violet stomped between us. "I told you to change."

"Oh, uh." I backed up the stairs. "I'm not going to brunch after all. I'm not feeling well—"

"What? No. Absolutely not." She rounded on her husband. "She is perfectly fine, Harry. She's making it up to get out of going and I won't have it."

"Ember, get in the car," Harrison commanded.

"But—"

"No buts. In the car. Now."

Fists balling, I seriously considered making a break for it. I didn't have time to sip tea and nibble on sandwiches. I had to get to Mom and Dad.

I can't make a break on foot, my voice of reason reminded. *I have to wait for one of the boys to pick me up. Sitting here or at the restaurant isn't much different.*

"Now," Harrison repeated.

Stiffly, I got in the car. Violet went into the house to get Eli and soon we set off for the Willow Raven Day Spa. My aunt spent most of her time there and why wouldn't she? It had everything you could ever want in one place. A pool, tennis courts, sauna, a café, and well-toned people ready to rub out all your kinks and worries.

The lobby was a pristine, relaxing paradise. Potted palm trees swayed with the air-conditioning. An indoor waterfall was a serene backdrop for patrons reclining on the lounges in their white robes. We bypassed them for the open entrance to the Willow Café.

My aunt stepped up to the maître d' and I claimed the chance to hang back. I dialed Clay first.

"Hello?"

"Clay, are you busy?" I asked. "I need a ride."

"My mom ran off this morning, Em," he said. "We're about to get in the car and look for her. But if it's important, I'll pick you up and help them search afterward."

"No," I said automatically. I couldn't ask Clay to pick my family over his. "No, find Virginia, bring her home, and tell her I found a great shampoo that helps with the dry hair."

"I will."

We said bye and I ended the call. I scrolled down to Hiro's name.

"Ember, where did you go?" Violet stuck her head around a palm tree and spotted me. "What are you doing? Come inside."

I followed her, dial tone chiming in my ear.

"Put that away, please," she said under her breath.

I did because Hiro didn't answer. "Call me as soon as you get this," I told his voicemail. "It's extremely important."

My aunt and I weaved through the intimate, linen-covered tables for a booth in the back. My uncle and Eli on one side while Ruth Slater and a man I assumed was her husband sat on the other. Violet and I broke apart. She sat next to Ruth and I claimed the space by Eli.

A waiter materialized promptly. He silently filled our glasses with lemon water and left as quickly as he came.

"Ember, thank you so much for joining us." Ruth extended her hand and shook mine warmly. "This is my husband, Edgar."

Edgar was a short man with thinning hair on top and ruddy cheeks. Still, his handshake was just as warm and his smile genuine. "We're glad we could have you here, Ember. When that check arrived in the mail and we realized you'd been looking for the money the entire time, we felt like such heels. Now that our lawyers have assured us this terrible business is over, we wanted to thank you in person."

"You're welcome, Mr. and Mrs. Slater," I said. "I wish none of this ever happened, but maybe now that the money's been returned, people can get back on their feet and the town can be like it was."

"It's hard to remember what Raven River used to be," Ruth said. "These days I barely recognize my home."

Under the table I typed a message to Hiro.

Me: I know where my parents are. Cabin off Chesil trail. I need to get there now. Please come.

I stared at my phone, willing it to ring, as brunch carried on around me.

"I spoke to Wren on the way here," Ruth continued. "She says Nolan Ives was found in the Outer Borough."

Violet gasped. "Really?"

"We hadn't heard," said Harrison.

She nodded. "He's in the hospital and his parents are arranging to transfer him here. Apparently, he was found half-dead and bleeding from a stab wound. A local doctor found him, patched him up, and delivered him to the hospital."

That's pretty much the true story.

"Oh my goodness," Violet breathed. "How terrible."

"Stabbed," Edgar said. "The boy was no saint but he should have been brought in by the police, not attacked and left for dead."

He did the attacking.

"It's further proof that the Outer Borough has gotten out of control. Drive-by shootings. The academy on lockdown and the Estate all but closed as well. The upcoming town meeting is a good call. It's past time we discussed what we're going to do about this, or our town will truly be lost."

My phone rang.

"Excuse me," I said, shooting up. "I have to take this."

"Em—"

I walked off on whatever my aunt was going to say. The ladies' room was straight ahead of me. I rushed inside and hit *answer*.

"Ember, I just got your text. Where are you?"

"I'm in the Estate. Can you come and get me? I'll meet you outside of the gates."

"I'm on my way now, but I don't understand. How'd you figure it out?"

"The memory just shook loose," I replied. "I asked my uncle and he said it's a rental cabin in the forest."

"Have you called the cops?"

"No. I can't."

"Why not?"

I peeked under the stalls, ensuring I was alone. "My parents are still fugitives, Hiro. If the cops get to them first, our big reunion will be separated by glass. Also, what if the police barrel through the forest with their guns, loudspeakers, and sirens, and the person holding them panics? I have to go—see if they are really there—and once we know what we're dealing with, I'll call the police."

"Okay," he said. "I'm almost to the gate."

"It's not that far a walk from here. I'll be there in twenty minutes."

"Ember."

I paused reaching for the door handle. "Yes?"

"After this, there's something we need to talk about."

"A good something?"

"I hope so."

Hiro hung up, leaving behind that cryptic parting. I put it aside to deal with later like he said. My first priority was getting out of this brunch.

The table stopped their conversation at the sight of me. "There you are, Ember," Violet said. "The waiter just left. I ordered you an avocado caprese salad."

I didn't sit down. "Thank you, Aunt Violet, but I have to go. I'm really not feeling well."

Her smile tightened around the edges. "Nonsense. There's no reason to leave. Sit down and sip some water, you'll feel better soon."

"I can't."

"Ember," Harrison chimed in. "Sit down. We'll get you home in a bit."

My temper flared. "Uncle, I'm nauseous and achy. I'd hate to ruin this nice brunch by spewing on it."

Ruth Slater unconsciously inched back. "If you're ill, we can do this another time—"

"She's not ill," Violet cut in. "Ember likes her jokes but now is not the time for them." She pointed to the chair. "Sit."

That's enough of this.

"I'm not joking," I said. "I'm pregnant and morning sickness is kicking my ass."

Ruth choked on her water. Harrison and Violet gaped at me slack-jawed and eyes huge.

"I need some fresh air, so I'm heading out." I bowed to the Slaters. "Thank you for inviting me. I'm truly happy you'll see your money soon."

I kissed Eli's forehead and turned my back on them.

"Ember?" My uncle found his voice as I reached the host stand. "Ember, come back. Come back here!"

I picked up the pace, running through the lobby and escaping outside. Black, angry clouds moved in during my short jaunt in the spa. Fat water droplets struck my cheek. The beginnings of what promised to be a downpour.

I jogged all the way to the gates and waved to my usual guards on the way out. Hiro's car idled twenty feet away, half parked on the grass. I threw a breathless hello as I slid inside.

"Do you know the way?" I asked.

"We'll be turning on to the trail in about twenty-five minutes," he replied. Hiro threw the car in gear and peeled out. "Did you get any more directions? How far down do we go? Is the cabin on the left or right?"

I shook my head. "All my uncle remembers is it's by the trail. We'll find it, Hiro. We have to."

"And when we do, I'll check the place out while you wait in the car."

"Why does everyone try to keep me in the car?"

"Because you're pregnant," he said bluntly. "Next question."

I gave him a look that he obviously didn't see because he was driving. "I'm not trying to be reckless, Hiro. That bubble you guys are constructing me—where I'll be housed, protected, and pampered until Bump Cassidy Tiara is born—is exactly where I want to be. After the last few months, I've earned it.

"But I've just learned my parents were blackmailed, threatened, and forced to hide from an unknown man who may have his hands on them right now. Whoever this guy is, he's wealthy and ruthless, and I'm not letting you run in to save my parents alone. We'll be smart," I said, brushing back his hair. "If the place is surrounded by armed guards, we call the police. If it's empty, we'll search and see if my parents left behind some clue."

"I have to get better at saying no to you," he mumbled under his breath.

"No, you don't," I teased.

The rain beat insistently on the windshield. The skies promised a storm and it would deliver.

"Also, Bump Cassidy Tiara? How is it possible the names are getting worse?"

I smiled. Hiro was distracting me from thinking about what we might find in that cabin and I loved him for it. "Do you want to kick in some names?"

"I like Kimi."

The piece of my heart that beat only for Hiro thumped twice. Kimi after his mother.

My fingers skated from his hairline to his jaw, indulging in the warmth of him. "I like Kimi too."

"Kimi Cassidy Bump Tiara," he announced. "She won't get beaten up at all."

I giggled. "Thank you."

Hiro didn't have to ask for what.

As we drove further from town, I tried to hang on to that smile. That laugh. I thought of names for my daughter and then names for my son. I remembered us together in Royal's apartment, safe and happy for the first time in some of our lives. I thought of everyone I loved until they grew smaller.

Smaller.

Smaller in my mind.

Then what I thought about was him.

Dark-haired, middle-aged, and potentially half the men in the Estate. Even Edgar Slater fit the description.

Who was this man? Why did he do what he did? If he's a Ravener, he's not hurting for money, so what drove him to dig up my father's past, stalk me and my brother, and demand they hand over everything?

Hiro arrived at the meeting of asphalt and muddy dirt. He veered left, setting course on the Chesil trail.

What are we walking into? My parents asked me to send help to this house. Were they being kept there against their will? Have they been for the last several months?

My mind offered no answer and I could only believe the cabin would.

"How did they end up here?" Hiro asked. "The same cabin your family rented fourteen years ago. That's not a coincidence."

"No." I scanned the trees, searching for a flash of purple. "It's not."

The Chesil trail stretched nearly five miles through the forest, winding and snaking past trees, dens, and the occasional home of a townsperson who wished to take the "town" out of the equation.

Three miles in, we stopped seeing the occasional house. Hiro and I squinted through the pouring rain at our surroundings. The forest grew thicker, throwing more trees in our way.

"Em," Hiro spoke up. "Is that it?"

I launched over him, straining against the seat belt.

Just off the trail was a slight decline leading to a driveway. There was a cabin. And that cabin had a bright purple door.

"I don't see anything," Hiro said. "No car. No overflowing trash. No sign of people."

"We have to look around."

"I'll drive further down and park. If someone comes, they won't notice the car." He pointed over his shoulder. "There's an umbrella under my seat. You take it."

Hiro drove off the road and killed the engine on a dirt patch shielded by a copse of trees. I rounded the hood for his side of the car. Together we pushed through the storm. Wind and rain whipped at us, soaking our bottoms in seconds and sticking wet leaves to our heels. Hiro drew me closer as the cabin again came into view.

"The curtains are drawn." He raised his voice over the rain.

"We'll check all the windows. There might be a sliver that we can see through. Split up," I said,

"No."

"Hiro, come on."

"We're not splitting up." He held me tighter. "You have the umbrella."

I let it go. Truth was I wasn't anxious to wander the property without him.

The covered front porch provided shelter as I searched through the living room. I made out nothing but darkness. Around the side of the house, raindrops bent and magnified my vision. I carefully rubbed them away and met with more darkness.

We continued on to the back, and my memories followed me. Faintly on the edge of my mind, they coaxed me with hushed giggles and a face so much like my own.

Hiro and I rounded the corner for the backyard. It revealed a trash can but if we hoped to use its contents to prove people were staying here, we were out of luck. The garbage was empty. Same for if a car had been parked there. The rain gleefully washed tire tracks away.

"We can't tell if anyone's in there," Hiro announced.

"We'll have to break in."

"Yeah."

I looked up at him. "You're taking that much easier than I thought."

"We can't leave until we know for sure," he said.

Hiro led me up the back porch. I dropped the umbrella next to an old wicker chair.

"I don't pick locks like Cassius, so this won't be as neat."

"Wha—"

Hiro lined up with the glass pane and shoved his elbow through it. I flinched, hearing the shards shatter inside.

Both of us held still waiting for someone to shout, run outside, something. When nothing happened, Hiro reached through the hole and unlatched the door.

I took a step. Hiro held up a hand, pulling me up short. He pressed a finger to his lips and followed it by gesturing to himself.

Be quiet and stay behind him.

I nodded.

He held out his hand. I grasped it, holding tight as he stepped inside.

The interior of the cabin didn't match the foggy memories my four-year-old self hung on to, but after all these years, that made sense. I recalled bright lights, rustic furniture, and the air of a family stitched together again.

Fourteen years later, most of the furniture was gone, and a lingering stench hung in the space, reminding me of stale food and damp, moldy carpets.

Rusty pots and pans hung from the ceiling hooks in the kitchen. They swayed gently, shaken by the storm battering the cabin. We passed under them and Hiro motioned to the garbage pail.

Overflowing.

Empty takeout containers, water bottles, and beer cans littered in and around the trash.

The thought passed through our minds at the same time. We might as well have said it out loud.

Someone was here.

We stepped into the hallway, observing the three closed doors in a new light. One would lead to a bathroom, and the other two might tell us who was staying here—whether by the stuff he left behind... or meeting the man himself.

I clutched Hiro closer. I didn't see myself as a person who scared easily and yet the cold, chilly rain soaking my skin did nothing to stop the beads of sweat prickling my body.

Is he here? Behind one of those doors. Waiting for me to come through.

Hiro kissed my cheek—wisely guessing I needed it. "Ready?"

"Let's go," I whispered.

Our footfalls fell in sync. We opened the first door nearest the kitchen and met with a bathroom. Moving on, I reached for the second door handle.

The cold metal bit into my skin. I twisted and released, letting it swing ajar on its own. A metal-framed bed and dust-covered dresser looked back at me. We poked our heads in to be sure. Checked the closet. Glanced under the bed.

There was nothing here. No clothes. No books. No belongings to point to anyone.

"I don't know if I'm disappointed or relieved we haven't found anything."

"Go with relieved." Hiro held my hand, ushering me out into the hall. "There's still hope, Em, until we have hard proof showing otherwise."

"I think I remember this room," I said softly. "The bed in there had metal frames and Rory hid under it during hide-and-seek. She always giggled when she found a good hiding spot. I got her every time." The scene unfolded in my mind. "There was also a huge antique vanity with a spinning mirror. We acted like we were all grown up, sitting in front of the mirror pretending to put on makeup."

"Maybe there'll be a message stuck to the back like in the movies. Giving us our next clue."

I let out a long sigh. "I just want to find them, Hiro. Safe and sound."

"We will." Hiro pushed open the door. "I promise."

I lifted my gaze, looking into the antique mirror, and screamed.

Reflecting in the surface that once held sweet laughing girls, were two skeletal figures, gagged and bound to the bed.

"Mom! Dad!" I raced inside, falling onto the mattress.

My parents were still—almost sleeping. My shouts stirred my mother, though the woman before me resembled my mother in the barest sense. The wavy golden crown I inherited had turned to matted straw. Her once tawny skin was so pale, I counted the blood vessels beneath her skin.

Mom peeled her eyes open and I felt the effort it cost her as if it was my own. "Mom, it's okay," I sobbed. I pulled out her gag. "I'm here."

Sunken cheeks fluttered as her jaw moved, forming her cracked, dry lips to speak.

"Em... ber," she rasped.

"Hiro, help me! Call the police!"

My love jumped to do both. Racing to the other side of the bed, he ungagged my father and tugged at his ropes with one hand. The other dialed the police.

"Hello! Yes, it's an emergency. Send the police and an ambulance down the Chesil trail. Three miles in to the cabin with a purple door. We found Frank and Lenora Bancroft and they need medical attention right away."

Tears blinded me. My fingers slipped twice undoing Mom's bindings.

I freed her hands and dove for the rope anchoring her feet to the frame. A bony hand gripped my arm, stopping me.

"Ember, you have to… go," Mom forced out. "Get out… before he comes back."

"We're not leaving without you!" I yanked on her restraints. The rope bit back, slicing my fingertips. "Daddy," I called. "Can you hear me?"

My father groaned, head lolling as Hiro lifted him onto his back. He dropped all of his weight on him, barely conscious.

Hiro bore it. Muscles straining, he pushed up. "We need to get out of here right now, Em," he said. "We can't be here when whoever did this comes back."

I threw Mom's ropes across the room and bent to help her up. Wrapping her arm around my shoulder, she was practically nothing in my arms. Mom's head dropped on me—too weak to hold it up. "I knew you'd figure it out, baby," she whispered. "I knew it."

"C'mon," Hiro ordered. "The police are on the way. Let's get them in the car. We'll meet the ambulance on the road."

Hiro hurried into the hall and Mom and I were right behind him. "What happened? Who did this?"

"We got it… all wrong," she said. "We thought we were protecting you and Eli. Instead we put you in terrible danger."

"Mr. Bancroft?" Hiro said. "If you can hear me, we're getting you help." Hiro threw open the back door. "You're going to be…" The words died in his throat.

I froze.

A man stood on the threshold, visibly as surprised to see us as we were to see him.

Average height. Dark hair. Early forties. Well-dressed.

"Monroe?"

The chauffeur's arm hung in the air, caught in the act of grabbing the knob. Beneath the other, was a tarp and shovel.

"Run!" Hiro bellowed. He slammed the door in Monroe's face, spinning with Dad.

I almost tripped over Mom whirling for the front door. She limped after me, her arm a stranglehold on my neck. "Go without us," she cried.

"No, I won't!"

A crash rattled the cabin. Roaring, Monroe charged after us. The *thud, thud, thud* of his footfalls shotgunned terror through my mind, shredding it in panic.

I bolted out into the storm, sprinting for the car.

"Argh!"

Thud!

Monroe leaped on top of Hiro and Dad, dropping the three of them on the muddy drive.

"Ember, don't stop!" Hiro shouted. "Run!"

He crawled out from under Dad and struggled to his feet. Monroe tackled him again. Their limbs flailed in the darkened web of wind and rain.

I raced to the trees, setting my mother down in the scant cover.

Hiro bucked, throwing Monroe off. He swung before he recovered. The man's head snapped around and his body with it. Monroe pitched onto the porch steps.

"Get out of here, Ember!"

My dad lay facedown in the mud. Unheeding of Hiro's shouts, I grabbed him under the chest, lifting with all of my strength. "Daddy, stay with me," I screamed.

I stumbled to the trees, preparing to lay him next to Mom. My vision cleared on an empty patch of grass.

"Mom?" I whipped my head around. "Mom?! Where are you?!"

My search landed me on Monroe and Hiro's fight. The chauffeur jabbed at Hiro and missed. Hiro followed through with his duck, using the opening to bury his fist in Monroe's gut. He collapsed on the steps again.

Hiro advanced on him, fist raised, and Monroe yanked the gun from his coat.

"No!"

The shot ripped through the storm, resounding through the forest as loud as my screams. Hiro stumbled back and crumpled onto the ground.

"No, Hiro! No, no, no, no!" Agony punched a hole through my chest. I fell on him, clutching him to me as heaven shed its tears on our fallen Angel. "Hiro, please, don't l-leave me." I pushed the hair from his face, cradling his head on my lap. "You promised me for the rest of my life! You—"

A hand tangled in my hair.

I shrieked, clawing and slapping desperately. Monroe dragged me from Hiro and tossed me roughly at his feet. I looked down the barrel of his gun.

Time slowed, freezing the raindrops in the air.

I looked into the dead eyes of the man whose motives I'd never know, and the oddest thought passed through my head.

At least I kissed Eli goodbye.

I blinked and time resumed.

Monroe raised his hand, leveling the gun between my eyes.

A blur cleaved through the rain and struck Monroe's temple. He fell headlong, gun sailing out of his hand and it dropped next to me.

The force of the hit knocked my weak mother off balance. She hit the dirt, body and shovel, but didn't let that stop her. "Ember, my baby." Forcing herself up, she crawled to me, pulling me into her arms in the first hug I received from her in three years.

"Oh, my baby," she wailed. "I'm sorry. I'm so sorry."

Sirens pierced the forest, bellowing their arrival as heaven and I wept.

Chapter Thirteen

"Miss Bancroft? Ember?"

I lifted my head from the bin of Hiro's personal effects. Tears soaked my face, dripping onto his clothes.

Agent Underhill dropped to his knees in front of me. He tugged on my hand and, after a hesitation, I let him take it.

"How are you holding up?"

"I'm a complete fucking mess," I said. "Which is just about right for the situation."

"Of course, I understand. I thought you might like an update on how things stand, but if now isn't a good time—"

"No," I broke in. "Tell me."

He inclined his head. "Your parents will have one or two questions to answer. As will Andrew Williams. But the evidence of duress is incontrovertible. I strongly suspect they won't face charges. For the money or, I'm sad to say, for the hit-and-run. The statue of limitations has run out."

"What about Monroe?" I spat.

"He will enjoy the state's hospitality for a very long time. So will Violet Bancroft."

I pressed my lips together, stemming the tide of vile curses I wanted to spew at the mention of her name. In the seventy-two hours since my parents' rescue, the truth came out.

Quite by chance, Aunt Violet spotted a golden-cheeked warbler while exploring the new lodge property with Uncle Harrison. She took a picture and looked up what she thought was just a pretty bird and discovered it was a protected species.

It turned out Uncle Harrison's security firm was struggling even before the lodge. Bancroft Manor sat empty because he was quietly fixing it up and seeking out buyers. To turn things around, he invested a heavy amount in a sure thing, and with one bird, Violet discovered the lodge project would never get off the ground.

"Monroe Stinson was an old boyfriend," Underhill said. "She convinced your uncle to hire him, hiding who he was, and they carried on an affair for many years. When she needed to blackmail the officials, she went to him.

"As you know, your parents found out and further incentive was required. Your aunt investigated Harrison a few years back to gain ammo in a divorce. She discovered the truth about the hit-and-run and connected the dots to Frank's involvement. She kept the knowledge to herself assuming the time would come when she could use it," he said. "That time came."

"Eventually they decided to have all of the money, and now here we are."

He patted my hand. "That was Monroe's influence. He'd been pushing her for a while to run away with him, but your aunt had no interest in returning to middle class. After the additional discovery of the floodplain and your father's resistance, Monroe swayed her that twenty-five million would buy them a nice life in a nonextradition country."

"I can't believe they did this," I said. "Explains why she was pushing for Monroe to drive me everywhere. They needed to keep an eye on me."

"It certainly turns the stomach. Attacking your own family like that," he said. "You won't hear me say I approve, but I understand why your folks contacted Mr. Williams and used your mother's real estate connection to rent that cabin in the woods and bury the trail.

They suspected someone close to them was behind it. They just never suspected Violet."

"That's how she got them in the end."

Underhill sighed. He must have seen worse in his job but he looked at me like our story was the saddest in history. "After I stupidly told the media the note was a secret message, they were scared for you. They broke down and contacted Harrison. Violet picked up the phone instead.

"She'd been searching for them and keeping a close eye on *unknown* numbers that called her husband. Violet answered and convinced them that she'd help in his place. Once they gave her their location, it was over for them."

I clenched thinking of what my parents had been through. The doctors rattled off severe dehydration, malnutrition, physical beatings, and the mental traumas we couldn't see, and I broke down thinking of all that time they'd been waiting for me to end their pain.

And I was late.

"Stinson tortured them for the location of the money. With you both in your aunt's care, he had an even better bargaining chip. But your parents held out because they feared Monroe would do worse to you if he discovered you were the only person with access to the account. They trusted deep down that Violet wouldn't let Monroe harm you. Maybe it says something for her that she didn't."

"It doesn't," I said, voice hard.

"No, I guess it doesn't." Underhill rose and claimed the seat next to me. "The breaking point was your return of the money. They denied it was real for a while. Your parents overheard the fights," he explained. "During a bathroom break, your mother took a chance while they were arguing to steal Stinson's phone and send you that message. Eventually, they accepted the money was lost to them and it became an issue of what to do with your parents. Letting them go wasn't an option, but Violet wouldn't agree to killing them."

"Then I shot my mouth to Uncle about the purple-door cabin with Monroe two feet away," I finished. "I was such an idiot. How did I not see that he fit the description?"

"You were expecting a wealthy man, not a silent chauffeur," he said. "Also, a psychopath by all accounts. He heard you speak of the cabin and decided to take matters into his own hands. He went there to kill your parents and bury their bodies without your aunt's knowledge. Someone had to get to them quickly." Underhill's kindly expression morphed to stern in a blink. "And that someone should have been the police. I thought we agreed the last time we spoke, that you'd stop trying to do my job for me."

"Is that what we agreed? Because I remember talk of an honorary badge and a party to celebrate the two of us solving the Frank and Lenora Bancroft case and bringing down the Horsemen."

"No, it was definitely what I said."

I cracked the barest smile. It went as quickly as it came. "I should have known the text was real from the beginning."

He rubbed my back. "You can't beat yourself up. You saved them in the end."

"It will take them a long time to recover from this."

"But they have that time," he reminded. "Soon, they'll be back on their feet and you all can begin to heal as a family."

I didn't reply for a spell. My mind was lost as I gazed at Hiro's things.

"What about the other projects I gave you?" I spoke up. "Did you catch up to the leaders?"

"Cillian Cavanaugh was picked up outside an apartment complex in Easthaven. He couldn't resist visiting his mistress one final time and we had the place staked out. As for Endo Ren, Marcel Noble, and Raymond Antario Cruz—also known as Rio—they've slipped the net. Though it's only a matter of time until they're caught. Their organization is in pieces," he said.

"As for Mallory Keene, I've turned her over to an Officer Rama-di. She'll have her arrested."

Underhill stood. "I must get going. I mentioned my wife. It turns out she prefers we spend our anniversary together."

I tsked. "Odd duck. Better keep an eye on her."

Chuckling, he held out his hand. "Goodbye, Miss Bancroft. Let us never meet under these circumstances again."

"Agreed. Stay safe out there."

He waved goodbye down the bustling hallway, turned the corner, and was gone. The guy turned out to be a decent sort after all, but I did hope I would not see him again.

Without his distraction, there was only the bin. I clutched it tighter, steeling myself.

It's time.

Rising up, I crossed to the hospital room and went inside.

Hiro lay still on the Egyptian cotton sheets, head cradled by memory foam. I made a great stink about him recovering in the Estate hospital. In his grieving state my uncle saw to it that I got whatever I wanted.

Placing the bin on the nightstand, I bent over him... and flicked his nose.

"Wake up."

Hiro's eyes flew open—his fake sleep over. "What was that for? I need my rest."

"You'll get plenty. The doctors say the bullet was through-and-through. Didn't hit any major organs. I swear you Angels truly are heaven-blessed."

Hiro stroked my cheek. His love reflected in his eyes. Me.

"Why were you crying?" he asked.

I bent my head, pressing into his palm. "Because I found something in your pants. Hiro Saito"—I held up the tiny box and the ring nestled inside—"what were you doing with this?"

Hiro took the simple silver band and single glittering diamond from the box. "This was my mother's ring."

"Why do you have it?" I pressed.

He looked me in the eyes. "Because I planned on asking you to marry me."

A flush surged up my neck, down my chest, and through my whole body. That had to be the answer but still I couldn't believe it.

"Why would you do that?!" I blurted.

"Because I love you." He smiled and my heart stopped in its tracks. "And I promised you forever."

"But we— But— We can't—" I swallowed, trying to reclaim my tongue. "We're only eighteen."

He shrugged. "If you can become a mother at nineteen. Why not a wife?"

"But I can't marry all of you," I cried.

"*We* aren't asking. I am."

He was enjoying seeing me flustered. One hundred percent enjoying it.

"It's not how relationships like ours work."

"Who says?"

"There are rules," I tried.

"No, there aren't." Hiro's grin grew wider and wider.

"What would the guys say?"

"They'd say yes." He slid his palm under mine. "I asked for your hand old-time-style and the guys are cool. Cassius even said I earned going first by taking two bullets for you. So, Ember Bancroft, what do you say?"

Heat steamed my face. "Hiro, we're really young and this is a huge commitment."

"It is."

"My family is going through a major crisis and I haven't dropped on them that I'm pregnant yet. Following that up with a marriage announcement might kill them."

"I get that."

"I mean, I'd be fulfilling every backwater stereotype!"

"True enough," he said. "So, what do you say?"

"Ugh! I say yes!" Tears burst out of me for no explainable reason. "Yes, yes, yes, you stupid, fucking, amazing, wonderful idiot."

I fell on him, kissing every inch of him that didn't hurt. Hiro captured my lips, searing away the last vestiges of my doubts for the future.

I had my Angels. Despite the troubles that were coming, I trusted in the promise that we'd make it through.

Together.

One Year Later

SHE BLINKED AT ME, staring with those big brown eyes filled with innocence and curiosity. She may be five months old, but my daughter was a deep thinker. Behind those eyes she was figuring out the world.

The baby tooted.

"Yep," Clay said, picking his head up off my lap and out of the firing zone. "She's definitely Cassius's."

I rolled my eyes. The boys had been playing this game since she was born. Any spark of personality she showed, they used to name her biological father.

The truth was we didn't know. Haven Lorelai Bancroft was born a little blonde beauty. Hair she could have gotten from the triplets, or from me. The boys played their game, but honestly, none of us cared. Haven was all ours and we were all hers.

Everything we built was for her. The baby that brought us out of our storms.

Our Haven.

"You guys are so bad," I said. "Tell me, who is her daddy when she's spitting up in my hair, hitting me with her little baby fists, and refusing to bottle feed just because she can?"

"Royal's," Clay, Cassius, and Hiro said.

"Fuck you," Royal called from the kitchen.

Giggling, I pressed a kiss in Haven's soft curls. Clay stretched out on my side. Cassius stood under the winding staircase talking on his phone. Royal was in the kitchen and Hiro sat at the table, playing hot nerd as he reviewed his textbooks, glasses perched on his nose.

My loves and my husbands in the home we made together.

Yes, my husbands.

It was still true that I could only legally marry one of them. And it was true Hiro and I held that legal wedding in an intimate ceremony with Raven River as our background. What most didn't know is in the following weeks and months, Clay, Cassius, Royal, and I stood before the people we loved and announced our commitment to each other with the same beautiful promise. On paper I had one husband. In all the ways that mattered, I had four. And we had the lives we always wanted.

Clay once asked how much it cost to buy one person a new life. It turned out a five-million-dollar trust fund went a long way toward buying seven people a new life. A home with a balcony that looked out over the city. Hot cocoa and onesie pajamas in front of the fire. Café brunches with my best friend. Wandering the streets with Eli. Taking my daughter to all the wonderful sights of old New York, taking ten times as many pictures of her as I did of the buildings. And, of course, tuition for Columbia, NYU, Chapman School, and Royal's tattoo apprenticeship.

The spring semester saw me and Haven rolling through Columbia on my way to my art history classes.

Royal strode out of the kitchen carrying a bottle and blanket. Eli was hot on his heels—dressed in his Chapman uniform complete with a baby blanket over his shoulder.

"You can't stay and feed her," I told him. *"You have to get to school."*

"I can be late."

"No, you can't!"

Eli snapped his head around, so he could pretend later he didn't see that final comment.

"Fifteen-year-olds," I mumbled. But there are worse teenage behaviors than loving your niece. I was thankful every day that the seven of us made it to New York. Even if the circumstances were difficult.

When the truth came out about Violet, Uncle Harrison fell apart. He couldn't handle his emotions let alone looking after Eli. Technically, custody should have transferred to my parents, but they were worried focusing on their recovery would leave Eli in the same position. After weeks of long, intense conversations, they agreed to let him live with me.

I waddled across the stage at graduation seven months pregnant, and the next day, the six of us were on a bus.

"Come on, princess." Royal lifted Haven off my chest and tucked the baby under his neck.

I sniffed. "You used to call me princess. When I was your favorite girl."

Chuckling, Royal shot me a wink as he walked off with Haven and Eli.

"Consider it, Dad." Cassius's conversation floated to my ears. "You could use the money to move up here. All right. Cam is coming over tonight for dinner. The five of us can talk about it then. Bye."

"Everything okay?" I asked.

"Dad's been approached by developers to sell the house," Cassius said. "They're offering a decent amount of money."

"It'd be great if he and Virginia moved up here," I said. "They could see Haven all the time."

Of course the plan had been to move his parents up months ago, but when the time came to sit down and get serious about it, his dad said no. Rio kidnapping Cassius and then taking off to leave the gang in shambles woke him up. He'd been relying on other people to take care of his family for too long. Glen swore they'd move up to join us when he could afford to do it himself.

"That's what I said." Cassius grabbed his laptop off the table and snagged a kiss as he straightened. "I've got to get to class. I'll get food for dinner on the way home. Camila requested lamb tacos from that Greek fusion place."

"And hot cocoa and a roaring fire to warm her up," I finished. "Can I just say I love having my best friend two stops away."

"You can say you love having me two feet away."

"I do," I whispered, grinning.

Cassius stole one more kiss and headed out.

I got up and strode to the balcony, passing my hand along Hiro's shoulder as I went.

The crisp New York morning welcomed me. Sun unveiling the pulsing, breathing city we made our home.

Life can't get any better than this.

Ten Years Later

"ARE YOU REALLY THINKING about moving? You love New York."

Camila questioned me from the circle of her fiancé's arms. The two leaned against the counter cuddling instead of peeling potatoes.

"Our family has gotten too big for New York," I said. "We need more space for the kids to run around."

"Have you considered looking here?" asked Mom. She dutifully did her job of prepping the yams. "The kids love coming to visit us at the lake."

"We're discussing a few places, Mom."

And it wasn't the first time Mom suggested Earnshaw Lake though she innocently brought it up every time. I couldn't fault her for wanting to be near her grandbabies.

"Timothy and I love it in Easthaven," said Gail. "I can't fathom why it took me so long to move."

My smile dimmed. I couldn't say why my former headmistress waited but I knew what finally pushed her out. Almost our entire ragtag family had been forced out of Raven River.

The town was a different place than it was ten years ago. It was a different place than five years ago.

Asa Ives's plans weren't noticeable at first. The people of the Outer Borough welcomed it when their rich neighbors offered to build a new hospital. Then a new school. Then a couple of restaurants. And when Ives's development company offered more than market value for their homes, they eagerly sold. Until one day they realized they could no longer afford to live in their own neighborhood.

Backed metaphorically and financially by nearly the entire Estate community, Asa Ives bought nearly every piece of property in the OB that wasn't government-owned, and he kicked everyone out.

Raven River Academy didn't revert to Raveners only. The sad fact was most of the "OB kids" were forced to pack up and use those checks to find homes in Easthaven or beyond, and Gail struggled with it until she felt compelled to leave.

The whole time Nolan's drive-bys weren't mindless violence. The shooting broadcasted live for the world to see and the second shooting terrifying the children of the Raveners were meant to scare their

parents into doing something about the violence-ridden Outer Borough. And they did.

The funny thing was no one called each other trash, OB kid,
Ravener, or backwater anymore. And three years ago, the town celebrated the Estate gates coming down.

The vision of Raven River that we talked about all those years
ago in Mrs. Seeger's communications class came true. Most of us just
weren't there to see it.

Hands encircled my waist. "What's that look on your face?" Clay
asked.

I relaxed, frown fading away. "What look?"

Some days my heart panged for my old town, and those days I
remembered that my home was wherever my family was.

Crash!

I groaned. "I don't even need to ask who is responsible for that."

Wiggling out of Clay's hold, I walked into the den and nearly
trod on a Joni Mitchell CD. The three-year-old grinned at me too
widely for innocence, standing next to the tipped-over CD stand.

"Royal," I called over my shoulder. "If you ever doubted it, you
can rest assured this kid is yours."

Royal's chuckles floated out of the living room. He didn't doubt
it. Angel "Ransom" Cruz popped out with a full head of raven hair
and the attitude to go with it. Every day he looked more and more
like his father.

A blonde streak shot past my knees. Hannah pounced on Angel,
throwing her pudgy arms around him and landed a big smooch on
his cheek.

Nose wrinkling, the poor boy looked at me for help.

I heard footsteps behind me. Julian held out a bottle of cream soda. "Here you go."

"Thanks." I gestured at the kids. "Like father, like daughter, eh?"

"Shut up," Julian said, laughing. "My girl is just excited to have a new cousin to play with."

Angel escaped her hug and ran off. Then, proving that Cruzes are a mercurial bunch. He spun around, grabbed her hand, and they ran off together to cause more havoc.

"Partners in crime," Julian mused. "If you're looking for a new home, consider California. Those two can grow up getting in trouble together."

"Tempting," I teased.

"Mommy?"

"Yes, Kimi?"

"Grandma can't find the pasta strainer."

"I'll be there in a minute," I said. "I have to clean this up."

"I can do it, Mommy."

Kimi slipped through us, bending down to grab the CDs. The long, voluminous waterfall Hiro passed to his daughter swept the floor as she worked. Sometimes I looked at our Kimi and marveled Hiro and I created this sweet, beautiful girl—filled with the love and kindness we sought in our childhoods.

"Kimi, where is your sister?"

"She's upstairs with Daddy Cas."

I patted Julian's shoulder. "I'll let you sway me on California later. I have to grab Haven and get started on the pumpkin pie."

"Ooh, please do."

Rounding the banister, I climbed the familiar steps of my parents' beach house. Haven would be in the room that used to be mine, reading the letters I left for the little girl I didn't know would be her.

"... apply light pressure," I heard. "Then push the pins up one by one."

I topped the landing. Haven bent over my old doorknob, obeying her father's lock-picking instructions with a serious expression.

"What the— Cassius!"

"Oh, shit!" Cassius scooped the ten-year-old and tossed her over his shoulder. "Run!"

Haven shrieked, laughing her head off, and swinging off her dad's back. They bolted into our bedroom and locked me out.

Shaking my head, I left him and his clone to it. Haven may look like me in nearly every way, but she matched Cassius mischief for mischief.

I drifted down the stairs, looking out over the family gathered together for our fifth Thanksgiving celebration.

My mom and dad sneaking kisses in the kitchen. Uncle Harrison and his new wife talking by the fireplace. Royal, Clay, Hiro, Julian, and Julian's wife, Marly, watching the game together while our children played at their feet. Virginia and Glen holding each other and swaying in a corner, listening to music only they could hear. A lot had happened in the last ten years and beyond but still we gathered here.

Rio's capture, trial, and life sentence did not tear us apart. Nor did the two years Harrison refused contact with us as he healed from his obliterated marriage. Eventually, we all ended up here in this lake house and we would always be here in some shape or form throughout the coming years.

My gaze swept the living room and kitchen. *There is only one person missing.*

I weaved through the happy family and stepped out onto the porch.

Eli gently pushed Morgan on the swing. His pregnant girlfriend tilted her head back, leg sweeping up as she awaited her kiss. Eli complied and pulled back with a smile on his face brighter than the sunbeams glinting off Earnshaw Lake.

He saw me, kissed her again, and then jogged over. I pinched myself all the time but still the short, cherub-faced brother I once protected at all costs remained this handsome young man. Successful and happy as a web developer with his own house and a baby on the way. Even so, I still kiss-attacked him. And he still knocked me out with pillows.

"*You okay?*" he asked.

I smiled. "*I was just thinking that life can't get any better than this. But then I thought that the day before. And the day before. You and I have come so far from those two abandoned kids with no one but each other. Sometimes I worry it'll all disappear if I blink.*"

"*Even if it did, you and I would have each other's backs,*" he said. "*But it won't because Rory wasn't the only goddess.*"

The door creaked open. Royal, Clay, Cassius, and Hiro fanned out around me, encircling me in their warmth and safety.

"*Angels were always watching over you, Ember.*"

Keep In Touch

Join Ruby's Mailing list for news, teasers, and more:
https://www.subscribepage.com/rubyvincentpage
Join Ruby's Facebook Reader Group:
https://bit.ly/3bNuCOq

Marked Sneak Peek
Prologue

Wide, terrified eyes gazed at me in the glint of the steel until they disappeared in the gush of the liquid. It flowed down the metal—hot and thick and seeking my fingers.

Someone was screaming. Horrible, piercing shrieks that made it impossible to concentrate. Impossible to understand what was going on.

Why wouldn't they stop? Why wouldn't they—

Oh, wait...

I put my hand to my raw, aching throat and smeared it with blood. The person screaming was me.

Chapter One

"Ugh. Size zero." Olivia picked up my uniform with two fingers and tossed it over her shoulder. "I used to be a size zero too, little show-off. Before you wreaked havoc on my hips."

My reflection rolled her eyes. "How many times should I apologize for being born?"

"Until I get my figure back!"

I burst into laughter, and after a second, Mom did too. Our giggles filled the room until a soft whine cut through our mirth.

I closed my lips with a snap and looked at Adam in the mirror. *Please don't wake up. Please don't wake up!*

The baby stirred from the comfort of my bed, scrunching up his little face, while I held my breath. After a few tense seconds, his face smoothed out and he settled back into sleep.

I relaxed and reached for my brush. Adam had fought his nap all morning, screaming and wailing so loud the neighbors must have thought we were murdering someone in here. It took so long to get him down that I was in serious danger of being late on my first day to Evergreen Academy.

"That was a close one," said Olivia. She reached over and pulled the blanket up to the baby's chin. She settled back onto the comforter, propping herself up on one arm, and watched me in the mirror.

Olivia, as she insisted I call her whenever we were in public, still looked amazing for her thirty-five years, despite how she complained about me ruining her figure. Mom's chestnut hair fell in soft waves to her shoulders, framing a heart-shaped face, Greek nose, and piercing green eyes with flecks of gold.

That face was my face. We looked so much alike people asked if she was my older sister and that pleased Mom to no end. Gray had yet to touch her brown locks and wrinkles dare not grace her skin. She was still young and in the prime of her life. Just ask her.

"You sure about this, kid?" The hand brushing my hair stilled as I pulled myself out of my musings. I met Olivia's eyes in the glass. "This fancy new school," she clarified. "Things have been different for you at Joe Young High. You've made friends."

"I'll make new friends," I insisted. I smiled at my reflection, drawing my lips across my teeth and grinning widely. The smile trembled as if the muscles had forgotten how to do this. It began to look like a grimace and I dropped it.

It's alright. Things will be different from now on. Soon... all of my smiles will be real.

"This is a great opportunity, Mom," I continued. "This is *the* opportunity. Of course I'm sure about Evergreen."

Olivia sighed. "I just don't want you to think you have to go because of—"

My grip tightened on the brush. "Mom."

"—everything that happened—"

"Mom!"

Adam shifted at my shout, but I didn't pay it any mind as I spun on Mom. She met my glare without flinching. This was Serious Olivia. This side of Mom and I were barely acquainted.

"Don't give me that look," she said calmly. "I only want to make sure you know that you're in control. If you don't want to go, then you don't have to."

The tension leaked out of my shoulders. "I know. I'm sorry." I took a breath and released it. "But I do want this, Mom. Kids from all over the world fight to get into this place. Having a school like

Evergreen Academy on your application pretty much guarantees automatic admission to any university in the country. I'll go, graduate, get into a good school, get an even better job, and then"—my eyes swept my room—"I'll get us out of this place."

Olivia studied me for a moment, then she offered me a smile. "Glad to hear it, kid. You get your mom a big house and deck her out in diamonds and pearls. It's the least you can do."

I snorted. "Let me guess, it's the least I can do after messing with your figure?"

She tapped her nose and winked. "Exactly."

I shook my head and took the five steps to the other side of the bed to pick my uniform off the floor. My room was just that small.

I gazed around the space with the royal blue monogrammed fabric dangling from my fingertips. My old life and my new.

To continue reading the first in a darkly tempting series, Marked, click here.[1]

---

1. *http://mybook.to/MarkedEvergreen*

ABOUT THE AUTHOR

Ruby Vincent is a published author with many novels under her belt but now she's taking a fun foray into contemporary romance. She loves saucy heroines, bold alpha males, and weaving a tale where both get their happy ever after.